Last Lesson
of the Afternoon

Born St Monans, Fife, 1944, Christopher Rush was educated at Waid Academy, Anstruther, then Aberdeen University 1964–68. He graduated with First Class Honours in English Language and Literature winning the Lucy Research Fellowship tenable at Peterhouse, Cambridge, but elected instead to enter schoolteaching. He has taught in Scottish schools since 1969, principally George Watson's College, Edinburgh.

He has written in many literary forms as: poet, short story writer, novelist, prose stylist, biographer, children's writer and screenplay writer.

His books include: *Peace Comes Dropping Slow* (1983), *A Resurrection Of A Kind* (1984), *A Twelve-month And A Day* (1985), *Into The Ebb* (1988), *Two Christmas Stories* (1988), *With Sharp Compassion* (1990), *Venus Peter Saves The Whale* (1992).

He has won two SAC Book Awards, has been twice short-listed for the Scottish Book of the Year Award and also short-listed the McVitie's Prize of Writer of the Year for the screenplay of *Venus Peter*.

He is currently working on the *auto*biography of William Shakespeare!

Last Lesson
of the Afternoon

a satire by
Christopher Rush

CANONGATE

Author's Acknowledgements

I am deeply indebted both to the Arts Council and to the Governing Council of George Watson's College for their assistance in the writing of this novel. Their generosity granted me the gift of time, without which the book could not have appeared from the pen of a full-time teacher.

First published in Great Britain in 1994 by
Canongate Press Ltd.

This edition published in 1996 by
Canongate Books Ltd
14 High Street
Edinburgh EH1 1TE

The publishers acknowledge subsidy from the Scottish Arts Council towards the publication of this volume.

British Library Cataloguing-in-Publication Data
A catalogue record for this book is available on request from
The British Library

ISBN 0 86241 649 3

Typeset by Hewer Text Composition Services, Edinburgh
Printed and bound in Great Britain by
Mackays of Chatham plc

This book is dedicated to
the memory of Alastair Mackie,
the real Mackay, Mackay;
George Sutherland:
An Iron Man with a human face

And to
Alastair Leslie, Eddie McGeachie, William Blair, Peter
Smith, Peter Howling, Randall Phillips, Herbert Soutar, Jim
Drummond, Charles Brown, Flora Mackay, Alec Watt, John
Robin, and all my old teachers.

And all poor sods of teachers whose last lesson has not yet
been taught!

Explicit hoc totum
Pro Christo da mihi potum

Author's Preface

Swift said that satire is a sort of glass in which beholders generally discover everybody's face but their own. In writing the preface to a somewhat different battle of the books nearly three hundred years later, I have to make a plea along the opposite lines, without detracting from the truth of Swift's dictum. My novel is not a mirror in which individuals are reflected for the purposes of satire, for that would reduce satire to the level of lampoon. This is a work of fiction. Those who wish to read it as a sequel to the semi-autobiographical *A Twelvemonth and a Day*, cannot legitimately do so, even though the author did indeed proceed from Fife to Aberdeen University (where he was inspired by Professor Duthie et al), and so to Edinburgh and into schoolteaching. In these pages the real world is granted its existence, but is made to accommodate Skinfasthaven, Kilminnis and Taft Academy in the same way as Orkney's Stromness becomes the Hamnavoe of George Mackay Brown's stories and poems, taking on the garb of fiction. The very setting of Blair's indicates its imaginary status, and after a quarter of a century as a schoolteacher, I believe I can safely say that there never could be a Headmaster as bad as Cranford. (Please don't write in all at once!) As the antagonist, he is the symbol of all that I believe has gone wrong in contemporary education in Scotland and indeed in Britain. For that reason he has to be presented as 'over the top', as does the protagonist, Campbell Mackay.

Having got all of that out of the way, I should be dishonest if I did not confess to the existence of some real-life elements in the following pages. Writers who say that their novels contain no resemblance etcetera to actual people living or dead, are quite simply strangers to a literary truth. We all lift from life both consciously and unconsciously. In point of fact I have obtained permission from three of my former teachers to re-create them in fiction. Thus Lachlan Campbell and Mackay Mackay have their roots in actuality. By agreement, the Goof retains his untranslateable nickname. There are no other meaningful resemblances. The true-to-life counterparts of these three men persuaded me to stay on at school just as I was poised to go to sea. But they are not the only teachers to whom I have to record my debt of gratitude. The real 'Shark' also encouraged me on the road to academic excellence and helped me along it, as did the real school Welfare Officer who, although she never taught me, was kindness itself to me, quite unlike the fictitious Fanny Fergusson of the book. Similarly my first French teacher was an unforgettably eccentric *bon viveur* and nothing more; my Music teacher was a marvellous enthusiast and that is where the resemblance ends. And so on it goes. If there was a degree of sadism in some aspects of Scottish education at one time, I never encountered it at Waid Academy. All my teachers were humane and enlightened men and women. Any unfriendly portraits, whether at Taft Academy or at Robert Blair's, take their rise from systems and situations and not from individuals, in spite of whatever similarities may or may not be found to exist between my fiction and past or present fact. But to those who do peer in the glass to find faces, I can do no more than to issue a final warning. Beware: for it is written that when Judas Iscariot goes out, he meets Judas Iscariot!

Christopher Rush
February 1994

Preface to the Second Edition

Humour is a great corrective. To what extent literature influences real life remains, however, an imponderable, and I would doubt whether the prose of Alexander Solzhenitsyn had much to do with the collapse of the Communist system in the old Soviet Union, or whether Swift's satire has done much to improve the human race, politically or morally.

There are examples, nonetheless, of battles begun by books and of words helping to win wars. It is said that the pen is mightier than the sword and somebody more recently added that it is also mightier than the *word*. It used to be believed that when my fellow-Fifer, Sir David Lyndsay's "Ane Satyre of the Thrie Estatis" was played before James V on Twelfth Night 1540, its effect upon royalty proved to be an influential part of the course of the Scottish Reformation. The real truth is that those in power are generally more interested in their own prestige, pay-packets and survival than in getting things right. Break not your sleeps for that. The problem only begins to bite when the power-people really do believe that they *are* right, in spite of what people and prophets cry to the contrary from heart and gut.

What James V really thought when he saw Lyndsay's satire is another imponderable. I do know that when *Last Lesson* appeared in 1994 I had high hopes that it would succeed in helping to promote an educational reformation. That was naive of me. The war against education as my generation understood it goes on as if I had never written a word about it. It would now be easy for me to conclude that I had wasted my time.

But no. One thing alone continues to give me immense private satisfaction and a warm glow of justification. I refer to the many letters I have received (to my astonishment not a single hostile one!) from schoolteachers throughout the U.K. who read my novel and were overcome with emotion in various and multiple manner: 'I grat with relief . . . I ran out into the garden and howled with laughter ... "Yes, yes, yes!" I screamed ... I sat among unironed clothes and unwashed dishes, dazed by the realisation that I was not alone, that at last somebody had found the words to express what we all secretly felt but hardly dared say – that something was rotten in the state of Denmark and we ought to burn out the cancer.'

Right now that is impossible. One of Tom Stoppard's characters explains why: "There must have been a moment, at the beginning, when we could have said—no. But somehow we missed it." When teachers do decide to exert their will and say no, I shall be pushing up daisies, and posterity, if it pauses by my pit, will perceive a bumper crop on that tremendous day. I hope.

Meanwhile I look forward to the second edition of this satire, which, though it has failed to sanitise education, has won the hearts and minds of many practising teachers, and, for a time at least, anaesthetised their pain. It is now my turn to express my gratitude. Thank you, colleagues, thank you. If my book made you feel that you were not alone, your letters have done the same for me. Teaching is still enormous fun, management and theory the dreary claptrap which ought to serve and feed us, not choke and poison us. And hey! – let's keep teaching out there, in spite of every attempt that has been made in these past two decades to dismantle what it is that we do.

Christopher Rush
September 1996
Edinburgh

O, Michelangelo! What hellish torment
This place must be for your creative genius.
I see familiar faces everywhere:
men of spirit, of untold strength of mind . . .
squashed in the mould of uniformity
by state and doctrine. O, this breaks my
heart!

Imre Madách, *The Tragedy of Man*

I have ever hated all nations, professions and
communities, and all my love is towards individuals . . . But principally I hate and detest that
animal called man: although I heartily love John,
Peter, Thomas and so forth.

Jonathan Swift,
letter to Pope, 29 September 1725

Lay not that flattering unction to your soul,
That not your trespass but my madness speaks:
It will but skin and film the ulcerous place,
Whiles rank corruption, mining all within,
Infects unseen.

Shakespeare, *Hamlet*

O, keep the teacher hence that's friend to men,
Or with his books he'll make them fucking
read again!
Bloody lecteurs . . .!

Last Lesson of the Afternoon

1

Yet once more, O ye laurels, and once more
Ye myrtles brown, with ivy never sere,
I come to pluck your berries harsh and crude.

SO WROTE THE great Milton, boys of Blair's, addressing himself
to his honoured Muse, poor girl that she was: sexless as a
schoolteacher in a seminary where semen never ran. A school
of nine sisters with strychnine in their knickers and carbolic on
their hair. Shampoo La Mort. You know the type.

O, Milton! thou should'st, old son, be living at this hour! (the
violet hour). And ah, sweet mystery of life! and ah, Chekhovian
childhood, with your tears and terrors, your comic Fords and
farms and blinding theologies of fruit and flowers, and old
hat—when do you end? And youth, sweet youth, when do you
begin? Forget Milton (and Larkin) for the moment, and let me
give you the reply biological, just to prove to you all that there's
life outside an English lesson.

Childhood ends at puberty, biologically speaking. The pituitary
gland is the key to the process. For twelve years it sits unturned
in the brain's secret lock, while we regress from Roald Dahl
to Stephen King, from hide-and-seek to trivial pursuits, stuff
ourselves with fast foods, Bruce Forsyth on the box, asinine
hours of soap, and learning off a few capitals and kings in the
classrooms of our Primary education, where computers crouch
now like blind beggars waiting to be unshrouded and fed.

Or that's how it was in your case, my dears. In mine I recall
only the capitals and kings. Other than that it was twelve years
of building beach fires and rafts, talking to tombstones and the
sea, watching the tide coming in, going out. Living in fear of
God and the Devil and most things in between, including my
teachers; packing in as much fun and fury as I could on the road
to eternity. It never struck me at any point during those dozen

I

years that there was another life to be lived before I ever reached the promised land of primroses or red-hot coals; that the iron gates of childhood would one day clang shut behind me, leaving me with a universe of echoes to be caught and canned before I died; and that adolescence waited like a witch and adulthood like an Arab to take me hostage into the land where there is no horizon: all boredom and bitterness and longing for the light. And for a long time indeed I thought that nothing ever would change. That I would be eternally trapped in the *Boy's Own* castle towers of my twelve years.

Then one day it happened; the key started to turn. I didn't know it was happening, naturally, nor was I certain what precisely was going on, but the process started up, inevitable as a Monday morning. My pituitary began to produce hormones which stimulated my reproductive organs. In turn my testes set about manufacturing sperm and the secondary sexual characteristics broke over me like a rash of toadstools. I stopped singing 'Danny Boy' for my grandmother in that pure soprano voice and an Adam's apple festered instead in my swollen larynx; my milk-bottle shoulders grew broader; hair smote me malevolently like an eleventh plague from Egypt, peach-furring my face, roughening up my chest, sandpapering my armpits, and, most awesomely, clutching hold of my crotch, invading that region and investing it with a besetting fascination that was entirely new to me. The hair sat like a flaming whirlwind over my prick—(I'm fair-haired, as anyone here can see)—typhooned into my navel and crept quietly around my balls, couched as they now were inside what had come to resemble a lizard's gizzard. The scrotum increased in size and weight, a pomegranate loaded with lethal seeds. The cock changed colour and texture, no longer looking as though it belonged with the rest of me. A god called to me out of the whirlwind. By this time I was well and truly a child no more. Young friends, I was on the very doorsill of my teens. I had drunk Dr Jekyll's diabolical brew. I was a monster.

At this point I could also give you the effect psychological, the analysis sociological, and call up an army of autobiographical data in charting the end of my mute inglorious childhood and the beginning of that second sultry movement in life's ever-unfinished symphony. Let us just say that I made the big break when I went to school.

Secondary school, that is: Taft Academy, Skinfasthaven, East

2

Neuk of Fife. On Scotland's schizophrenic east coast, tinfoiled in summer by a glittering firth and in winter battered by storms and self-contempt. Thank you, Calvin. Thank you, North Sea. You tempered our Mediterranean mythologies of optimism, escape, amelioration and the dream, with a steady drip at the nose and a pain in the groin: half the year frozen like brass monkeys, the other half throbbing with guilty fear of a most just damnation.

The school was built in 1886 by the bequest of naval lieutenant Andrew Taft to accommodate the sons and daughters of drowned sea-captains and to set them on a course somewhat safer than those taken by their ocean-fated fathers, so it seemed to me. For in 1957 the school still boasted its Navigation Hall, into which we filed on a sweltering morning under a tall August sky. A hundred First Formers from farms and fisher-houses all along the coast of the East Neuk and inland: from Earlsferry to Fifeness, from Kilconquhar to Crail. We were a Chaucerian collection of reluctant pilgrims, God's plenty and the Devil's delight, sporting a proliferation of faces and physiques which eloquently proclaimed variety, sheer variety as the proudest consequence of evolution's enterprising thrust. A hundred ejaculations accomplished in darkened rooms, on hire-purchased bedsprings, within a radius of six miles and six months, to the sound of hooting boats and crapping cows, had produced the inevitable school quota for that year; and until this day we had lived out our close, secret existences, to the twelfth year of our age, in villages and homesteads only a mile or so apart, but had never once come together as a vast cloud of witnesses to procreation's miracle. Or for the most part even so much as set eyes upon one another. Such were the levels of social immobility achieved in that seemingly distant era of four decades ago.

Our common language was a strident set of variations upon the Doric, the accents varying according to village or farm. The physical types also diversified in compliance with the bleak inbreeding practised by each particular community. I was appalled by nature's obscene inventiveness, its gallery of possibilities hitherto hidden from my eyes. There were lanky big-boned boys with scarred knuckles and boys that looked like sides of beef: brutal characters that would be beating me up, I well knew it, before the end of the week. There were lads leprous with freckles and blistered by boils; boys with broken noses, stewed eyes, harelips and hunched backs, albinos and albatrosses pouring into the ark.

3

A very thin sprinkling of pale, intelligent-looking lads frightened me even more. Their pink-rimmed National Health spectacles were bandaged with elastoplast over the breaks and stared at me with cold superiority. There was surely something pure and deathly about being so clever. Even the boys who had travelled with me that morning from Kilminnins, the village playmates of my once familiar childhood, seemed caught up now in alien orbits of their own.

The girls were even more elaborately varied. From carroty minxes and honey-thighed blondes, they shaded into dusky Cleopatras who looked ready to be rowed in purple down the Nile. Except that when they opened their red lips there clattered out clanging volleys of Scots oaths to blunt the spears of incipient Antonys. We had one thing in common: we were all nervous and sweating, and underneath our red and black blazers, grey flannel shorts, black and navy blue skirts, there were the same taut bodies eager for action: girls complete with egg-laying ovaries, periods and breasts, armpits dark with lust, hips aesthetic as apples; and, tucked away out of sight, like sinister silk handkerchiefs, the black shark-fins of their pubic hairs, further than which we dared not think. We had cast off the flesh of innocence and had taken on the uniform of adolescence: the badge of beauty, the badge of suffering, the emblem of all our tribe.

My suffering started at once.

No sooner had it been established at roll-call that we were who we said we were, than we were shepherded out of the Navigation Hall by a burly Sixth Form prefect, immensely tall and with dark brown hair bristling out of his nose. His nostrils gaped like twin inverted pipe bowls into which the tobacco had been badly tamped by a hastily lavish hand, leaving the strands dangling loosely like antennae in the heights well above my first year head. O, sweet heavens! I thought, was this what happened to you by the time you reached your final year in this place? was this how I was to look? I felt my fingers groping at the end of my nose, tentatively exploring the double opening for developing shag. No, thanks to whatever nose-governing gods might be; all was perfectly hairless as yet.

'Stop picking your snout, you disgusting little brat! Yes, you boy, come here!'

The voice sounded for all the world like a man's, deep-chested and gravelly, but it emerged from a middle-aged, horsified

4

beldame whose enormously sagging breasts, slung out contemptuously in a slack grey cardigan, pronounced her, biologically at
least, to be unmasculine. A bleak scowl from the stark-lipped face,
capped by close-cut, iron hair, gave nothing either way. It was
yet possible she was a man with tits. Tiresias, perchance. Ah, but
there were other signs of femininity: the stumpy varicose calves
bandaged by thick brown nylons with a sheen that set my teeth
on edge and a tweed potato sack draped about a pair of bulging
buttocks. The latter would be encased (I registered in passing)
in brobdingnagian bags, a set of those colossal, cream-coloured,
elasticated knickers, biting masochistically into the white wobbly
thighs—between which there would be lodged something with
all the antiseptic sensitivity of a pot scourer (steel-wool variety)
and at her age lightly dusted with Dettol powder and Vim. This,
I was to learn later, was Fanny Fergusson, a Maths teacher who
doubled as the school matron. Bid them wash their faces and keep
their teeth clean. That was her watchword, O boys of Blair's,
when not perched astride a phallic tower of mathematical Babel,
spouting Pythagoras (Greek to me) to my uncomprehending
brain, out of all the bitterness and frustration of her pent-up
years. A right bitched-up old bag.

The first lesson she ever taught me was in sadism. She lifted me
by the ears out of the shuffling line of new blazers and bundled
me through a door immediately behind us. A brown baize door:
the trapdoor to the bloated spider's parlour. I found myself among
dark-green filing cabinets bloomed with dust, a scuffed desk with
a stained pink blotter, and a Red Cross first aid box big enough
to contain a stick of bombs. In an open drawer I glimpsed some
unfamiliar cotton pads with laces attached. Were they for gagging
and blindfolding miscreants like me? Her eye caught my furtive
glance and she swiped the metal drawer shut with a blotched fist
The echoes returned the shuddering clang.

'So you're a nose-picker.'

It was a statement which I was not invited to question or to
qualify. Nor could I have done so even had I found the courage.
My tongue clove to the roof of my mouth and my bowels
melted to wax within me. How could I possibly explain my
nose-fingering, the wrongful accusation, with reference to that
prefect's shaggy caverns and my own little frisson followed by
the instinctive act of self-exploration? In a flash the two worlds
of reason and imagination came into collision, harsh, incongruous

5

and astonishing, and altered my existence. Not so very long ago I could have come out with just such an explanation as would have befitted a child. All that innocence had gone down the plughole and now I stood naked in the bath before this squat fart of a martinet, this abomination on the name of Eve. I was utterly exposed, without the words to clothe me, to hide my shame. She placed the palms of her hands (toad hands, naturally, to go with the prune face, the ash hair) on the coathanger hoops of her harris-tweeded hips and sneered at me blearily.

'A nose-picker. Well then, let me see what you pick with.'

My tongue laboured to find its way round a word.

'Fingers, boy, fingers, let me see your fingers. Hold out your hand!'

I offered her these trembling appendages in a gesture of the most abject appeasement and did an impression of Charles Darwin lampooned as a gangling, shambling chimp. It produced no softening effect whatever. She whipped from the cardigan pockets a pair of folded nail scissors which she flicked open with the expertise of dire practice—Taft's female counterpart to the teddy boy and SuperGran of the Elvis era. The little silver points gleamed between us. Would a knuckleduster appear on the other hand? But no. Ready to operate, she seized me by one wrist and spat the words at me spitefully.

'Filth! I knew it! Absolute and utter filth!'

I could not believe we were looking at the same hand, as I may tell you I was very particular about scrubbing my nails, even as a little peevish boy, and could not bear the sight of a grain of dirt lodged thereunder. I did, however, keep my nails a little longer than might have been expected in a lad—the spectacle of ragged, bitten-down finger-ends offended me —and it was obviously the length of my nails that had outraged Miss Fergusson and not their degree of uncleanness, though I did not dare suggest to her that they were in fact spotless. Perhaps she read my mind and even came close to offering an excuse for the impending surgery, for she twisted my wrist savagely, flapping my hand in front of my eyes like an alien amputation and spat even harder.

'Do you know how many germs you are harbouring in these claws of yours? how much microscopic filth is breeding invisibly under there? Answer me!'

Did she want a number?

'Speak!'

A globule of Miss Fergusson's saliva (a consequence of the unvoiced bi-labial plosive) flew through space and landed on my lower lip, where it hung and stung. It was poison. I did not dare swallow, let alone speak. She was still squeezing my wrist and at the same time jabbing the air with the scissors; a rather crazed image of Aristotle flashed into my mind—expounding a point in a children's encyclopaedia I had once opened in error. I imagined a beard on her (which was not difficult) and a toga. Then balls. (No problem). A cock crowed out of the Brillo pad, the desert blossoming as the rose.

'Still can't speak, eh? But you can howk your hooter well enough. Well then, understand that these nails may look clean enough to you, boy, but I'm telling you that you could plant potatoes in them. Potatoes!'

I thought about brushing away her bit of gob with my free hand, but even as I did so she came at me again.

'Do you know what you're fit for, nose-picker? I'll tell you what you're fit for. Potato-picking. Yes, nose-picking and potato-picking you may indeed be fit for, boy, but you're certainly not fit to come to school. Not this school, no, and for that matter maybe even the clodhopping farmers wouldn't want you coming onto their land looking like that. They'd say you were a cissy, to grow your nails that length!'

> To plough and sow, to reap and mow
> And be a farmer's boy

'Did you say something? Do you think I'm a lip reader or something? If you want my best opinion for you, boy, I believe it's chimney-sweeping, the dirtiest trade of the lot! Where do you come from when you're not in the ash-hole?'

'Kilminnins,' I managed to get out of my poisoned lips.

'Kilminnins, *miss!*' she thundered.

Kilminninsmiss. It was too tortuous for me to produce. I made the attempt and she slapped me hard in the face.

'Kilminnins!. Where the drunkards and the ne'er-do-wells live out their lives, and low lives at that. And where Lord Lumsden himself sweeps the lums, when he's sober once a fortnight.'

Lord Lumsden (nickname naturally) was notorious in the East

Neuk for his lumbering drunken ascents and sudden sobering descents.

'Well then, you can pick your way up the lums with him, my boy, starting from tomorrow, for you're not coming to school in the condition you're in now, you filthy little shrimp!'

I felt another prick of spittle on my eyelash this time. Her teeth were her own but they were as brown as a sailor's in spite of her dentist's breath.

'Have you heard of Nebuchadnezzar, boy?'

I knew all about Nebuchadnezzar from my Sunday school days. My head managed to wobble once in slow affirmation. Heavy, ugly and brainless as a turnip.

'Don't nod at me, boy! Head bobbing up and down there as if he was sucking on a tit! Got the palsy, have you? Nebuchadnezzar. His nails grew as long as a wolf's and he went about on all fours and ate grass for a living. I'll have you on all fours all right, my lad, if I catch you at any more of your germinous ways around here, master Nebuchadnezzar!'

> *Nebuchadnezzar the king of the Jews*
> *Ate the grass and shagged the coos.*
> *When the coos began to roar*
> *Nebuchadnezzar shagged the door.*
> *When the teacher saw his claws*
> *Nebuchadnezzar got the tawse.*

'What are you muttering about again, boy? How dare you stand there dreaming when I'm talking to you? You can just find and write out the chapter about Nebuchadnezzar's nails from the Old Testament ten times for tomorrow.'

It would not be difficult. I practically knew it by heart. The Old Testament had been one of the stories of my life. The New Testament had been the other.

'In the meantime these filthy talons are coming off!'

She dug the scissors so deeply into the quick that the breath was taken from me with a shock, Snip, snip, snip. Each of my nails was treated in exactly the same way: a cut on the left hand side, another on the right, followed by a pitiless, slicing pass along the tip of every finger, leaving me with a set of hideously blunted stubs, some of which were smarting fiercely where, in her deliberate fury, she had punctured the skin. Tears of pain and injustice sprang to my eyes and the chimney-sweeper's cry to my mouth. I fought them off quickly though, because I now had other problems to contend with. Ordering me roughly to get along to Assembly, Miss Fergusson bundled me out into a corridor bristling with tall files of senior pupils and I was carried along captive, an alien reed on the rivers of Babylon and ready to sing the Lord's song in a foreign land.

The concourse bore me down to a vast sea of bodies that filled out the school Assembly Hall. The hall was remarkable for its towering windows which would have flooded the room with summer but for the black blinds that hung like tall tapestries of mourning, so faded, so threadbare that they permitted just enough leakage of sicklified sunlight to remind me of how I had been so brutally snatched from the blue uncomplicated world of skylines and sea and immured instead in this monstrous hutch. To make matters worse I knew I was in the wrong section of the hall and could see no sign of my fellow First Formers. Minutes ago I had been hating them: now I longed to be safe in that seething anonymity out of which Miss Fergusson had plucked me burning. Nor did it take the older pupils too long to become aware of foreign tissue and they quickly invented another problem for me.

'My God, it's a first-year trog! Step on it, Jocky!'

Jocky looked as if he could have stepped on a bull and broken it like a beetle. His close-set eyes nearly met in the effort to formulate the question beamed from the back of his brain. Finally the message got through the bushwire that was his head of hair and out at the front end, where the mouth was.

'Who the fuck are you?'

I held my peace and looked as silly as I could, hoping that I would be pitied and left alone.

'Bugger off!'

Fingers like blotched bananas touched my chest so lightly I thought for a moment he was going to award me a playful tickle for my idiotic impudence in thus invading the territory of the upper forms. One second later I found myself flying backwards into a battlefield of boots and blazers.

'Hey, watch who the hell you're shoving . . . Bloody Mary, it's a bit of first-year shit! Back where you came from, turd!'

I was returned on a flying visit to Jocky and his cronies, who

9

promptly sent me spinning off again into another shield-wall of irritation. Their annoyance soon shaded into amusement and I grew almost content for a space to become the shuttlecock of their better nature. Until it all ended quite abruptly with a frenzied whisper.

'It's the Shark!'

A red-skinned, sweating hot potato by now, I was flung out into exile, utterly disowned, landing brokenly on the slippery chocolate-brown knots of the newly-buffed floorboards and burning my knee so exquisitely it made me yell out—the old chimney-sweeper's cry for the second time that day. At that point the double doors swung apart and in swept a pale personage, white-haired, walrus-whiskered, sternly bespectacled, his gown flowing out in his wake in black flames. God with a haircut. Wearing his executioner's robes. His Old Testament dress.

This was the Rector. Mr Aeneas Sharkey.

A name to conjure with. A name too fine for quotidian utterance, for daily repetition, like bread, for pupil use. Shorten it, then, to what is functional, direct and bluntly, derogatorily descriptive. Of his awful power to horrify, to gorgonise, to chill. Very well then: the Shark.

The Shark.

He fixed upon me one long, baleful stare and pointed to the rostrum. I took his gesture to mean that I was to be elevated to public ridicule and correction before the assembled school and I began fearfully to mount the steps.

'You fool!' he hissed. 'Down there!'

I was merely to stand by the podium throughout the Assembly. There were delighted sniggers from my audience. Trembling, I adopted my position as directed while the Shark took up his imposing stance above that sea of faces whose slightest ripple he could quell with an eyebrow but to whose dumb mockeries I was now exposed.

'We shall sing hymn number 640. Open your hymn books. Music please, Mr Dalyell!'

The organ lurched obediently into life and after the few bars of rousing introduction six hundred voices burst into the verses of a hymn which I had never once heard sung in the holy city of my childhood, in spite of all its churches militant and all its warring flocks.

> *And did those feet in ancient times*
> *Walk upon England's mountains green?*
> *And was the holy Lamb of God*
> *On England's pleasant pastures seen?*
>
> *And did the Countenance Divine*
> *Shine forth upon our clouded hills?*
> *And was Jerusalem builded here*
> *Among these dark Satanic Mills?*

O, boys of Robert Blair's! How can I describe to you the effect first wrought upon me by these words? how give you my testament of joy? If I had a hundred tongues and the eloquence of Nestor, of Hermes, I could not do it. From the very first chords that music broke over me like a cleansing sea, more mysterious, more beautiful by far than the praises of the Congregationalists and the Salvation Army—the Holy Rollers on whose simple rhythms, easy cadences and simplistic sentiments I had been reared. Blessed Assurance; When the Roll is called up yonder; Shall we gather at the river? This is my Story. It was as if something had entered my side and let out all of that hysterical evangelism, the water and the blood, in a crimson flood.

> *Bring me my bow of burning gold!*
> *Bring me my arrows of desire!*
> *Bring me my spear! O clouds, unfold!*
> *Bring me my chariot of fire!*
>
> *I will not cease from mental fight,*
> *Nor shall my sword sleep in my hand,*
> *Till we have built Jerusalem*
> *In England's green and pleasant land.*

The images came at me like a quiver of darts; I was gloriously transfigured, transfixed. William Blake was no mere fire in the guts, he was a white-hot sword in the bowels, a flaming skewer in the groin, a terrible churning in the brain, turning the world red. This school was ugly. Its architecture was Victorian ugly, its brown doors and towering blackened windows, its tigerish teachers and braying pupils, they were all part of an ugly world and I was a piece of scum shivering on its skin. But I had heard the chimney-sweeper's cry and he had heard mine. I had heard the music of chariots—not those sweet chariots that would one day be coming for to carry me home, but the chariots of fire, the chariots of Elijah, the chariots of the gods. And for a blessed moment I was the Church Triumphant, swept up in glory.

And was it not then that something other than True Religion also pierced my soul? Oh, yes, a thousand times yes. It was England, my dears. Yes, England. Entered my consciousness for the first time in that strange mysterious way that has been with me ever since. Not the England of my Primary School history books that we'd tashed at Bannockburn by digging pits, and that got its own back a couple of centuries later when shivered was fair Scotland's spear and broken was her shield; and again at Culloden when *bugger you, Butcher Cumberland* and *go and fuck your cannon* proved such an inadequate strategy replacing the old Highland Charge, led by a piss artist. England that has been getting its own back ever since, as we are well aware. No, Flodden and all that was just a dusty page from an old text book, enlivened for me at the age of six by an engraving of a weeping Scottish knight, who with vailed lids looked for his noble comrades in the dust. It was that which had turned England in my mind into a massed army of bloody bastards, nothing more—the Ancient Adversary, the innocent rose with the serpent under it. No, that was not the England that took possession of me now. And it was not the England whose capital city was London, population fifty million, and whose Midland towns made knives and forks. That particular England was as meaningless to me as the banal pronouncement that Sheffield gives us steel, stuck in my brain like some throbbing thorn from Primary Three. What had I ever cared about Sheffield and its steel? What had knives and forks to do with me? But it was now that the first intimations came thundering up the sands of youth with a golden leonine roar that here was another England, a literary England, with treasures on offer far richer than the folk culture of my early days, the stories round the fire, the writings on stones: an England whose green and pleasant land I should one day rape and plunder in an orgy of aesthetic lust. Genuine poetry communicates before it is understood, as T.S. Eliot said (and wisely was it said, defending his own verse) and while I had no understanding, as I stood there, of what was happening to me, the trick had been worked. I had heard the sound of great poetry. I had heard the pre-echoes of this New England and it became at once the balm of my hurt mind.

This was the music that crept by me upon the waters in the

twelfth year of my age: the waters of the Firth of Forth where I had sat down and wept for the king my grandfather's wreck and for the king my father's death before him.

My head was swimming when the music ceased, its reverberations still surging backwards like a red beating sea. I could not see for tears, or hear for the blood in my ears. Dimly I became aware that the rector was droning out lists of instructions and regulations for the day, for the session. For life. Earth-shattering principles of existence such as that taps must be turned off after use, chewing gum must not be stuck in inkwells or on the undersides of desks, obscenities must not be scribbled on the walls of toilets—which must be flushed after use.

And so it went on. Thou shalt not cease from mental fight, nor shall thy pen sleep in thy hand. Catapults are forbidden in the school grounds and the arrows of desire must not be fired till we have built Jerusalem in the East and *not* in the West Quad. And keep the red flame burning. And always, always, keep to the left . . .

Assembly was dismissed so that the school day could begin but I was kept standing, under the Rector's lofty glare, inscrutable behind the flashing glasses, while the forms filed off, out of the filtered black sunlight, out of the double doors, Jocky and his cronies assuring me with sly swiping gestures accompanied by winks and pained grimaces that I was certain to be belted.

I waited with dry mouth and thudding chest.

When the hall was empty and the double doors swung shut, the Rector turned to me in the sudden silence.

'Name?'

I gave it.

'You are a troublemaker, boy. I can see it. I can smell it from you. I can sense it in your face. You have come here to cause trouble and with no other purpose in mind. Am I not correct? Is this not true?'

Whichever reply, affirmative or negative, seemed bound to displease. Why did teachers ask such stupid questions? I pursed my lips, furrowed my forehead, screwed up my eyes, hunched my shoulders, flexed my buttocks, whined a little and tried to look as cringingly vile as the doziest sinner ever to stand before the big white throne. The combination seemed to work a little in my favour.

'Perhaps,' he said slowly, 'perhaps you are stupid enough to wish to go on being a troublemaker. Alternatively you may just be too stupid to succeed. Either way I have a quick cure for you. For the moment I shall be content to wait and see. Now get along to your Maths class. Miss Fergusson, Room 9.'

I shuffled towards the door.

'But remember,' the grating voice harried me, 'I know the name that God gave you, I know your surname and I know that stupidity and trouble are your middle names. I don't want to hear any of them ever again. Now go!'

I went.

'Geometry,' said Miss Fergusson, is the *measuring* of the world.'

'Geography,' said Mr Blythe, 'is the *drawing* of the world.'

'History,' said Mr Munro, 'is the *story* of the world.'

'Ah, but science,' drooled Mr Drummond, 'science, boys and girls, is *knowledge* of the world. If you know science you know everything. Everything you need to know.'

Science. From the Latin *scienta*, meaning knowledge. Look at your blazers, boys and girls, look at the badge of your school, *your* school, Taft Academy, and tell me what you see.

Two tall towers and a ship passing through the portals, pennants and flags proudly fluttering, the colours of Lieutenant Andrew Taft, mariner, scarlet and black, and underneath the insignia an unfurled ribbon of Latin, an erudite streamer of blood, telling us of our rite of passage. Many pass through . . . And knowledge shall be increased. *Et augebitur scienta*.

And knowledge was increased, boys of Blair's, by Jesu it was.

By the formidable right arms and bloody razor-sharp brains of Mr Munro, History; Mr Sterne, Latin; Mr Macdonald, Art; Mr Dalyell, Music; and even Mr Peter Periwinkle, Maths. And English teachers I shall come to by and by. Men who took the time not merely to instruct—but to teach.

Teach? Yes, *teach*.

You see, anyone can *instruct* with a book in one hand and a piece of chalk in the other. Instruction is easy, with a computer in the corner and a check-list in the file and a conference to go to and an in-service to attend and a committee to sit on after school. And a father to bury and a filly to fuck and a field to plough. But these fellows at least had some soul. They taught out of themselves, not out of a book, and that meant that when occasion required it of them they laid aside the ablative case, the diminished fifth, the seventeenth Euclidean proposition, the policies of Bismarck—and gave us instead the Sermon on the Mount, the cock-ups of Churchill, the psychology of dreams, the spawning of the salmon, the Big Bang, the buttocks of Catherine the Great (another Big Bang), the Song of the Volga Boatmen local songs by vulgar fishermen, Le Saint Prepuce, the Harlot of Jerusalem, the story of their lives—just as I now give you mine—and the mating habits of trawlermen and giant female skates when times were tough and chip shops not so fussy.

Little did I know when I myself passed through the twin towers of Taft Academy on my very first day, was near circumcised by Miss Fergusson, crucified by Jocky and his henchmen, suffered under the Shark and was resurrected by William Blake's 'Jerusalem', that this was the school that would actually inspire me to get wisdom and to become a teacher myself, a dealer in life's most precious commodity. Understanding. Not the base external trash of human existence, too servile and illiberal for me, but the choicest apple from the bough, that would enable me to do unto the young what my teachers were destined, in spite of all appearances on that first day, to do for me. To stand on the very pinnacle of creation and practise the noblest profession of them all.

O holy simplicity! O felix culpa! O tempora! O shit! Where ignorance was bliss, 'tis folly now to be wise. But all's too late for that. The question of exile from the Eden of childhood was no mere matter of the reply biological and the hell of puberty. It also had to do with the lie academical and the pursuit of false gods.

Oddly enough fame was never the spur. That last infirmity of noble minds that leads some clear spirits to scorn delights and live laborious days. Which ought to bring us back to Milton . . .

Except what would be the point? When what we really need is Milton brought back to *us*. Back to the classroom, from which he has been much missed of late. Scotland hath need of thee, old friend. And England? Oh, bugger England. The green and pleasant land is fencing off its literary pastures too, so that sheep may safely starve, uncorrupted by clover and battened on fast and useful . . . A no-nonsense area, pedestrian precinct. The hungry flock look up and are not fed. Stuff that. What happened, then, to your friendly neighbourhood teacher? Yours truly will be impossible in the next squeaky clean millenium. Milton? Who'd he play for, boyo? God? Aye, not heard from *Him* this while back. English? What the fuck's that, when it's at home? Ah, you means Communications, Media Studies, Life Skills, Every School's Service Industry? That sort of thing . . .

That sort of thing.

No, that sort of thing would never have stopped a donkey on the road to Damascus, would it?

But Milton did. And Shakespeare, and Homer, and Handel, and Bach. And William Blake. And a hundred more where they came from. They worked the magic . . . and put me under the spell.

2

MY FIRST GENUINELY educational experiences at Taft Academy after William Blake had nothing to do with English or History or Physics or French. With the square on the hypotenuse, the conjugation of *être* or the chemical constituents of water.

Ah, no, O, no, O, noni noni no.

Alack alas, amo amas.

They were solely concerned with my prick.

Which brings us not to Milton, I fear, but to the revelation sexual.

And Wanker's Wynd.

Yes, Wanker's Wynd ... and the Revelations of John the Divine. It will not have escaped your notice that I have omitted the bit about John the Divine's being a saint, which normally forms part of the tag. That is because the John about whom I am going to talk to you this afternoon was not a saint. As a matter of fact he was the furthest thing removed from saintliness that a gnostic God could possibly have devised to throw himself into comic relief. We called him John the Divine simply because he wasn't (divine) and because his father was one of the parish ministers.

John Cranford could have made a mint in the Middle Ages posing for cathedral craftsmen when the master mason said, 'I think we'll do gargoyles today, boys—and be sure and make 'em ugly!'

Cranford was ugly all right. To say that his face was the arsehole of creation would be a blot on all backsides ever bared, even one of those you sometimes see on a chimpanzee, with piles like the Hanging Gardens of Babylon. The merest suggestion that his physiognomy was pockmarked and moonshaped would be unfair to smallpox, lunatics and centuries of Romantic verse. To describe his actual complexion as rough, purple and blotchy would do offence to a blighted plum. And his nose was an affront to the very worst effects of syphilis on an old-time Neapolitan.

Well, perhaps I am exaggerating a little, just a little, mind you, allowing myself a modicum of poetic licence and a degree of drift—drift, my boys, as Milton did when mourning his Lycidas and attacking the abuses of the Church instead. The purest purist may be puritanical and the converse may be true too. But to return to the medieval theme—Cranford could have understudied for the part of Satan (without the use of make-up) in a thirteenth-century miracle play. He'd have done Judas Iscariot as easily as shinning up an elder tree. A little later on in the evolution of the drama he'd have been able to walk straight on stage as Caliban, his brains in his bollocks. Fancy might yet find him even in the bathrooms of a Spike Milligan stately home, decorated à la Puckoon, his frightful visage engraved in porcelain on the insides of bidets and toilet bowls as a sure cure for piles. O, pardon, gentles all! We're back again to the medico-lavatorial, but it's true that one look at that grim visage and the little devils would scurry back to their hell of fiendish invention, thus relieving the sufferer of his bunches of black grapes.

You probably think by now that this is going too far, much too far, over the very top. Bear with me, boys of Blair's, and I believe that in the end you will come to understand and even accept my strength of feeling. I know you will. You see, no one who is intelligent and sensitive can ever really be described as ugly, no matter how conventionally unhandsome his features may appear to be. Take Laughton, for example. He was never ugly—not even as Quasimodo, or Bligh. Or take Socrates—that picture of henpecked misery. Xanthippe didn't marry *him* for his looks, and as for her, she no doubt showed all the brains she had when she took off the bottom half of her two-piece toga. Who is't that can define true beauty, pray? The real trouble with John Cranford, you see, lay underneath his looks. He was not blessed with a single grain of sensitivity, nor had he a grain of intelligence. He was a moron.

An utter moron.

Speak that last sentence, if you will, rather slowly, pausing briefly between each word, achieving increased emphasis and augmented pitch on the 'utter', and you may begin to feel—(sound affecting meaning, as I have always taught you)—something of the degree of Cranford's stupidity: his crassness, his coarseness, his contemptible depravity. These are what compounded his ugliness, translating it into a myth of our time and place. As schoolboys, however, we considered it hitting below the belt to refer in conversation to our classmate's evil-favoured features. After all he could not help it; it was a matter of genetics. When he was born he was at once pronounced the ugliest baby to appear north of Berwick-on-Tweed since the Reformation, so an unkind cleric was heard solemnly to whisper outwith the doting father's hearing. His stupidity was equally a matter of heredity, a booby prize gifted to him in the genes: there was plenty of family intelligence but he had opened the wrong box. Yet somehow we did not see it that way, preferring the view that oafishness, unlike ugliness, was a chap's own fault, a condition he could do something about if he simply tried to pull himself up by the jockstrap and get what brains he did possess onto the top storey.

So there were a great many jokes invented in our year about John Cranford's incurable dopiness. Jokes of which I can remember three.

1. What do you call a fly on John Cranford's head? Answer: a space explorer.

2. What do you call a brick on the top of John Cranford's head? Answer: an extension.

3. What do you call John Cranford with half a brain? Answer: gifted.

With such schoolchild ironies and images I have striven to bring him before you, our antagonist and anti-hero, if I may marry the twain. At least these pleasant introductory remarks may afford you some idea as to just what sort of a person we are talking of. Very well then, now imagine this baneful boy, grinning from ear to ear. (You wouldn't expect he had much to grin about, would you? And yet, Cranford's greatest asset as a youth—possibly his only one—was this shallow geniality of his, a quality which was to be hideously destroyed over the years. Oh, yes, the pity of it, you might be tempted to say, if you did not get to know him better—as you will—oh, yes, the pity of it, Iago, the pity of it, ha ha!) Imagine, as I say, this twelve-year-old Quasimodo bearing down upon you, with a great grin slashing apart his monstrous phiz, rendering him like unto some out-of-season turnip lantern, and you not knowing him from Adam or Old Nick. This was the position in which I found myself on my very first day at secondary school, the startled recipient of a most unorthodox lesson that was hastily interpolated in five seconds and one easy part between Physics and French, and as foreign to my experience as either of these alien disciplines. The subject was put to me quite simply by this catastrophically ugly son of the manse who (I should inform you now) was new to the district, having moved up from London during the summer with his dog-collared pater.

'Listen,' he whispered, stealing furtive glances around the class-room that was already bustling with blazers, some of them with girls inside them, 'listen . . .' His eyes glinted with the light of the most reprehensibly wicked revelation and for a moment he resembled Robert Newton, not quite certain whether he was playing Bill Sykes, Ancient Pistol or Long John Silver. He settled for the Pistol. As ever.

'Listen, did you know . . .' (evil pause) 'did you know that if you go into the bathroom and rub your prick for a few minutes, it'll start to *foam*? Did you know that? It's called *wanking*!'

I did not know. There was scarcely a boy in the class who knew. Our pricks were for peeing through and that was the extent of our private knowledge. The serpent had not as yet so much as indicated the attraction of the apple, but Cranford had arrived and on our very first day had split it to the core and his fruit was sweet to our taste. We were magicians; henceforth we should do tricks with our wands, and we should be as gods. Yea, and I said, ye shall be as gods. By the start of the period the whispered wildfire had caused something of a sensation in the room, to be suppressed by the entrance of Mr Fat Boy Farquhar, French teacher extraordinaire, Francophile by taste and pederast by popular repute.

'I shall begin by showing you how to roll your Rs,' he said, pronouncing it *arrs* so as to emphasise the pun and at the same time turning his back upon us and swivelling his own Billy Bunterish bottom on his out-thrust pelvis with decidedly comic effect.

'Now, each time you come to your French r's, just think of my rump—and roll away!'

We were quite taken aback by this unorthodox figure. Never had our Primary education—a series of unloved misses, all buns and no breasts—thrown up such an oddity. We were to see a lot more of Fat Boy's arse-rolling before he was done. Meanwhile we paid scant attention to our first lesson in French pronunciation, so eager were we to run to the bogs at morning break and subject our privates to this very first experiment according to the newly discovered principles of John the Divine.

The bogs were an outside affair, open unto the fields and to the sky, courtesy of numerous holes in the roof through which the noisy elements whistled at our willies. This whitewashed brick byre bore the scribbled obscenities of yesteryear, an accumulated mass of filthy doggerel and intimations of immorality, many of them amply illustrated for the benefit of those for whom words alone were not sufficient to convey the awesome wickedness of boys' first confrontations with sex.

> *In days of old when knights were bold*
> *Their balls were made of brass.*
> *Their dickies clanked and when they wanked*
> *The sparks flew up their arse.*

A perfect specimen of the ballad quatrain: alternating tetrameters and trimeters, rhyming *abab*. Not that I appreciated that at the time, but clearly the act of wanking belonged to an old and noble order.

And so, surrounded by similar incitements from the hands of our progenitors and scholarly precursors, we fell to with a will (excuse pun) upon our hitherto innocent members, John the Divine setting himself up like Satan in Pandemonium as leader of that execrable orchestra, criticising someone's tempo, suggesting here and there a smoother rhythm, urging upon us a universal concentration.

At first nothing happened, other than a natural enlargement of each penis present—I counted thirteen in the group—and we hauled away in grim silence. Was it some idiotic lie? Who was this Cranford? And then at last understanding began to dawn and a beatific smile o'erspread each countenance in that occult assemblage.

'I can feel something . . . my balls have gone all prickly . . . it's like I'm on fire . . . hey boys, this is great!'

After which the grins tightened into an expression of that kind of desperate ecstasy with which some of you will long since have grown familiar: each particular mouth widened to a yawning red chasm, the hands flew faster, the breathing quickened, conversation was strangled for several frenzied and unprecedented seconds . . . Until it finally hit us: the first wave of orgasm. The first wave to assault us in the twelfth year of our age. There would be many more such waves before the castle of innocence crumbled. And fell into the sea.

John the Divine (High on a Throne of royal state) had conducted us well. We arrived virtually together in a baker's dozen of euphoric roars that must have been heard across continents. Oceans. Unserpented Edens I believe every voice in the class broke in that single split second of release, from Welsh tenors to Russian basses, and we lay back for a few trembling moments, new made, each boy astonished by the bursting of his own bud. Not much on this first occasion: just a thin hot wire of sap shooting upwards and a crown of creamy white petals garlanding the already drooping phallus. Not much to look at—but we had flowered and deflowered, we had shown our colours, fluttered our white ensigns and now we had the masts to nail them to. We were men. Able-bodied and ready to set sail. We looked at one another in admiration of ourselves. Boys no more, we had initiated ourselves into the grand and noble order of Wanker's Wynd, with John the Divine presiding as high-priest of the phallus. We had done what our forefathers did before us and were now one with knights of old and fucking old wankers the world over.

The irony was that at that moment of first ejaculation there were few of these twelve-year-old comers-of-age who actually knew for a certainty the precise and ultimate purpose of the act that had just been carried out. There was no reason whatever to relate it in any way to the girls in our class. The facts of life were as yet unknown to us and we awaited the further mystic revelations of John the Divine. Somewhere in my own head a childhood voice whispered to me that boys came from the Bass Rock and girls from the May Island, and though reason would have told me, had I ever seriously wondered about it, that this was untrue, the simple fact is that I never did wonder. Nor did I wonder now. Not yet awhile. At that moment nothing else seemed to matter. We had stumbled upon a new pleasure that cost nothing—And it's free, boys, it's free!—so we were innocent as batsmen without balls, revelling in the glory of our theoretical strokes. Rather like those ingenuous Elizabethan poets of Golden Age Verse, hitting off conceits harmlessly, for fun and without a solitary point of artistic advancement. Until John Donne appeared on the scene and hit every one for six.

22

We were a long way from that.

There followed weeks of total absorption in this new and delectable recreation. We practised it individually and in groups; met in solemn conclave to compare notes on the matter; speculated long and loftily on its putative advantages. It increased the size of the prick and energized the balls; it caused hairs to appear, encouraging pubic growth especially, and also on chest, arms and legs; it deepened the voice, made manly shaving necessary, kept colds at bay, prevented insanity and stimulated the heart.

Until darker doubts assailed us and gathering clouds of guilt. Wanking had its fearful side-effects, apparently ranging from the undesirable to the positively lethal. It gave you spots, turned you blind, induced cancers, haemorrhages and high blood pressure, caused impotence by the time you were twenty, led to premature baldness, deafness and senility, reduced intelligence, weakened the bladder, and in extreme cases caused failure of circulation in the prick, making it wither and so, ignominiously, drop off. This last was the long expected apocalypse in the awful iconography of Wanker's Wynd.

The worst moment came when it was announced that the school Medical Officer was arriving to conduct a full frontal examination of every child in the Academy. The senior boys warned us with grave assurances as to the ulterior motives that underlay this exercise. *It's to find out if you wank!* And instant panic spread throughout the ranks of the entire male population of the first year as we listened to what the seniors had to say.

They'll look for the usual signs: an enlarged cock, a slack foreskin, hairy balls, prominent blood vessels, and loose tendons in the wrist. And what happens if they do find out? A letter home to parents, naturally, followed by automatic expulsion and an indeterminate period of hospitalisation, accompanied by whatever surgical steps were necessary to rectify the damage we had wrought upon our private selves. But they can't expel all of us, surely! And what will our mothers say? Think of the disgrace. We all began to rue the day we had hearkened to the wicked disclosures of John the Divine. His feet went down to death and his steps took hold on hell.

'You've got one chance,' we were gravely advised by an old salt of the Sixth Form who had survived this hazard and was known to possess the wiles of Odysseus. 'The doctor will pull down your pants and ask you to cough. As he does this, Fanny Fergusson will bend down and watch your balls. If they fly upwards while you're coughing, you're done for. It's the ultimate test. If you're a wanker then try to cough from the chest—that's your only way out.'

The thought that Fanny Fergusson would spy out our naked-ness was bad enough but was swallowed up in the greater fear of detection. To picture her bent double, with her gorgon's eyes riveted to our testicles was a hideous prospect, but to consider that she would then know precisely what we had been doing, how we had been spending our time behind locked doors—it was unthinkable. All of us ran home that afternoon to spend a naked evening coughing in front of the mirror. I even rigged up a second mirror, tilted strategically at the testicles so that I might observe their slightest movements. To my unmitigated horror I found that no matter how hard I tried I simply could not manage even the daintiest cough without dislodging my bollocks from their low-slung quietude into an upwardly mobile, guiltily buoyant movement. I tried coughing quickly and sharply; slowly from the larynx, with throat-clearing deliberateness, avoiding the diaphragm; mockingly, casually, politely, savagely, until my mother shouted at me from the other side of the door that I'd be sent to the doctor if I didn't desist. Affrighted beyond measure, I coughed a few more times, watching in dismay as the balls bobbed like uncontrollable corks inside their ball-bag, helpless little betrayers to the practised inquisitorial eyes of Fanny Fergusson, witch-pricker unwonted and finder-out of abuses and self-abusers.

It was just too late: the damage was done and I was doomed to discovery and condemnation along with the rest of my class. What scenes of ignominy were to be unfolded after tomorrow? I considered running away, faking an accident. Self-castration. Suicide. My mind moved dreamily to the very point of the breakwater, far beyond the harbour, where the lapping tangles of kelp and laminaria salaamed and beckoned out of the deep waters in slow dark sarabandes. One little jump from the utmost pier-end of civilisation and I'd be entangled in the cold caresses of congers and sea-cats and crabs, dumb beings of the sea, whose imagined attentions held far less horror for me at this moment than those of Fanny Fergusson and the school Medical Officer in a few short hours from now.

I pictured the suicidal scene.

Boys of Blair's, have you ever been half in love with easeful death? Let me tell you I was more, much more than half in love with the prospect. I was head over heels, arse over tit, and was really beginning to get well into the kind of poetic atmosphere that the great Milton creates for the drowned Edward King—or Lycidas, if you prefer, to the literary circles in which you will justifiably move once you have completed your study of this poem. Ah, the sea-imagery of *Lycidas*! I didn't know it then, at that tender age, prior to my literary conversion, but I had no need of it, for the real thing called to me to come and end it all. To sink beneath the watery floor, just like the day-star going to bed, to have the shores and sounding seas wash me far away, hurling my bones beyond the stormy Hebrides—

> *Where thou perhaps under the whelming tide*
> *Visit'st the bottom of the monstrous world.*

It sounds almost pleasant, doesn't it? Like a package tour of eternity beneath the sea, with a bevy of mermaids to keep you company and cool your fevered brow while you feed deep, deep upon their peerless breasts. Yes, I was convinced, and I believe I was just about ready to take the long journey down to the edge of existence and off—when at that crucial moment in my agonisings there came a loud knocking at the back door.

O, the sweetness of unexpected succour! O, lovely knocking at the door! O Person from Porlock who kept me from another world!

It was my bosom crony of the first year, Peem Peattie, bearing with him the news of our salvation, and from the beatific aspect of his face that day, I felt in my very soul the saving grace of the message before it was even uttered. O, it came o'er my ear like the sweet sound that breathes upon a bank of violets, stealing and giving odour. And what were the tidings, pray? Carried by fiery cross, they had already spread up and down the coast from the manse at Kilminnins where John the Divine sat like a monstrous worm at the heart of the apple. In the Old Nick of time that archetypal reprobate had come up with the solution and had sent it out by the feet of winged Mercuries through farms and villages for miles around. How beautiful are the feet of them that bring the gospel of good news! I could have kissed Peem's, at any rate.

And the missive was quite simply this:

You must, when called to the Medical Examination Room, behave normally, even when stripped down to your underpants. But as soon as the doctor makes to pull down your kegs, you must quietly, unobtrusively, flex the muscles of your buttocks and pull upwards on your balls, holding them up for as long as your private parts remain exposed. The crucial part of the examination will last only several seconds. That way, when you come to cough as requested, you will find that your balls have no upward distance left through which they can possibly travel and consequently there will be no tell-tale testicular ascent. The moment you are allowed to pull up your pants you can relax your buttocks and balls and bob's your uncle.

'I've tried it,' said Peem. 'It works.'

We ran to the bathroom and tore off our clothes. It was true. It was simple. It was sublime. It was ridiculously, fiendishly easy. It was yet another of John the Divine's diabolical masterstrokes.

We hared out of the house and down to the harbour, screaming to the very skylines, to carry the glad tidings to fellow wankers throughout the town, to unlock them from the miserable prisons of their guilt and drag them with us, whooping, down to the breakwater, along whose crumbling ramparts we charged in a wanton frenzy of freedom. This was no suicide mission now. Waving V-signs at the dark waters which could not claim us as yet, we pulled out our pricks, yelled defiance at the invulnerable air and wanked in mad abandon into the firth. After which we stripped to our underpants and dived with one accord into the deep waves. Normally we kept to the harbour when swimming, being rather wary of the longer, colder pulses of the open sea, with its oozy woods and cold-blooded, sharp-toothed things that crept and slithered among unseen weeds. But we were as euphoric as dolphins, so full of valour that we smote the very air for breathing in our faces, and for more than an hour we splashed and struck about ourselves in a charmed circle of sanctuary and relief. The setting sun dripped like a burst rose, making the green one red, and we tore the sea's net to shreds with our wild shrieks that beat upon the water like gongs. Then we pulled our clothes over our wet bodies and marched home in single file, singing 'Jerusalem' at the tops of our breaking voices. We would not cease etcetera, nor should our swords sleep in our hands . . .

It came as something of a massive anti-climax when next day we were each subjected to a gruff grunt and a cursory inspection by the school doctor, who peered at our privates so wearily we concluded he must have seen more pricks than a King's Cross bog and was doubtless dying to get on to the girls—a thought which led Cranford to aspire to medicine for the remainder of the day. Fanny Fergusson was not even present.

Decades later, when fond memory brings the light of other days around me, what I remember best is that long baptismal hour at the point of the breakwater. I had intended it for my Hades and it became instead my glad immersion in the water of life, my sweet Siloam's shady rill where sweet the seaweed blows. I shut my eyes upon you now, O ye of little faith, O nest of vipers, O well-taught boys of Blair's, and I see instead a generation of innocents who knew not what they did, or were. Dear Christ, the very houses on the shore did seem to leap along with us—a city on the inconstant billows dancing—the kirk steeple was a clenched fist, punching the sky, the seagulls immortal souls in bliss, their cries rising in ascending thirds and floating and fluting like Delius, and the sea drift was endless and tomorrow was another day. And what see'st thou else in the dark backward and abyss of time? Much more, much more, but for now only that magic circle of swimmers, that sunset—a dripping rose, a flushed firth. That holy city dancing on the waves. That dolphin-torn, that gong-tormented sea.

Forgive the arcane allusion to Yeats's 'Byzantium' and forgive me when I tell you that for several days after these events there was, I am afraid to say, a mad outbreak of wanking among the guilt-liberated First Years. We came in from rugby, our loins girded with sweat, and wanked in the steaming hot showers. We wanked in smirking coveys at the bottom end of the sports field, far from the madding Head's ignoble wife (the top end adjoined the Rector's back garden, you see, where Madame Shark skulked among the flapping yellow camisoles. And stays. And at any hour, of any colour, believe you me.) We wanked on the beaches, we wanked on the benches, we wanked into test-tubes—we surrendered our sperm at every opportunity, indulging in that frenetic affirmation of the life-thrust that made the folk of the Dark Ages fuck with joy as soon as they got it into their skulls that the world was not, after all, about to go up in flames at the end of the first millenium Anno Domini, as they had been well warned that it would by no less a person than Wulfstan, that Benedictine beater of the drum, in his Monster Raving Loony Party prose. And when the year One Thousand came and went, I wonder if Wulfstan then went—and came? Into his vestments. With the same apostatic ecstasy as took us of Taft when we knew we were safe. Or as put the peoples of the Middle Ages into the jim-jams during the great decimations of the bubonic plague, when they ran in droves to the graveyards and gang-bashed audaciously in presence of their foe, the old Grim Reaper himself, bringer of the Black Death. Our particular bone-man, with hour-glass and scythe, was the pale Shark; Fanny Fergusson was the Angel of Death; and the plague we suffered from was, alas, the plague of adolescence, spots and all, the end of innocence, and the onset of the most exquisitely painful period in the whole human span.

It blew itself out, however, this storm of concupiscence and glee, and by the end of that first term we had rounded our Cape Horns and wanking was a subject barely referred to except in the most bored tones adopted by those world-weary wankers who had been through the excitements of youth and bravery and saw nothing new under the sun. Such ingenuousness was natural, I suppose. The era of girls had not yet dawned, you see, and we little knew what torments we had to suffer when we marched under Cupid's banner. But the hour of the female had not yet come and that of wanking had passed into ordinariness. We divided our time between football and French and dodging the Shark. There was one boy in the class, however, who simply never stopped wanking, who remained a wanker all his life. Those of you with an ounce of literary intelligence and critical imagination (enabling you to discern the metaphorical force of this entire recollection of wanking) will note in passing that Milton has much to say in *Lycidas* about wankers. Those of you with even half an ounce of that same critical gumption will not be surprised to hear that that one boy who carried on wanking after childhood into manhood (and doubtless age and death)—was John the Divine.

It is time, I suppose, to come out with my own particular revelation about this wicked revealer of the facts of life, this corrupting companion of my earliest youth, this serpent in Eden. Time for me, as they say, to come clean. It is early in the lesson to play this card, I agree, and to lose whatever suspense I may have generated about this boy, but for reasons which will shortly become clear to you, I have no choice. You see, I have to tell you that John the Divine (though he himself was the lyingest knave in christendom) is no mere figment of my creative imagination or instrument of my lost poetic licence. In a word, I must confess to you that all of you *know* John the Divine. He is here among you now. Yes, his identity is known to you, and yet it is not yet known. And here, I perceive, your puzzlement begins.

Let me make it a little easier for you.

John Cranford was, as I have already informed you, a moron: an intellectual prat of the first order. That did not, of course, prevent him from taking his Leaving Certificate, with Higher passes in English, Maths, French, Physics, Chemistry and Geography. Wonder not that I can class as a moron someone who succeeded in tucking no less than six academic passes under his belt before he left school. They were not brilliant passes; they were sufficient to equip him for entry to The University. CAMBRIDGE UNIVERSITY.

Ah yes, you are protesting by this time—I can see it in your faces, those of you on whom the first light is beginning to dawn. I can hear you telling yourselves that my comments about Cranford's lack of intellect must surely be quite unjustified. How in the name of the wee man could someone stupid actually make it to university, let alone Cambridge University? Ha! Dear children—let go the rosy glasses and the scales drop from your peepers. Step into the light of my greater understanding, behold, and see! Dear juveniles this happens all the time. Such people not only arrive on the university door-step in a state of brainlessness, they actually graduate from the dear old institution even more beef-brained than they were when they first enrolled. And that cocked-up rite of passage is even more certain to be their portion should they happen to attend the universities of Oxford or Cambridge, which are the academic antique shops of this sceptred isle. Art thou incredulous, O kinchins of mine? I can well understand why. But bear in mind, if you will, that I am speaking only of the Cranfords of this world. Added to which, you labour under those burdens of ignorance that your masters wish you to bear, poor sweating little asses that you are, because the heavier the load of crassness and crap that you carry, the harder will it be for you to shake it off and frolic in the green pastures of comprehension. List, list, O list! (as Hamlet's father once said, making his tastes in classical music crystal clear to one seriously unenlightened member of my last year's Higher set!) Listen again, let your millstones roll away, wake up and smell the morning. And learn of me.

Firstly, intelligence and intellect are not one and the same gift of nature. You can't have the second without the first, but you may be blessed with heaps of the first and not own a mustard seed of the second—which is the case with many a university graduate, believe me. They can tell you all about the causes of the French Revolution, aspects of symbiosis in the orchid and the fungus, the eighteenth-century background of cultural primitivism and its relevance to Wordsworth's poetry—but they haven't the feeblest clue what to do with the knowledge they've accumulated in the dark lumber rooms of their tiny brain cells. They may even be brilliant mathematicians and yet remain intellectual morons.

Often—though not always—you may spot such schmucks a mile off, by their fondness for cricket and golf and their attraction to sterile pursuits such as chess and ballroom dancing. Morons United. Naturally I use the word *moron* in my own deliciously idiosyncratic application of the term, to mean an intellectual prick, a knobhead, nothing more. And I needn't be more precise, for you all know what a prick is and dickheads are common as condoms, for which they are most excellent advertisments. That is why I can say, without fear of contradiction, that, added to university graduates in general, and PhDs most of all—(because you really have to be imbecilically stupid to spend three years of your life studying the menstrual cycle of a cat and its influence on the Egyptian funeral service)—most pricks do go to Oxford and Cambridge and emerge from these waxworks even greater wallies than God made them, ever intended them to be, or even thought possible. Not all, mind you—lest I be thought prejudiced—but many.

Oxonium veniunt multi
Redeunt quoque stulti

So runs the medieval proverb. Many go to Oxford and return home none the wiser. 'Twas ever thus, and I have Latin to prove it. It was that way, friends, with John Cranford—except that he went to Cambridge. Well, what's the difference? I have heard so much crap about Oxford and Cambridge in the same breath that I have almost come to believe they're one and the same and that a truly successful pupil doesn't just go to Oxford or Cambridge, he goes to Oxford-*and*-Cambridge and comes back double-glazed. But to be particular about it—yes, there is a difference (he says grudgingly) which is that Cambridge is Oxford's inferior in terms of the *intellectual* quality of its pricks. Butterflies from Oxford, caterpillars from Cambridge has been my finding during a quarter century of teaching, if you really want to know.

So Cranford went to Cambridge.

And he even graduated. (Eventually.)

In Geography.

This untalented dumbo got into Cambridge for two reasons only. *One*: his old man had studied theology there in the fourteenth century or something and so he knew folk who were still there, screwing their students (gaily) and passing the port (blearily). Actually they had died centuries ago but no one had noticed and influence is strong in the House of the Dead. *Two*: Cranford was good at sport, the champion of the Taft Academy 1st XV, 1st XI and the athletics team. Not for him the sober meads of Academe where the cloistered clerks sharpened their quills, toasted their sandalled toes at the brazier, cracked open an egg and fondled the college cat—but in their stead the ruggah pitch, the wicket, the race-track, the boozy dens of macho man and the swaggering upspring reels. Cranford kept more wassail than wicket down south, I can tell you, and as he drained his draughts of Rhenish down he scored many a hole in one—but more in fannies than on fairways, oh yes. Using his favourite club.

And this is how it was.

No sooner had he got among the Cambridge men than Cranford was shafting their maidens, rekindling their matrons, cutting capers on their fields, guzzling their strawberries, their pasties and piss-like beer; swanking around their buttery bars (I did say 'swanking', didn't I?), wearing his true-blue blazers, and making a complete and utter arse of himself, like everyone else on the campus, by tearing up and down the bloody Cam in a punt (I did say 'punt', didn't I?). He'd found a use at last for his formidable right arm other than the exercise of his insatiable knob: the noble art of rowing.

Not that his efforts helped them much in their boat races, even during the interminable years it took Cranford to get a degree. But that's a trifle. By the time he'd failed his Finals he'd cut such a dashing figure that they couldn't find it in their hearts to award him the inevitable Third or Fourth or Fifth, could they? And in any event there was something else that softened these donnish hearts. What was it, think you?

The hidden factor.

Hidden to you, that is—but grip fast, my kinchins: all will be shortly revealed. After all, what did the degree matter, subject or number? He could have graduated in wanking for all anyone cared—with Seventh Class honours (though he'd have got a First in that department any time of the week). The point is, he'd graduated from Cambridge. From *Cambridge*! He was a made man. Made, that is, for professional success back home in a Scotland that goes weak at the knees at the very mention of these consecrated names, Oxford and the Other, irrespective of whether the graduate in question has a brain in his head. It's the name that counts—the name at which we must fall down and worship, sing praises, be joyful.

Our Oxbridge, which art in heaven, hallo to thy name. Thy lingam come, in every bum, In Scotland, as it doth all over. Give us this day our Oxbridge Head, and forgive us our Firsts—from the wrong universities, as we forgive them that did not travel south. And lead us not into temptation to study at home, but deliver us from the evil of our awful Scottish tongue. For thine is the key to the kingdom of promotion, and to power, and to glory—and the free Merc every eighteen months with the house chucked in to boot. Hey, man!

In the face of such Anglophilia and the apotheosis of Oxbridge, how could this fourth-rate prick fail to make his way in Scotland the Grave? He became a teacher of Geography, then a Head of Department, and then Headmaster of a Scottish school. Aha! I begin to see in your faces the dawning of the light. Up until now you have passed off certain facts as coincidences and now you are agog with the prospect of the truth. And yet your incipient understanding is clouded by one great question, one remaining doubt. I know in what your bewilderment consists. Let me put an end to it at once and forever by slotting in for you the final piece of the puzzle.

You see, there was one other reason (as I warned you) why the Cambridge dons, in their gratuitous wisdom (genuflect, you Scottish bastards!) decided to confer the degree of Bachelor of Arts, Second Class Honours, upon John Cranford, and not to award him the intellectual mark of Cain he so richly deserved.

It was because of his accident.

O, now I see you stand like greyhounds in the slips, straining upon the start. But stay awhile and hear me out, if you will. I shall be faithful.

This piss-head Cranford, well-used to drink and drabs, got himself so deep into both one wild night in darkest Cambridge that he suffered a most grievous miscarriage from which it has to be said that he has in no wise recovered. I should state at this point that it actually took him five years to achieve even his miserable version of a degree and that this simply meant for him an extra two helpings in the flesh-pots of the university beer bars, pissing his allowance up against the wall, poking the local tarts and shinning up the bedsit drainpipes of whatever old whores or fallen freshers would drop their knickers for a drunken bum like him. Which was not a few. This night, at any rate, was in the summer term, in early June, when the academic piece was over, bar the rabid shouts of huzzah and howzat and all that suddron claptrap. Cranford and his cronies went out on the town as was their wont and got themselves utterly sloshed, as was also their wont—even by their debauched and Bacchanalian standards. After which they picked up a flock of floosies and brought them down to the boathouse, which was always a handy place for a quick bang, two to a boat, when wardens and landladies were on the prowl in stairwells and on fire escapes for any illicit midsummer fucking. But instead of resting content with the usual spot of dry land wick-dipping (a couple of sozzled stabs and a squirt) Cranford took his boat with its giggling bit of skirt out onto the river for a last laugh, as it were, and farewell and adieu to the carefree days of getting stoned for yet another session. Afloat on the English waves, he soon got stuck into his southern strumpet who, full of Southern Comfort, raised her knees supine on the floor of this narrow canoe, and between the pair of them I have little doubt that they had a jolly passage, rolled to starboard, rolled to larboard as he rowed and rode his filly ungently down the stream.

And indeed life would have been all a dream for John Cranford had it not been for the fact that his was not the only thing that got up that night. A freak storm did as well. Summer lightning, rain and tempest, wild winds, the lot. King Lear Act Three come down to Cambridge, and Cranford and his courtesan caught in the throes of the whole caboodle. They were whirled along like scum (no comment) in the screaming darkness—quite dramatic, it must have been, I suppose (more

Lawrentian than Shakespearean, on second thoughts)—but with Cranford doubtless too drunk to appreciate the qualities either of metaphysical grandeur or human mire in such a scene, even if he'd had a brain in his head to provoke contemplation. Rumble your bellyful, spit fire, spout hurricanes, pour on, I will endure. Not a chance. And even if he'd been sober and well-read he'd still have been shit scared for his skin and nothing more. Such a literal sot. Born to write Headmaster's prose.

In such frightful circumstances an oar might have helped, but guess who forgot what in the cock-up of their midnight embarcation? Cranford had only one well-plied oar in mind when he left the shore and by now that had served its purpose and gone to sleep. So there they were, in a right old stew (a favourite place of Cranford's) with some of the bold boy's inane companions hurtling along the streaming river-banks on foot, keeping time with *le bateau ivre*, some singing pissed songs, some shouting phallic encouragement, using the usual vocables of gentlemen without brain, others just sober enough to realise that there was actually an element of danger here.

They all woke up to the immediate exigency of that danger when they saw the lights of the little pleasure cruiser flashing upstream and heading for home at the rate of how many knots I couldn't have told you even if I'd been on that particular piss-up, which thank heaven I was not, but I have no doubt they were breaking whatever speed limits, legal, moral or practical apply to English rivers. Naturally the boat, a chartered bastard, was in the harmful hands of yet another crew of university tosspots and dullards who'd taken on board their own bloated carcasses a cargo of drink voluminous enough to float the boat itself. Putting it Pinteresquely, for a change, these crapulous Cambridge bums were pissed from backside to breakfast time and Cranford and his little minx stood no chance whatsoever as one flower of Oxbridge ivresse bore down inexorably upon the other, Dionysus himself unable to judge which was the more besotted. Too late the blootered captain of this bibulous band heard a few wispy cries in the wind, saw the white hands fluttering, and so, gropingly, answered the helm, crazily steering the vessel hard a-port. Only to drive Cranford's straw coracle straight into a concrete-enforced section of the river bank, slicing it in two, the prow pinning the hapless matelot to the map of England by what was left of his skewered leg—which was not a lot. The bigger boat was jammed fast and quite apart from the inevitable broken heads and hands that resulted from that collision, Cranford himself was trapped for over two hours in agony, the river level rising rapidly under the furious onslaught of the irreligious elements. Or maybe they were sent by God.

By the time the rescue services arrived he'd shipped so much water down his gullet that he was swamped from arsehole to elbow and screaming like a French whore. They pumped in the morphine, did some cutting and hurried him off to the sawbones. The doctors took one look at his leg and disconnected it or whatever they do to well and truly knackered limbs. It was a cruel blow for the great Cambridge athlete, the unkindest cut of all to a blue star of the campus, but at least he was alive. The same could not be said, alas, of the little *fille-de-joie* who'd gone down with the wreckage of the boat. They dragged her out next morning—no knickers on and mud up her crutch where she had been invaded by the sucking ooze of the ungentle Cam.

O, where were ye, nymphos, when the remorseless deep closed o'er the pretty head of one of your loved number? Wert thou shagging, perchance, on the steep tops of Mona, or dropping your frillies by the Dee? Wherever you were, you let her down, too literally, poor Naiad, to muddy death, poor knickerless, buggered-up Ophelia—and buoyed up in her stead her drunken swain, till rescue came. O, it could have been better done! He could have lost his head, for example, instead of his leg. Down the swift Hebrus to the Lesbian shore that brainless visage might have gone, singing its drunken songs en route, and this ultimate amputation would have left him with no call for explanations. He'd have been a Head of different sorts. As it was, his ancient, trusty, drouthy cronies saw to all that. The explanations, that is to say.

You see, Professor, you see, Inspector, you see, your Worship, my Lord, it was like this. Returning from a modest pass-the-port sort of evening, following a perfectly innocuous little schooner of sherry and plenty of good wholesome roast beef in between, John Cranford and his lady companion went for a quiet stroll along the banks of the sacred river, only to find, when the storm blew up, that some irresponsible person had left one of the college boats too loosely moored and in some danger of being swept away. Heedless of harm, and his heart transfixed as ever by love of the College Boat Club rather than the call of good old-fashioned amour, he leapt to the attempted rescue of the barque, accompanied by the plucky little lady, only to be whisked off by the freakish gusts without benefit of oar or sail. That same night a pleasure boat manned by stout lads celebrating the end of their exams, spied the stricken vessel and, changing to a doughtier tack, tried to come to the rescue. Alas, the power of nature proved too strong even for Cambridge men bent on succour (doubtless an Oxford crew—of genuine suckers—would have perished one and all) and the gallant Cranford lost his leg, while his trollop—er, sorry, fair companion—lost her knickers and her life. (Spot the zeugma, by the bye, O scholars of mine? Condensed sentence to you Dogberries who never learned a thing from your poor old Holofernes, not in six whole years, and are now preparing to slum it through the rest of your quite unliterary lives!) At any rate the bobbies bought it as it meant less paperwork, and more importantly, the dim dons bought it too. Instead of being expelled, Cranford was hailed as a hero: martyred, sainted and crowned overnight. He had put the college first and had paid the scholar-soldier's price. Well, not the ultimate sacrifice but quite enough to be getting on with, thank you. The grave, grey heads that might have wagged and tutted over his shambolic Finals Papers the following year met in sympathetic close circuit and awarded him his Second. The newspapers glorified him in the Douglas Bader tradition—Sports Hero sacrifices his career for College honour, and all that futile crap—and his reputation went before him. His destiny as the Headmaster of a famous public school (Carry on!) was duly sealed.

So: there you have it, O mes enfants chantant dans la coupole! Even now, even now, after all that build-up, you can scarcely believe it, can you? But it's a fact, oh yes, it's incontrovertibly correct, unshunnable, like death. Nothing so terrible, nothing so true. That grey nonentity, that can of clichés, that bureaucratic turd, that foul-faced chimera that shakes his greasy locks at you from the dais, that masquerading ruffian with the tin leg that clanks along the corridors of power—is none other than John the Divine, Your Headmaster, John T. Cranford B.A., the Principal Thing of Robert Blair's College, is John Cranford the Very Same who went to school with me at Taft Academy, tonked his way through Taft and Cambridge to shipwreck, laceration and a sham degree, taught me to wank and has never ceased to wank ever since. In the metaphorical sense, of course. But why 'of course', I hear you ask? Why metaphorical? Quite simple, O youths to fame and fortune yet unknown. It has to be figurative because it cannot be literal. And it can't be literal because, on that fateful night in June 1968, in the murky waters of the sacred Cam, when the rain came down in biblical proportions and drenched the steeples, drowned the cocks—John the Divine's own fine cock was given more than a mere wetting. John T. Cranford B.A. (Cantab), in fact, not only lost a lady and a leg—he also lost his balls.

It brings the tears to your eyes, doesn't it? I don't mean tears of compassion, naturally, for who can feel compassion for a turd? No, I mean it brings the tears to your eyes just to think of being rammed by a pleasure boat and actually castrated. The loss of the leg is more acceptable somehow, in line with the literary and historical traditions: Long John Silver, Captain Ahab and all those gallant lads who got in the way of whales and cannonballs and cutlasses and polar bears and sharks, to peg about in after years in dark-raftered seaside pubs, cadging drinks off the white-clothed ones—the kind that love to have such local characters around as rustic props to boost their middle-class, tennis-tripping urban egos. No, no, you can live without your other pin, grin disreputably and learn to make a virtue of necessity. And if it's cost you a leg, then it's got an aura round it, after all. A touch of atmosphere. Of class. You've crouched in the fo'c'sle, stubbly with goodness, walked out on the whole crowd of craps, undone her dress, clubbed women with your sex, broken them up like meringues, shouted Take that, you bastard and Stuff your pension—and you've got the stub to prove it.

So the leg is acceptable, yes; though regrettable for a rugger oaf such as Cranford, so used to the foul tackle, the boot applied to the knee, the studs to the other guy's scrotum. But to lose your own balls, oh no! No visible wounds to smack of gallantry there, I'm afraid. Knackered in that department, there's not much you can do to siphon off a little sympathy from the surrounding world, where the fat and greasy citizens sweep on, swigging their pink gins regardless. You can scarcely swagger the nut-strewn roads if some of them happen to be your own. (Nuts, that is.) Still less strip your jock-strap and show your scars to gentlemen of England now abed (blessed with full sets of balls, the bastards!)

and shout like Larry the Fifth that this you got upon St Crispin's Day. No such luck.

Quite an event, though, when you do come to think-about it. After all, who among you can boast of having caught a whole crutchful of cruiser and lived to tell the tale? John Cranford did it. Only he didn't go for the re-telling bit. Not much of the Ancient Mariner in chummy, as you all know. The minute details of the circumstance itself evade me, of course. Whether his testicles, so well-tried in their day, were mangled to an unprocreative pulp. Or were simply sliced clean off to float downstream, singing their swansong to the frenzied lesbians of the sybaritic south. I know not, neither do I care. The point is they were now—as President Richard Nixon said at one hilarious moment in the Watergate trial, of all his previous statements—'rendered inoperative'. A classic euphemism for a string of lies. A classic periphrasis for the inability to fuck.

Whatever the method, I have no doubt that Cranford suffered, yes, suffered. Physical pain is not what I am talking about. That goes without saying. I am thinking of his spiritual suffering, inasmuch as a bastard without a soul can ever really be said to experience incorporeal pain. Perhaps I should rephrase myself, then. Let us say that Cranford sustained, in addition to his physical injuries, immense psychological damage. Just as he was preparing himself for years of asininity, propping up the bars of rugby-clubs, rowing clubs and sundry F.P. drinking howffs, where he planned to stand in his Pringle jersey, the little woollen lion on his left tit swelling to the sound of his coarse jokes and stupid songs—suddenly he went and lost his leg. And all his future glories on the field went down the jakes. So he'll go no more a-whoring, so late into the night. That was bad enough. As to the private agonies he suffered in losing a man's two best friends—and I have neither wife nor poodle waiting at home for me—who can ever assess the extent of the impairment? It almost draws iron tears down Pluto's cheek, O unlettered lads of modernity, who cannot tell me to which poem by Milton I have just alluded. Would almost win mine ear and wet mine eye. Almost. For that uncaring miscreant Cranford cared about only one thing when he was at school and that was his tool. His one talent. And what use is a tool if you cannot make it work, and that one talent which is death to hide lodged with you useless? So there you be. Now I have told you, fully and frankly, the mute and miserable chronicle of John T. Cranford. Poorer than piss, don't you think? And undoubtedly the most pin-headed, pin-legged, ball-less bastard ever to run a school.

Do you detect here a crude but happy symbolism? The pin head, the pin leg, the want of balls? I'm sure you do, though I should say that with regard to imagery I am referring to a purely aesthetic felicitousness when I employ the word 'happy'. Cast your minds back a term or so, to Chaucer's portraits of the Summoner and the Pardoner in his *General Prologue* to *The Canterbury Tales*. What do we find here? Two monsters of depravity: one with a hellish face and the other with no testicles. In the Summoner's frightfully disfigured countenance—ravaged by syphilis, perchance?—you may read the diseased soul of the medieval church, its money-grubbing cock rammed tight up whatever hole is on offer, on trial, on compulsion, on the squeeze, back or front, male or female, sheep or tup, hole-in-the-corner, hole-in-the-wall, holy-of-holies, Sodom and Begorrah, the Summoner's not fussy, so long as number one goes into zero. How many times? Every fucking time.

While on the other front there's nothing. The Pardoner's emasculated condition reflects a church that has lost its stones. It's got no spunk, no vigour, no verve, no spine, no direction, no drive. It's going nowhere, it's a no-go institution, an affront to Jesus, its spiritual juice has gone dry, it's as barren as a strumpet's bum.

Now, leapfrog over six centuries, with everyone going to school but only five percent to church, substitute a school for a church—and handy dandy, what do you find? Cranford combines the perfect features of Chaucer's two most perverted creations and in himself is a perfect symbol of the appalling condition of secondary education today: disfigured, distorted, ugly, castrated and mean. No brains, no balls, no poetry of soul, no scruples, no scrotum, no spiritual depths or drive. It's lost its leadership, its springs, its liberating fancy, its soul, for God's sake! It's a gelding, an epicene little runt. An impotent sham.

3

I HAVE AN ingrained habit—and I'm not ashamed of it—of thinking in metaphor. A moment ago I employed a branch of metaphor (personification) to convey to you my contempt for an educational system that has lost its manliness. Or, for that matter, and if Cranford had been a woman—its womanliness. Its sex. It's an old bit of imagery, in fact, the poetic depiction of any institution as a *body* of sorts. Shakespeare wrote about the body politic in anatomical terms, St Paul about the church, though neither man, playwright nor apostle, got down to the nitty gritties of actual testicles. They left that for D.H. Lawrence to make his territory. But each saw the state of man as like to a little kingdom a microcosm. And a school, you will easily appreciate is just such a little world: the sort of microcosm in which a multitude of novels has been set. Such as an island, a boat, a cancer ward, a prison camp, a castle—all images of this mighty world.

Or a train.

I jump at that last image not because I am thinking—as an English master who is broad-minded enough to read good trash—of Agatha Christie's *Murder On The Orient Express*, or Graham Greene's *Stamboul Train* (slightly better), or anything nearly so exotic. As a matter of fact I have nothing literary in mind whatsoever. I am simply remembering a little steam puffer that used to chug its way along the east coast of Fife, like many another engine in many a neck and armpit of these Happy Isles before the dreaded Doctor Beeching came along like Death in *The Seventh Seal* and axed them away overnight. The unromantic bastard.

This was the train that was wont to carry us to school. The first pupils embarked at Elie as the engine came wheezing north-eastwards along the coast from Edinburgh to Dundee, stopping at Kilminnins and Pittenweem and the various fishing townships, to gasp and shudder and take on board a cupful of water, a scuttle of coal (ah, the simple life!) and the seekers after secondary knowledge. Stage after stage it filled up with bags and blazers, hurled before them into battle as it were (like the casketed heart of Bruce from the hand of Douglas) by droves of youngsters aged twelve to eighteen, the pipsqueaks and apples of their race. At Skinfasthaven we alighted as one vast tribe and made our way towards the pillar of smoke and fire, the tower of Taft Academy, for a day's education, the milk and honey of science and humanity, after which the returning teatime train would trundle us all home.

For me the journey from Kilminnins to Skinfasthaven was one of only three miles. Including the momentary stop at Pittenweem, the train barely deigning to pause before it began pulling its way out of the station again, it used to take nine minutes precisely. Looking back on it now I am amazed to calculate, with what little mathematical wit God gave me, that our iron horse must have been travelling at a mere twenty miles per hour on average, though for a jiffy it might have topped an astonishing sixty before decelerating in preparation for the stop at the next village, so close at hand. At the time, though, it seemed to be fairly rollicking along past flashing fields and breakers at nothing less than breakneck speed.

What made it seem to travel so fast, now that I look back on it in the light of fond remembering, O ye who come so variously to Blair's by bus or car or Shanks's pony, is not merely the faster beat in the heart of heady youth, but the urgent excitement of the events that took place in those carriages during those vital nine minutes, when pleasure and action made the hours seem short. And what action, think you, induced such sensations of pleasure on these rocketing mornings as to make time run faster than a dial's point with life itself the span of but an hour?

I can give you the answer in one word.

Feeling.

Permit me to explain. I am using the word 'feeling' not as an abstract noun—a gerund, you might have thought—pertaining to human emotion, but as the present participle of the verb which describes what we actually did during those nine Muse-inspired minutes when the first flush of youth suffused our morning faces.

We felt the girls.

Felt their fannies, to be round with you once more. *Groping*,

41

I believe you term it in these crude socio-linguistic shallows of today, though I have no partiality for the word myself. Granted, it conveys something of the first blind awkwardness of young people getting to know about sex. Yet it contains nothing of the warmth, the intimacy, the deep fleshly excitement contained in the verb 'to feel'; nothing that registers that word's possibilities of emotional experience, the admiration and awe, one's frenzied fear of the opposite sex when confronted by one's first awareness of its naked existence: the hidden pathways between the knees, beyond the hemlines and beneath the blouses of beings who, a stone's throw off in time, had been curious enough little planets, apart on their alien orbits, of no real consequence to our rough-and-tumble lives. The girls had skipped and street-rhymed their way through four thousand days on the sidelines of our consciousness, while we barely paused in our stone-throwing, ball-booting circumscribed existences to interrupt their salt-and-pepper nonsense by anything other than a haughty wave, a catcall, a command, a crackle of saliva spat out in their direction coolly, contemptuously, on a frosty morning.

All that altered in the school train.

Yes, feeling the girls in the school train was a new beginning for us all. And it was initiated, naturally enough, by John the Divine. But bear with me awhile before I come to his dubious laurels once more, and I shall sketch in for you a little helpful background. And local colour.

When the train, three-quarters empty, pulled into our tiny station at 8.30 sharp each morning, it was assailed, as I have told you, by a boisterous horde of youngsters, clad in Mephistophelean red and black, who boarded it like pirates spoiling for a prize. Most of the carriages boasted a corridor which enabled you to perambulate from compartment to compartment, much of the length of the train. But there was usually at least one coach without the interlinking corridor, and this coach consisted of a sequence of separate compartments, each seating eight to ten passengers. Once you had entered such an isolated compartment you were lodged there for the whole of your journey and there was nothing you could do between stops should you wish to leave, the two doors on either side opening straight out onto the hurtling countryside and broken limbs at thirty miles an hour or death at sixty. A setting ripe for many an Edwardian crime yarn, complete with deadly struggles for the communication cord. So that, given our rather less desperate circumstances, if you found yourself drafted into an uncongenial group—(perhaps of older pupils, who would savage you every inch of the way, or of toffee-nosed snobs from Elie, Hooray Henrys and Hilarys, plummy-mouthed bastards who wouldn't deign to piss on you if there wasn't a toilet from here to the back of beyond because your own Scots-spoken mouth wasn't good enough to contain their urine)—well, there was simply nothing you could do about it. And yet, in spite of these manifest disadvantages, each morning brought without fail a madly contentious scramble for the coveted compartments whose intactness from the outside world for the precious nine minutes provided the ideal circumstances for all kinds of fun and folly.

Each morning, therefore, we swarmed across the treasured coach like wasps on a hive, each one of us itching to find a cell in the rich honeycomb of adventure, many finding themselves knocked off by the bigger brutes and sent flying backwards onto the platform, some even clutching frantically onto footplates and door handles as the train pulled away—to be hauled off by infuriated porters and bundled in elsewhere with a final slamming of doors on the gallop. Then, when the shouting and red-faced elbowing died away and the train chugged through the first tunnel, it was not uncommon for you to find yourself among ten, twelve or even fifteen youngsters in a compartment designed for something nearer half that number of souls.

It was on one of these occasions that I found myself, like Daniel in the lions' den, lodged with Jocky and his cronies, who had already discovered my usefulness as a shuttlecock during my first morning Assembly. Though Jocky's memory cells did not re-open upon events so far gone by, his travelling companions speedily reminded him of my identity and of how invaluable I had proved as an instrument of brainless exercise. I spent that particular journey being violently batted from one side-end of the compartment to the other betwixt a double row of grinning jackasses, all outvying one another in the ferocity of their serves, and each team attempting to make it impossible for the other side to return me. The manner of achieving this was to catapult me so hard that I became a dangerous missile to the opposing row of thugs and they were compelled to react accordingly, attack being the surest method of defence. It need hardly be said that Jocky's team prevailed. It was the longest nine minutes I can recall.

When they had done with me they threw me up onto the luggage rack and dared me to come down before Dundee. Chug, chug. We arrived at Skinfasthaven. It was time to disembark. With malice in their souls they held on to the very last second before making good their exit and banging the door shut upon me just as the whistle blew, the funnel screamed and the long crocodile of carriages resumed its shuddering peregrination of the coast of Scotland. I rolled off the rack, bouncing from seat to floor, shouting blue murder for the engine driver to stop, and flew out of the compartment to land with a sharp bone-jarring crack on the edge of the platform, leaving the open door to be flapping wildly in the wind all the way to Crail and the enraged station officials hurling capfuls of oaths at me as I hared away at high speed for the Academy.

That was a minor skirmish. In my later years at Taft, on one of those fun-filled return journeys, as antidote to a day's schooling, I have seen a poor unfortunate stripling of the first year pinioned to the inside of the carriage door, his wrists secured—almost guillotined—by the sliding window which used to be held in position by a broad leather belt (Eeeh by gum variety) secured by a brass stud through the last eyehole. There the sorry youth stood, debagged, naturally, by the Jockies of his generation, his bare backside exposed to the jeers of the assembled travellers as they left the train, his dangling parts ready to greet the first platform porter to investigate the flapping hands, the wild white face at the window, while the perpetrators slipped sniggeringly out on the wrong side, landed on the naked rails and fled to the safe anonymity of their homes, over fields and fences and castles of foam, the sky filled up with their sharp young cries like the blaring of geese on October mornings.

Ah, but look how I prattle, sweetings, with guilefully digressive tongue, to keep you from your fun and final exit. Very well then—to our tale, and to the quick o' the ulcer. When I think of the school train, it is not to that coarse horseplay that my mind romantically returns, indeed no. I shut my eyes, smell remembered steam, hear the rumble of iron wheels on glinting rails, and I associate these nostalgic sensations, as I have already intimated, with my first discovery of girls. And the wonderful feel of.

Girls. One two three a-learie, knit one purl one, catch me if you can, hop step and jump the bed, cissy-ribboned, can't

44

climb can't swim, don't be rough, silly whining snivel-nosed and tall-tale tell-tale tale-bearing pig-tailed girls. All that gone now forever and ever amen from the simple streets of our childhood and in its place—The Girl. The female of the species, beautiful womankind, daughters of Eve, the eighth wonder of the world, fairest of nouns, common, singular, plural, feminine gender, young unmarried maid and made for loving, not yet ready but able and apple-breasted, expectant cup-bearers of sexual bliss, girls.

Girls.

Forgive, if you will, that momentary flurry of emotion in my voice, blurring my language, furring my syntax, the number of verbal grace-notes there disgraceful in one of more than middle years—declined, you might even say, into the vale of years, or tears (yet that's not much) but designed nevertheless to convey something of the youthful perturbations of half a lifetime ago, when I first woke to the realisation that girls now had the spirit to enforce, the art to enchant, and carried the meaning of life betwixt their budding breasts, the secrets of the sea between their dreaming thighs.

My discovery of the female was an event that occurred in two distinct stages. The second of these was by far the more important of the two. This was my awakening to adolescent love and I shall return to it in the course of this lesson with well-remembered passion. It hit me hard, let me tell you, and it was at least one revelation that had absolutely nothing to do with John the Divine.

The first revelation did. It was the more primitive and rudimentary stage of sexual understanding which comes to you—shall we say about the age of thirteen?—when you first put your hand up a girl's skirt and a fiery pain floods your groin and spreadeth upwards throughout your flesh and frame, making your very fingertips flame and tremble. Not that it would ever have occurred to me to conduct such an awesome experiment had not John Cranford shown me the way in his usual brash fashion. And even so it took many weeks of watching him at work before I could bring myself to imitate the action of the tiger.

It began one morning—one morning, one morning, one morning in May—on the outward-bound train journey to school. Following the usual battle for places, I found myself sardined in a single compartment along with Peem Peattie, John the Divine and five other first and second year boys who had crowded in after Jenny Miller. Jenny was not like the rest of our tribe. Even by the standards of the village Cleopatras among us she was a dusky doll, possessed of an air of indefinable apartness—exotic, mysterious, redolent of Lebanon and food for Solomon any night of the week, with spiced breath, incense in her nostrils and honey under her tongue. A mane of black hair swept her Egyptian brow, beneath which her eyes shone even blacker, like pebbles polished by the Nile. Her white socks showed off the dark-skinned legs on which her hairs glowed in golden points of light. She was utterly contained. And those unspoken passions, the enemies of reason and content, were locked away behind the poppy-garden lips, the sparkling gates of her teeth.

I say all this now, mind you, with the conscious hindsight of the adult under whose bridges a great deal of sexual river hath come and gone. Well, I remember it coming, all right. Where it actually went to is another question.

On the particular morning I am describing, when I was dipping my toes into the great tide of my teens, it very probably did not even occur to me that Jenny Miller was beautiful, still less that she oozed sexuality from every pore. Until, that is, John T. Cranford suddenly leapt from his seat with a whoop, threw himself upon the startled Jenny and thrust his hand straight up her skirt. Her response was vigorous. She punched, kicked, yelled, scratched, bit, tore—and Cranford collected a fast crop of cuts and weals in reward for his assault upon her virtue. He was driven, however, by his usual obsessive determination to lead and succeed and would not leave off until his hand was well and truly inside the leg of Jenny's navy-blue knickers, where he fumbled frantically, yelling yahoo under the rain of blows and bites.

I will confess to you that I was shocked. This was a far cry from wanking: this was a total invasion of another person's utmost privacy, an unthinkable intrusion into another realm; not forbidden because entirely unthought of hitherto, yet ultimate, awful and full of fear. I was not only shocked—I was fascinated, and watched the entire assault with the horrified recognition of something that was also within *me*; a secret uncoiling in the groin, a sly flame that was far off and yet urgent, demanding, entering the universe from light years away and bringing to birth a new order. The girl's skirt had been pulled up in the struggle well past

46

her waist and as she lashed out with her fists and feet I caught my first quick glimpse of female pubic hair, in Jenny's case a cluster of coal-black curls sprouting out of the side of her pants—oh! dark as Erebus, my boys, and not to be trusted, the jungle of human passion, the heart of darkness, the forests of the night in which Cranford alone burned and I could not bring myself to follow, so mesmerised was I by what I felt and saw.

The other boys in the carriage responded without complexity to the first trumpet call of sexual war. They too now threw themselves upon Jenny like lions on the helpless hind and she disappeared beneath a scrum of backsides and bare legs, her silvery protests swept along unheard in a rush of steam and pistons between the coastal villages. I longed to participate but still I was anchored to my seat, hypnotized, transpierced. It was too fundamental, too extreme, like striking a knife into someone's living flesh, like stealing or lying or taking the Lord's name in vain. It had the primal eldest curse upon it. Not in the Ten Commandments, it was lodged somewhere in Genesis, it had to be. It lurked somewhere between the gates of Eden and the spot where Cain killed Abel. I knew that if I took part in this coarse communal invasion of Jenny's virginity that the voice of her innocence would surely cry out from the carriage and would be heard all along the coast, betraying me to the world.

Do you recall that marvellous moment in the play when Macbeth, on his way to murder Duncan, imagines for a moment that the very stones he treads upon may shout out a warning to the sleeping king? Wake up, Duncan, for God's sake rouse yourself! The treacherous Glamis comes to stab you in your sleep! In Macbeth's horrified psyche the entire universe has come alive, even inanimate nature, and is about to bear witness against him. Well, that is precisely how I felt at that moment. I feared the wrath of God and the Rector, the pale Shark, parents and teachers, the voices of my own beleaguered conscience, trumpet-tongued. And pity like a naked new-born babe, and heaven's cherubin horsed upon the sightless couriers of the air—yes, they were all there that day, making learning impossible and night hideous. And yet I knew that to feel a girl was now my most immediate need.

Cranford's assault upon Jenny unlocked the floodgates and a torrent of lust swept the school train for many mornings afterwards. Most of the girls took it as a form of sport in which they were the goals—and if goals were scored, well, that was the name of the game of being female. Sometimes indeed the goals were left undefended and generally a broad humour prevailed upon either side. But there were other occasions on which things went really a trifle too far. Many a time and oft upon the Rialto I have heard the shrill screams from an adjoining carriage, rising above even the thunder of the wheels, and on sticking my head out of the window, have seen, projecting from the adjacent car, a metre-stick let us say, and, fluttering outrageously, preposterously upon the extremity of that highly unexciting object (filched from a maths room at the end of a day), a pair of knickers—yes, knickers, ungallantly removed from some poor female's loins by the marauding hands of John the Divine and his band of coarse-grained acolytes. The metre-stick would be discreetly retracted at Pittenweem, lest the station master be made privy to this highly irregular flag-waving and banner of inter-village disrobing and so make a denunciatory phonecall to the Shark that would have us on trial for weeks to come—and then out would go the metre-stick again as the train picked up speed for Skinfasthaven. How well I recall the flying clouds, the plume of steam, warm and white and wet on my out-thrust face, the glittering firth flashing by and the green fields—and those silly knickers flapping wildly in the slipstream, an emblem of our daft and happy youth.

Alas, had it but ended there! Unhappily, Cranford had a somewhat nasty trick, just as the train was approaching Skinfasthaven, of giving the metre-stick the wickedest little flick, thus sending the wisp of underclothing fluttering across the fields to come to rest upon a bunch of thistles, a fence stob, a bull's horn perchance, a cowpat? Or even under a gooseberry bush, like Richard's crown? These are imaginary, if not impossible, destinations, of course. In reality the poor demented lass had the choice of either running back across the fields for her knickers and so being late for school, or spending the day without them, to be pursued along the corridors all day long by Cranford and his hoarse, coarse cronies, with their embarrassing shouts, their loud innuendoes and their relentless probing arms.

He really was an absolute turd.

What was it beyond fear that kept me from joining in these innocuous little feels? Some grain of decency, perhaps, sticking to my soul, from the innocent years? Something sufficiently Calvinistic squatting in me too? Or plain old-fashioned shyness, timidity, the gaucheness of the ultra-sensitive adolescent, which is what I was. Ay me. 'But the undiscovered country of the cunt was to open its frontiers to me quite without warning and my day of baptism arrived—a shade late in life even by the standards of those halcyon days of deferred sexual experience. I was almost thirteen.

It was winter and there was a massive flu epidemic which had cut away the school attendance like swathes of corn. For some weeks there had been none of the mad jockeyings that marked the boarding of the morning train and so we had taken to arriving on the platform—those of us who were still well—later than usual, sometimes cutting things rather fine. My house was not far from the station, and from my bedroom window I could see the plume of smoke from a fair distance; on a still morning could hear the tell-tale whistle a full two miles off and saunter up to the platform in good time and with idle unconcern.

I found myself sitting in one of the prized compartments and having the entire accommodation to myself. It was a rare moment for me and I hoped no one would enter as I prepared to lord it all the way to Taft, the prince of the eastern seaboard. Just as the train shuddered and prepared to pull away, I was mightily aggrieved when the door was thrown open and a late arrival came flying indecorously aboard. When I saw who it was, my irritation evaporated and was replaced by a different panoply of emotions.

It was Jenny Miller herself.

The divine Jenny. Flushed and frozen and breathing heavily from her last-minute bolt from her bedroom, she threw herself into the corner furthest from me, fixed the luggage rack with a resolute stare, and settled herself down as though I were invisible and she would not dream of addressing an empty compartment.

Silence then. Broken only by the hot frost-clouds of her breath. I knew now that the moment had arrived, the moment I had winced at and shrunk from and dreaded. Time was drops of gold. As we picked up speed, the platform and its porters falling away, I slid along the seat until I was sitting next to Jenny, hoping that she herself might do something, even if it were to clout me on the ear. She never did. I might as well not have been there. Clearly the rest was up to me. Soft you now. Shaking uncontrollably, I placed my hand gently on her cold, locked knees. Still she did nothing. Did she know I meant country matters? I waited, trembling on the brink of her passivity, afraid to make the extreme move without at least some little show of consent. She put out not the faintest flutter, neither harbinger of love nor war. The ice-capped knees stayed implacably together.

I was considering withdrawing my hand when the train shot into the one long tunnel in the journey. We were suddenly together in several seconds of comforting, liberating darkness. Jenny must have sensed the rightness of it too because she abruptly unlocked her knees, parting them just wide enough for me to slide my hand upwards between her thighs. I did so—and with a little shock arrived at her crotch, felt my fingertips stopped by its mysterious softness and warmth, so different from her legs, which had the redness of the morning frost on them still and had felt like marble. I tucked one finger probingly underneath the elastic of the left leg. It was much too tight and Jenny made a tiny sound protesting her discomfort. At the same time she slipped back just a little into the corner, shifting her bottom forwards so that she now lay slightly flatter on the seat. I found my hand responding to this gracious concession by moving up across her abdomen as far as her waistline. My fingers touched the nakedness of her sides and belly, the middle finger falling accidentally into her navel. She squirmed just a little. Then, gently prising, I entered the private world of her knickers, and slipping downwards now, arrived at the sancta sanctorum, the hairy of hairies. I felt female pubic hair for the first time.

The effect was electrifying. A white shock went through my hand, surged swiftly through the rest of me, a wet flame of excitement. Shivering, I stroked the strange, silky stuff which I could not see, imagining its ebony enigmas, its bold exotic brushwork, not wishing to explore further at that time. No, not even daring to think about it, to breathe. After that Jenny herself never moved an inch. We were in that tunnel for scarcely any time at all and yet it seemed to me afterwards as though we had experienced an eternity of togetherness in that blessed darkness, my hand on fire inside her knickers, and yet, insensible of fire, staying unscorched, fingertips drinking in the satisfaction of that soft roughness that was hidden from me, my heart and head pounding madly, my groin besieged by the golden arrows of desire.

O, boys of Robert Blair's! Such epiphanies are few—they are like life itself, swift as a shadow, short as any dream, brief as the lightning in the collied night, that ere a man hath power to say 'Behold!', the jaws of darkness do devour it up, so quick bright things come to confusion. But this was life in reverse, my younglings. The darkness swallowed us up and I came alive. When the train shot out into the day once more the immediate witchcraft of the thing was over, though it bore along with it a comet's tail of associations that will never quite fade out into the light of common experience. The fields around us crackled like a rimy sea, the rising sun a blood-orange bringing a hectic flush to the acres of whiteness surrounding us, flooding the coach with an unearthly glow. Dawn's rosy fingers joined mine in creeping steadily, Homerically, up the length of Jenny's thighs and stroking her fanny through her knickers, still making no effort to touch the sacred seal itself, warming it merely, the sun and I. Thus we stayed as we were, Jenny with her eyes closed, a breathing statue, myself a man on fire, a boy no more. At Pittenweem she moved her head slightly, peering out of the window, with eyes like Nefertiti, to protect our sanctuary from intrusion. No one came in. And so we were borne along in this silent communion of souls, she yielding herself for this one precious moment which we both knew would never be repeated, I claiming her as mine forever. Into my school satchel she went, yet more alms for oblivion, and the very first of her line.

When the train came hissing into Skinfasthaven I removed my hand and she smoothed down her skirt—but not with automatic hand, oh no! Then we took up our bags and left the carriage without a solitary word to one another. Nor would I speak to any other person as I made my way to school that morning, deaf to questions, bellows, hoots and jeers. I was triumphant, transported, touched by a new consciousness of things. I had felt Jenny Miller. Felt her more than physically. I had felt a girl for the first time and she had wanted me to do it. No one else had seen our little act of unification. Only the sun had been there. It had nothing of the coarseness of Cranford and his crew attached to it and I knew now why I had been unable to imitate his public lecheries. They were a desecration of something divine. But this—oh, this was something far beyond their ken. I believed Jenny to have been grateful for the healing balm of our solitary deed of love, which had soothed away the indignities visited upon her in the past; grateful for our tacit understanding, the sweet peace of the darkness and the pinked white fields as the train thundered through fragile time, cementing us together, my hand—*my hand*—in her knickers, her ultimate atom extended to *me*. Bliss was it in that dawn to be alive, but to be young was very heaven! Then felt I like some watcher of the skies when I felt Jenny then, or like stout Cortez confronted by the Pacific, silent upon that peak in Darien. The silence is what I remember most of all—not a word spoken as the train hurtled through the virginal white wards of fields, pristine in the still quiet frosts, the sheer silence surrounding the calm excitement, the discovery and the dream. And those wild, wild eyes.

And that wild surmise.

What a time it was! When I look back on it now I can hardly believe it existed, that there ever was an era when children were ingenuous, adolescents sexually untutored, and that for a large portion of our early lives we young men fleeted the time carelessly in the golden world of not knowing. Cranford was the worm in the apple, the maggot in the sickening rose, the bringer of knowledge, of the white light of information and murderer of the dark innocence of sleep. The false thane. He was born to be an educator. An instructor. But Cranford too was a child of his time, a serpent that stayed curled beneath the innocent flower for many a day before even he woke up and smelled the coffee, smelled sex and stardom on the morning air. For it was in the realm of sex above all else that we were allowed to hold on to our childhoods, to languish in ignorance, if you will have it that way, to run wild and unsexed in Eden until we were literally into our teens. You see, when I lay with my hand in Jenny's knickers on that magical train-ride through the tunnel of puberty, I was in darkness in a metaphorical sense too; sexually, that is. For I, who had been taught by John the Divine both to bring forth sperm and to invade a girl's underclothes, even to the extent of stroking her pubic hair, still had no inkling whatsoever of any possible connection between the two experiences, women and semen. Young gentlemen, I still did not know the facts of life. I knew that the old story was no longer a truth: that boys did not come from the Bass Rock or girls from the May Island. I did have some blurred awareness that between man and woman something vaguely medical happened that would produce a baby: something that was solely the concern of hospitals and doctors and the closed confessionals of ambulances that took women from their homes and brought them back to their doorsteps clutching babies and bouquets. I began to understand at last that they did not encounter God or bishops or even storks en route, that I myself had emerged from a mystery of whispers and antisepsis. But that I had come out of my mummy's tummy was a fact still unknown to me as I turned twelve. I was still largely in tune with that guilt-ridden but ingenuous world in which Duncan's blood was golden, leprosy divine, the saints stood like coppers on every corner (God's friendly fuzz, keeping an eye on you), devils came down with the rain and got into your lettuce, ignorance was bliss and flourished like the plague—and sex was out in the pastures, an innocence of froth among cowpats and cow parsley, long purples, liberal shepherds, cold maids and dead men's fingers; and your sperm on show with thistle-milk and cuckoo-spittle, slug slime and shagging bulls and all the birds of the air and all the beasts of the field.

I had not yet entered the era of information. As I stood there shivering in the shallows of my teens, my feet cold with expectation and my hand still on fire from Jenny's pubic hair, I was still three years from the Chatterley Ban and six from the Beatles' first L.P. old age, atheism, communism, cancer, mental breakdown, Cemetery Road and spots on the bum—I believed in none of these. History had granted me my childhood and left my imagination intact. A diet of secondary education was set to fire it to furnace point.

O, gone now are the trailing clouds of glory in which we came out of our classrooms not so long ago, drunk on the dreams of poetry and with the heaven of our infancy still clinging round about us. The visionary gleam is fled and the shades of the prison house are closed about the growing boy. That vision of the universe which I had myself when I was less than five years old, before I'd even heard of Wordsworth and Shelley and the Romantic Movement—all that has faded into the light of common day for you, my poor aesthetically undernourished children of the western world, the intellectual playboys and yuppies of your generation, imagination's poor. No longer are you so young and easy under the apple boughs about the lilting house, nor do you sing in your chains like the sea. You are fathers of the next millenium and the adult emerges stillborn into the brave new world of the future. Your old world is dead. And you yourselves are dead. You are the dead. You are the dead.

4

HAVING LEARNED TO wank and having felt Jenny Miller, with no suspicion that the two experiences could be in the remotest sense biologically connected, I settled down at last to the business of my secondary schooling.

Which fell into two halves: the first three years being principally the agony without the ecstasy, so to speak; and years four to six delivered the ecstasy all right, but with heaps of agony thrown in.

Let's get the misery over with first, shall we?

As a matter of fact, unecstatic though these were, they were not years of totally naked affliction, though there was much that caused me pain and trembling: the shock of being tossed into a noisome whirlpool of seeming abnormals in an institution many times larger than the sequestered backwater of my old Primary school; the consciousness of other people's surliness and sweat, their apparent readiness to hurt, to humiliate without cause; the sheer gratuitous brutality of this many-headed, multi-limbed monster that stank and swore, played with its private parts and indeed anyone else's it could get its hands on. Anyone else's? What am I saying? There *was* no anyone else; there was no you or I. Here was a grotesquely distorted fulfilment of John Donne's injunction to forget the hee and shee.

And so it came about. Difference of sex we knew not any—in the sense that we were all excrescences of this vast and hideous hydra. My prick was not mine own; the girls' fannies were public property and pubic belonging, part of the massive communal coarseness of things. The private walls of the self were breached and razed. I was on parade. Very quickly I grew a second skin to protect my evaporating ego, to trap the fading reality of self within what was left of my head and hands, my feet and fingernails, the armpits and anus that seemed to be exposed, accessible, on universal show.

Such was the agony.

Will that do? If not, there's more; much more. For I found myself confronted now by the brass mouths of iron angels: a terrible host of schoolteachers, all singing the praises of their own terrifying new disciplines, bugling excelsior and promising hell to them that did not understand.

Algebra at once presented itself to me as a conceptual knot which daily complexified and grew tighter in my gut till I felt my stupidity begin to hurt and spread like some awful disease. Geometry on the other hand I managed pretty well at first because it consisted largely of the learning by heart of Euclidean theorems and because it gave me images to work on. In the later stages of the game, when it came down to making more advanced geometrical deductions without the help of Euclid, and knowing what cosines were, I realised that there was not one ounce of mathematical brain in my head. I had simply been enjoying the patterns, the pretty pictures, like Dr Faustus, enchanted by the mystery of the new: lines, circles, letters, characters! Very pleasing until you look a little closer and ask yourself what you really know about them, what you really know about anything. Ah, Mephistopheles!

Arithmetic I struggled through with some primitive ability while thoroughly detesting its power to transform the world into an aesthetically unpleasant dimension where water gushed at so many gallons per minute through so many pipes of a certain diameter, only to change course into pipes of smaller or larger circumferences, thus requiring me to calculate the difference in fluid volume or rate of flow, as though it mattered most horribly to the picture of universal reality which now broke open on my equally horrified consciousness. Everywhere men were busy digging holes for so many hours per day, shifting unbelievably precise weights of soil at rates of pay that had been worked out by the most sadistic of employers, eight shillings and elevenpence halfpenny per hour in a nine-and-a-half hour day, changing to another rate halfway through the week if one of the men fell sick. All that kind of thing. In all my dreams, before my helpless sight, they come at me now, these workmen—their bellies bulging with pints of beer converted to gallons, their pockets laden with loose half-pennies collected from the complexity of their shifts. But at least I had learned to count. Unlike the bright little buffs of today's educational shitheap who, when asked—*Now, if I give you nineteen computers and then take eleven away, how many computers*

55

will you have left?—look utterly pole-axed and fumble cretinously for their rinky dinky pocket calculators.

And worse things than Arithmetic, after all, were waiting to break me on the wheels of incomprehension, tedium and terror. Even those subjects I thought I might have liked quickly began to bore me. French was a clutter of unfamiliar snorts, History a catalogue of dates and inventions: incredibly dull facts concerning spinning jennies and percentages of the franchise. It differed little from Geography, which failed to capture my interest regarding the lengths of certain rivers, miles per inch maps, population distributions and the availability of iron ore. Berlin, Birmingham, Belgrade—what did I care? They had absolutely nothing to do with *me*; I did not feel them upon my pulses and therefore they simply did not exist. And as for Science, it was the ultimate brick wall. Other disciplines yielded just a fraction as I thudded my skull against them and I was vaguely aware that they must have some relevance that must concern someone other than the teachers and the taught; that they must even matter to somebody, somewhere. After all, people did at least vote; ate carrots, spoke French, lived in Vladivostock. Even the world of numbers, in spite of the fact that I was lost in it, possessed a certain purity of form, an inviolable abstractness that sealed it off from any possibility of my contempt.

But Science. Oh la, sirs! Chemistry revolted me with its noxious smells and its formulae that resembled Chinese calligraphics. Anything beyond H_2O paralysed my brain. Physics was without a doubt the most impenetrable mass of concept I could ever have believed it possible to exist, designed for dullards and drop-outs from the university of the imagination. Even biology, which I was actually disposed to enjoy at first—counting the segments on the drawing of a worm was as far as I reached in my inquiries into the nature of life. No one ever brought in a living worm. Biology was a world of dead specimens, the deadest of all being they that taught it. Oh yes, they were the dead. Had they ventured into reproduction they might have come alive for me and made the unbelievable connection between the First Revelation of John the Divine and the feeling of Jenny Miller—but alas, they taught the science of death by day and at nights they went home to steep and sleep in jars of formalin, emerging each morning brain-dead and chalk-faced, dead hands disembodied and scrabbling on the board like white ghostly crabs.

It was not, of course, the place's fault, the fault of the subjects or their teachers, do let me be fair. Partly it was I who was dead—to the deadness I thought I saw in them. Time, I have to confess, has done little to bring the water of life to many a parched academic area of my existence, such as Mathematics and Geography. And the deserts of Chemistry and Physics have failed to blossom as the rose. Even so, it would be entirely wrong of me, sirs, to blame too much too many of my former teachers for faults and failures that were largely my own. And yet, blame them I do, in some measure. For as a teacher myself, albeit in his final, finest hour, and teaching his very last period of what hath sometime passed for English—as a teacher myself, I say, I think that some of them could actually have done a good deal better, had they applied themselves, dug a little deeper. Got into the part. But you see, the chalk was flowing in their veins and the iron runners from those old oak desks had already run into their souls before I got to them, or they to me.

And yet, and yet.

What sayest thou, noble heart?

I wish to say that there were, even at that early stage in my schooling, during the years of my agonising, many teachers who stood out from their boring brethren in bold relief. Not because they taught me anything of an academic nature, for they did not, but because they were *characters*, oh sweet Jesus, yes, they were characters of the like of which you guys have seen the absolute end of their line, for I am myself the last of the Mohicans, Joxer, and I am retiring while I have a little spirit left in me still, albeit I drink my cup a round or two before the rest, and what o' that? Be Jasus. Yes, they were characters, that they were, who'd have made old Geoff Chaucer's eyes twinkle with mischief, Will Shakespeare's pen twitch out whole volumes in folio and never a line blotted out—and the inimitable Boz run screaming through the Strand to tot up zeros on the royalties and memories for middle age.

Bring them before the bench, then, like the ghosts that peopled Dickens' mind, motes in the sunbeams athwart the study chair—for yet again I summon up remembrance of things past, to vitalize the present time. Who shall be the first to have his name echo cheerly down the great hall of fame? Bring them before us, I say.

Lazarus, come forth!

One Bugsy Blythe, Geography master extraordinary if ever there was such a one, sat alone in his room, day in, day out, and never seemed to move. Indeed it was bizarre, but I have no mental record of his actually moving from the teacher's desk at which he sat, his brown suit growing browner by the year upon his faded person. His hair was grizzled, no? A sable-silver, greying by the period, the century, the term—the rags of time had no place in Bugsy's seamless movements. Naturally I exaggerate: he must have moved, it stands to reason, to micturate, to defecate, to hibernate, to browse and sluice. He came, he went. But we never saw the coming in and the going out, whether at the rising of the sun or at the going down of the same, old Bugsy Blythe was simply to be found at this desk, part of its intrinsically unaesthetic sculpture.

Were there not exercise jotters to be given out?

No, not given out, exactly. We came up to his desk one at a time and received them from his correcting hand, delivering them at the same collection point once we had completed the next stage of our work.

Was there not a blackboard, then, to be written upon?

Undeniably, there was a blackboard, but with equal conviction I can vouch for it that there was never a word written thereon. Once and once only, when expatiating vaguely upon volcanoes (this I recall vividly) Bugsy twisted slightly in his chair, half turned in the direction of the board that loomed black and blank behind his perennially immobile presence and looked for one second as though he might actually draw something. A volcano, peradventure? The class held its breath that day. But the fit was momentary, overcame him as a summer's cloud, made him seem suddenly weary, as though even thinking about it had exhausted his invisible reserves. In a twinkling he had slipped back into that benign torpor that was his alone and the opportunity of seeing the unseeable had gone.

Did he not eat and drink?

Neither at the staff table in the refectory, nor in the Staff Common Room, of a surety. A flask sat on his little teacher's table, a tartan flask, as I do recall, containing all the tea that he required. And a McVitie's shortbread biscuit tin housed his humble sandwiches, always with the crusts cut off (to give to the early morning birds, he kindly explained) and wrapped in greaseproof paper. Such was his repast, for he coude in litel thing han sufisaunce, like the humble Parson in Chaucer's *Prologue*. Remember? Of course you don't.

Very well then, were there not maps?

Mais oui, there were maps, be in no doubt of that, there were maps, and what maps! Huge yellowed ones, cosmographic colossuses that unfurled like Old Masters' canvasses to be nailed to the walls and in bygone days perchance pointed at and examined through their ancient varnish. Maps left over from Marco Polo and discarded by Columbus and Da Gama as long-time obsolete, archaic as Alexander's empire and not worth a ducat. Yes indeed, as you may surmise from my all too palpable memories of them, there were such maps already upon Bugsy's walls, hung up like monuments. But he never once addressed himself to these maps; he studiously ignored them. How can you teach Geography without maps? How indeed. Bugsy accomplished it. Easily.

He taught me Geography for my first two years at Taft. Two whole years of mapless Geography. Throughout the second of these years the words MR BLYTHE remained stiffly chalked upon the blackboard. At one point during the opening day of the session he must have bestirred himself to tell a first year class his name, and for this elect number he actually wrote it down! Alas it was not our class and I never witnessed the great event, never beheld his glory. Had I done so I might have gained some weird notion that Bugsy was actually alive, a live schoolmaster teaching a living subject. I might even have become interested in the discipline, if you can call Geography a discipline. As it was, the dead hand of Bugsy lay eternally asleep upon the globe, preventing it from turning. The world and the drawing thereof slumbered under his heavy, fleecy fist. For Bugsy was an hairy man, as I do recall. One of those creatures upon whom the thick fur that clusters round our secret clefts has radiated outwards to blacken every part of the body: sprouting out of the shirt collar above the Adam's apple, befurring the wrists and finger joints so that these protruded from white starched cuffs like the half human extremities of Rat and Badger and Mole, waving to us from our childhood in the wind among the willows.

Bugsy did have a sense of fun, though. Let me not be unjust. Good, serious, intellectual fun.

In what did it consist, then, this academic junketing?

Perpend.

When our scheme of work was completed and each term

drawing to a close, Bugsy dutifully suspended the teaching of geography and, leaning down from his chair (not actually leaving it!), withdrew from the contiguity of the cupboard a cardboard box, stuffed with copies of an erstwhile publication entitled *The Children's Newspaper*. He possessed every issue ever published, spanning many volumes, mouldering back numbers that were leprous with foxing and mildew, dog-eared from the dog-days and dog-fights of time, tattered and torn, yellowed with years, turning up their corners in disgust, as it were, at their own indeterminate condition somewhere between preservation and decay.

These riveting items of reading material Bugsy painstakingly unpacked from their box labelled 'Eggs' and allowed them to be distributed throughout the class for what he fondly imagined to be our delighted perusal. On every occasion, and in spite of his exquisite fastidiousness, corners and quarter-columns of print crumbled away at a touch, floated off under our library-silent breaths and turned to dust like mummies and vampires on the classroom floor. This left gaps in many a scintillating paragraph concerning the activities of certain groups of schoolchildren from countries that had long since altered their flags, their names, their allegiances, their politics; had even disappeared off the mappa mundi and were now mere historical-geographical expressions, or lost Atlantises, drowned in gloom, corals encrusting the empty desk and chair of some Minister of Bananas, psychedelic fish flicking apart the weeds that slapped the sunken walls of the Department of Coconuts and Radio Sound Effects. These children had by now produced children in their turn and were themselves kirkyard clay and coral reef. We knew that whatever relevance they once possessed to our time and place had long vanished. Yet Bugsy watched us read these papers with a hugely beatific smile settled on his square features. He genuinely thought we were enjoying ourselves, just as he himself must have revelled as a youngster of ten or twelve or fourteen, who knows, devouring the up-to-the-minute happenings, as they then were, of the somewhat younger world. He watched us with a vicarious and a nostalgic eye and we tried our hardest, by our expressions of assumed rapture, not to disillusion the poor dear man.

The truth of the matter was that Bugsy was a shy and gentle soul who had lost any real interest in the world time out of mind and now held up Geography, of all things, as the most ironical of façades to conceal the fact that he was on this earth but not of it. In a word, he was a deep believer in God and a follower of Christ's lore and that of his disciples twelve. A Christian. Most of his day at his tiny table was spent steeped in the Greek New Testament. It was known that a Sixth Form boy, a bible and classical scholar, came to Bugsy's room during certain periods to study New Testament Greek. I stood in complete awe of this astounding fact of Septuagint scholarship and in the backwash of that knowledge Bugsy's room-took on the moth-eaten musty silences of empty upland churches, and I sat in the dim religious light of the drawn blinds and thought how privileged I was not to have been taught a single geographical fact that I could remember by this genial authority on the things that were not of the world.

Once, on the homeward train journey from Taft, I entered a solitary compartment which I had taken to be unoccupied, and was startled, upon closing the door and sitting down out of breath from the run at which we always seemed to take things in those days, to see Bugsy sitting chameleon-like in the corner, his brown suit humbly at one with the upholstery, his little brown suitcase perched on his knees, his Greek gospel flattened out on the makeshift lectern, under the gaze of his soft devouring eyes. He looked up, saw me, nodded, and smiled his secret, half-uneasy smile. For the next nine minutes his gaze flitted anxiously, apprehensively between myself and the safe, dead Greek columns upon his knees, his expression shifting from the absorbed ecstasy with which he pored over the original scriptures to the timorous smile he bestowed upon the awkward pupil in the opposite corner, so inconveniently alive and requiring to be acknowledged, so he thought—and so back again to the ravishment of his seventh heaven.

Dear old Bugsy. Of the dead but kindly hand. Hold him, boys of Blair's, hold him in your hearts and heads for a moment, before we wish him God speed. You could never imagine, could you, that anyone would wish to do harm to this bland scholar, this dovelike denizen of Room 42? Of course such a figure as Bugsy would be torn to shreds nowadays by the shitehawks of the contemporary classroom. Well, we were rather more civilised in our day; more restrained. But not even the rodents of today, who prey upon the weaknesses of such meek spirits—I mean not even your generation could countenance the possibility of anyone's wishing to hurt such a man. Or could you? But here is where I come to one of the most genuinely shocking parts of my spiel, an unpalatable lump in the lesson which I would rather were not there. Would that I could remove it by the surgery of lies, or sinful omission. But no, that is not my way. Great is the truth and the truth shall prevail, as an old shag said, and it wasn't Kingsley Amis. So here goes. Someone did hurt Bugsy. There was such a one who did set out deliberately to wound and pain him, and who succeeded. Most horribly. And you don't want telling, do you, just who that person was? But I'll tell you anyway.

Listen again.

I had just turned fourteen and it was the day of end-of-session pranks: that day of Unreason in the academic calendar of Taft when all-licensed fools were permitted to roam the corridors and to pursue their antics both in and out of classrooms. Within the bounds of decency, that is. Of moderation. It was acceptable, for example, to lock a teacher in his room for a period, send round spoof notices requiring everyone to strip to the waist and run three times round the school, singing *She'll be coming round the mountain when she comes* at the tops of their voices. To dress up in somebody's gown and teach a mock lesson to a chortling class. A sedate old Classics master would even allow himself to be paraded about the corridors in a wheelbarrow, garlanded with lupins, wearing full rugby kit, and to be wheeled into room after room of appreciatively guffawing youngsters, applauding the shrunk shanks, the white knobbly hairless knees. Fat Boy Farquhar was dressed in lady's floral attire and wore lipstick for an afternoon, his great gravid belly shaking with sunflowers and laughter. And if Mr Drummond's bicycle were to appear, surmounting the school tower like some fantastical emblem of the pedalling pedant, designed by a sober-hooded medieval futurist—well, that too was all part of proceedings that were considered harmlessly euphoric. There were, after all, known limits. You couldn't, for example, have removed Fanny Fergusson's knickers and run them up the flagpole to engulf the whole school in an antiseptic bell-tent and fumigate all thoughts of fornication into extinction—but short of that almost anything could go.

The traditional Day of Misrule ended two years after I enrolled and it was Cranford who put an end to it. His crime killed the golden-humoured goose, making it impossible for the Shark to allow things to continue as they had been. For this particular jape o'erstepped the bounds of all propriety. As we like to say in Blair's. His jest was too cruel a one. Too cruel anywhere, dear Duff, even in Blair's, even though 'twas but jest. Poison in jest. And it was unspeakable.

Briefly, and a short tale to make, (for I could take no pleasure in dwelling upon this), the damned Cranford stole Bugsy's box of precious children's newspapers from their cupboard and took them down to the farthest corner of the sports field, where he and his cronies stuffed them into a litter bin and set fire to them: a quick red end to years and years of devoted hoarding. The fluttering black ashes were then returned to their cardboard box—the label 'Eggs' being prefaced by the one word 'Fried' from the scrawling hand of Cranford—and re-lodged in the cupboard, waiting for Bugsy to discover them.

He did not have long to wait.

Bugsy, whose absent-minded absences from school assemblies were long tolerated, did always manage to attend the last gathering of the session, and it was while he was out of his room on this rare occasion that Cranford did the deed, following it with an act of wickedness intended as a forerunner to the great jest itself: a harbinger of doom. With a pocket lighter (nicked from the local café) he stood by Bugsy's door for a full ten minutes, heating the door handle to a golden temperature. He held the little flame steadily under the brass knob, while his followers lay around clutching their sides in attitudes of exaggerated mirth. This carried on until the rumble of multitudinous feet signified that Assembly had broken up—upon which they fled to the nearest corner, and safe cover. By the time Bugsy's own ponderous step was heard, the handle had cooled a little, though it was still hot enough to administer a quick sharp shock to his honest palm . . .

Bugsy withdrew his hand sharply from contact with the hot metal and stared at it for a few seconds, more in astonishment than in pain, watched from the corner by a cluster of red faces that were bursting with suppressed mirth. Using his jacket pocket to open the door, Bugsy stepped within and was forthwith confronted by a giant size notice chalked up on his board. STOP PRESS. FIRE DESTROYS CHILDREN'S NEWSPAPERS. LOOK IN THE CUPBOARD, BUGSY, OLD BOY!

On the quick tips of their toes the hellish band then sped from their covert, *Twelfth Night*-style, farcically to peer round the open door of Room 42, as from the box-tree. What they saw silenced and dismayed them. Bugsy stood in tears before his beloved box.

He was weeping and shaking uncontrollably, his fingers full of black flakes, the hot scalding drops raining into the ash. Stood in tears amid the alien corn. And the one member of the party who did not at once turn white and creep away in deep shame—was John Judas Iscariot Cranford. The holy glimmers of regret shone in every eye but his, and on every brow but his the pallor was Bugsy's pall. Cranford boasted of it, in fact, for years to come, so gross of soul, and though rewards were unofficially offered by the Shark for information leading to the discovery of the perpetrator of so heinous a crime (a prank poorer than piss) and many a knowing confederate longed to finger him, they also feared for their own hides as accessories to the fact. On top of which our age-old code of loyalty forbade us to point the digit. So Cranford carried on unimpeached and the bloody deed was in time forgotten.

But not by me.

And not, my friends, by Bugsy. He retired from teaching the following year, intending to study late in life for the ministry. Alas, he died ere he completed his course. I sometimes wonder, quite seriously, if Cranford killed him. The king 'ath killed 'is 'eart, if you take my point. If so, Bugsy's was but the first of many noble lives disposed of by that murdering bastard.

Tropically, of course.

Well, there's the story of Bugsy. Not a pretty tale in the end, young shavers, and would that I could untell it, but I can't, and, Ancient Mariner that I am, I must go over it from time to time, to slough off some of the common guilt into which we were all plunged by the unbelievably coarse crime of John the Divine Cranford, the archetypal crap on your shoe, the knot in your shoelace, the bounce in your cheque, the fine on your car, the red in your bank balance, the Mormon on your doorstep, the prick in your letter-box, the crud in your coffee, the turd in your tea. Your teeth. O, had I but time! But patience, thou young and rose-lipped cherubin, I here look grim as hell. So damn him, I say, damn him, chop him into messes! And let us proceed.

Who is this, then, that cometh up from the wilderness of past years? One Bulldog Drummond, Physics teacher, long departed this life, riseth now like a wraith, out of the bell-jars of the mind, white-coated genie, permeating the walls of mine own classroom with the alien odours of leaky batteries, prussic acid and all the sulphurous fumes he ever concocted, malodorous bouquets of pandemonium and the pit. A pity, really, because Bulldog deserved neither his pet name (bestowed upon him simply because of the literary connotations of his surname) nor my olfactory association of him with the infernal regions. He was, in fact, like Bugsy, a rather muted man, a gentle dreamer behind whose gold-rimmed glasses the world of Physics flashed before me in incomprehensible coruscations. Sleek, silver, aristocratically austere in appearance, he purred quietly, contentedly to himself (most of the time) about the enigmatic movements of matter and its constituents. He did so with the serene assurance of a man who knew that the universe obeyed certain laws and so was, by that immutable truth, governable, civilised, subdued. It was a matter of profound regret to him that he failed to draw me intellectually into this comfortable fold wherein the insane howling of the wolves without—the cries of chaos—were voices from a wilderness he knew nothing of. Academically I was one of the damned and his red biro sweated and bled on my behalf as he covered my disgraceful work with his detailed drawings and assiduous attempts to elucidate my incredible ignorance. It was useless. There was nothing he could do to make me think like a scientist. I picture him now, staring at my answers with disbelief, as though he half wondered whether I might be playing a joke upon him. No intelligent person—he was thinking—could possibly be so ignorant, could fail to comprehend the laws of Physics and Chemistry so utterly and with such consummate blindness. No one could be so beyond the pale. But one could—and I was. So he turned back sadly to his world of inevitabilities: equilibrium and slow assured precipitates, reposeful under the balmy breath of the Bunsen burners. Ah! And he smiled again. Content.

Contentment for Bulldog (oh, never was Adam's kin so cruelly misnomered!) consisted in the contemplative man's recreation, the first and last retreat of noble minds, the tranquilliser of classroom-weary souls—the gentle art of angling. I say all that not from the fishes' point of view but from the fisherman's, and in particular Izaak Walton's. Every now and again, when the weather was right and the trout were rising, Bulldog would not go home at the end of the school day—(he too travelled to and from work on the train, taking it from his home in Burntisland)—but would tie his fishing tackle to an old bicycle he kept in the Chemicals Room for that purpose, and pedal peacefully up to the Carnbee loch, by the slopes of Kellie Law, well above the farmlands and the shut-eyed villages with their steeples standing guard. There he would sit a whole summer's night through, watching the moonlight flash on the flanks of the leaping trout, dreaming of catches on the subtle gilded fly meticulously prepared by his own cunning hand; from time to time bestirred by bubbles and eddies and sudden whirlpools of silver teasing him out of sleep. Dawn drew her finger along the dusky skyline, scribbling in the pinks and golds above the grey glimmering firth. The steeples caught the sun and bounced it up and down the coast, awakening the sleepers outside the kirkyard walls. Boats stole off quietly on a first wrinkle of tide and the early morning train left Edinburgh and headed north to pick us up nearly two hours later and take us all to Taft again. Bulldog packed up his catches and sailed ecstatically for school, a freewheeling piscatorial Einstein, downhill all the way, to distribute the fish among his colleagues, fussily pleased by their appreciation of his generosity and skill. Then he would teach us about the laws of nature and how the fly is drawn by fatal instinct to the sunny waters, merely that it may be snatched up at once by the quick-eyed trout or darting salmon; just as the poet Thomson tells us in the second of his great meditations on the four seasons. It is all engineered, you see, by a hand higher and mightier than our own. Who can understand how some scientists fail to see the workings of God in the universe and so incline to the darkness of atheism?—that cannot I, said Bulldog—when even the great Newton himself admitted he'd been like a child playing on the seashore, amusing himself with trifles like the laws of light and the movements of planets, while all the time the great ocean of God's truth lay before him undiscovered. Thus would Bulldog hymn to nature, as though he'd been left over by mistake from the eighteenth century. God said, Let Bulldog be—and there was light.

But there were these very occasional mornings when he failed to appear for morning school. A Sixth Form prefect would then be sent to cycle up the couple of miles to Carnbee, to arouse Bulldog from the golden slumbers which had kissed his eyes and to which he sometimes succumbed, still wearing his waders, his line trailed in tangles across the loch, the dew bedabbling his silver hairs and the early sparrows feeding off the night-time sandwiches lying on offer by his dreaming fingers. Had not God made Bulldog fall into a deep sleep merely that the birds might have their breakfasts? It was all pre-ordained. Hail, Source of Being! Universal Soul of Heaven and Earth, who with a master hand hast the great whole into perfection touched! And did you not also create the monarch of the brook simply that a tittering class at Taft Academy could spend its first two periods firing paper pellets and studying the trajectories thereof, instead of entering into the enthralling realms of thermodynamics?

'Sir, sir, waken up sir, it's morning! You're to come and teach your classes.'

'Dear me, boy,'—through a haze of good-humoured awakening—'is it really that time already? I must have dropped off. Good Lord. What period are we in?'

It says a lot for the dreaded Shark that he tolerated these lapses and never turned Bulldog in. For all his outward sternness the Rector was like others of his kind in the high and palmy days of education before the bureauprats arrived on the scene. Education was about personalities rather than grids; it was about allowing, yes, and even encouraging people to develop their differences, teachers and taught alike. A splash of character and colour mattered more than another box ticked, a grade allocated, a checklist checked, a name minuted, success and failure quantified, catalogued, and sent up the line in triplicate to die thrice over in the filing cabinets of the promoted. The drearily, untalented promoted. These days the dreamy Drummond would have been appraised, weighed in the balance and found wanting. Thy days are numbered, sunshine. The writing is on the wall, the Philistines are upon you, making sure your hair is kept cut, your nose clean, your face and boots wiped, your jacket on, your top button done, your tie knotted, your balls tucked back. Teach them Physics without passion, please and never, never, never lapse into those languorous rhapsodies in purple quoted by rote from the pages of your beloved Walton when you ought to have been explaining the fulcrum—digressionary recitations for which class 3b were truly thankful.

And if I might be judge, O ye who will never read Walton because Walton will never be videoed, God never did make calmer, quieter and more innocent men than the like of Bulldog Drummond and Bugsy Blythe; and, doubtless God *could* make better people, but doubtless God never will. I am struck by the fact that while I learned from them nothing whatsoever about geography or science (and indeed to this day I know not one iota pertaining to either subject) I remember the men themselves with poignant gratitude. They communicated to me something that went far beyond any understanding of mere physical matter, its motions, its principles, its elements, its designs. Something of the stuff of life in its spiritual essence. I recall them sometimes in the late sunsets and in the sharp sweet scents of elderflowers, in those moments when the symphony of life slows to the bleeding of a single violin, the book drops from your listless hand and you ask yourself what, of all the things that you know, is actually worth knowing. Somehow then all the Maths you ever mastered crumbles to a useless abstract ash.

And what remains is people. Folk. And the love of. What will survive of us is love. That is why, in the end, I took to literature and the teaching of the same—because literature is about love of people. It is about love of words too, but it treats of people in their ultimate attar and pith. Other disciplines tell you everything about William Shakespeare except what you really want to know. History will tell you exactly when he lived, Geography where, Sociology how; and from that point onward we can wheel endlessly round this man, collecting data regarding his anatomy, his organs, his complexes, his political beliefs; how he spent his money; what he thought of God, the Catholic Church, ghosts; whether he had venereal disease. We can isolate his willie or his will. We can reduce William Shakespeare, Gent., to carbon and water if we choose. Computers can even date his plays for you or futile cranks prove that he didn't write them. That he was a homosexual. Or wasn't. That he asked for tea in an American-Irish accent. Or didn't. Or couldn't. And when we have done all that we have not even begun to pluck out the heart of his mystery—because that is the business of literature, to explain without explaining away, to give answers that open up even more questions. So literature receives the human individual pigeon-holed, anatomised, labelled by economics, medicine, science, then puts him together again, adds the immortal soul and hands him back to God, saying What a piece of work is man! the glory, jest and riddle of the world! Thank you, God, for a bloody good show! Now what's next on the universal agenda?

Next is Fat Boy Farquhar, dotty as a leopard and—to all appearances—as queer as a coot. Man and Woman created He them and after that He created Fat Boy. Fat Boy who waddled about the classroom in a hairy tweed blazer which would barely button across his mighty belly and which changed its colour at the start of each new session yet which never looked exactly new. Which led us eventually to waken up to the conclusion that Fat Boy must have dyed it during each summer vacation and so contrived a reasonably newish look without too much expense. Even with the growth to maturity of my own school generation, however, his weight and girth increased astonishingly, so much so that by the time I was in the upper school the blazer had long ceased to be buttonable and—all pretence dropped—was permitted to retain the puky puce that must have been the last on Fat Boy's colour catalogue of cunning dyes.

Along with this diehard blazer went the archetypal grey flannels, without the benefit of a crease, the equally archetypal un-ironed shirt, with permanently puckered collar—and the old Etonian school tie that was indeed so old, concertina'd, corkscrewed and wrinkled, it looked as though it had been tug-o'-warred in boyish battles of long gone by, when Fat Boy was a lad himself, deep in the sybaritic south, singing bum-titty bum-titty titty-bum and we're all queers together, in the dorms of yesteryear. Now he was a bachelor gay with no one to darn his socks or cook his meals.

Not that the latter mattered much. He was always dropping in for tea.

Uninvited.

The method was simple.

Incredibly, for a chap of his Falstaffian proportions, Fat Boy helped out with rugby practices, heaving his Herculean belly about the field with all the nimbleness of a Walt Disney hippopotamus in ballet shoes. Whenever a boy was injured during a training session he at once became the object of Fat Boy's tender concern. Solicitous to bless and bemoan the pulled muscle, the broken collar-bone, the torn ligament, the booted testicle, the bruised shin, the black eye, Fat Boy would materialise on the home doorstep at the stroke of tea-time, anxiously inquiring after Jimmy or Jock's medical progress since period seven. Still in a bit of pain, is he? I've brought some Sloane's Liniment along with me here—and an elastic bandage, if that would help. Bit old and hoary now, I'm afraid, but it's seen me through a scrape or two. Stay for tea? Let me see, I don't know if I can . . . Ooh, sausages and chips, did you say? and plenty to go round. Well, why not? We'll see how his French verbs are getting on over the pudding. Oh, my hat! Steamed apple dumplings, with raisins! I'm won over—putty in your hands, dear people. Just say steam pud to me and I'll sing 'Bless This House' in French all night long and 'Alouette' in the morning.

And he did too, with many another ditty and many a witty rhyme—brought on by the port, which had never breathed since the last New Year or family funeral had pulled the ritual cork, but was deemed fitting beverage for a personage of Fat Boy's academic standing (such was the respect accorded by the community to teachers once upon a time) and his professional associativeness with all that continental finery and finesse. No, go on, finish it, please. It has to be a new bottle anyway for next Hogmanay and we won't be needing it before then—not unless someone dies. And Fat Boy would throw up his hands in mock horror. Oh, my sainted aunt, madame, don't talk like that! Now I do need a drink! Pass me the decanter again, *mon garçon*, and reckon not the cost. We'll swig to your quick recovery and chase *diablo* from the chimney top. Fill all our midnight bowls, I have room for six scotches more! *Santé*, sonny boy, we'll soon have you back in the front row, booting Bell Baxter in the bollocks. Oops, pardon my French, folks, *pardonnez-moi, s'il vous plait*. Well, cheerio then, here's luck—and bottoms up every time.

Thus he ate, drank, quipped and quoted his way through the households of the school rugby teams, the repertoire always the same. All streets in time were visited. Fat Boy was like an ambulance. There was a school of thought among us boys, naturally, that Fat Boy even went out of his way to procure himself free wines and dines by deliberately causing injury on the field, delivering each one personally and with subtle innocence. Nothing fatal, you understand. Nothing Gothic. He stopped short of strewn brains and gushing bowels. But it began to be noticed that a remarkable number of casualties occurred when Fat Boy happened to be in the vicinity. His was the boot that was ever near the banged kneecap, his elbow pointed at the purpled eye—for he was a demon hooker in the scrum and we learned to scatter when we saw him coming, lumbering among the troops, ostensibly to spur them on, but reputedly intent on producing another teatime patient.

All coincidence, I'm sure, and if not, then all good clean

harmless fun. Especially afterwards, when Fat Boy showered with us.

I do not jest.

The first time I walked into the changing rooms and saw him standing there in his nakedness was an eyeful that stopped me dead in my boots. Steam from the showers had invaded the changing area to such an extent that when I first stepped inside I could see only hot white clouds that swore and sang and chanted ribaldries—and a host of human shapes becoming vaguely, pinkly semi-visible among the hot fogs; indistinct armies of bathers in the springing geisers (of which Bugsy had once droned) were what they reminded ine of. Yellowstone? New Zealand? Someone would know—someone paid to know something stupid. It was as if the gods were having an Olympian knees-up and all was cumulus and disembodied talk. Peering into the Turneresque interior, I dimly discerned one shape bigger and bulkier than all the rest put together, and, bobbing and swarming about it, like pilot fish around the mighty whale, the materialising bodies of my team-mates, dancing attendance on the master blob. Do you want me to dry your shoulders, sir? There's still a few drops of water on your back. And then I heard that drawling voice, as high and glib as an angel's. *Merci, monsieur*, a little higher *s'il vous plait. Ah, c'est magnifique*! What satisfaction! I'm up to my chin in heaven. Well, up to me bollocks, anyway . . . And indeed there he was—standing fatly pink and naked among the parting veils, wearing only his rimless National Health spectacles that were so steamed up he could not see a thing. Blind as a new-born baby, quite helpless I am, putty in your fingers, do with me as you will. What, dry my glasses, would you? Would you be so kind? Thank you, my boy. There you are, sir. Ah, that's much better. Oh, hello, here's our young friend (referring to me) just come in, with his little winkle still white as a beansprout and innocent as an acorn. Haven't done too much wanking yet, have you? Oh yes, I'll bet you wish you had a whopper like mine to tuck yourself up with o' nights, *n'est ce pas*? *Oui, monsieur. Non, non—si, monsieur*. Always the *si* after the negative, remember? Oh, Lord help us, the boy's mesmerised.

I had been trying to look everywhere except the obvious place, but amid the clearing clouds of shower steam, fifteen pairs of adolescent eyes were fixed on that cynosure of phallic excellence, the Fat Boy's private parts—and I joined in the general stare.

71

Swinging below the pendulous white overhang of his belly hung the Farquhar penis. Delicatessens had yet to appear in our isolated quarter of the world in the fifties, and so images of sleek thick German sausages did not occur to me at that time, but years later, when I first saw one, I was instantly reminded of Fat Boy's willie, standing out in salaami red-and-purple, ample in circumference, interesting in inference, and generous in size, glistening still with beads of moisture and succulently on show. The Sixth Form prefect's shaggy conk had been one thing—but this was quite another. Was it for this the prick grew tall? But Fat Boy was proud of his prick and revelled in our boyish admiration of its qualities. A boy once more, in our company, he let himself go, and sang loudly and lewdly his version of the Eton boating song. If I had the balls of a bison and the prick of a great buffalo . . . for we're all nice boys at Eton, excuse us while we go upstairs, yes, we're all nice boys . . .

And yet and yet and yet.

Yes, here comes the playful crunch.

I have to tell you, that in all his posturings and seeming pretensions to pederasty, there was not one ounce of harm in him: not a solitary hint that his hand might carry out what his mind never even conceived; not one. Not once did he lay a lawless leg on one of us; not in shower or changing room was as much as a fingernail extended in our direction. Only on the rugger field was there physical contact, where his flailing boots and barging belly bore down upon us mercilessly and knocked us into injury time. But all was innocent on that score, as I have already explained to you, totted up to free fish and chips and left-over Christmas bottles all the year round. He had all the nancy boy's pecadilloes but none of his pederastic passion or even inclination. In short, he was a bohemian, that's all, an innocuously eccentric figure among us, a misunderstood and somewhat lonely misfit who bravely tried to face out the social emptiness around him (God knows what brought him to Skinfasthaven!) with lines from the ever-flowing script he carried in his head, to suit the rôle appointed for him by that most arbitrary of casting managers, fate. Hiding unhappiness by bad acting. Perhaps in some ways a bit like me? I tell you, I should not be ashamed to think so.

And in the classroom he switched to the rôle of the dotty but impeccably gifted schoolmaster, hammering French into us by deftness and wit, then side-stepping into the shower and basking in our strictly off-the-record praise of his prick, a scenario that would never spill over into the classroom beyond the usual risqué witticisms. He compartmentalised the thing beautifully. A poor player, perchance, who strutted and fretted his hour upon the stage, but who loved his part (public or pubic) and lived it, and did his best for it. A genuine teacher whose like would not be tolerated today—the sponging, the shameless chit-chat with parents, blarneying his way to the booze and the beef-steak pie, sitting there on the couch with his feet up and holes in his socks which madame darned (indebted, good woman!) eating chips and sucking orange through a straw. And the naked swanking in the dressing rooms, boasting like a latter-day Bunter of that one talent which to a schoolboy is death to hide, but of which poor Bunter was never permitted to speak. Not in that prickless literature of Etonland where the lingams do not grow, but where the obscenities of faggings and thrashings proliferate, yea, and are even hailed by the very flower of English enlightenment—(made men o' them, it did! our wars won on the playing fields of our public schools, they were!)—as having been no bad thing.

Goodbye, Bunter, O Etonian maverick that you were! *O garçon gai*! *Au revoir, monsieur* Fat Boy! I wonder where your mighty blazer fails to button now? Perchance among the angels, who titter when you castigate their sexless ways and tell them tales of Taft and your exploits on the pitch. And then (to switch mythologies) you doff your dandies, trip the light fantastic through Elysian fields, on deep-blue beds of asphodel, and chuck your discus-halo through undimensional space, innocently to injure the little cherubs at their play, letting the ichor flow. (Who, me? I was miles away!) And then to go soliciting of Jove at tea-time what's for grub. Ooh, goody gumdrops, ambrosia washed down with a little Chateau Paradiso, Appellation Dante—now that's what I call nectar! Clay in your hands, my darlings, putty for your pleasure, for we're all queers together . . .

Ah no, no, no. That's just the stuff as dreams are made on, boys of Blair's, mere words that I put together, nothing more. A vapour that vanisheth away. The reality and the awakening are chiselled on a marble gravestone in Suffolk. (I once made a pilgrimage there myself.) Barry Neville Farquhar, B.A. Down his carved name the raindrop ploughs. And, as they might have said in the good old days, when the cadences of language unadulterated could be heard in country churchyards, spelt by th' unlettered Muse, whispered by stones to the weather—sometime teacher of French in Scottish schools, principally Taft Academy, Skinfasthaven, East Neuk of Fife. And of his age 52. Died of leukaemia, dear departed Fat Boy, quitted this life anno domini nineteen hundred and seventy seven, now larding the lean earth as he lieth low, and not a quip to serve as epitaph. Where be your gibes now, your gambols, your songs? your flashes of merriment that were wont to set the classroom on a roar, the showers on a steam? No parting shaft at the bottom of the stone? Nothing to halt that raindrop as it plougheth past your name? Accept then, O Fat Boy, these words of mine, spoken in my final lesson, a lesson of which you would have been proud, and laid down as offerings, as flowers at your feet. Goodbye, Fat Boy. These fragments have I shored against your ruins.

And who goaded him into leaving Taft before we had reached the end of our fifth year? Who brought down his menopausal mid-life hairs with sorrow to the grave before they'd even had the chance to turn grey? Who chalked HOMO all over his board and POOF across his classroom door? Homo! Poof! And even—sinful shame that it was, alas the day, scrawled a sentence in thick white paint to desecrate his sweet little bubble car. (You will not know about these rinky-dinkies of the roads of thirty years ago that had such a lamentably brief reign.) Fat Boy should have driven a Cadillac at least, if not an armoured tank, but he contented himself with his bubble car, which he'd christened Claude. A vivid orange, was Claude, and stood out boldly in the quadrangle among the Morris Minors and the Austin Cambridges of the few staff that drove to school. And there stood Claude, parked in full view of the Shark's study windows and with the terrible scrawl available for horrified Rectorial regard: *Cave, cave, homo fuge!* And Cranford's own waggish translation to accompany the text: Careful, careful, Fat Boy *fucks!*

Poor old Sharkey. He knew at once that he had to lose a brilliant French master. Knew that he would never stay. Knew, in any event, that he had to go. Knew he was harmless, of course. A harmless old pussy. (Old in our young eyes, in his thirties.) Eccentric as an eel, queer perhaps to the external eye, but in reality as innocent as the driven rugger ball directed to the nearest crutch and a quick painless tea—and even that was never proved. Oh, hell. But there was nothing for it, for there it was, the easy lie, Etonian homo in our little East Neuk midst. And *homo fuge*

74

it had to be. Fly, O Man. Fly, O Fat Boy, depart, O cursed into everlasting death, for you carry on your noble brow the mark of the Great Beast. Branded. Bohemian. Different. Individual. Not to be tolerated. Cute as a dressed cucumber but now no-go. It's no-go, my honey love, it's no-go, my poppet. Out! *Raus*! Black sheep, tainted wether of the flock, what was it that you used to say? My ventures are not in one *bottom* trusted. Good one, Fat Boy. Big joke. Joke's over now. We know you not. Depart from me. Goodbye. Goodbyee, goodbyee, wipe the tear, baby dear, from your eyee. Chin-chin, napoo, toodle-pip, toodle-oo. Goodbye. Goodbye.

Thus did the hand of Cranford strike Fat Boy down. By the Scaean Gate.

The bastard.

There was assuredly something wicked about that . . . bastard, yes, about that genuine first-class turd who, even at that pimply stage of his career was rehearsing for a career in murder: killing off the characters of the classrooms and bringing on the robots in their stead. For what he did to Fat Boy and Bugsy amounted to a slaughter of the innocents: exile followed by premature death. In my own mind I make no bones about it, boys. It was delayed assassination, nothing less. Sounds a trifle posturising, do you think? a bit melodramatic? like something out of Jean Brodie? Of course you'd think that. You may even be right. But at the end of the day it makes no difference, no essential difference. Bugsy Blythe and Fat Boy Farquhar might well have been destined to be delivered unto their maker at the appointed hour, irrespective of the slings and arrows of outrageous Cranford. It is what Cranford has done since then that really matters. What he has done to this school. What crimes he and his kind have committed against education throughout this country. Laid an entire system to waste: laid the axe to the roots of a glorious tradition; laid the Fat Boys and the Bugsies as low as to the fiends. Laid the Great Whore of Clichés in a billion fucking sittings of a million clucking committees, raped the Muses one and all, and brought on the clowns, the veritable clowns. Brought forth a brood of bores and fellow wankers, the brood of folly without brain cells bred, to promote in turn their short-life working parties, their long-life cock-ups, impoverished courses, bad spellers, desk-boys, bum-boys, jobs-for-the-boys, windbags, shitebags, shameful examinations, asinine assessments, continuous crap, crassly writ-ten documents, foul-papers, shit-papers, dreary development offic-ers, syllabus-sycophants, ask-me-another-advisers, front-of-school brown-nosers, backseat-bootlickers, at-home-honeys, conference-crawlers, arsehole-adulators, anus-appraisers, in-service-earwigs, glib-grovellers, all manner of feet-on-their-belly-gasteropods, inspectors of how-many-inches-have-you-rammed-it-up-today, O toad?

And above all a generation of half-taught kids.

For it was Cranford who brought death into the world and all our woe, He and his fallen angels.

More of which anon, good people (good repose the while) when the whirligig of time comes round at his proper hour.

And brings in his revenges.

Forgive, if you will, these satirical squalls—and the waves of bitter lyricism that blow up from time to time in my teaching. 'Twas ever thus, I'm afraid; for I am, as you have been these many years aware, passion's slave. So what o' that? So was Hamlet, O, my sedentary friends, Hamlet, that self-labelling loser of himself in speculation. And loser altogether. And so was not Horatio: the brick; the good egg; the good listener. Like the good books, the good bed, the good china—and your life in perfect order, like Horatio's. Reprehensibly perfect. Ah no, I'd rather be the cracked heart than the hackneyed commentator, worn in its core; the snail rather than the sparrow. Any day of the week. Wouldn't you now? So again I say, forgive these wild and wandering cries, confusions of a wasted youth, for it is above all the tragic sense of waste that maketh me thus to cry out in anger and contempt.

Waste. I shall have occasion to return more than once to the theme in this afternoon's lesson. For this is *Lycidas*, without a doubt. Alas! what boots it with incessant care to tend the homely, slighted teacher's trade and strictly regulate the lunch-time booze? When all is waste, complete and utter waste. Waste of intellect, waste of talent, waste of unfed youth, waste of effort on the part of Pound's poor old toothless bitch, still awaiting the putting-down after long and honourable pedigree, followed by decades of dead-dog-maggot-breeding toil. Waste. Waste of the lives of certain men who took their First Class Honours, every one, inspired me to take mine, by the sheer quality of their schoolmastering, and so equipped me for a style of teaching that hath since been deemed worthy of the poor brontosaurus. By the whizz-kids of that roller-coaster run amok which we are pleased to call contemporary educational theory.

Oh, yes—and waste of a great tradition. No: a Great Tradition. Go on, scoff at the very phrase, you slick debunkers of whatever is past, part of the establishment, smacking of high seriousness, Miltonic-Arnoldian, and of good literary repute. I stand on the shoulders of better men than myself—and you petty piss artists, you walk under their huge legs and do piss about to find yourselves dishonourable graves. And are not worth the shit which the rude wind blows in your faces. O, I know you all, you bourgeois Goths, and have too long upheld the unyoked humour of your crappiness. From Beowulf to Virginia Woolf and so on down to you. Or should I say to *youz*? From Homer to haemorrhoids. O the bathos! O the crappy ending! Is this the way the world ends, dear Thomas, were you right? Was it for this the clay grew tall? Is God's Minister of the Arts responsible for this? Who wrote the script and failed to put it into scripture, pray? Yes, pray, you bampots, you miscalculating, unprophetic Yiddish turnips that you are, ye blind guides! What was it that you saw? Earthquakes and famines in divers places?—yes. But Jackie Collins and Jeffrey Archer to be sold at the top end of the temple—that was never written down. Wolves in sheep's clothing and a surplus of false gods?—indeed yes. But feet of clay in Ironmills—oh noninonino! And the sky shall be darkened?—yes, yes, yes, a thousand thousand times! But Sky television! That's no apocalypse now, my poor, let-down theatre goers who have been crowding out the auditorium all these years, watching others strutting the earth's stage and waiting for the second Big Bang. Not to come, though, is it? Not with a banger but a wimpy, is the Word. O, what limp rag of a last Act, what swizzle of a final scene! What lines thrown away, what costumes of blood cast off, what speeches undeclaimed! What men or gods are these! what supine sluts! what mad pursuits! what post-punk timbrels! what low-grade ecstasy! what porn! what vomit! what balls! what pigshit! what trash is Scotland and what offal when it doth serve for the base matter to illuminate so vile a thing as Cranford, the piss and marrow of our attribute, the acme—no, the acne—of our enlightenment, the best it could do, our crazy cankered culture! O, whip me, ye devils, roast me in sulphur, wash me in steep down gulfs of liquid fire—anything is better than bromide! For this is our armageddon, this age of amentia and unteachable, unspeakable excreta. Our civilisation.

Civilisation.

Civilisations are usually won by fighting, are sustained by fighting and are finally lost by fighting. Yet here's fine revolution an' you had the trick to see it. Our own pathetic little accomplishment is being laid waste and not a fluid ounce of blood is being shed. Not a longship launched, not a nuclear prick peeping from the conning tower, no chariots of fire or balls of brass, no Milvian Bridge, Poitiers-Tours, no Charlemagne, Marathon or anything that would step up the adrenalin of a wimp. Boredom is upon us, the boredom of barbarism; the Reign of Dullness is here. Hail, Emperor Ennui! We who are about to die of platitudes, salute thee!

Culture? Pah! Don't talk to me about culture! Top in all subjects at school, fair Lycidas, and hath not left his peer. Accounting, Business Studies, Computing, Economics, Modern Studies and Technical Drawing—passes in all six, how's that for contemporary culture? O come and mourn with me awhile, for Lycidas is dead, dead ere his prime and hath not learned a line. O sit we down and weep—by the rivers of Leith there let us sit, hang our harps upon the willows thereof and lament the passing of the age of elegance, when talking was not an educational mode but an art form and words grew like flowers on Yorick's vanished lips.

This is the age, says your Friendly Neighbourhood Teacher, not of Aquarius but of the dark, the Newly Dark. O dark, dark, dark, amid the blaze of noon, irrecoverably dark, total eclipse without all hope of day.

There is a Dark Age poem called *The Ruin*, in which the Anglo-Saxon poet contemplates the crumbling remains of masonry in a deserted Roman city—a thought-provoking edifice in the dreary landscape. And in *The Wanderer* a similar picture is evoked, where walls stand beaten by winds and hung with frosts, the builders lie low, the laughter is heard no more—and idle stand these old works of giants. Aw, 'tis a daarlin line, is it not now? But do you honestly imagine that the boredom of the first Dark Age was worse than this? Let's have the line again. And idle stand these old works of giants. What works be these, think you? Virgil? Spenser? Dante? Shakespeare? Webster? Milton? Wordsworth? Dickens? And idle stand these old works of giants. They do indeed, sirs, they do indeed. And what would that Dark Age poet think if he could take a peek at western civilisation now? Oh, it's easy to say he would be impressed, and at first sight—once he'd recovered from his stupefaction, poor guy—I dare say that is exactly what he'd be. But on the other hand, as a poet—maker, prophet, seer into the life of things—I wonder what he'd really think, given time . . .

Or what would Aeneas think, if he were cast up in contemporary Britain and had the leisure to take a good look round? He'd find a dildo quicker than a Dido, I dare swear, in these tainted isles. Not strong on Didos, the modern Brits. O blessed Virgil! It's one of the greatest moments in literature, you know. Aeneas and his men have just been shipwrecked on a coast which they are afraid may be inhabited by savages.

Looking fearfully around, Aeneas suddenly experiences a surge of relief. There, carved in bronze before them, is a scene from the Trojan Wars. Look, he says—there's Priam! It's all right, boys, our problems are over. This isn't a savage country after all. The men who did this couldn't possibly be barbarians. These men know the pathos of life and mortal things touch their hearts. *Sunt lacrimae rerum et mentem mortalia tangunt*. Well, it was only a work of art. Only a bloody picture! But he fed on it until his face was wet with tears. Poor guy, what would he see around him in our brave new world that would assuage his fears? Shop fronts ablaze with television screens flashing forth the latest art in bold bright colour from coast to coast: *Neighbours*, *Home And Away*, *Coronation Street*, *The Price Is Right*, Terry Wogan, with the third world and *The World at War* thrown in as heavy relief: famine and genocide, meat for the sandwiches of Robbie Coltrane and Russell Hunter slumming it in the adverts. Can you picture the scene? Oh God, I'm sorry to tell you lads, we're in trouble. This is actually the planet of the apes. Was for this we fought at Troy? Was it for this the world grew old, now with old woes wailing its dear time's waste? O world, world, thou bad and faithless servant—getting and spending you've laid waste your powers, laid waste your talent.

Waste.

But the greatest waste of all lies in the perversion of values in our education's fast-expanding cosmos of ambition, where fair is foul and foul is fair. They pay out the big fat readies to the administrators, the deskmen, the managers, making the grievously mistaken analogy between education and industry, while the genuine schoolteaching talent, the gold dust, those who remain in the classroom, are kept on the thin parish gruel. Richest in giving, they are given least. They are the unpromoted; they are classed as failures. They have clung to that one talent which to them is death to hide and instead of receiving just recognition from those who run the show, they get what they deserve for such outrageous idealism. They are the dead.

And such am I. Of course.

Dead.

5

DIGRESSING AGAIN, old scout?

Not necessarily, young sprogs, not necessarily so. For you shall also discover in the course of the lesson that what I so oft return to is one of the major themes of our poem: the antithesis between idealism and ignorant, cynical self-seeking. But of what use is *Lycidas* unless you relate it to life? Of what use is anything? No, I am being entirely relevant when I tell you that I was once an innocent little lamb, well looked after by good shepherds that have long since left the pen.

The good shepherds I refer to were in themselves as Chaucerian a selection of characters as the pupils they sought to edify and inspire. I have already acquainted you with the characters of three of these, besides glancing at the dreaded Fanny Fergusson, she of the well-scoured yoni and the mill-sharp shears, sterility in her bones and vasectomy in her heart. But there were many more who, in the six years I schooled at Skinfasthaven, crossed the threshold of my teens and invaded my mind with their passionate eccentricities, their deep learning, their inspiriting zeal, their genius for education. Gradually they won me over, by their wizardry transforming me into gold from the base metal that I undoubtedly was.

When to the sessions of sweet silent thought I once more summon them, they flock to the bar to give evidence on both sides. And the sound of their murmuring is like the rushing of many waters. Is like the twittering host of souls on the anchorages of the Styx, each one clamorous to be heard. A crowd flowed over the Forth Road Bridge, so many, I had not thought death had undone so many. (Waste, did I say? Waste? I tell you, boys, we are crushed under the tragic weight of it.) Flowed up the hill and down King William Street (high above Dumbiedykes) to where a clutch of churches kept the hours, with a dead sound on the final stroke of nine, when Robert Blair's opens for business along with all the other factories and offices, labour camps, cancer camps, salt mines, Iraqi mines, Safeways, Strangeways, motorways, turnings aside from the Ways and any fucking ways but the old ways and the right ways in all this intricate uncaring world. Its dead nine o'clock humdrum bell beating in ghastly harmony to the strokes of time laid down in Ironmills Road, Dalkeith, Edinburgh, offices of the Scottish Examination Board, where the educationists yawn from their yawning coffins, sharpen their fangs, and prepare to suck the blood of any they can find who has actually confronted an *idea* in the past twenty-four hours and who has actually had the audacity to think for himself today. Let him become one of the undead, they say—or death to his hopes of promotion! Hey, Stetson! you who were with me at the chalk face! That corpse you made a Headmaster last year, has it stayed buried? Is it one of us? Or does it threaten to bloom this term? O, keep the teacher hence that's friend to men—or with his books he'll make them fucking read again! Bloody lecteurs! O those dark Satanic Mills! O tempora!

But you, my mentors, are of the dead, not of the undead, and you can speak for yourselves. Approach then, like the rugged Russian bears that you were, the armed rhinoceros and the Hyrcan tiger. Growl, gentlemen, please. Let me hear you say your speeches over again, those famous one-liners, the verbal mannerisms that made you immortal in the firmament of our youth. And identify yourselves, if you would, according to your subjects, as you once more make the ghostly flame quiver with your speaking. Minto Munro, you with the peppermint in your mouth, slipped in halfway through your lesson, making parts of the Congress of Vienna sound as garbled as the House of Commons on a difficult day—will you be the first, Minto?

Mister Munro to you still, if you please! And take your hands out of your pockets when you address me—as *sir*!

Yes, Mr Munro, yes sir.

Very well then, let us proceed.

MR MUNRO, History (speaking of martyrs and statesmen, as always): *Here is a fine man—come, let us kill him! Here is an unprincipled idiot—let us make him Prime Minister! Such is the key to British History.* Good one, Minto.

MR FORSYTH, Chemistry: *If you lick this you'll be pushin' up daisies!* Tongues hang out all around the bench.

MR DALYELL, Music: *And now, Tschaikowsky, at this point in* the concerto, does exactly what I should have done had I written it myself—which I sometimes feel I did! Followed by general snorts of scorn, with here and there some residual hero-worship and interest in reincarnation.

DR CASSIDY, History, Second in Command (he whose doctorate thesis had dealt with the economic policies of King James VI of Scotland): *Today I'm going to lekchah on the Empah!* Groans, but pencils sharpened all the same.

And the same man again: *Nobody had ever unravelled the complicated finances of James VI. Not even James VI! I did.* Dumb admiration on each and every face.

MR GREEN, Mathematics: *Aha! the gilt's come off the gingerbread . . . Algebra soon sorts out the mathematicians from the morons—and that's how the world is divided!* The unalgebraic tremble.

And the same gentleman, in an attempt to simplify the theory of Calculus, with erudite reference to Jonathan Swift: *Big fleas have little fleas upon their backs to bite 'em; little fleas have littler fleas, and so ad infinitum!* Total nonplussment.

MR PERIWINKLE, also Maths: *There are those who understand the theory of Relativity—and there are others. If I'd understood it just a fraction better, I wouldn't have been teaching you lot today.* Genuine attempts at sympathy.

And again: *Don't ask me why. I never answer questions beginning with why. That's metaphysics. Leave that to the Religious Education Department. I am only concerned with how.* Smug assumption by some, of Mr Peter Periwinkle's brazen conviction of superiority. How noble in reason, they think, though how circumscribed in faculty.

And yet again: *Ah, mathematics is a noble subject! Merely to think about it beautifies and ennobles a man. Just look at me!* All look—and wonder. And still they gazed and still the wonder grew, that one small head could carry all he knew.

What a character!

MR MACDONALD, Art: *Wen you reach de Fift and Sixt Forms, you'll find that teachers are but human* (pronounced yooman). *You'll also find that women are best wen dey're lyin down!* Hoots of laughter, mingled with interested incomprehension.

MR STERNE, Classics: *Latin, the Rod of Life, Greek, the Staff of Life. Adam's Ale and Bread of Heaven, that's the Classics.* Awe.

And on hearing dirty remarks: *Salt and water, salt and water! Mouthwash, mouthwash! You must keep your minds pure if you're to study Homer*. True. Not strong on sex, old Homer. But what turned him blind?

MR BLAIR, Technical Studies: *I'd rather be a lamp-post in Skinfast-haven than Provost o' Pittenweem! Here you may learn your craft—at the centre of the world*. What world?

MR SUTTER, German (a man of acerbic temperament): *Open your teeth, man! I'll give you a touch of the tawse, my boy, I'll come over your fingers in a minute!* Naked fear. Sutter's arm was strong to smite.

And every other period when Sutter's Law held sway: *Modern Languages? Good grief, you can't even speak English! Too much Classics! To hell with insolent Greece and haughty Rome, I say!* But who could be more insolent than Sutter?

MR LEES, Biology (on being told how many of his class intended to study medicine): *I pity the community. Pray God I never come under your scalpels*. Delight from the medically disinclined.

DR ORR, School Chaplain (a deep divine): *The Scriptures tell us that the people could not see Jesus for the press. Thus the language of the Authorised version with unintentional irony provides us with a wry comment on the art of journalism!* Dim awareness that Dr Orr had cracked an erudite joke.

And still they come. What, will the line stretch out until the crack o' doom? Stop then, and let me say a word or two of women.

Women? What women?

Very few women teachers flourished in Skinfasthaven in the fifties, in point of fact. I don't know why. My Primary teachers, on the other hand, had been women to a man—to the last hair on their heavily moustached lips, poor breastless creatures that they were. But Taft Academy was a man's world, teaching being a more respected job for a man in those days. A profession, even. Wow! Maybe it was even better paid, relatively speaking, than it is now. Don't ask me. I'm not an economist. I'm a child in such matters. A Skimpole.

Fanny Fergusson was one of the few. She divided the class into the good side and the bad side—no anti-élitist, egalitarian crap muddled the minds of our clear-thinking pedagogues: you could either *do* Maths or you bloody well couldn't!—and we were assigned our places according to our current performances, that is to say according to whether we could or bloody well couldn't on the particular day, the hour, the minute. The good side was on her right, the bad on her left, the best pupils going to the right wall and the worst to the left. As the rows on either side neared the centre of the room, the line of demarcation between the mathematically and the non-mathematically minded grew less distinct and the middle passage where the two sides met was a no man's land patrolled by a perpetually fretting and fuming Fanny. There was also an upward and a downward order of merit in each row. Top right hand corner was thus the highest place of honour: bottom left, the diagonally opposite corner of the room, was the lowest of the low, reserved for the greatest dumbo. And so, quite apart from the pull and counter-pull between left and right, there was also a bottom-top battle for places—places that altered from minute to minute, involving a constant movement of bodies, like chessmen on a board gone mad. Down you come, boy! Across you go in his place! Two rows into the good side for that answer, and five seats up. You can change seats with the fallen angel who has just given me the stupidest answer of the week. How art thou fallen from heaven, O Lucifer, son of the morning! Out you come, boy, move!

And so on.

Fanny shared Mr Green's belief that Algebra was the killing field on which the mock mathematicians were slaughtered. Geometry was mere recreation, so she maintained. So when I slunk in for a period of Algebra she would jeer at me, 'None of your drawing today, dunderhead! It's pure Maths—better get over to the bad side!'

Yet I know this for a truth: that had it been possible for me to learn Maths, Fanny Fergusson would have taught it to me with all her heart and soul and mind and strength. And fist and foot and spittle and strap. And with all her sheep-and-goat tactics, the saints on her right hand, the sinners on her left—and nothing in between but the yawning certainty that the one could become the other in a moment, in the twinkling of her Calvinistic eye, when she sounded her trumpet and judgement issued from her great white throne and a sterilising sword from her scrubbed cunt. As it happened, not all Fanny's horsiness nor all her man's muscles could ever succeed in putting together for me the humpty-dumpty egg of Mathematics. And a broken vessel it remains for me to this day.

There were, it is true, a sprinkling of benign spinsters besides Fanny Fergusson, but Miss Fergusson is one of only two female

85

teachers who remain in my mind. The other was the girls' P.E. mistress, Miss Myfanwy Jones, to whom I shall come by and by. But the teaching at Taft Academy, Skinfasthaven, was, as I have told you, a mainly male affair, the masters referred to not by their surnames but by a variety of nicknames, sometimes attached to their proper names, and which ran through the incredible alphabet of human types who taught us: Auntie Andy, Baldy Briggs, Boosey Brown, Bugsy, Bulldog, Codface, Dorando, Dozy, Fat Boy, the Goof, the Gowfer, Hot Lips Harry, Liquoroso, the Madcap, the Odd Man, Piggy, Pimple, Plumbeak, Pongo, Ratty, Sleazy, Tich, Tinribs, Vladimir, Zapper. Most of these tags graphically suggest the physical and personal peculiarities of their owners. Such characters belong now in educational museums, along with books and blackboards, teachers who can spell and earn a decent living, children who can write French and count in their heads, grammar and graceful gestures, answering in sentences, hymn singing, Homer, holding doors open and saying good morning, history before 1989, the poetic tradition, the Oxford song Book, Hereward The Wake, the Scottish Paraphrases, Cranmer, the Authorised Version. And much else besides that has gone down the school toilets in the name of progress. All of which old-fashioned values were championed by those giants of yesteryear. And by none more valiantly than by the Goof: calling from the wall-bars or dancing out upon the beams a philosophy of life that I have not forgotten to this day.

The Goof was our Physical Education teacher, and must take the credit to this very hour for the quality of my physique, my standard of fitness, and indeed the general condition of my carcass, which, as you can see at a glance, is not too run down, as it happens, for one who must now be described as past the perfect age of man. As others at Taft Academy inspired me to examine my mind, my morals, my imagination, my soul, through the academic medium of what they had to teach me about the world, so the Goof succeeded in convincing me that my body was there to be looked after with the utmost care; that my intellectual faculties would be the more efficiently employed if I kept the flesh they adhered to in good trim—and indeed that true fitness was no mere matter of how many press-ups I might perform in the gymnasium or the number of penalties I could score on the field.

'True fitness, boys, is nothing to do with muscles; it's to do with mind. A healthy mind in a healthy body.'

And he quoted the Latin tag—a cliché, of course, but one which he took a stage further. To be fit for the rugby team or the athletics field was just the beginning, he told us. We had to move on from there so that we should be fit for the world, and, laying aside then the flesh which we had hopefully tended all our lives, fit for the next world too. For eternity. 'And fit us for heaven to live with thee there' he sang to us on our very first day at school, so that we half wondered if we had strayed into the Religious Education Department in error or had misread P.E. for R.E. when copying down our timetables. The Goof watched our wondering faces and smiled a gap-toothed smile.

'Some of you will learn what I'm on about sooner or later,' he said. 'Others never will.'

And he told us that the first stage in getting to heaven was to turn our faces away from it, towards hell, prostrating ourselves on our bellies like the serpent, of all the beasts of the field the one without legs, and then to take the first step upwards, using our God-given arms and that equally angelic ability to aspire out of the dust: faculties denied to the serpent. In plain terms this meant doing press-ups: as many as we could manage. Which as far as the Goof was concerned meant that we had to push and punish ourselves physically until the very moment that our beating brains threatened to explode out of our skulls and our biceps quivered like red jellies. We soon learned that the man who broke softly into parts of 'Away In A Manger' and wept over a dead hedgehog was no gentle Jesus meek and mild when it came to the basics of day-to-day physical education. He was a lamb who acted tigerishly for much of the time but whose ultimate aspirations were gentle and benign.

Tiny and trim as a ballet dancer, lithe as a monkey, hook-nosed and aquiline as an archetypal Sherlock Holmes (a stunted Basil Rathbone if you care to visualise him) and with a pipe to match and a match always to his pipe, the man we knew affectionately as the Goof had been a commando during the war and had performed daring deeds (so we believed) dangling from the end of a rope while scaling impregnably severe cliffs on unimaginably moonless nights of slipperiness and naked steel, to the absolute confusion of Hitler's war machine. Whether or not this image of our P.E. teacher matched the facts of his career prior to his days

87

at Taft mattered little to us. We admired his spirit, believing it to be the lever that could move mountains, pivot the world. Give me the Goof, Archimedes might have said, and I will move Jupiter.

'I don't give a damn about the result!' he would storm at us during half-time pep talks—pep talks being an understatement for those wild scenes when Mr McGonnachie (let's name him, once at least) foamed at the mouth and gnashed the few dagger-sharp teeth which had demolished so many German rope-bridges, while the rains lashed down, plastering the strands of his flaming red hair close to his skull. 'No, no, I don't give a monkey's toss what the score is at the end of the match. You can beat them ninety-nil if you like, or they can take it from you by no more than a ballhair! What does that matter to me, do you think, after all I've taught you? Sweet Fanny Adams, if you really want to know! It's the spirit I care about, nothing more—the spirit of the game! And it's the spirit that's missing here! Now get back on that field and show some spunk before I have to come on myself and make damn sure some of you never show spunk again!'

Once he really did come on—in the course of a match in which we were all subsequently disqualified. A famous defeat, remembered by us with some pride, although the Goof preferred not to be reminded of it at all. We were playing Bell Baxter at Cupar, an away game, and we had allowed the superior size and weight of the opposing side to convince us in advance that we had no hope of winning. Even so, we had succeeded in holding them to a single try lead with only ten minutes of the match remaining and had contented ourselves with the thought that this would not represent too bad a result considering that nature had so clearly endowed the other side to our disadvantage and the odds were stacked high in their favour. Again and again our thin red and black line broke their charges, though we drummed up no assaults of our own, resigning ourselves to a merely defensive endeavour for the rest of the match, the tactic we had rested on from the very first blow of the whistle.

This was not good enough for the Goof, who had been silently fuming at us from the touchline since his half-time diatribe. His patience finally snapped during a scrum, back in our twenty-five, when the ball had gone in and had failed to emerge after nearly a minute of fruitless wheeling and veering about in the usual thick brown soup of mud into which our efforts had churned the field. Grunting and cursing we were as always, heads down like embattled bulls, eyeballs bulging, mouths frothing, necks sweating, noses ploughing up the filth, our shins being booted to buggery, our ears getting torn off, the fury and the mire seething in our veins—when to our astonishment we heard a hysterical Goof screaming at us from two inches away, followed by an abrupt vision of his inverted face bobbing like a demented gargoyle just inside the scrum.

'My God, this is hellish, it's bloody terrible! I've never seen the like! Have you got balls in there or haven't you? It's not the First fucking Panzer Division you're up against, it's only a few clodhoppers from Cupar, for God's sake! Have some belief in yourselves, you poor milkwet things that you are, and throw away those bibs! By God, I wish I were playing for you! Push, you bastards, push, push, push, push, push!'

How much of the Goof's unacceptable language had been overheard by the momentarily stunned referee I cannot say. He might have let us away with it had it stopped there, but it didn't. Suiting the last word to the action, the Goof dived to the back of the scrum and added his weight in our favour. It wasn't the extra ten stones that mattered. The Bell Baxter bumpkins still surpassed us easily in that department. Each one of them looked well enough able to plough a field before breakfast with the jawbone of an ass—and then eat the ass. But the Goof had a way of releasing our adrenalin and along with it torrents of sublunary energy. With the little man screaming and spitting at our backsides we carried off a sudden surge that completely toppled our confused opponents and freed the ball for our scrum-half to feed to the wingers. They took it with a whoop and flew down the field like geese to score the try. Roars of indignation, naturally, from every player on the Bell Baxter side, the referee, and every spectator in the touchline crowd that had witnessed this atrocity. Wild cheers from our fifteen. Or should I say sixteen? The Goof stood there in the midst of the waving arms, the whistling and jeering, the pointing fingers and shaking fists. Stood there in his muddied rumpled tweeds, a huge jagged grin slicing his scarlet face, looking for all the world like a cartoon scarecrow, undaunted by the angry yokels that surrounded us, howling for his blood, snarling their outrage. Stop the game, ref! Send them home! Cheat, cheat, cheat! Off, off, off!

And of course he was sent off. We all were—and were sent home in disgrace, the Goof to be officially reported to the Shark as a shocking example to boys of bad sportsmanship. The Shark simply smiled. He knew his man. But after he had emerged from his fit, the Goof was naturally mortified at having allowed himself to become so utterly carried away. Not a whit abashed were we, however. All the way home in the bus that morning we sang 'For he's a jolly good fellow' with the gusto that properly belongs to victors—until he begged us to desist.

'Even so, boys,' he conceded blushingly, 'it shows you what you can do if you've just got the spunk!'

One of life's great characters, the Goof.

It was the Goof who started me long-distance running, across country, a form of exercise with which I have kept the faith right up to this bank and shoal of time on which I now stand, poised for the big jump, the life after schoolmastering. How well I remember my former teacher's advice and his goal for life. Start running now, he said—ten miles a week, that's all—and before you retire, each one of you will have run right round the circumference of the earth: a distance of twenty-four thousand miles! Alas, boys of Blair's, I confess I find myself retiring from the once noble art of pedagogy somewhat before my time—and, as this truth is palpable and therefore must be known, actually *well* before my time. What though we do not weep for Lycidas? I shall weep for much else besides and will come to Lycidas by and bye. And I shall take an oath right here and now that for as long as my God-given limbs and lungs last out (and all other necessary parts of the machine whilst this machine is to him) I shall continue in my retirement to pursue the Goof's goal for life, as a tribute to a great schoolmaster if nothing else. So help me God.

I bring God in not as a mere theological flourish to an oath taken in your presence. God may well have to come into the great scrum of life as did the Goof, to help me out, ere I am done. I am not as strong as I was wont to be—where is the life that late I led?—and various forces take their toll. This long disease my life is most inexorable in its daily grind, and this fell sergeant death is strict in his arrest. Does that sound dark? Naturally I entertain high hopes of eluding the long arm of the ultimate law (dissolution) for some little time to come, relative though time may be, but even so, the odds of life do begin to gang up on you like the Bell Baxter bucolics (and no Goof to bustle in) when you arrive at Middle Age, this all too ample ante-room to decrepitude and dust, and one in which we fall back all too often on the great Miltonic consolation: they also serve who only stand and wait.

Still, were it rightful for me to bow down now and worship a graven image, I should genuflect and kiss the golden feet of the Goof, who first took us out to run.

Skinfasthaven was built on a gentle seaward-sloping hill and the Academy stood on the high ground, its south-eastern frontage facing the firth, its rear windows looking out across the fields and farms of Fife, a flat and fertile landscape. The terrain was ideal for running, with its network of footpaths, lanes, dirt-tracks, hedgerows, verges, bridges, burns—and waves of quilted meadows rolling away for miles in a green sea westwards, northwards, eastwards to the sea itself. Nothing was more idyllic after the end of the rugby season and the start of the summer term than to be following the Goof out of the school gates on a morning in April or May, knowing that he had made an arrangement with the appropriate departments for us to miss our next two periods, the subjects to be made up next time round the timetable on a *quid pro quo* basis. No Goof the following week and a double helping of Chemistry or Maths. What did that matter? 'Today is thine!' shouted the little man as he trotted along at the head of a steadily lengthening streamer of vests and shorts. 'Misuse it not.' And he stopped to shout encouragement to the expanding ribbon of runners, letting it pass, panting and spitting, so that he could complete the quotation. 'Tomorrow perchance cometh not.' No, tomorrow we might never see that extra period with Fanny Fergusson. Today was ours. Yahoo! And the Goof came tearing back up the line again, pert as a pony, to remind those at the front that they were opening up the day for the others, blazing a trail through Tuesday so that Wednesday might be better when it came, if come it did. Sufficient unto the day is the evil thereof, he warbled. Above all we should not be at the front because we wanted to win. Winning was not what the race of life was all about. It's the attitude that counts, that's all, he said. Oh yes, win the race if you can and bloody good luck to you, mate! But the Goof had no time for anyone who won too easily, without balls, without backbone, without character. Without mettle and fire and vision and love.

Love?

Yes, that's what I said. Love. And what does love have to do with it, you will be wondering? It was the Goof who taught me that love had everything to do with it. 'I love my competitor because he brings out the best in me.' That was his favourite line and he quoted it many a time and oft upon the hoof, did Goof, nailing the words to the sky, pinning them to the clouds with his busy breath, which he never stopped to take enough of. It doesn't matter if your competitor beats you, but it matters much if you beat *him*, or if he beats *you* down to the ground and you haven't even tried.

Oh, you chivalric fool! (I hear a voice cry)—as if the way that one fell down mattered! And I hear the voice of the Lion in Winter and Richard Coeur de Lion say quietly again that when the fall is all that there is, it matters. The Goof did not believe that the fall was all that there was, or that a single sparrow fell in vain, and he saw a special providence in every human action. But an action in itself, the movement of a muscle this way or that, an action without a human spirit behind it—that's hopeless, he said. That's just another brick without straw, slung into a jerry-built life. A life that is no house at all for a person to live in. A house of life that God didn't build. I want competitors, not winners, he sang as he danced up and down the line, three miles out into the country, St Andrews bobbing on his shoulder and the earth spinning like a ball beneath his feet. But if you win as well, that's a bonus from the gods. 'Listen boys, listen.' And he stopped the front runners to let the others catch up, and when fifteen sweating boys stood in a red-faced circle among the bluebells and birdsong of a brilliant spring morning, the Goof stepped into the centre of the ring and told us a story.

There were two men who once argued over some land and it was decided that they should run a race in order to settle their dispute. Winner take all. One of the men was less fit for the race than his competitor; he simply didn't have the muscle. But he had more determination, more stamina, more grit. In spite of his inferior physique he battled ahead and managed to build up a convincing lead. Then for a time it looked as if his rival were about to eat up all the ground that had been gained and would succeed in overtaking him. The gap closed foot by foot as the finishing point came in sight in the far distance. This was no short sprint—it was long-distance stuff. They were running all the way round the disputed territory, miles and miles of it. Nearer and nearer came the stronger man until the one in front could feel his breath on his shoulder blade. He hovered there for a few agonising seconds, a certain threat, poised to strike, to snatch the race. The last two hundred yards had just opened up before them when the stronger man made his move and began to push out easily in front. Ah, but a race is never over until it's finished. The beaten man decided to try the last. Digging deep and setting his teeth he put on a final spurt and regained the lead. The stronger man fought back but it was no use—the one in front snarled his defiance and tore on, devouring the ground, drinking the air he was determined should belong to him. His chest was now heaving like a blacksmith's forge—his lungs were the bellows, his heart the hammer, pounding against the anvil of his ribs, his head was a raging furnace, his feet were the burnished hooves of a war-horse, shod with steel, his legs flew like pistons, a sword of victory had been fashioned out of his left arm and as he reached out for the tape his fingers burnt it and he came through to win. Then he collapsed, clutching his arm, and died.

Winner take all? The loser took the disputed land and as for the winner, well, he got all the land he needed: six feet of it. And six feet of earth, boys, is all the land a man actually needs. No more than it takes to bury you. Remember that.

But he didn't stop there, the Goof. The lesson continued.

Think about that story, boys, and while you're thinking about it, think about Hamlet looking at the skulls in the kirkyard. Remember the skull of the lawyer, full of fine dirt? The lawyer who, in his time, had been a great conveyancer, a great buyer-up of land, his head crammed with zeros and how many more zeros he could add to the existing pile. A head that now lies deep in the earth, stuffed with the ultimate zero: dirt. Land. Where does it get you, that brash concern with possession, with property? All that getting and spending, what is it worth? You can see what it was worth to the man in the story, the man who won and lost the battle. Didn't Christ say something about gaining the whole world and losing your own soul? And all he had when he died was six feet square of seamless raiment. The man in the story—the man who died—he had lost his soul before he lost his life. I don't want you to run like that man—for greed. In spite of his pluck he didn't run with his soul, he ran with his legs and his lungs. But legs and lungs are just machinery; the soul is the vital spark that makes everything work in the right way. And his way wasn't the right way.

It's a matter of principle, really. Of honour. There's Hamlet again, you see—ask your English teacher—comes across twenty thousand men, Fortinbras's army, on their way to attack Poland. Why? What's at stake, Hamlet asks the Captain? Oh, he says, a tiny patch of ground. I wouldn't farm it myself if you paid me. Wouldn't give you five ducats for it, seriously. Well then, says Hamlet, surely the Poles will never even go to the bother of defending it. Oh, but they will, replies the Captain. It's already garrisoned in fact. This rocks Hamlet back on his heels. It turns out, into the bargain, that the bit of land these Norwegians and Poles are about to fight it out for, to the death, is not big enough to hold the two armies that will meet on it; not even large enough, in fact, to bury the casualties that will result. Even as a potential graveyard it's inadequate. And yet these men on both sides are not only willing to die for it, they are going to go to their graves as blithely as though they were going to bed. Why? Because it's not a piece of land that's at stake, really. Nor is it just the old territorial instinct. It's a principle, an ideal, a matter of honour.

You can play for a sixpenny bet. You can fight for a farthing if honour's at stake. You can run for a straw. An eggshell. But you don't run to win no matter what. You run because you love the race itself. To have taken part is the great thing, to be able to say at the end: I was there, I was part of it. Life itself is like that, isn't it? If you can say at the end that you took part in your own life and that you weren't just a passive spectator, that you were like Beethoven, who took life by the throat in spite of what it did to him—then you'll be a happy man, smiling through shit. And happy is the man who can truly say that he loves his competitor. In the last analysis, do you know who your greatest competitor is? *You are.* Especially in a race like this, where time and terrain and distance and stamina are the main factors.

So when you feel like giving in, like slacking off—don't. Resist. When that happens push yourself all the harder and you'll come through.

Like Pheidippides.

And then the Goof was on to Herodotus and he told us the story we knew already. Of how, before the Battle of Marathon, this legendary soldier had run for help, from Athens to Sparta in two days—which wasn't along tar-macadamed roads, either, or neat little byways—and even had time to chat to a god on a mountain top! Yes, we all knew it, of old, that story. Who didn't?

But it was something about the way the Goof put in that little bit about the god Pan on Mount Parthenium, above Tegea, that made you feel that if you ran like Pheidippides you might meet gods on the way—even if your way lay just between Skinfasthaven and St Andrews.

After the battle that other great runner raced from Marathon to Athens to take his countrymen the news of their victory over the Persians. He died too, coughing up his blood (the Goof dressed it up for us) after the immortal words 'We conquer'. Only he didn't die like a man coughing up his life's blood for land or loot. No, he had triumphed over himself and that was the victory. Nowadays, said Goof, they would just lift up the telephone and no one would die. Fine. But then a man doesn't triumph over himself that way. There's nothing triumphant about lifting a telephone. Any wanker can do that.

Thus waxed the Goof lyrical-philosophical, from literature and history, through ethics to religion and the pursuit of self-knowledge. Man, know thyself (quoting us the original Greek). And don't forget old Polonius's advice. To thine own self be true. Polonius may have been an old buffer but there's never been a better bit of philosophy, more succinctly put. To thine own self be true. What more is there to say? Then he suddenly remembered he was a P.E. teacher and we were standing in the middle of a field deep in the countryside, attracting an outer ring of curious cows. Ducdame, ducdame, ducdame.

Righto, boys, to rest is not to conquer! Off we go again to strive, to seek, to find, and not to yield!

And off we went—fertilised by bullshit, but fertilised all the same. Inspired.

And where was Cranford, pray? Was he not present to hear the Goof's inspiring declarations of his philosophy.? Not he. He'd had enough of clichés, he, and more than enough of exertion. Elsewhere he was, unnoticed by the ecstatic little man, whose eyes shone as he addressed a whole clump of boys but never saw or missed the individual trees on those flights of his. No middle flights indeed.

Where then was Cranford? Lying low, is the answer, and dodging anything so gruelling as a cross-country run with a slice of philosophy in the middle. Wonder not that Cranford could be a shirker in this very department in which you know he shone.

When I told you that he was a sports hero of his time and place I told you true. He enjoyed in physique what he lacked in intellect. But please do not let that mislead you into thinking that Cranford went in for hard work if he could possibly avoid it, oh, dear me, no, 'pon my word (Artful Dodger voice), perish the thought, no. He did his share of training, no question. But he was inclined more to the short bursts than to the long hauls. Definitely not a marathon man in any sense of the word. Not strong on the Pheidippides bit, old Cranford. And on cross country days it was his habit now and then to pull a neat little dodge. Artful, as I told you.

Less than a quarter of a mile from the school, the Goof's preferred route passed over an old Roman bridge, still spanning the peaceful Dreel river that slid down to the sea soundlessly in summer and in winter advertised itself as a much noisier affair. We train-travellers came close to this bridge each morning on our walk from Skinfasthaven station to the Academy, and on the morning of a cross-country day Cranford would make a detour under the bridge, open his briefcase (never a schoolbag for him) and deposit a couple of bottles of beer into a natural ice-bucket of boulders over which the burn flowed coolly on its seaward journey. Thus when the class started off on its morning slog, the Goof well in the lead, spurring us on, Cranford and a chosen crony would lag well behind and, choosing their moment, dart beneath the bridge, leaving the rest of us to the pursuit of exercise and instruction. There, where the ancient Roman bridge-builders had first laved their dusty feet in the Dreel, the latter-day drones would sit with their screwtops nicely chilled by now, boozing mildly and smoking the odd cigarette (another Cranford vice which his sports stardom never seemed to keep from him) until the thunder of feet in the fields nearly one hour later told them it was time to dowse their dog-ends in the burn, send their empties downstream to litter the sands, like the philistines they were, and prepare to sneak out and rejoin the crocodile at a point appropriately close to its raggedy tail. Had the untaxed Cranford slotted himself in near the front and produced an easy spurt, as he frequently threatened to do, we should not have given him away, of course, but he was clever enough not to want to come to the Goof's attention as a potential long-distance runner. A hundred yards a time was his motto and his style.

Even had Cranford bothered to listen to the Goof's philoso-phisings, I doubt if he would have heard what the little man was saying. Some have ears but hear not; some have brains but understand not; and some have no brains at all but a plentiful lack of soul. And I cannot conceive that it would have made any difference to Cranford's own educational philosophy in later life. Besides being an anti-belter in the seventies, he threw in his lot briefly with the anti-élitists. He joined that crowd of crappers (sociologists mainly and such like loonies) who believe that competitive sports are bad for the child. I won't even pause to piss upon that one in passing, if you don't mind. Arseholes like that—as bad as the Raving Right in their own way—are pissing on everything that the Goof taught us. But of course you'll appreciate that Cranford had to drop this particular pose pretty quick after he decided that he wanted to become the Principal of an Edinburgh Public School. And yet, having gone back to élitism, he became, as you all know, an élitist in the very sense that the Goof detested. He became what Goof called a heart and lungs man, a boot and biceps bum of the first order. If you don't win you're of no use to the school and you're of no interest to me. And if you're not a filthy rich buyer of land and real estate, sod off! Results. That's what I'm interested in. None of that spirit bullshit. Thus spake Principal Cranford. And all the Goof's education for life went right down the sewers of Cranford's many-holed mind. And in the Cranford educational establishment of today—and Robert Blair's is just one tiny cog in one small machine in one little factory in the great new Education Industry—there is no room for a Goof. Such a one would not be tolerated and in fact could not even survive. So busy are we drilling and assessing and profiling and generally pissing about with bits of paper, that we have no longer the time (nor the energy, nor the confidence, nor the will) to impart the kind of wisdom that all of us *got*, as the bible sayeth, from the Goof: the P.E. master who quoted Shakespeare, Herodotus, the Gospels, Fenimore Cooper, anything that came to hand, not simply because he was a character in his own right, but because he was fortunate enough to teach in a system that gave him the time and conviction so to do, and to live in an age (only a few decades away, for God's sake) when practising the teaching profession was closer to practising medicine, or law, or indeed Christianity, than it has been for far too long a day. Televisions can be switched on at any time of the day or night, information photocopied at the push of a button. Only a teacher can communicate the spirit that goes beyond the dust of data, the ashes of administration, the sterile bones of those mechanistic drills that have replaced true learning: the spirit of justice, fairness, cleanliness, self-knowledge and truth—yes, all that crap. Can you wonder, therefore, that the Cranford crowd wants such teachers killed off? The old world pedagogues are all too uncomfortable a reminder to them that education was not always top heavy with bureaucracy, that a Headmaster and a single Deputy used to run a school with much greater efficiency than is possible today, that bureaucracy has created *more* inefficiency, by creating unnecessary work, which creates stress, which creates tiredness and muddle; that only a special kind of person *can* teach, that the education business has defined itself most devastingly in its bleak new profile: antiseptic as Fanny Fergusson's fanny; pure and cold and pointless as a nun's vagina. Where no waters breed or break. Where only those with a clerk's mentality can survive. And no dinosaurs give birth. And old teachers are expelled. And Shakespeare is stillborn. And old shags never shag again. And Charles Dickens is dead, is dead, is dead. Is dead.

6

An engineer told me before he died
And I'm fucking sure he never lied
He knew a whore with a cunt so wide
That she was never satisfied.

So he built this tart a prick of steel
Driven by a fucking great wheel,
Two brass balls he filled with cream
And the whole fucking issue was powered by steam.

Round and round went the fucking great wheel,
In and out went the prick of steel.
Till at last the maiden cried:
'Enough! Enough! I'm satisfied'.'

Up and up went the level of steam,
Down and down went the level of cream.
Till again the maiden cried:
'I'm fucked! I'm fucked! I'm satisfied'.

Now we come to the tragic bit,
There was no way of stopping it.
She was split from cunt to tit
And the whole fucking issue was covered in shit!

NOT EVEN THE Goof, who stopped to spout Robert Burns at a daisy on one of our morning runs, could have prevented us from pursuing that predilection for crudity which seems to be ingrained into most males from the age of three upwards, even Mozart, and which I fear we carry with us like shithouse doors to our graves.

God made man in his own image, yes, but yet there yawns a world of difference between man and man. And God, who made it possible for Blake to write 'Jerusalem', also made possible 'The Engineer's Wheel' and other such rugger ditties, sung in the steamy atmospheres of communal baths and drink-laden buses, after 'away' games in particular, when the grape was illicitly quaffed. Songs of such grossness as would make Beelzebub blush.

Thus sang the uncouth swain to the oaks and rills, with many a song and many a lecherous lay. But although I myself did not find such songs risible, I found them—as did we all—fascinating. Because, as our choirmaster Cranford stirred this diabolical sub-broth of bawdry and libidinous laughter, gradually it exuded the seminal vapours out of which a new order of awareness was formed. I had learned to sing-a-long-a-Cranford for quite some time without having the faintest clue what many of the words really meant. But it was out of the rugby world and its lewd lyrics, the musical rutting and roaring that went on in the buses on the journeys home from Kirkcaldy, Cupar and Dundee, when the Goof's pipe was out and his senses shut, that the facts of life first emerged for me in all their fearful nakedness. In point of fact I could not bring myself to believe, in the beginning, that they were true. Surely they were as mythical, as spurious as the songs we sang so lecherously and so loudly, with such salacious thirst after the absurd and the unreal.

It was Cranford—ever in the vanguard of education—who assured me that this particular story was no joke but a fact of life: *the* fact of life. Solemnly he instructed me in the mysteries of human reproduction and all its associated horrors and delights: foreplay, penetration, pregnancy and birth itself. He talked of semen and spermatozoa, of eggs and cells and strange canals. He drew back the veils from the female orgasm, from menstruation, her time of the month, which he called her *period*.

—Her period?

—Her time of the month, I've told you. What she uses fanny pads for, when she bleeds. (It was all too terrible to take in. I had seen such articles lying on the beach and floating around the sewage pipe, like anaemic fish stained pale with blood, and there flashed into my mind again the contents of Fanny Fergusson's cabinet.) Are you listening? You can shag her a few days before the period and a few days after it and she won't get pregnant. That's one way of avoiding a baby. Another way is to pull it out and shoot your spunk on the ground—or into her belly button. It can't get in that way! (Snorts of lecherous laughter.) There's a Latin name for it: coitus interruptus, or cock-no-come-in-puss. (More laughter.) But that's frustrating. The best thing is to use an F.L.

—What does that stand for?

—French Letter.

—How can that work?

—It's not really a French letter. I don't know why it's called that. Wait for it, though—it's a bit of rubber tubing that goes on the end of your prick and catches the spunk. Neat idea, eh? Of course you could probably use a balloon or something, but it mustn't hurt too much. An F.L.'s the thing.

—Where do you get them?

—Aha! The chemist is one possibility but they won't sell them to you there if you're under a certain age. Anyway they'd go straight to your mum and dad and tell them and then you'd be in the shit. The other place is the barber's.

—What's it got to do with him?

—Think. Your dad has just had a haircut. He doesn't want to admit to it in front of all the other blokes that he's going to go shagging his wife again tonight, so he says to the barber, casual like, 'Keep a shilling for yourself, Sam' and winks. And when Sam hands him the change he slips an F.L. into his hand as well. Simple.

—Are they quite small then?

—Don't know. I haven't seen one yet. But listen. You know Logan—his dad has the barber's shop in Pittenweem. Says he knows where's they're hidden in the shop and he's going to get me one. Going to bring it to school. Then we can all try it on.

—Wow!

And so indeed Logan did arrive the very next day, bearing the awesome article. But to unwrap it we betook ourselves far from the school, up to the loch where Bulldog did his fishing, and further still, climbing the slopes of Kellie Law, Druidic and solemn in our ascent towards the moment of this hitherto occulted truth, the discovery of which was a species of guilt that only God would know about as He strolled around heaven all day in the cool of the clouds. As He knew about all things. There on the summit, with the farms and villages and steeples spread out beneath our feet, we were at least showing ourselves before God's universal eye, his cirrus hair, his cumulus-pressing feet, aware that we were pursuing a dubious branch of knowledge, but perhaps (and with a little bit of luck) Goof-like and benign on this occasion in shutting his eyes and ears to our live, advertised imperfection. After all we were only human and our forefathers had fallen like dominoes before us all the way from Adam, the first of the pack.

The pack. Ah, yes. Logan handed it to Cranford, who opened it with trembling fingers. Plain stiff brown paper concealing a packet labelled 'Durex', inside which sat another sealed package: a riddle containing a mystery wrapped inside an enigma, (as Winston Churchill said of *Hamlet*). Carefully Cranford tore apart the inner wrappings and pulled out its contents.

And there it was, the French Letter.

The Contraceptive.

Neat and innocuous as a piece of chewing gum. Sterile and chilling in its implications as a surgical swab. The little teat at the end, as yet unfurled, would venture into an unknown darker than Africa, a secreter passage than the northwest, as it made its fantastic journey into the future, the worst journey in the world. It would probe the unplumbed mysteries of Jenny Miller's womb, remote as Uranus to my Greek yearnings. It would boldly go where none of us had ever gone before, where up until yesterday I had never dreamed of going, not even knowing what such things were, that we did speak about.

'Shall I put it on?' asked Cranford, a little hushed.

And we all nodded in affirmation, holding our breaths tightly as the specimen from Logan's Hairdressing Establishment for Gents in Pittenweem slid easily over Cranford's erect cock.

'Now I'm going to fuck the first sheep I see!'

Not strong on refinement, Cranford.

But we didn't laugh. Another new planet had swum into our ken and we gazed out at the blue firth in the distance, a dumb, innocent dream, and stared at Cranford's shrouded knob, clothed in white samite, mystic, wonderful, stout as old Cortez in the glory of its six stiff inches. And looked at one another with a wild surmise. Silent upon that peak in Fife, somewhere west of Darien.

There was in the school library a Chaucerian tome, unread by human eye, but much fingered by human hand on only one of its archaic pages, so thumb-marked that the print was almost worn away. Even had it been in pristine nick, it would have been far from easy to interpret; for not only was it printed in the original Middle English, but the edition had been put out—as it flashed upon my remembering and better-educated mind in later years—by the press of William Morris, with its gorgeous antique type. Some enterprising thief made off with it eventually and it went the way of all fine books. Into someone's private collection. Unless of course it was purloined out of prurience, which I doubt. A vandal such as Cranford wouldn't have weighted himself down with the whole tome. He'd simply have torn out the titillating page and left the violated volume on the shelves along with all the other crap that was there. In the Battle of the Books he was destined to become quite an educational hit-man, was Cranford: the Butcher Cumberland of anti-bibliophiles. Anyway, to get back to the business of the book. I said 'enterprising' a moment ago because the book in question was a first edition of considerable value.

It was the famous Kelmscott Chaucer.

I thank the good Lord it was not Cranford who drew me to this well of English undefiled, this bubbling fount of medieval fun. Of knowledge made fun—which, by the bye, gives you my own definition of education in three words. I first came to Chaucer by accident. Or instinct. Something sufficiently bibliophiliac squatted in me even then—in my third year at Taft, was it?—to make me want to pick up the book and examine it as an object. Inevitably it fell open at the place that must have been scented by intuition by the first trail-blazing troglodyte in a blazer to come through these walls, sniffing after sex and seeking like me, blindly after illumination, acquaintance with mystery. I looked, I saw, and I read. And these were the words that flashed out at me:

> Derk was the nyght as pich, or as the cole,
> And at the wyndow out she pitte hir hole,
> And Absolon, hym fil no bet ne wers,
> But with his mouth he kiste hir naked ers
> Ful savourly, er he were war of this.
> Abak he stirte, and thoughte it was amys.
> For wel he wiste a womman hath no berd.
> He felte a thyng al rough and long yherd.

What was it that sent a thrill through my bowels, clutched at my cock, tickled my testicles and swept a wave of fire across my chest and arms so that my fingertips trembled? I like to think that there were some dimly discerned literary values even in that first ephemeral experience of Chaucer, of whom I had not at that point in my life even heard. That something of the beauty of the book, with its monkish borders, its mock medieval initials and woodcuts of pale Burne-Jones heroines, was borne in upon me. Even then. That even as I sat there staring at a piece of poetic bawdry six hundred years old, with Fanny Fergusson's disapproving breath bactericidal upon my back, I had some unconscious sense that this is what would come to matter to me more than anything and would form the nucleus of my intellectual adult life, my professional life. Perhaps. Perhaps not.

What did strike me with great force was that here was a story from a very long time ago (I had no notion then how old) in which the same fascination for the female anatomy could be apprehended, albeit in a manner made deliciously absurd. A woman had stuck her arse out of a window like the moon in the middle of the night and a chap called Absolon had gone up and pushed his face right into her pussy. *A thyng al rough and long yherd.* Imagine actually doing it! Imagine sallying forth on one of these indescribably balmy nights, dripping with summer stars and honeysuckle, and going for miles up country, where Goof had lightly trod, to one of these isolated farming cottages. Such girls as Alyson lived out their sly separate lives up there—I had seen them looking fawn-like over dykes, with their darkened eyes and swinging tits. And imagine, on keeping an impossible assignation at a window, with one of these succulent wenches, imagine coming into contact not with a pretty farmgirl's fáce but with a different set of lips entirely. A mouth surrounded by a beard, as shockingly rough and shaggy to the touch as it was to a lover of centuries ago, a mouth that could not speak but which could be kissed and entered. A forbidden mouth. *A thyng al rough and long yherd.* The steeples of Skinfasthaven, Pittenweem and all the other fishing townships would stand sentinel as lips encountered lips, and the same quiet stars would glitter on the firth, stars like satyrs, winking with connivance as they did when Absolon first came into contact with the holy of holies, the fabulous pussy, the female pudenda, dark as old Egypt, mysterious as the Nile.

I made to share my bookish experience with Cranford but he showed no interest. Not strong on words, remember, old

Cranford. And the younger Cranford was even less interested in the world of words: one essential difference between him and me. More of a pictures man, our Cranford. And was then too. You can see hi. style all over the place, more pictures than print on every page you turn. Visual stimuli, as they are called nowadays. Or non-print stimuli, if you like. More gobbledygook to keep the crappers in their jobs. The stuff you actually read is what they now term print stimuli. We used to call them books. Remember?

Oh, Cranford was interested in books all right, even when he was a Third Form nipper, but they were strictly picture books, and the only print they ever contained said things like 'Gloria: 42–21–44'. Girly magazines. We first came across them in Dundee after an away rugby fixture. Usually the Goof allowed us an hour or so out on the town before reporting back to the bus for the rude songs and ribaldry that in those days carried us home. So we'd spend a shilling or two on sweets. Money was tight then and didn't rise to the price of naughty mags. Cranford put forward the plan that we should spend less on sweets in future and club together for one of these forbidden publications—which we did. Only to find that some shop assistants refused to sell them to us. 'It's a present for my dad,' Cranford would then say, and sometimes actually succeeded in obtaining the goods on this pretext, having taken his father's name in vain. It is to me one of the great mysteries of genetics that the Reverend Arthur J. Cranford, whom we all knew to be the mildest and ablest of men, could have sired such a son. As sensitive as a horse's bum and as thick as its shit. Doubtless the sire would have said that this is good theological ground, solid evidence that biology alone does not produce people. God is in there somewhere, even if it is to see to it that a blameless Christian gentleman in a dog-collar and with a most respectable lineage to boot, should be given a good-sized cross to bear. I don't know how the poor chap thought of his son, mind you, but I scarcely think he could have seen him as a boon and a blessing. More a bane and a burden. The old guy did not live long enough to see his son become Principal of Robert Blair's College. Anyway it was this abortion of a boy who seemed God-ordained to bring dubious knowledge into our midst and he was the one who naturally procured for us our first obscene literature.

Obscene. Boys, permit me to place my hand across my mouth and titter, will you? The Victorians put out naughtier erotica than anything we could find on sale on the shelves of John Menzies, even at the end of the fifties, when you had more chance of picking up hornbooks than anything genuinely horny. Convinced of our wickedness, however, we sped down to the banks of the River Tay with our filthy bargains and feasted our eyes in wonder upon sights that nowadays would hardly cause a lusty lad of twelve years old to stop in his tracks and adjust his wandering willie. Gloria would be seen standing on a beach wearing white trousers and no top. She'd be holding a beach ball and laughing toothily as she prepared to throw it to the camera. Her bare breasts were exposed and looked a little as if they were there for playing with, once she'd got rid of the ball. Or she'd be standing with her back to you in her living room, quite naked, looking round as though slightly surprised by your presence. Oh, hello, come to take my photo, have you? Hang on a minute, I haven't got my knickers on yet. Matter of fact, I'm starkers. And her bum would be as smooth and polished as an apple. One of those plastic apples, shining in bowls of artificial fruit. Not one for biting into, though.

Then there were the sultry poses: the tits thrusting out of the page and dangling like dangerous melons about to go off. Play with me at your peril, they seemed to say—and our hearts beat faster with excitement and fear. How could such women be handled? But if there were full frontal nudities they were always toned down to something safely anodyne that would not offend a still-touchy sense of public decency, unbelievably nunnish now, set against the nefarious nineties. The crotch was never exposed, the lower abdomen usually masked by a table or a knee, and if the pubic region were on view at all it was always impeccably shaved. For a time I wondered if pubic hair were a phenomenon peculiar to the females of east Fife. Come to think of it, I had only ever felt one girl myself. Maybe there was something mannish about Jenny Miller. Ah, but I recalled my Chaucer. Something rough and hairy sticking out of a night window, for Absolon's deluded delectation. Anyway, Cranford assured me, Gloria always had to keep her fanny shaved. It's the law, he said. If the photographer showed you her hairs he'd be fired or fined. What he does is to have a bloody good look at them first himself and then he shaves them off for the camera. With one of these new electric shavers. God, what a job to have, being one of these photo men! If I had a job like that I'd ride every woman that came to my studio. That would be my fee. Sometimes I wish I'd been born a girl (he added in one of his rare moments of wistfulness). If I were a girl I'd be able to look at other girls' tits when we were changing. And I'd sit and feel myself all day long!

I considered this interesting prospect and thought it not unreasonable at the time.

If the dirty magazines had been communally purchased they were brought home and loaned out alphabetically, one night per boy, and if your name came last in the team then you'd have to languish a fortnight for the book to be smuggled into your bedroom, where, with a torch beneath the blankets, you goggled at Gloria's breasts and backside for a clandestine hour until your prick could stand the strain no more. Sometimes the magazine came to you already crackly with earlier emissions that made the pages crinkle and stick together. Then you grumbled if a tit was torn off in the turning and demanded to know the identity of the stickler who had marred your pleasure. If pleasure can really be said to be the word which correctly defines that deep surreptitious aching for experience which was kindled in us by such books.

I wonder what Gloria is doing now?

Judging by the firm state of her tits and the freedom from fat, the plunge of her back, the sweep of her hips, the waist like an arctic swan, the flab-free thighs, the general tautness of her satin flesh, what might one say? Look at her all round, except up her cunt, which is not allowed and doesn't help to age her in the way you can a horse when you part its rubbery, fanny-like lips to examine its teeth—(no teeth up a fanny, except Fanny Fergusson's, naturally, and well-brushed ones at that, all ready to deal you vasectomy with a vengeance)—but laying all that aside and taking a good round look at her roundness, I should say that Gloria was in her early twenties and had perhaps ten years on us at the most.

Where is she now then? *Ubi sunt que ante nos fuerunt?* She's between fifty and sixty, that's where she is, and by the end of the sick mill she'll be an O.A.P. for sure, if she's not one already. I wonder what her tits would do to me now? Now that they've been sucked and stretched by a brood of vipers who have probably given her fifteen grandchildren by now. Poor Gloria. Have you had your eyes tested? got your subsidised specs yet? your varicose veins stripped? your womb hitched up? whipped out? your slipped paunch tightened? your sloppy cunt fastened?

your slack jowels lifted? your cancered bowels lasered? your wig on? your dentures in? eyelashes attached? fingernails glued? pacemaker set? deaf aid receiving? labia taken in? And which one of those glorious tits of yours, O Gloria, is not your own? Not so glorious now, I fear. How beastly are the bristols when one is gone away! Stands the left mammary where it did—or is it silicon that swings there now? O sic transit Gloria's Monday, for she's now at Larkin's Friday—Friday afternoon, actually, and tomorrow she dies. Just the day before me, as it happens, O you young fry of lechery, you Monday's children you! So fair of face. Thus runs the world away, alas. And it goes with a lass. And alack. So *carpe diem*, seize the day.

O, go for it, boys, go for it now, while the young sap shoots in your stems, while the genie drives the goodies of green age through your throbbing pink fuses, go for it—and may the force be with you! Go tell it on the mountain, halleiujah, ah se-ee-ee-n the light, brothers, go tell the virgins, the blue girls, to make much of time, as Herrick bade them long ago, and many a wise old shag before his day, ever since Catullus imagined Lesbia's pink lips flecked with his semen, white as winter snow on the sweet, little yoni that caused him so much prick-ache, so much pain. Erotia? Yes, but not half as taking as all those poems to Julia: upon her clothes, her voice, her ribbons, her petticoat, her breath, her breasts, her bed, her legs, her hair, her lips. There's nothing we don't know about Julia, down to the notch on her left nipple, the mole under her armpit, the electricity in her tongue, the egg-white smoothness of her calf, the swaying of her buttocks and thighs to which her underclothes would cling—then fling themselves away again as she moved, sending our Herrick into his melting swoon. Nothing like Julia to keep a man from butterfly nets and bibles. His verses may be an inventory of clichés but at least he takes the trouble to give you a guided tour of the bird and the boudoir. It may be lust, my friends, of the most impeccably decorous variety, but it's God-given and goodly and let's be thankful for it. A far cry from both the shower songs of semen and syphilis and the horrified intellectual analysis of the ego. Don't analyse love, just make it, in verses or in bed, but for God's sake don't go all pure. Just keep your eye on your cock and hers on the clock and never stop reminding yourselves how time is running out. Oh, why do they never listen, hoarding their maidenhoods all the way to Hades, the Sabine spinsters with the revolution-sized boobs and the ice-cold cunts, leaving the joys of Cypris to lie unfucked in Acheron, a pile of bones and dust?

Who cometh next? John Donne?

At the other end of the pole from Cranford. Much too intelligent by half, too conceited, too frenetically afraid of being just possibly wrong about his God and his girls and having to prove it over and over in verses that bristle with uneasy confidence. Wha daur meddle wi' me, ye bastards? I'm intellectually watertight as a cod's behind. *Nemo me impune lacessit.* Or, in Cranfordese, fuck off. I'm impregnable. *Antes muerto que mudado,* and I'm not arguing with you anyway, I'm telling you. In poem upon poem. *Cogito ergo sum.* My cock is up and flashing fire doth follow, so stand out of my way or get shot. With the pearls of my semen and my cerebellum.

No, Donne will never do. John Donne. Undresses a girl in the most public rooms in the world (such pretty stanzas) for all posterity to see, but at the end of the day posterity doesn't see a single part of her. Glitterati literatti, eyes on the Harper's Queen gear she takes off, piece by glistering piece, and him counting them all the way to the cunt: the breastplate and bankrolls, the bodice and brass, the busk and the bread going neatly together in a glorious sexual-economic fantasy that has him dribbling at the mouth; girdle and gravy, laces and lucre, dolman and diadem, sparklers and shift, readies and ruff, folding and Frenchies, lolly and lingerie all at one sitting. Bring in the booze then, I've got the bird and lashings of blarney. Go on, gel, gerremoff, gerremdown, you chic expensive scrubber of the nineties, fifteen or nineteen, sixteenth or twentieth, what does the century matter? what your age or your wardrobe? Just be my cocktease, with buckets of champers and ice to cool down my ego, and I'll be that shit in the shuttered chateau as long as the poem lasts. O.K. Not too fast now, and take your time as you take them off: the Laura Ashleys, the Levis and loot, the shoes and the sugar, the gown and the greens, the girdle, the corsets, the boob-tube, the boodle, the ponies, the panties, the pearls, the tawdry, the tights, monkeys and morning-wear, yashmak and yen, dollars, décolletage, stockings and shekels, petticoats and pelf, it's going on and coming off all over the world and up and down the ages, the G-strings, the grands, the spondulicks in your suspenders, the needful in your nicks. O, my bank of America!

my gold mine of Africa! my angel of England! my creme de mint! my Eskimo Nell! rip your knickers away, you archetypal tart and make me the ruler of the world! In bed. For money makes the world go round, not love, in spite of what I seem to be saying in the poem. Money money money money money money money money money money money money, yeah. Money is power, though I have none. The Court is power, though, I never got me there. (And shines like rotten wood.) The Church is powerless to give me what I want. (Says what's good and doth no good.). No good to me anyway. Sex is metaphysical, power is real. All you need is love, love, love. No, all you really need is money and power. And as I have neither I shall sit me down and think. All I *can* do is think. I think therefore I am.

Thus John Donne.

How witty, how ambitious, how arrogant! How massive his ego, how aspiring his erection! How false his convictions. But sucked on country pleasures we were, before we met, just fucking around with any old cunt. But to fuck *her* is to be free. Her cunt is a chapel. Her birthday suit bijoux richer by far than all the expensive attire she has just kicked off . . .

And yet it's only the fashionable Bond Street wear that his eye actually sees. His fingers fondle grammatical parts only. Behind, before, above, between, below. What a line! The five sexiest prepositions in the English language, made so by Donne. Brilliant. But they're still only prepositions. Rephrase, please: the buttocks, the pubes, the tits, the thighs, the cunt. Not so poetic—but less prurient, you might say, and that is what is lacking here, in the famous undressing elegy. Do we learn anything about this woman of his in her nakedness? What colour was her dress, her hair, her eyes? were her breasts apples or pears? was her skin smooth like a nectarine or downed like a peach? lips like a thread of scarlet or full with a Cupid's bow? small neat ears or ones with large lobes? wanton tresses or curtailed? Birthmarks, moles, broken toenails? Dimpled bum? Yoni small or large? Anything at all? A freckle?

Nothing. Let's admit it, we learn nothing from Donne about his women. From Donne we learn about Donne, the be-all and the end-all from bedpost to bedpost and nothing else is. Princes do but play him. In bed he is king, emperor, pope. God. Now that's not love, because for all the puns on his prick there's simply not enough genuine lust there. Not short on lust, the Elizabethans. Look at Barnabe Barnes,—who wished he could be the wine gurgling down his girl's gullet, so that he could go a progress through her gut and come back into the world as her urine, refreshed by the ultimate rite of passage. Not 'I could go a glass of wine with you, love', but 'I could go a trip through your uterus! Drink me off will you, darling?' Brain-boggling maybe, but it's honest-to-goodness desire, taken to extremes. Donne never felt for a girl like that, never stopped to chat to you about her as dear Herrick does, about his lady as a person, as a visible entity that moved and talked and had eggs for breakfast.

And what of Andrew Marvell?—so much more enjoyable and urbane than Donne, so much more relaxed. A little frisson, yes, but elegantly controlled, and if his tongue is in his cheek you can guess where it will be next. He looks at his mistress, so succulent, so coy, and imagines a courting as expansive as an impossibly ideal day, stretching from the Creation all the way to a biblical never-never time and comprising a ritual dance from India to Hull. How slowly his erection would come on—but how vast it would grow! And how refined his love: evolving from a stiff cucumber at the Cranfordian level of vegetable existence to the uncategorisable intricacies of empire and art. Just ponder the prospect. He could take the Hundred Years War to admire her forehead. Her tits would use up the High Middle Ages in their entirety. Not that he couldn't have allowed even more time if he'd felt so inclined. Even the Elizabethan Age might have gone on a nipple. By the time he has sung paeans to her pudenda the human race would be three hundred centuries into the future.

Well, what do you think of the prospect, boys? Do you approve of the prospect, sirs? And how do you like the amatory arithmetic? He didn't invent the fashion, as any seasoned critic will tell you, but what a compliment to any lady, so gracefully phrased! And so clever of him to tell her that she is worth this amount of adoration, with the ages of earth's history set aside solely for the contemplation of her private parts and the sun shining out of her arse.

> But at my back I always hear
> Time's winged chariot hurrying near:
> And yonder all before us lie
> Deserts of vast eternity.

Ay, there's the rub: the ticking clock. Breathlessly he brings it into the bedroom and the bedroom becomes a desert, the alarm clock melting in its midst: a clock no longer but a cock, a surrealistic cock, wilting like Salvador Dali's, inducing the panic of the proud male when facing the prospects of impotence and eternity. Eternity. Only, you see, Marvell would have pronounced the line *Desarts of vast etarnity*, with that luxurious, lugubrious lingering on the back vowels. A line of dark resonance that makes you shiver. Before you know where you are in this featureless fear he has created for you, the clever sod is busy surrounding virginity with all the usual associations: sterility, tombs, graves, dust—but doing it in his own inimitable way. Should she die unentered by human cock, it is only a Fabian tactic, a delaying of the inevitable. Other cocks will have a go at her in the grave. Disembodied pricks that crawl about among clods and sodden roots and centipedes and things—the phallic worms that now seduce her where she lies powerless to halt their erotic advance.

> *Then worms shall try*
> *That long preserved virginity.*

No man has ever experienced her—but the cold worms will.

> *And your quaint honour turn to dust*
> *And into ashes all my lust.*

And her quaint honour turn to dust. It takes a Marvell man to produce that pun on *quaint*, used as a substantive by Chaucer when arse-kissing Absolon's rival caught Alyson by the *queynte*. The ancestor of our word *cunt*. That's what it means. Imagine the cold pink segments of an earthworm as it inches its way up your cunt, a cold pink prick parting your rosy lips, pushing and probing up the vulva, spearheading a hundred others to breed in your belly. A wormery in the womb. Imagine allowing first access to such slimy pricks—and yet refusing *me*—your warm, turgid lover. Is that the way you really want it? That's exactly how it will happen, if you don't drop your knickers now, now while your quaint is hot and moist and the only worm in the room is powered by balls and ready to make you die a different death: the ecstasy of orgasmic release, in which you will abandon the macrocosm for a brief moment or two . . .

> *Now therefore while the youthful hue*
> *Sits on thy skin like morning dew . . .*

And he visualises the love-making that will result from her

submission: not a sedate billing and cooing of two turtle doves, but a terrible tearing and clawing as two birds of prey devour one another hungrily, with bestial appetite eating Time too, biting back at it, the bastard, fucking the last enemy, King Death.

Let's give it all we've got, then—

> *And tear our pleasures with rough strife*
> *Through the iron gates of life.*

Through those awful, invisible iron bars that keep the cunt locked: the rosy gates of guilt and fear, the iron blood-blushed lilies of the labia, portcullising the castle of ultimate experience. Can't you open these gates? No, never. Even though you say yes in the end ten times over like Molly Bloom, the gates always stay locked, imprisoning the rose, as they do from adolescence, when we first know the rose is there. And our fierce frail pleasures must be ripped through those unforgiving bars, a million separate petals coming apart and floating free. Weird, isn't it?

My favourite poem, I suppose. Perhaps because Marvell does best what poets have been doing for centuries, from Ovid to Amis. Go on, Kingsley, have the final word.

> *The best time to see things lovely*
> *Is in youth's primordial bliss,*
> *Which is also when you rather*
> *Go for old shags talking piss.*

Trust old Kingsley to hit the nail on the head—all too neatly, as it happens. All of you are looking at the old shag. Precisely. And you can hear all too plainly what passes for piss. I pass it every day. You've been hearing it for years now, some of you, and you're off to college very soon to hear much more. Do me one favour, chaps. See that you stick in!—the advice I was given years ago, remember? Listen hard. The piss is potent; you can't live without it; it's the water of life. But in all your listening, get wisdom, always remembering that Wisdom is not the Principal's thing (not *our* Principal's, anyway). And in all your getting, don't forget to seize the day. And to tell your girl to seize the dick. Every time. *Carpe diem.* And to gather ye hymens while ye may.

And get stuck in.

Getting stuck in was all that I could think about for weeks on end, following Cranford's latest revelation of the means by which human life was created. Not that I was eager to procreate: simply to follow the natural promptings of my prick and fuck somebody. Anybody. The identity was of no matter. She could be dark or fair, fat or slim, old or young, ancient or modern, asiatic or albino, Heloise or Eskimo Nell. Dead or alive. Just so long as she let me stick my prick through the iron gates of life. Or if not the whole way in, then just a little fraction through the keyhole in the door. *Oh, the keyhole in the door! the keyhole in the door! I'd take up my position through the keyhole in the door*! Or if she were even to allow me the merest morsel of the gift of mercy, no more than a peep—this destined 'she' of my suddenly acquired desires.

And as I had to fix on somebody, I suppose it was natural that I should follow the path taken by nearly every other boy in my year by selecting as the immediate object of my passion Miss Myfanwy Jones, aforementioned in this lesson, but, in case you have forgotten, the girls' P.E. mistress. She was the first female I consciously lusted after with the full force of my terrible new knowledge concerning the true facts of life as never before known, and as lately revealed by John The Divine Cranford, dispenser of the apples of knowledge, for a price. Miss Jones was indeed an object worthy of any red-blooded male's mounting concupiscence, though a decade out of my reach in her mid-twenties: tall and supple as a poplar in the wind, bright-haired as a rowan on fire with the spring. (Do my comparisons reflect my ingenuous romanticism? Ah, what a time it was!) Her limbs belonged to the bronze—nay, golden—world of the billboard girls (before Titch Thomas got to them with knife and tuberous cock and balls) as did her complexion, so different from the pasty pimpled faces of our generation—rather short on vitamins, I fear, and continental holidays.

Miss Jones did not come short on anything. If she had a flaw, it lay in her too-full gobful of teeth. A glinting white arsenal. So that, when she laughed, which she frequently did, I was reminded of Burt Lancaster and Charlton Heston about to do battle with six-guns—just look at all them teeth!—grimacing at one another from fifty yards apart in that expensive American way that threatens death and speaks of porcelain crowns laid in at a thousand dollars a time. Oh, but Miss Jones's teeth were her own, all right. Just a little too manly, perhaps. Such noble molars! Such moulded lips concealing such white weapons of war!

Or love?

There was no sign of that. We looked hard and thought even harder but no lucky bastard on a motorbike ever roared up to the school gates and whisked her off through the fields for a frolicsome fuck as we half hoped, and half feared. It seemed that Miss Jones was made for war, not love, after all, destined for a platonic relationship with her hockey stick, followed by a barren life with some old fogey pursuing a shared interest in riveting china and incontrovertibly less riveting books and bed. In good order. A life reprehensibly perfect. And a life without children.

We watched her on the hockey field, moving with lethal grace among her girls, whacking the ball with a force that made our rugger look tame by comparison. Or in summer we looked on with hopeless longing when she coached the girls for tennis. The short navy winter tunic was doffed for the even shorter white pleated skirt, and each time she served we edged up to the court behind her, as close as we dared, watching her, round-eyed and drooling as the skirt flew up to reveal her knickers, so immaculately white and tight against the titian flesh. I had expected to see a pair of frillies—a flash of pretty froth beneath the hem, the sun glinting on a wild sea-horse mane, something poetic. But no. Instead there was this other something that could not be defined, something unbearably arousing about the simple cotton that covered her skin. Did that tan of hers creep all the way up, under those Spartan tide-white knickers, burnishing her buttocks like the rest of her infuriating flesh? It seemed probable. And if that were the case, then where did she receive the lucky old sun that looked down upon her Welsh nakedness, the busy old peeping tom that he was? Was there a sun-lamp tucked away in one of the private staff apartments off the gymnasium somewhere, used only by Miss Jones? O, such agonies of pleasure! such pains of prurience! O wolves of memory! If only, if only . . . O, love at fifteen.

I ached for the sight of female flesh and the wonderful feel of girls as the desert longs for water. As the hart panteth after the waterbrooks. As the mother mourneth for the lost child of her loins. As the saint hungers and thirsts after righteousness. As the mystic longs for God. That is not sacrilegious, I trust. In fact there was truly something religious about my yearning. A divine lust for revelation, to be slaked (so I often imagined) in some wondrous way—Venus herself surfboarding into the harbour right in front of my windows, posing in her cockleshell, powered by its little

Botticelli outboard motor, her hand on her tits, her hair covering her cunt, ready to reveal all. A woman that would come naked to me out of the sea. I dreamed about her, my Marina. I scanned the skyline hungrily.

She never came.

But Miss Jones did.

Right out of the school swimming pool.

It happened at a time when reconstruction work was being carried out in parts of the P.E. block and new changing rooms were being built for both pupils and staff. At an early point in this project the dividing wall between the boys' and girls' changing areas was demolished and a temporary partition was erected. As a barrier it was adequate but being composed of wood was more amenable to improper penetration than the solid stonework which had kept males and females properly apart since the school was built. They were indeed most ancient baths.

We watched breathlessly one Saturday morning as Cranford bored a tiny hole through this partition at a conjectural point, cunningly plugging it thereafter to avoid detection. The aperture afforded a direct view into one of the temporary cubicles, though we had no idea who might make use of the facility, if anyone. All that we could discern was a convolution of cables with a workman's lamp attached—not much promise of pneumatic bliss there. But again and again we crept in whenever we had a free moment and applied our illicit eyes to this spyhole. With never a result. The cupboard remained bare and so we very soon forgot about its existence and the work went on.

Until the great day came when I ran back from the station one afternoon after rugby to retrieve my forgotten schoolbag from the changing rooms. As I took an illegal short-cut past the swimming pool, I could see, through the glass windows of the double doors, two figures emerging from the water. One was Jenny Miller. Miss Jones had been coaching her. Jenny was turning into an athletic girl, a lusty gymnast, and I was struck by her shapely figure as she stood there in her costume, listening to what Miss Jones was telling her, confidently shaking the water from her hair. They disappeared together into the girls' changing rooms and I ran on to collect my books.

On the way out again I paused. Supposing . . .

It was irresistible. Dropping the bag I turned back quickly into the boys' area and crept up to Cranford's old plughole. No sooner had I removed the tiny wooden stopper and screwed up my eye against the breach, than the door to the cubicle opened and a form filled it up, standing among the clutter of cable with such inescapable thereness. My heart began to beat so fast and hard it hurt me till I nearly cried out. I couldn't actually see the face but everything was visible from the neck down. The costume didn't belong to Jenny Miller. It was Miss Jones.

It all happened so fast.

Off came the straps, down came the upper part of the one-piecer and out bobbed my first pair of breasts. The first mammaries I had seen that had not been drawn on a bog wall, viewed in the mind's eye, made in the monstrous images of the rugby showers, or gawped at helplessly as they hung on the inaccessible, unreal Gloria, torchlit beneath the bedblankets. The workman's torch in the cubicle was now switched on, imparting an Old Masterish brightness to the paps of Miss Jones as they poppled and dangled just in front of my wild Cyclopean eye.

Before I had time to take them in, she had stripped completely and I was staring into the dark brown tangle of her pubic hair, on which the waterdrops glittered, strung out like scattered pearls, like drops of dew on spiders' webs of a gossamer morning . . . Oh, boys, boys, she stuck the towel between her legs and started to dry her crutch, the undiscovered country of the cunt. Even at that moment I heard the whistle of the train in the distance and knew I'd never catch it now, knew I could stay here and watch all, through the keyhole in the door, the keyhole in the door. Knew she was entirely in my power. In the power of my knowing. I would *know* Miss Jones. And she would not know that I knew.

But do you know what?

I couldn't do it. Even at that age of merciless and unprincipled lust I could look no more. Some drop of propriety sitting in my soul that made me turn my back on the knowledge I rutted after? I know not. What I did know then was that here was something more beautiful by far than Gloria, than Eskimo Nell and the Harlot of Jerusalem in all their fantastic randiness, something so pure that all the sewers of our groping ignorance would not succeed in defiling it. To look upon it further would be to besmirch it forever. It was sufficient unto the day that I had been granted this glimpse of paradise. It would stay locked within me. I would not tell Cranford—or indeed anybody. And here, years later, I find myself telling you. Unburdening myself of something, like the Ancient Mariner again.

Maybe I missed my chance with one of the lords of life. Should I say 'ladies'? No, somehow 'lords' is the word I want. But as I walked home that day the three miles to Kilminnins, my feet springing effortlessly off the face of the planet, the fields and firth knowing my secret, rustling together with conspiratorial glee, the sky blotting up the picture that kept pouring out of my eyes, I marvelled at the sharpness and plenitude of the vision. It was not the firmness and symmetry of Miss Myfanwy Jones's bosom that filled me with wet fire; not the sight of her roseate nipples, erect with the cold water and the rubbing; not the dark dripping lushness of her pubic hairs in which the droplets blazed and burned like tigers' eyes in the forests of the night. I bring in these images in spite of myself, you see, but they are beside the point.

No. It was my apprehension of the fact that when a woman you have known takes off her clothes in your presence for the first time, she is, quite simply, more wholly composed of flesh than you had ever imagined she could be. You don't know where or how to look. You drink to her only but she is impossible for your eyes to drink in. It is as if she were a different being entirely from the clothed specimen with whom you have talked, drunk tea, seen on the bus, stepping off the train, closing a known door, known in the unreal city of the dead, where we work and worry our lives away. I now had visions of reality that were ready to transport me far above the visible sphere of Cranford and his cronies. They were set on their course, I on mine. My eye had sported with Amaryllis in the shade of a changing room. Had played with the tangles of Neaera's pubic hair. Now that eye of mine was preparing to play the painter in those same hairs, to heighten raw experience, create the universal art form of amour. Dark lust was ready at last to flower into the brightness of love.

7

BUT THE COURSE of true love never did run smooth, as the old shag, Shagspear himself, once said, and I found that for a time my teens were troubled by that same body-and-spirit conflict as curseth middle age. The latter is a general falling apart, as I have already advised you—if you were listening. In my later adolescence there was, however, one specific physical affliction which caused me untold agonies. Untold as yet. Boys of Blair's, you are about to hear of them.

It was the scourge of spots.

At the very time my oyster mind was busy forming pearls of understanding—of literature, music and art, and of woman above all else, romantic, sexual woman in all her pride, plume, plump and majesty—my body had decided it was time to blast the newborn ecstasy of mine with this most gruesome of curses. It began innocuously enough, as most things do: a little red mark across the mouth one day, that faded away as doth the early dew; a yellow pinhead on the nose that could be flicked off like an overweight bubble; a lump on the chin; a blotch on the brow; the merest blemish.

Hey, but what's all this then? What's going on?

O, had it pleased heaven to try me with affliction in any other area (pubes not excluded), rained all kind of shames on my young head, steeped me in Chemistry to the very tits, given to crassest Cranfordian ignorance me and my utmost hopes—I should have endured it, preferred it, I should have found in some part of my soul some drop of patience, stolen from Othello (yet that's not much), left over by Job, in spite of the sizeable amount used up by that holy stoic. Well, then. But what *is* going on?

Well, you see, sweet youths, when sorrows come, they come not single spies, but in battalions—and that's a Black and Tan fact, so it is.

They arrived on the doorstep like Goldberg and McCann one

morning, just as I speak it to you, and before I knew what was happening there was Nat and Ben and Simey and Seamus and Dermott, all raising their plooky standards in my face—and I too was having an identity crisis.

Who *is* this spotty bastard?

I tell you true, it was an identity crisis of Pinteresque proportions, worthy of a breakdown.

A crisis which drew me daily to the mirror—my new-found friend, my confidant and bosom pard, my other self, my counsel's consistory, my oracle, my cousin of Buckingham and sage grey men, my intimate, my self-publisher, my priest, my angel, my frank discloser and disguiser of the awful truth about myself.

What self?

That thing in the mirror.

O, mirror, mirror, on the wall, what do I look like?

You look like fuck-all.

The trouble was that I actually began to look like Cranford. I knew within my soul that we were essentially different beings, earth and fire, not being too short at this stage on vanity—a useful enough commodity at times and especially in one's teens. But my outward ugliness now made me feel inwardly vile, unfit to inhabit God's universe. On a really bad day I'd wake up and find myself looking into a dappled field of acne in the midst of which my hitherto inalienable features were proving a little difficult to distinguish—had all but disappeared, so it seemed to me, under the multi-coloured hail of spots—and my lunar face, till now fruitless and pure, was horribly cratered after its first meteoric shower, the moon map assuming its terrain, the seas of tranquillity and dreams ravaged now by storms—smouldering, stigmatised, scarred for life. To the east crouched a softish red blob about the size of a shilling; to the west a cluster of hard yellow knobs. Somewhere between these landmarks there burned what used to be my nose, barely recognisable beneath its barrage as the noble tower of Lebanon that once had been. See what a grace was seated on that brow, the front of Jove himself! Gone with the wind. What sat there now was an army, the campfires of mine enemies, come to stay, to sit out the siege.

Yet go away they did, only to be replaced by reinforcements, an ever-changing display of constellations that swept across my face, relentless as the seasons, vivid as Van Gogh, puky pulsars, red giants, white dwarfs and supernovas by which I learned to identify myself. Naturally I tried to chase them on in their appointed orbits, gritting my teeth and squeezing them till they burst and the glass was spattered with pus. There goes another bastard! A spent star. Out, out, damned spot! Such a deliberately scuttled cosmos would take days to disappear, however, and my face became an obvious enough battlefield, a no man's land through which my eyes crept on stalks. I should have been a pair of ragged claws, of course. O, hide me from the world, I prayed—or let me die.

Two things made matters worse.

One was the latest horror of having to shave. Proud of it at first—O wise young hairs! O honourable tufts!—I quickly learned to hate the morning chore of picking my way delicately with the razor among the growths that had been so diabolically planted there overnight. Mine enemy had come in the dark and sown his tares. Tiptoe through the tulips (red ones) sang a smarmy Max Bygraves on the morning radio (and through the daffodils too, mate) as I scraped and sliced away, scarcely knowing the difference between blob and bristle. There is a garden in her face? I tell you there was a plantation in mine and on some mornings I felt like lopping off the flowerheads every one with the razor and cutting my own throat to boot.

From my boyhood reading I remembered the story of The Man In The Iron Mask and wished I could be whisked away into the reign of Louis the Fourteenth and hidden on the Island of St Marguerite; plunged deep in the Bastille of anonymity, my terrible facial disfigurements gratefully concealed by the cool black velvet over the iron mail. Then came the Phantom-of-the-Opera-life-in-death-wish. A television set had been fanfared in all its majesty through our front door before the end of the fifties and I had watched the old black and white film with horrified sympathy long before Lloyd Webber learned to hit the money note in a mint of memories. The jammy bugger. Jenny Miller would pity me, oh so deeply, as I sang like Caruso in the sewers of Kilminnins, except that the only sewage system the place afforded was a single pipe, eighteen inches in diameter, which jutted out between rock-buttocks and expelled the town's turds into the ocean. No, I could never be the Phantom. Or Harry Lime, who looked on the T.V. screen as if he'd never suffered a spot in his life, the greasy, Brylcreemed smoothie that he was! The world was bristling with people who didn't have spots.

There were even one or two boys in my class who escaped

spot-free all the days of their appointed puberty (the pricks) and swanned about grinning at the girls, confident of their clear looks, their dates, their feels by right, their open flies by night, left hand cupping a mound of Venus, right hand an uncupped D-cup tit, and laughing all the way to the crutch. Bastards. They were the rareties, the olive-skinned types from richer families, their hairy chests glistening with suntan lotion, their wrists dripping with gold watches, their fathers the town bankers, God knows where they'd come from, the foreign dago scum.

The other factor which increased the agony of the spots was the fearful feeling of guilt which was their concomitant. Guilt? Oh, yes, let me not fail to do full justice to this, my younglings, for the spots were the angels of guilt and of that I had no doubt. The fact that there were perfectly natural reasons for this facial plague was quite unknown to me at the time. On the other hand it seemed to me a reasonable assumption that the uglification of my facial appearance was due entirely to my own wickedness: an external projection of an interior evil that was now being paraded across my countenance for the whole world to see. Be sure your sins will find you out, my old Sunday School teachers had assured me. The very hairs of your head are numbered. And now, behold, my sins were being numbered according to the multiplicity of spots. A recording angel, in charge of spots, Andrew the Immaculate or something, was sitting up there somewhere hurling them down in handfuls, exquisite thunderbolts to torture the squirming adolescent. Yea, verily, I was a multiple sinner, each and every one of the spots resembling a soul burning in hell, like the flea on the end of Bardolph's nose, my spirit punished twenty times over every day in a colourful prefiguration of what would happen to me eventually one day.

In hell.

But that was one day. The trouble was today. Each day, every day, any day, I had to leave the Bastille, the Vienna Sewers, creep out from among the gnawed bones, the rat piss, the dusty props, the gloating turds—and make my way to Taft on public transport. I had to sit with my classmates under the scrutiny of teachers, under the narrow eye of Fanny Fergusson, who knew very well (although I had escaped detection in the first-year medical examination) just what was causing these spots. Blindness will be the next thing, boy. Just wait until you can't read the words on the page—then you'll get your come-uppins! It was the same sin that had caused my voice to break, my chin to flourish, my prick to sprout, my clothes to shrink.

It was wanking.

At least that was what had started it off. The first wank had been the turning of the key in the box, the Pandora's box of the world's manifold evils, metamorphosed into spots and visited upon me. There was no shutting the lid now. And wanking was only the first cause; there were all the other lustful thoughts and deeds, the rugby songs in the bus, the vile talk in the showers, the filthy stories, the jokes, erections over Gloria's tits as she did the hoovering without her clothes, the feeling of Jenny Miller, the trying on of contraceptives, the lusting after Miss Jones, the wet dreams of taking down her white cotton knickers and biting into her burnished bum, the peeping-tom episode that no one knew about but God—Satan at the bower door, watching her pluck a rose, drying her red cunt . . . Sshh! Don't even think that word! Why not? Cunt, cunt, cunt, cunt, cunt. There you are, an iambic pentameter of cunts, spondaic, multiple, monosyllabic, Miss Jones's cunt, done over and over in blank verse, scenes individable and poems unlimited . . .

But I didn't look! I turned away! My conscience screamed as I was hauled out before the bar for cross-examination in front of a gallery of horrified hearers. I turned my back to the wall, I did! I shut my eyes! I didn't see between her legs!

Shut your mouth, you worm! It doesn't matter a whit what you saw or didn't see. Not one jot or tittle, not one tit or nipple, not one mite or mitred miss or private piss, don't you see? That's not what counts. The thought was there, that's the point, and the thought's enough to hang you! to burn you! You imagined her cleft and that was evidence enough of your rutting libido. He that looketh on a woman to lust after her hath committed adultery with her already, in his heart. Matthew Chapter Five Verse Twenty-Eight. Oh, yes, my bonny bairn, came a voice from earliest childhood, you'll get something to cry for in hell! Though Christ's blood could float a battleship it'll not save you, you're sunk already, you're damned, you're guilty, guilty, guilty, guilty, guilty! Trochees of terror, syllables of shame. And I was five years old again, hearing the great-aunt's grandfather clock and the small marble one on the mantlepiece tick out the words between them in a deafening duet, the words that fitted in so well with the double pendulum strokes. Eternity, eternity, eternity! Hell, hell, hell hell, hell . . .

> *My grandfather's cock was too tall for the shelf*
> *So it stood ninety years on the wall*

No, no—I had to shut out these sniggering vulgar voices from the brain-cave. Make them go away, please God!

> *In watching his pendulum swing to and fro*
> *Happy hours he had spent as a boy*

Ha, ha, ha! Excellent, i' faith! Of the chameleon's dish! It was no use. I was vulgar, I was wicked, I was vile. The spots proved it.

Could nothing be done? If Christ's blood could not save me then how could spot remover? If gold rust, what shall iron do? I crept down to the chemist's and skulked around the shelves, searching for something to burn or bury the bastards. The youngish pharmacist watched me warily from behind her lipstick and powder, culled from the latest range. White-coated, spotless, virginal, elegantly coiffured, she was a tide of eau-de-cologne. She thinks I'm looking for French letters, I thought to myself, or sanitary belts to try on. (Cranford had stolen a box once and we had used them as face masks in a mock gunfight on the beach, to the horror of the ladies of the Salvation Army band and to the glory of the Devil and the delight of the town daftie.)

Eventually I selected a small tube of flesh-coloured unguent that was supposed to dry out and act as a fake skin for a brief hour or twain while doing its work of medication. But as I handed it over the counter and saw the dark, antiquated drawers at the back of the shop, I suspected that I required a form of treatment considerably more potent than what I was about to buy. Something that might just be hidden away in those Hippocratic arks.

> *Ther nas quik-silver, litarge, ne brimstoon,*
> *Boras, ceruce, ne oille of tartre noon,*
> *Ne oinement that wolde clense and byte*
>
> *That him might helpen of his whelkes whyte,*
> *Nor of the knobbes sittynge on his chekes.*

The beautiful assistant handed me the bag and my change and smiled at me professionally, a smile of lavender sweetness. My heart leapt—and sank. How could she even bear to touch me? Without white gloves at least. Up to her white elbows. *Her* unfriendly bust gave little promise of the old pneumatic bliss, unlike Miss Jones's. Uncorseted it would never be for me, and she would never smile like Grishkin under my poised prick, her hair laid loose and spread out like watery lightning over a white pillow. She was as full of sexual potential as a razor blade.

'And a packet of razor blades, please.'

I wondered what it would be like to fuck her. Probably she used something from the shop. Something sterile and remote from human taint.

No, it was not a fuck I needed; I needed a needy apothecary to appear from the Mantuan shadows, where murderous Machiavellian corruptions lurked in jars, and take me into the very reaches of the back shop, the penetralia, where the stuffed alligators hung, the tortoise and the ill-shaped fishes. I needed that man with famine in his cheeks, oppression in his eye, misery in his bones, contempt and beggary hanging from his back: to rake about among empty boxes, green earthen pots, bladders and musty seeds, and come out with a phial that would kill or cure me. Forty ducats and cheap at the price. Something shittily Italian. Or faecally, fatally French.

And a French letter, please.

Did I say that? Or are my thinkings audible?

What though his deadly dram did take me off? Someone had told me that Brigitte Bardot (corseted and pinned to the back of my bedroom door from the Dundee days) had at one point attempted to take her own life because of the very same affliction. I knew not if 'twere true, but I was desperate. I was also, as you will have gathered, at the stage where I was beginning to identify myself with the characters I read about in literature. My skin had erupted, but so had my interest in books.

And there were other awakenings too.

The mirror, that had drawn me to itself for horrified self-scrutiny, became from now on no mere reflection of reality, but a view to reality itself, a window into another world, an order of existence that was fundamentally removed from the coarse banalities on this side of being. The furniture, the walls, the domestic objects that constelled my life—the blue ginger-jar, the rose-bowl, the Yarmouth crockery, the willow-patterned plates—all these remained as they were, underwent no sea-change rich and strange. There they were, on the other side of the mirror, as drearily, unalteringly fixed in the orbits of days as they had ever been. Summer put roses in the bowl: September came and peeled their petals away, dropping them soundlessly round the crystal's slow circumference to lie on the polished walnut dresser, soft and unmoving, totally without meaning. I looked away from the mirror, faced the objects themselves—and found them to be no different. But when I looked back into the glass and saw myself—ah, that was different. I had seen this self all my life and had taken so little care of it: a shape that had come and gone for fifteen years, brushing the glass fleetingly, leaving no impression, forking no lightning, registering nothing of reality. Visitations as quiet and purposeless as the rose-petals kissing the coffin-lid fixity of the dresser with its black shine, the bright darkness of hours.

All that had changed now, like the world outside the house. Looking into the mirror, I could see through the bedroom windows the ungrammatical clouds floating past, behind them the griefless sky, and the leaves of May coming out like the notes from Spanish mandolins, trees like guitars, fierce and tremulous and green against the wild blue sea. God, what was happening to me? What was this restless ecstasy? Who was this ugly, elephantine oaf on the other side of the glass, so gauche to behold and yet who felt so keenly, had visions of things unknown until this day? It was not I, that was for sure. The real me was something immaterial and pure, something that had been wedged in universal error into this gross calamity of a body, as surely as Ariel had been so rudely thrust into a cloven pine by Sycoraxian malice a dozen years together; after which time Prospero had turned the key. The old pituitary was my Prospero and had also turned in me after twelve long years and now I was a soul split in two, my schizophrenia spread out against the sky, the adolescent's ultimate empty auditorium.

I talked to it, naturally, this thing in the mirror, this Frankenstein. I talked to it under the sky, in my closet (as I was sowing), the poor monster that wanted to lock itself away yet wished to come forth and meet its creator, to converse a little higher than the beasts, a little lower than the angels, to meet somewhere on a middle earth. It looked back at me, fearful and half-formed, ungainly, gangling, gauche, green and raw—and so I left the mirror and stood behind the bathroom door, the garden shed, the corner shop, the bus shelter, the church porch, the kirkyard dyke, the sailors' stones, the harbour wall, the breakwater, the rocks, the bathing huts, the brambles, the blasted oak, the twisted lime, the initialled beech, the carved cross, the haystacks, the dovecot, the standing stone, the Roman bridge, the rooky woods, the fields of rye (that clothe the wold and meet the sky), the distant hill, the quiet loch, Kellie Law, Kilimanjaro, the South Pacific, Darien, beyond the sunset and the land of lost content and the baths of all the western stars until I die . . .

And wherever I stood I tried to break through my own skin, to let this thing that was me find its bolthole, decamp and vanish out of those few pathetic cubic inches of brains and bones and muscles and blood—and meet that other me that communed with the air and ran like lightning through the sharp crackling veins of the earth, pure energy, pure Ariel that I was, uninhibited, omnipresent, unfettered, free.

Narcissus had me by the balls and would not let me go. Never has. But though he held me green and dying to get away, though I sang in my scrotum like the sea, weather-beaten sail of spirit bent to shore, weighed down by body's ballast, still the mind was free to contemplate the wonders of the old world that opened up before me now, courtesy of the teachers of the Old Guard. The Old Soldiers. The Talking Heads. Chalk and Talk, those outmoded, much derided weapons, yes, these were the swords with which they opened up the world's oyster of words and proclaimed the pearls.

Of learning? Of eloquence? Of exploit? Of art? Of wisdom? Of truth?

Of what you will, dear boys. They were all pearls without price because, genuine swine as we were, they had the power to transform us, to change us back into our human shapes. (Some of us anyway.) My first gifts from other worlds and other seas, the oceans and continents of the imagination, the vast river of history, islands of literature and art, the songs the Sirens sang along the way. The realms of gold. In which I travelled then, have travelled much in my time, and in the essential sense will never cease to travel, though my old travel agents have long gone bust.

Let us now praise these glorious, undistinguished, undersalaried men and women and the system that begat them. For this last lesson will be their memorial, and if I do not build it then they may perish as though they had never been, for no one has done it yet and it's not looking likely that anyone will, so I'm the man to do it, by force of destiny, else the fault is in me and not in my stars, Oh yes, boys of Robert Blair's, you've got to have that Miltonic vanity to believe yourself capable of the task. I shall say, therefore, *Exegi monumentum aere perennius*. I have built a monument more lasting than bronze—if I could but write it down! Ah, but I lack self-discipline, you see. And, sadly, the concentration. After all, what happened to poor Lycidas? You may well ask. And those of you who are still with me will say that he is not quite dead and that this lesson is far from over. When that happy moment has been reached, then I shall say again, I have built a monument more lasting than bronze.

Sleeping within mine orchard, the orchard of my ignorant East Neuk Eden (for innocence is but a form of ignorance, as you should know), upon my secure hour did Danny steal, with juice of—No, no, no, not cursed hebona in a vial, stop the quotation! Thank you. Not cursed hebona, but something wondrous strange, for sure, did Danny bring. Something which, laid on my slumbering eyes by this tubby Puck, made me awake and hear the power of music.

Danny Dalyell, maestro, maestro.

Strong on technique, mind you, old Danny, make no mistake about it. Boy, know thy harmony; girl, know thy counterpoint; pianist, practise thy scales, fiddler thy pizzicato, piper thy grace notes (a great piper himself, was Danny!) soprano thy top C, bass thy deep breathing, flautist thy fingering—there was nothing Danny could not sing, play or encompass within the sphere of music and he was a tireless taskmaster, losing patience only if he suspected you of having come short on practice. You can't be an authority without technique and you can't have technique without practice. Danny's watchword.

'But technique is nothing,' he said to us one day. 'It's nothing without vision.'

O Danny Boy, thou singest sweet music! What was that you just said? What word did you just utter?

I said where there is no vision, the people perish.

> *Oh Danny Boy, the pipes, the pipes are calling,*
> *From Ironmills and down by Causewayside,*
> *Your sun is set—and all your standards falling,*
> *It's you, it's you hast gone—and I must bide.*
> *But come ye back, when sanity hath tarried,*
> *And every mandarin and manager lies low.*
> *I'll not be here, but though I'm dead and buried,*
> *From up on high I'll laud the great—maestro!*

No need for all that, you know. Call that 'The Londonderry Air'? And your breathing's lousy!

Never mind, play it again, Sam, say it again, Danny, and a little louder, please, so that the Iron Men of the Mills can hear you, tin-eared as they be. They do not hear so well these days, you know. What was that you said again? About vision?

Ears, boy, ears! Who are you to talk about ears? I've told you before, your ears are weak, though your voice and fingers are very fine. Sharpen your ears and we'll make you a musician yet. What I said was that all the technique in the world won't help you unless you've got something to say. I mean, just look at Haydn. He had nothing to say. Well, nothing much. All those symphonies, churned out as nice as ninepence, neat as you like, every note in the right place, nice little numbers, beautifully composed, not a quaver wrong—but quite worthless, really. I mean, we could actually have done without them, without much loss. No vision there, none. String quartets much better, of course. Then there's Benjamin Britten. Clever as hell, but oh dear. I'm not saying he didn't have something he *wanted* to say. But oh dear . . .

It's when you look at giants like Mozart and Beethoven that there's just no comparison. Bach most of all. Take Bach now, yes, the best example. Now look over here, at the shelves. The Complete Works. All these volumes. Organ, piano, orchestral, choral, unaccompanied—just look at the scores. Now tell me what you see. What *do* you see? Go on, tell me. Notes. That's right, musical notes. Millions of them. Maybe billions, I don't know. Even Shakespeare wrote just over a million words, you know. But Bach! Just take a really close look at all these little black notes, and white ones. Like leaves on the trees in some pure black and white forest, a place of pure ideals, even though it looks like a jungle, doesn't it? It's incredible. You wonder how he had the time to do it, even physically, a busy man like Bach. But even then—all these notes taken together would have been useless without one thing that's behind it all. And do you know what that one thing is?

Faith.

It's faith in God, faith in the talent God gave him. Faith in his mission to use that talent to the full. Faith in what he knew he had to do. And did. When you look at it that way it's only then you begin to realise that any distinction between the sacred and the secular music of Johann Sebastian Bach is a false one—the kind of division which has been made purely to satisfy the cataloguing instincts of historians and examiners and folk like that, folk who like to put things into little boxes. That's fine if it keeps them happy. But it doesn't keep me happy and it won't do for you either. There's no essential distinction, really. It's all sacred, you see. Play Bach in a barn—just a two-part invention—and the barn becomes a church. A cathedral. It's the vision that matters. Listen to this.

And he sat down and played unaccompanied Bach on the cello.

With technique. With authority. With vision.

The first Gavotte from the Suite Number Six in D Major.

'Secular, do you call that? Maybe so. But people don't dance like that—only angels!'

O Danny Boy, O, Danny Boy, I love you so.

He didn't *look* like Rostropovich, playing the cello. As a matter of fact he didn't look like a musician at all. A stocky little Bacchus, a purple grace flushing his honest grinning cheeks. Butcher's hands. How could these hands do what they did to ivories, horsehair and gut? But they did, and the results were divine. He raised a mortal to the skies, he drew an angel down. War, he sang, is toil and trouble, Honour but an empty bubble. Music is the most persuasive and the most spiritual of the arts. It's the greatest of the character finders. Find out a man's musical tastes first of all. If he doesn't like music—great music—never employ him. Never befriend him. He can't be credited.

The man that hath no music in himself
And is not moved with concord of sweet sounds
Is fit for treasons, stratagems and spoils.
The motions of his spirit are dull as night
And his affections dark as Erebus.
Let no such man be trusted.

Salt of the earth, old Danny. Ex-soldier, actually. Oh, the stories he told of the war! And of old Beecham, his hero, whose *bon mots* he was forever turning over, dressing up and making more outrageous, especially the notorious remark to the lady cellist. Madam, that which you have between your legs has given pleasure to man for generations—it was not meant merely for scratching! That made him double up. Every time.

One flaw. Only one. His fondness for madeira. He kept a decanter of it behind the Groves musical dictionaries and occasionally applied himself to it a little too assiduously. When that happened he became maudlin and went to the cupboard where he kept his pipes. The whole school had no option then but to wait until he had finished. It wasn't the noise—it was the tune. When he was tipsy he always played 'The Flowers of the Forest' (It's for the fallen, I can't help it, you see, it's for the fallen). and the terrible torrent of that lament, with its dark haunting soulfulness, flooded through the rooms and produced a gorgonising effect on the teachers, only the lumps in their throats moving. The mathematician laid down his compasses, the chemist his beaker, the artist his brush, and every master one and all his textbook and his chalk, everyone down to the Shark in his study observing the impromptu two-minute silence which was the emotional imposition universally accepted every time Danny happened to get into this mood. Back in the music room after his lone stand in the quadrangle, the lachrymose piper would wipe his glasses, blow his bulbous red nose, pack up his pipes and say to me, 'Run down to Shore Street, would you, lad, and get me a packet of King Size from the café? I need a cigarette after that.'

A robust Christian, like the Goof, Danny played the organ in the parish church and frequently declaimed his religious views. They were astonishingly simple, really. Two things among others convinced him of the existence of God, so he argued. One was music, the other was wine. I can just see God sitting up there looking down at us and thinking, 'These guys need a little cheering up. I know what I'll do.' And he invented music. And after that he invented a little something to go with it. The two should *always* be taken together—out of school hours, of course. (Chuckle, chuckle.) Danny's religious beliefs in a nutshell.

> *Bacchus' blessings are a treasure,*
> *Drinking is the soldier's pleasure:*
> *Rich the treasure,*
> *Sweet the pleasure,*
> *Sweet is pleasure after pain.*

Under Danny's sometimes stern, sometimes soppy, but always civilising tutelage, I fell in love with the works of the great musical masters: Handel, Bach, Beethoven, Byrd and Tallis, Mendelssohn, Schubert, Tschaikowsky, Elgar, Wagner, Shostakovich, Ravel, Vaughan Williams, Verdi, Delius—it was a varied diet he fed us. As strong on musical history as he was on theory and practice, Danny fired my imagination when he lectured on the lives of the composers. I was shown the difference between Mozart's and Beethoven's manuscripts: the former written straight off, right out of the computer of his brain, where notes ran like billiard balls, each one to its appointed, preordained place; Beethoven's rubbed at so hard, as deletions and alterations followed thick and fast on one another, that the original paper had been worn away under the storm of erasions.

I saw Siegfried cutting his way through mountain forests, Brunnhilde burning, the Rhinemaidens teasing black Alberich with their gold and their flashing tits (which I knew I should not call tits any more but breasts—for all experience is an arch wherethrough gleams the untravelled world, and I was leaving Cranford and his vulgarities behind as I headed for that world whose margin faded out forever and forever as I moved). I saw lovers beating their breasts at casements, maidens and mill-streams letting their north-flowing hair run wild, Salzburg serenading the eighteenth century, England packed like squares of wheat, cathedrals and cornfields soaring and stretching endlessly into time and out of time. I watched Tschaikowsky conducting with one hand on his head to stop it falling off, married to melancholia, drinking his cup of cholera. Liszt the hungry traveller, Schumann the introvert with his face to the wall, Handel on his knees, screaming Hallelujah, Delius dying . . .

I saw Beethoven, the first signs of his early deafness come upon him, a frightened young man, running down into the cellars and smothering his head in pillows in a frantic effort to hold on to the remnants of his hearing, while Napoleon's guns thundered and boomed at the gates of Vienna. My God, what a place Europe must have been when people like that were around! I saw the famous picture of him by Batt, sitting in his workroom in the old Schwarzpanierhaus and I stared into it for haunted hours in dismay and disbelief. How could this happen to genius? How could the Mozarts of the world be slung so casually into the anonymous black pulp of the pauper's burying ground, to disappear forever, their music an eternal remonstrance to the world, to their high requiem become a sod? Still wouldst thou sing and I have ears in vain! How could this man Beethoven have been left, stone deaf, unshaven, old and ill, to eke out his time in a clutter of books and inkblots, tattered papers, putrid food, ear trumpets, scattered, unspent coins, guttered candles, broken pencils, the manuscript in his left hand, the quill in his right, his hair a grey tangle of strings, his forehead a line of crooked staves, where the notes knotted themselves into black crucified songbirds beneath the bone, behind the desperate eyes? Eyes that saw angels and daughters of the gods, ears that heard nothing of the sounds in the street beneath him, the people shouting, the children squabbling. *O Freunde, nicht diese Tone! Sondern lasst uns angenehmere anstimmen, und freudenvollere*! And behind him his old grand piano, its keys brutally dismantled, its strings burst and coiled in stilled parabolas of rage, the whole instrument smashed by his frenzied attempts to hear his own playing. While underneath the wrecked piano sat his chamber pot. Unemptied. Unemptied! As a distinguished visitor recorded, with breathless politesse. He didn't describe the turds, sludging like ruined battleships through a yellow sea of piss. And yet, out of this unbelievable degradation, quite literally out of the fumes of urine and excrement, arose the indomitable beauty of the last quartets and the glories of the Ninth. He was thinking of freedom perhaps, like Schiller. And if freedom were too loaded a word for the times, then what of joy?

> *Freude, schöner Gotterfunken,*
> *Tochter aus Elysium.*

O, Joy! All men shall become brothers where thy gentle wings tarry.

So I left the mirror and stared instead into the scores of the masters, the black and white forests of human emotion and ideals, finding my way through the woods, Danny handing me the twin keys of understanding and appreciation. Imagination and authority. Excited on the one hand by the jigsaw of notes, the sheer technical marvel of it all, I found myself at other times to be crying, quite literally, I kid you not, young masters, crying as I listened. The sheer sense of anguish, of desolation and loss in Elgar's Cello Concerto, burst into my life with the sudden vividness of a distress signal, lighting up the pain of being long before I had learned what that pain really was, really could be. All squandered lives, all lost infants and broken marriages and miseries of desire were laid bare in each terrible sweep of the sabring bow, that had no mercy even on its creator. I was stilled to sorrow by the naked yearning of the slow movement in Schubert's C Major Quintet. And when I listened to Byrd's Mass for Five Voices or to the Prelude to Lohengrin, the walls of the visible world fell away and earth-shattering events that made strident morning news—butter is up by tuppence in the pound—made me want to laugh and cry. And did.

Danny said this to me one day.

You know, when I was on duty in a surgical unit during the war, I saw a brain on an operating table shortly after it had been removed from a soldier who'd received fatal injuries. I looked at it, this brain, and realised that all Bach's works came out of that, and all Shakespeare's plays and all Christ's teaching. Out of that grey blob of jelly. Well, that's when I realised that atheism just couldn't stand up any more—that there must be more to life than that. The symphonies of Beethoven no more came out of that mound of matter than I came out of the moon. If you believe that, then life's just a Chemistry lesson—and I get more out of life than that, thank God! Music's not chemistry, for God's sake. And the notes Mozart heard when he was playing billiards didn't come out of his brain. They came *into* his brain. Not out of it. The question is, where did they come *from*?

Another of Danny's arguments for belief in the existence of God. The scientific, philosophical or theological soundness or unsoundness of it is quite beside the point. The point is rather that such Dannyisms will not be much heard these days in the music rooms of our secondary schools. Or, come to that, in any of the rooms, rules and rubrics where the Ironmills Rules rule O.K.

Not strong on such educational unorthodoxies, the men of Ironmills.

How would Danny have fared, I wonder, if subjected to that craziest of contemporary orthodoxies in education, the Appraisal System? Or how would Dr George Orr have fared, when weighed in that crass balance—and found wanting? As would have been inevitable in the case of the brilliant and gifted scholar who was not of this world and had nothing to offer us except his erudition, his eccentricity, and his eternal esteem of the things that were of God. This ancient divine was a Victorian anachronism who had forgotten to die. I say this not unkindly but with benign irony, for I worshipped the man. A state of idolatry he in his humility would have deprecated deeply. He hailed from Fochabers, a village in the north-east, as his accent more than suggested. A lad o' pairts from farming stock. In his reputed youth—for it was hard to believe that the egg-headed, hoary-headed, benignly bespectacled doctor had ever known a youth at all—he had laboured in the fields, shawing turnips, in order to provide himself with the money to get to university. Which he finally left with five degrees. The letters are carved on his stone to this day: M.A., B.Sc., B.D., D. Litt., D.D. The most lettered skeleton in the East Neuk. In his earth-bound days he was the most learned man in the district, certainly; in Scotland, probably; in the world, possibly. So we believed. And it may be that we were not far wrong.

Dr Orr lived in the oldest inhabited manse in Scotland, among thousands of books according to local tradition—more books than there were in the school library. More books than there were even in the chemist's library. He emerged from this fastness of learning, clad in black from the broad-brimmed clerical hat down through the long frock-coat to his polished presbyterian shoes; not quite brandishing a butterfly net, but always pegging along with his rolled black umbrella, in spite of strawberries and the sun, as if his theology had taught him to expect the worst. Blue and gold were the medieval colours of eternity and had nothing to do with the weather.

Thus garbed, he appeared, ready to set off on his parish rounds, to pray with the sick, to visit the school and to preach his unbelievably long sermons, classics of erudition that have long been lost. They were, like his raiment, uncompromisingly austere, and I recall one on Greek fire, an end of session bumper, lasting over an hour and delivered in his strong northern burr, like the crust on old wine as Hazlitt said of the voice of Wordsworth. A voice that stood commandingly between us and our summer holidays. A medium suitable for such a theme. When visiting any house he stood for several minutes outside the front door, his eyes fixed on the colossal time-piece in his hand, awaiting the agreed hour, not a second less or more. For all the days of my appointed time will I wait, till my changing shall come. And he attended our school dances with unfailing courtesy and impeccable grace, sitting through the era of bobby socks and rock and roll and so on into mini-skirts and Beatles, like a kindly black inquisitor who never passed judgement. Rather lonely in his corner—too scholarly, so we fancied, for any of the teachers to dare engage him in conversation, lest their ignorance be revealed. He also acted as the sole invigilator during our Leaving Certificate examinations, using the same gigantic watch. The Higher Papers were coloured green and I remember his words to us as we opened fire on the very first paper—the English paper.

'It is time now for you to begin—and for the next two hours you will see nothing in front of you except that little square of living green!'

Once, during an afternoon lesson, I was posted to his telephone-less manse to take the message that the time of the Burns Supper that evening had had to be changed. To my great delight and consternation I was shown by the little white housekeeper into the famous library. There sat the good doctor, bent over his books in a puddle of anglepoise light palely augmenting the fading skies of late January. He was surrounded, just as the legend had it, from ceiling to floor with shelves upon shelves of ancient books, bound in vellum and buckram and calf. I stared around the room in open-mouthed awe. At that point Dr Orr looked up, became aware of me, saw my expression and at once understood. He nodded and smiled, read the proffered note, laid it aside, motioned to me to take a chair, folded his hands across his church-clock-ticking fob and smiled again, his enigmatic smile.

'I read most of these, young man,' he said gravely, 'when I was studying for my thesis of Doctor of Divinity.'

I asked what topic he had written about. He brightened suddenly.

'The chronology of the Old Testament,' he said, 'which never fails to amuse me.'

I asked him why.

'Well,' he said, 'the University of St Andrews decided to make me a doctor simply because of my interest in the mere passage of time!'

And the book-deadened walls of the library rumbled suddenly with deep sepulchral laughter.

When I left that study I knew that I wanted to become a great academic.

8

IT WAS IN my sixteenth year that a double catalyst arrived at Taft Academy one fine day on the doorsill of the sixties. One fine day. Worthy of an aria (or two) any day of the week. I' faith!

What was it that arrived?

Two new English teachers. Bosom colleagues come down from the Highlands, from the northlands to Fife. Two north-easters. They saw that the game was afoot and they captured my hungry spirit and fed it with friendly rivalries, delighting me by their opposed but complementary styles of teaching.

Name them now:

I shall, my lords, I shall.

Lachlan Campbell.

Mackay Mackay.

Deal with them briefly, please, for the silent hours steal on.

Brief let me be.

They were talking heads. Their finger-ends were whitened with chalk and their biros sweated blood. First Class Honours dominies of the kind it is now fashionable to decry—indeed necessary to condemn if it's promotion that's your dirty little game (I'm sorry, boys, forgive that Freudian slip of truth, and permit me to re-phrase), if it is preferment that you are seeking.

Preferment? They preferred to stay where they were—in the classroom—and *teach*, like all decent teachers, all good men (and women) good and true. And when I say 'stay in the classroom' I don't just mean generally speaking, I mean every single fucking period in life.' Every one that they were paid for. To the death. They weren't like the corrupt spiritual teachers of pluralism, well condemned by Chaucer, those that swanned off to London for a weekend or a week of conference-wanking, no sir, they were no shitten shepherds that didn't give a monkey's toss in reality for their sheep, but were the salt of the fucking earth—and where are they now? Gone to graveyards every one. The graveyards where the paper angels play—filling in forms for all eternity, to the last syllable of recorded crap.

How then are the mighty wiped out! But come, step forth from the shadows, both of you, and let us hear something of your sparring partnership. Who's going first? And on what subject? Come on, Campbell. You that were wont to make the classrooms ring with your *sic probo*. How about hearing you on *Beowulf*?

LACHLAN CAMPBELL: *Beowulf*! Ah, if a man had *Beowulf* alone he would be rich beyond the dreams of avarice! It's got everything: characters, dialogue, drama, history, sociology, economics, philosophy, psychology, God and the Devil, old age and youth, war and peace, heroism and humanism, love of the light and fear of the dark, all the themes and genres rolled into one—and to crown it all, it's a poem. And a damn marvellous one at that. What more do you want?

MACKAY MACKAY: I want something a bit less tribal, that's what. And maybe a little less Tory, aye, and maybe a little less English Tory. A bunch of aristocratic Saxons down in the Lothians, looking up at a bunch of Picts north of the Forth and thinking, 'God, what savage brutes these fellows are!' And so you see Fife was their hell. Listen.

> *Waes se grimma gaest Grendel haten,*
> *maere mearc-stapa se pe moras heold,*
> *fen ond faesten, fifel-cynnes eard.*

So your grim ghoul, Grendel, the mighty pacer of the marches who held the moors, the fens and fastnesses, the land of the Fifelkin, was just a bloody Fifer! How do you like that?

LACHLAN CAMPBELL: You can't prove a word of it. The word *Fifelkin* simply refers to a race of monsters.

MACKAY MACKAY: Just my point precisely: the folk of Fife. That's how I derive the word *Fife*.

LACHLAN CAMPBELL: Tripe. The word is cognate with the old Danish word *fibhe*, which means 'the wooded country'.

MACKAY MACKAY: Too modern a derivation by half. I fetch my derivations from well before Danish invasions. The Anglo-Saxon just happens to be coined from this old Celtic word . . .

Learned men, my masters. My masters.

How they loved to lock their horns.

LACHLAN CAMPBELL: Poor Marlowe—dispatched in a tavern

by an assassin's dagger, an adventurer in blank verse and espionage, cut down in his prime. What a tragedy!

MACKAY MACKAY: Marlowe? A heady youth, over fond of bombast—and of *bum*bast too. Horribly stuffed with epithets of war—and Thomas Kyd's tool! A writer of little consequence. Got knocked on the head in a pub. No great loss to literature.

LACHLAN CAMPBELL: On the hills, like gods together, careless of mankind (his favourite quotation from Tennyson). Only the great melancholic himself could have written that line! Tennyson makes you realise that writing is a form of illness. And when you looked at Tennyson, you *knew* he was a poet!

MACKAY MACKAY (with Joycian scorn): Lawn Tennyson! Frightful fellow. Went about sniffing young ladies' bicycle seats (anguished cries of protest here from Lachlan Campbell) and sometimes seemed to forget entirely that consonants do exist in the English language and are there for the use of.

LACHLAN CAMPBELL: And that wonderful satirist Pope. With a friend like him, who needed enemies? He took the age apart.

MACKAY MACKAY: Too much of his age, that was his trouble. Poets transcend their time: prose writers get stuck in it. At the end of the day he had a prose mentality and was just a vicious dwarf.

LACHLAN CAMPBELL: Ah, but Wordsworth! The voice of a mountain torrent!

MACKAY MACKAY: And the bleat of a drivelling goat in his old age. You can live too long, you know—unless you're a painter. The older painters grow, the better they get; the longer writers go on, the further down the hill they slide. Hardy was an exception, of course, but Wordsworth is the best illustration of my conviction that writers should have their hands cut off after they've turned sixty. If somebody had put a plough into old Wordsworth's hands, he wouldn't have waxed so lyrical about the land. Burns knew better. Even Shakespeare . . .

LACHLAN CAMPBELL: Shakespeare's philosophy came out of a rag-bag. The culture that produced Dante was much the superior one. Human civilisation peaked in the Middle Ages. From the Renaissance onwards it's all downhill—nationalism, secularism, specialisation. And the death of Latin.

MACKAY MACKAY: The Middle Ages? Forget 'em. I'd rather know I know nothing than not know anything and think I know everything and accept every damn thing on intellectual credit. The only good thing about the Middle Ages was Middle Scots!

LACHLAN CAMPBELL: Eliot disagrees with you.

MACKAY MACKAY: Eliot!

LACHLAN CAMPBELL: A man who brought prophecy back to poetry.

MACKAY MACKAY: Clap-trap. And what's more, Anglican clap-trap. And what's even worse, high Anglican clap-trap.

LACHLAN CAMPBELL AND MACKAY MACKAY (together): One thing we are agreed upon: if we ever do agree then one of us has stopped thinking.

Never agree with either of us, they said: it's a sign of brain death.

If you will look upon this performing duo for a moment as a kind of Flanders and Swann act, Flanders playing Falstaff to Swann's Hamlet, then Lachlan Campbell would qualify temperamentally for the part of the fattie. Except that he was not fat. Quite the reverse. Genial, sanguine, extroverted and relaxed, his gaunt face and large spectral eyes gave the lie to the ectomorph-endomorph classification of physical human types. Mackay Mackay, on the other hand, though similarly lean, possessed the introvert's personality. A handsome weasel face, a waspish temperament, an enormous supply of passion in his side-tanks, he was intellect and emotion held in alarmingly taut equilibrium. He smouldered, occasionally erupted, was always tense and tight-lipped in his delivery, never fully relaxed. The longer he taught us, the closer we crept to the rim of the crater, fearing his sudden flashes, marvelling at the intellectual intensity, the imaginative glow radiating from the packed heart of the man. Some of us learned to dance like Dickens around this deep and daunting Vesuvius, occasionally coming away singed. He was no ordinary teacher.

Lachlan Campbell was the milder-mouthed of the two. A drawling Aberdonian with a deep, crackling baritone voice, a Double First in English and History and a huge love of both and of talking about both. When he became enthusiastic, which was impossible for him not to do, he could not refrain from dramatisation of his theme, and in no way did this please us better than in his rendering of one of his favourite pieces, *The Bells*, by Edgar Allan Poe. This poem of over a hundred lines he would recite from memory, beginning quietly enough, with his sparkling green eyes closed and his hands clasped:

> *Hear the sledges with the bells —*
> *Silver bells!*
> *What a world of merriment their melody foretells!*
> *How they tinkle, tinkle, tinkle.*
> *In the icy air of night . . .*

as his harsh baritone hammered each word like a nail into the walls of the room, he began moving stealthily from his desk to the blackboard, picking up sticks of chalk from their grooves and snapping them in little pieces as he returned to face the class, breaking the pieces in time, so it appeared, to the metre of the lines.

> *While the stars that oversprinkle*
> *All the heavens, seem to twinkle*
> *With a crystalline delight . . .*

His stealthily measured tread brought him nearer to the front of the class, where he then stood motionless under one of the large white lampshades that hung like dusty moons high above our heads.

> *Keeping time, time, time,*
> *In a sort of Runic rhyme,*
> *To the tintinnabulation that so musically wells . . .*

This was the moment we waited for with rapt anticipation. As he spoke the final three lines of the first stanza, he threw the pieces of chalk one by one ceilingward with such unerring aim and with such skilful timing that each one entered the inverted bowl of the shade to coincide exactly with his enunciation of the word 'bells', and as they did so they produced a series of echoing, bell-like chimes, an unforgettable auditory aid to our appreciation of the poem. The word 'bells' occurred seven times consecutively towards the end of the stanza and Lachlan Campbell had, of course, broken up the seven pieces, no more, no less, in precise readiness for this moment. As the flying objects hit the inside bottom of the lampshade with astonishing regularity, this display released from our admiring throats loud and raucous cheers. This in turn caused the grin on Lachlan Campbell's honest face to grow broader. The louder our cheers, the broader his grin, and he continued with an ever-widening smile to complete the verse with repeated volleys of chalk.

> *From the bells, bells, bells, bells,*
> *Bells, bells, bells—*
> *From the jingling and the tinkling of the bells.*

There are four stanzas in the poem and there were four such large lampshades in the room, and as each stanza ends with this sevenfold repetition of the word 'bells', you can guess how the operation proceeded. Four times Lachlan Campbell went to the blackboard during the first part of each stanza; four times he returned in time for the remaining three lines, and each time with the required number of chalk pieces in his hand. At the end of the poem, if he had succeeded, as he sometimes did, in his successive assaults upon the lampshades, in hitting the inside of every lampshade seven times, and producing twenty-eight chimes in all, there arose from Room 23 a standing ovation of such volume as would have raised Mr Edgar Allan Poe from his grave, had the old saying contained any truth, that a sufficient amount of noise would awaken the dead or the fox from his lair in the morning. The whole school knew that Lachlan Campbell had recited *The Bells* and that he had, as we said, done it again! It came as little surprise to me in later life to learn that he was a superb darts player. And there you have it. There was no lesson on the poem—there was simply the poem, brilliantly dramatised. A performance that required no follow-up worksheet and on which any comment would have been irrelevant. A performance that will not be ground out of the slow small grindings of the Ironmills. Not though they grind a thousand years. Which God forbid. Even in my own lopped professional lifetime I have seen classrooms grow grimmer for their grindings. Classrooms where Standard Grade Rules O.K., where paper takes the place of education, where the only bells to be heard are the birth-bells of the New Managers and the death-bells of the Lachlan Camp-bells. And of course the period bells, ringing in another generation of swine to be slaughtered by genuinely artificial pearls. A merciless bell, that one.

La Damn Bell Sans Merci.

Thank you, Lachlan Campbell. It was you who first made me long to be an English teacher. You must take the praise and the blame. Not your fault I can no longer teach it. Not your fault the subject as you taught it me exists no more. You handed me the torch, old man. A wind from Ironmills Road blew it out. But you gave me the vision and the faith, which still burns brightly within, like Milton's inner sight.

For which belief much thanks.

'Tis bitter cold and I am sick at heart.

Now go back to sleep.

And arise now, Mackay Mackay, and show thyself in all thy formidable splendour, bleak though it be. Return, return, O Shulamite!

Mackay Mackay.

It was Mackay Mackay who opened up my mind to the literary glories of my own country, handed me the Scottish tradition and an awareness of what had happened to that tradition, courtesy of our educators. It had never occurred to me to question the assumption that the accent and vocabulary of our street speech, the East Neuk dialect, was anything other than a quaintly slovenly corruption of English and that it was by some quirk of lone genius that Robert Burns had succeeded in turning his particular dialect into something memorable. I had never heard of Barbour, Blind Harry, Henryson, Dunbar and Douglas, Sir David Lyndsay, Alexander Scott, Ramsay and Fergusson; had no idea that for nearly two centuries between the death of Chaucer and the flowering of Shakespeare, Scotland had produced a literature that was second to none in Europe.

He repudiated and poured reasoned scorn upon the idea, complacently contained in much current English literary criticism—though not in American—that the writers of this period could be classed as *Scots Chaucerians*. While this was true, up to a point, of King James I whose *Kingis Quhair* took its rise from the English master, it at once became clear to us that none of the major writers of the period owed anything of their lasting qualities to Chaucer. Dunbar, for instance, threw off a few imitations but quickly became his own man, busking his way through the late medieval twilight at the court of the brilliant, doomed James IV. A volatile virtuoso, like his monarch, was Dunbar, a court-wise wide-guy, willing to write a poem on anything from a headache to the fall of man—for a price.

In teaching the work of this man, Mackay Mackay gave me my

first lesson in an important critical commonplace: that literature is not simply the record of an inspiration, it is the practice of a craft. Dunbar was a craftsman right down to his bollocks—which he wrote about too. His poems taught me something else at an early age—that there was no such thing as a poetical or unpoetical subject. The scrotum would do, if it was troubling you and needed a poem to scratch it. There was something Mozartian about the range, the readiness, the sparkle, the soul, the well of inventiveness, the gallery of inventions, love or fury fear or fun, laugh or cry, arses and angels, sacred and sexual, all from Dunbar's pen. As Mackay Mackay's dry passionate Mr Apollinax tones devoured the stanzas from the *Lament for the Makars* with its sonorous refrain, my heart sank at the names and numbers of dead poets catalogued by Dunbar, their works lost, some of them, as though they had never been, now only a reference in an obscure stanza. What a record of riches and ruin!

This same Mackay Mackay, O Boys of Blair's, having introduced us to a new language and literature, that of the entire Old Scots and Middle Scots periods, went on from there to study with us the love poems of Alexander Scott, the sonnets of William Drummond of Hawthornden and those of Mark Alexander Boyd, including his Latin poems . . . And the ballads.

On the ballads Mackay Mackay was in an element of his own and a ballad could appear without warning on the syllabic horizon, though he preferred to teach them in the lateness of the autumn.

Look!

We followed the direction indicated by the Harris-tweeded arm, the long forefinger (and thou art long and lank and brown as is the ribbed sea-sand), the staring, black-bespectacled eyes (yes, there was something marinerish about him)—and what did we see? We saw the sea, as the old song has it. But not the grey emptiness that bores the balls off fucking old wankers everywhere, browned off with bromide and randy for anything big, wet and slippery—and not the bloody boat! No, it was the kind of sea that always hit the East Neuk harbours at this time of year. A sea that came crashing over the breakwater and ripped through the piers, tearing the fishing boats from their moorings, flinging them into a wild waltz across the harbour. We could see the houses down in Shore Street clothed with the sudden white castles that pinnacled again and again, aspiring to the height of the kirk steeple, only to be sucked back into the formless ferocity of the firth. It was an awesome sight. Mackay Mackay opened the window wide and the gale tore in, shredding our hair and sending our papers everywhere.

'Feel that?' he roared. 'Yes, feel it, you little people, feel it! You're on your way back to Scotland with the little Maid of Norway, but the storm is upon you and your ship is knackered. You've had it!'

What do you feel?

Yes, it was true. Mackay Mackay did not simply *teach* us the ballad of Sir Patrick Spens: he *was* the ballad. We all became the poem, the classroom was the deck and we were the panic-stricken sailors, wading waist-deep in water with fear in our groins and death in our bowels.

The curtains rose on numberless other dramas as Mackay Mackay led us like Virgil through the otherworld of the ballads. Lord Randal returns home from visiting his true love, the poison already in his heart and the world weariness eating away at his sick soul. Thus a man comes back to his mother when love and the world have failed him. Edward confronts his mother, with his father's blood still redly wet on his sword—he has done her dirty bidding and has killed him dead. His towers and his hall, his wife and children, the things that mattered, that matter, are nothing to him now. The fine dwellings will be companions to cowcrap and grasses and rottenness and the dust into which they will tumble; the loved ones to destitution; the self-seeking, whingeing, wheedling hypocrite of a mother to hell and damnation. The material and emotional worlds vanish away before impulses stronger than a man can stand. The wind harps through a bleached skeleton by a pile of turfs—murder and nihilism are the grim melodies picked out by the invisible fingers on white bones. A lover weeps by an unquiet grave, a lady combs the gold hair of her lord and cups her hands in his blood, to drink his soul into her own. Marie Hamilton's to the kirk gane, wi' ribbons in her hair. With a prick in her cunt, with a bastard in her belly. With the sea in the mouth of her baby. Marie Hamilton dangles from the gallows in the Grassmarket, so fast the tragic consequences fall out to ruin these ill-starred lives: young men cut down in their prime, infants knived to death, ladies doomed and lovely, lords betrayed and butchered and laid

146

out on the green, their ghosts walking the glens and grasslands, the voice of innocent blood bubbling out of the ground, the cries of havoc and the clash of standards. The primal passions prevail, love, hate, ambition, greed, and the awful emotions that bind and break families, the demands of kinship, the rage of gain. Of course the hypocrite and poisoner are there, the toad in the winecup, the snake in the bed, the sword at the pillow—but they are seldom petty. Even in their malice there is something scriptural, larger than life, about the people who inhabit this elemental world, so different from the small-time shittiness that we inhabit. They carry out the grand gesture, adhere to the high ideal, pursue the heroic code, embrace the tragedy of life with an actor's ample sweep.

By the time Mackay Mackay had finished the ballads, the world outside school was not the world I had known. I was ten years old again, emerging from the cinema and adjusting from technicolour with a new uneasy perception of reality.

And Mackay Mackay did not stop there. He went on to study Burns and Scott and Stevenson, Grassic Gibbon and Hugh MacDiarmid. Pretended to pish himself before us, as Holy Willie, incontinent with emotion, quaking in front of the class, totally carried away by the poem, clutching his crutch. Crooned the cadences of *Sunset Song*, like a piper lamenting the forever lost but impossible to forget—and hauled Danny up from the Music Room to play us through the last pages of that novel. Championed a culture despised and rejected of Scotsmen who had betrayed their own heritage: a culture pierced in 1560, left behind in 1603, sold down the river in 1707, slandered, neglected, demeaned, lampooned, misunderstood, trivialised, mythologised, brutalised, sentimentalised, self-slaughtered and shat upon ever since.

Golden days, think you? Well, there was no buggering off to conferences and courses in those days: the days when ships were made of wood and men were made of iron and the teachers chalked and talked and the Goof invaded the pitch and Danny got drunk and Lachlan Campbell fired missiles at the lights and Mackay Mackay taught what the fuck he liked and an entire school was run by one Headmaster and a Deputy and the teachers did the fucking rest and arselickers were unheard of because men and women went in each day to teach and not to manage and leapfrog up the ladder to the apotheosis of Ironmills and tin divinities and inspectorial crap.

And Mackay Mackay was Mackay Mackay.

Golden days, McCann, believe me. Golden days.

The halcyon days of Mackay Mackay. There was a Caesar! When comes such another?

Never.

Come back to Erin, Mavourneen, Mavourneen.

Never.

Come back, Paddy Reilly, to Bally-James-Duff, come home, Paddy Reilly, to me!

Never.

Goodbye, Mackay Mackay. Rest, rest, perturbed spirit.

Oh, and just one thing before he goes.

Of course.

Mackay Mackay was also a poet, as I mentioned one moment ago. I don't simply mean that he possessed the poet's temperament and vision, inasmuch as he taught us literature dynamically and (like Lachlan Campbell) histrionically. He wrote the actual poems too. Wrote them up on the blackboard for us, building them up, line by line, stanza by stanza, revealing to us something of the hermetic inscrutability of the creative writer's instincts, approaches, industry and art. He wrote both in Scots and in English, but principally in a highly literary, erudite Scots, teaching us the principles of poetic composition, of practical criticism too, and filling me with the intoxicating desire to become a poet myself.

If Lachlan Campbell was the *primum mobile* in turning my thoughts to the teaching profession, it was Mackay Mackay who made me long to pursue the writer's lonely vocation. One put a red biro into my hand, the other a blue one. And of course now you will have guessed that the name by which you know me, the name by which the school in general knows me, by which the little world itself now knows me, the pseudonym I adopted for myself as a new writer in the early seventies – yes, Campbell Mackay – is not, as I have just revealed, the name I was born with, but something of a portmanteau name. When pondering a nom de plume to grace my first volume of poems, it occurred to me to do honour, if I could, to two remarkable men, my former English masters, by putting their names together. And though poetry has not earned me the wherewithal to live—thou foundst me poor at first and keptst me so, remember?—and teaching has been my livelihood until this afternoon, it is as Campbell Mackay that I shall choose to be known until mine ending. And that is the name the raindrop can have fun with when it dances on my stone.

When I tremblingly brought my first poem to Mackay Mackay, he castrated me without any show of mercy.

'Inchoate rubbish!'

'But,' he then added, 'you have the potential. We must work on that.'

And we did.

There and then he put into my hands a large hardbacked science jotter. Never mind about the science label, he said. I nick them from the Chemistry stockroom. That's your first writer's notebook. I want you to start making entries. I want you to keep yourself sensorily alert each day. Write down what impresses you. It may be the shape of a cloud, the scent of the wind, something somebody says, a line out of a book, a feeling in the gut. Much rubbish will be accumulated. Doesn't matter. Rubbish can be made to speak. The fishbones of Skara Brae were made to tell a tale. And make good music. Throw nothing away. Later you'll pick over the rubbish tips and find what you want. When you feel lousy. Or lonely. Or fall in love.

Then you'll write poems.

And he gave me this warning.

Look, my lad, literature is literature and life is life. They're both bloody marvellous, though like you I prefer literature any day of the week. But for God's sake don't confuse the two, that's all. Not life and art, for fuck's sake, man! Once you start doing that you're in deep trouble.

Yes, he saw that danger ahead for me, even then. A seeing man, Mackay Mackay. But even as he spoke he had set in motion a train of events from which I was never to escape. Any more than I was ever able to get off the school train when I was caught in one of those funny little compartments. The corridor is missing. The platform never comes. I was held in thrall.

9

A damsel with a dulcimer
In a vision once I saw:
It was an Abyssinian maid,
And on her dulcimer she played,
Singing of Mount Abora.

WHEN THE TIME of love arrived, it was a damsel with a dulcimer that my heart fastened upon. A dulcimer? Well, pretty close. And a dark damsel. Her darkness was not in doubt. Of that there was no question.

It was Jenny Miller. (Surprise, surprise.)

From the back of the Music Room I watched her one day as she sat with Danny. She had been learning the classical guitar, taking lessons from him at lunchtimes over the past year. She was playing for him Francisco Tarrega's *Recuerdos de la Alhambra*. And *naturellement, mes enfants,* I was transfixed. I never was any other way, of course: a softie, a patsy, a catspaw for poetry, O, what a chump! But on this occasion it was the beautifully idyllic mood created by the music, combined with the memory of our innocent childhood intimacy in the train nearly six years earlier, that brought me out in a sweat. The real thing. A spring of love gushed from my heart, etcetera. This was it.

Whether it were this vision that gave me to drink the milk of paradise, or the vision of her emerging out of the school swimming baths with Miss Jones, or the memory of that secret feel, I know not. But I do know that from that day onward our fates were sealed. For in the morn and liquid dew of youth, contagious blastments are most imminent and the plague of spots was now followed by the plague of loving. Everybody had caught it—even Cranford—and I was not going to be left out. Jenny had been marked out by destiny for my adoring attention and I tried to capture hers by the device that seemed to me the most natural at the time. I began writing love poems to her. And no—I am not about to make your afternoon by quoting you one. Not a line, not a line. A class of thirty years ago already enjoyed that particular joke at my expense (wince, cringe, blush), for my passion was public rather than pubic. And futile. Jenny did not respond. She did not even deign to look at me, except with occasional flashes of the utmost indignation and disdain. I was rejected, rebuffed, unrequited—and food for worms.

Was that a problem, then?

Mais non, mes amis. In terms of *amour courtois, pas de problème.* The lady's contempt was all that I, as a mere mortal man, could possibly hope for at this stage in the game. I set about the usual elaborate procedures of ensuring that she understood me to be her willing footstool. In school I became a general discomfiture to her, devouring her with stares and quickly averting my eyes whenever she happened to turn in my direction; mooning at her from an aesthetic distance while she besported herself on the playing fields or chattered with her chums. She could not eat but that she would find me spellbound by a nearby table, my mince untouched, my chin heavy in my pensive hands, my stone shoes heavier on my dreaming feet, my eyes feeding deep deep upon her peerless brow. On the train I positioned myself as close to her as I could decently manage, hypnotised by wheels and whispers, having to be shaken from my love-trance by friends long after the train had halted and I had ears in vain. I followed her home and waited for hours at street corners for a glimpse of her. On Sundays she would find me sitting outside the church door among the gravestones, like patience on a monument, smiling at grief, afterwards shadowing her in the maddening wake of her perfume on the traditional Sunday afternoon walks. On the cold nights she would look out of her bedroom window and see a lapidary silhouette etched against the westering moon, keeping lone vigil, sighing my soul toward the Grecian tents where Cressid lay that night. Even the rainy Pleiades did not persuade me from her door. My lover's eye outstared Aldebaran, outwatched the Bear. (Did somebody mention Milton?) The gull on the kirk steeple was not more patient, the night fishermen slogging at the Dogger Bank while the tides slurped coldly over the globe, the shoals and the seasons came and went.

Round the year to spring.

The spring of our sixth and final year at Taft Academy.

By this time Jenny was now inseparable from the inner life I was leading under the fire of lessons by Danny Dalyell, Lachlan Campbell and Mackay Mackay—and under fire from my own fired and out-of-control imagination As I sang my futile longings to woods and waves and bathroom walls.

> *Voi che sapete che cosa e amor*
> *Donne, vedete s'io l'ho nel cor.*
> *Quello ch'io provo vi ridiro,*
> *E per me nuovo, capir nol so.*

Danny heard the tremor in my voice and applauded the drama-tised renderings. Good lad, good—sounds like the real thing! It *was* the real thing. Higher Music was being learned upon the pulses. I was freezing and flaming and pleasured and pained and not really knowing just what was happening to me, like poor Cherubino. She was Eurydice and I was Orpheus. We were Lola and Turiddu, Mimi and Rodolfo, Alfredo and Violetta, Carmen and Don Jose, Tristan and Isolde.

And she was Fanny Brawne, Anne Hathaway, Mary Shelley, Mary Hogarth, Wordsworth's Lucy, she was Juliet, Perdita, Viola and Rosalind, she was Cathy, Estella, Eustacia Vye, Little Blossom, doomed or heartless, she was Josephine, she was Sarah Siddons, Madame du Barry, she was Flora McDonald, Charlotte Corday, Lady Hamilton, Mona Lisa, Aphrodite, Annie Laurie, Barbara Allen, Molly Malone, Polly Oliver, Juanita, the Snowy-Breasted Pearl, the Lass of Richmond Hill and the Girl I Left Behind Me, south of the border down Mexico way, she was Phyllis, Amaryllis, Laura and the rest, gathering mussels on the shore outside my windows, singing to sailors on the rocks, figureheaded on the *Fisher Lass*, as she made for harbour, her bare breasts dipping low into the firth, wetted by waves, her hair flying with the clouds. I met her coming through the rye, spent sweet green hours with her among the rashes-O and rode up to her father's tavern in the moonlight, the sound of iron on stone, while the redcoats waited behind the door and her finger curled around the trigger, even though the muzzle pressed deep into her own luscious left breast (and still could be and still could stand so nigh) to give the warning shot, to shoot that gorgeous breast right off and burst her heart, to save me with her virgin's blood. O, there was no escape from her and from my bondage to her being! She was all States and all Princes I. I read *Green Mansions* and she became the embodiment of the spirit of nature. I fell upon the life story of Dante and she was Beatrice on a bridge in Florence; of Swift, and she was Stella, awaiting my tutoring, my wakening. She was ringed by Nordic fire, which I would brave. She was Golden Marie. She was Ophelia and I stalked the harbour walls by the glimpses of the moon, varying between the parts of the Ghost and Hamlet, preparing to enter her closet, to lie in her lap and propose cuntrie matters, to cost her a groaning to take off mine edge. And I skulked along to the kirkyard and assured a maritime Yorick's skull, carved in stone and with lichens for eyes, that I would penetrate my lady's chamber and make her laugh at that. Then I looked across the wine-dark sea and resolved to carry her off with me to Greece once more, where burning Sappho loved and sung . . .

But in reality there was just no approaching her, no hope of winning her love with anguished pen, crazed looks or constant devotion. My poems fluttered to her like gulls on broken wings. I had all but reached the point where I could see *no* point in continuing with my exquisitely internalised pursuit of Jenny, when something happened which brought us magically together. Who can explain it, who can tell you why? Not I. Mine but to recount the moment to you as it occurred one enchanted morning—and allow you space to ponder.

It was the middle of May and Danny Boy was preparing us for the Inter-House Music Festival which always crowned the end of session in early July. Madrigals formed an important part of this musical feast, I am pleased to say, and (praised be fortune) Jenny and I both belonging to the same House, we were flung together in the same madrigal group, she a rich contralto, myself attempting a bass from the position of natural baritone. Danny coached each group impartially and worked his usual wonders with all of us.

'Too nice a morning for indoor practice,' he announced when it came round to our turn. 'Get the tuning forks from the cupboard, lad, we'll sing to the sea!'

And twelve of us trooped down past the harbour.

We followed the line of rocks right out to the waterline, where Danny grouped us carefully—don't fall in, now!—thumped a boulder with one of his forks, found the harmony and began conducting. We were already well practised by now at this particular number, but as we sang it that day, down by the sea's blue edge, I tell you I shall never forget it.

> *Since first I saw your face*
> *I resolved to honour and renown you;*
> *If now I be disdained*
> *I wish my heart had never known you.*
> *What, I that loved and you that liked,*
> *Shall we begin to wrangle?*
> *No, no, no, my heart is fast*
> *And cannot disentangle.*

Grouped as we were, Jenny and I were facing one another, and as we sang this amorous complaint, I can only suppose that something of the hopeless lover's longing which showed in my face, was aided by the words, the music and the sea setting, to soften her feelings. I know not, neither do I care, and as I have already said—mine not to reason why. Mysteries do not interest me—explain them and they vanish away. I know only that as we sang earnestly, plaintively, of absolute love and deathless adoration, I saw a new expression begin to creep into her face, into her so dark eyes. At once I knew what it meant. She was giving me permission to love her. At last.

> *If I admire or praise too much,*
> *That fault you may forgive me.*
> *Or if my hands had strayed but a touch,*
> *Then justly might you leave me.*
> *I asked you leave, you bade me love.*
> *Is't now a time to chide me?*
> *No, no, no, I'll love you still,*
> *What fortune e'er betide me.*

Something else happened here. Jenny and I, our eyes fastened upon one another, were singing to one another only, and our mutual awareness brought a new edge to our interpretation and delivery of the music, one that was heard by the others in the group and taken up. Danny caught it instantly and pricked up his old ears.

'Good! Good, damn it, good, good, good! Now you're singing! Come on, let's have it—with feeling!'

The lines rose and fell with the sea's blue dress—and with Jenny's bosom a white strong curve, like a swan under her blouse. The seagulls circled. Far away the village houses shimmered with bright watery cobwebs of reflected light and far over the rooftops a field of buttercups yellowed the green distance. A field in which I would surely lay Jenny down soon and taste her sweet buttercup lips.

'Come on!' Danny roared. 'Concentrate! Don't lose it now!'

> *The sun, whose beams most glorious are*
> *Rejecteth no beholder,*
> *And your sweet beauty, past compare,*
> *Made my poor eyes the bolder.*
> *Where beauty moves and wit delights,*
> *And signs of kindness bind me,*
> *There, O there, where'er I go,*
> *I leave my heart behind me.*

By the time we had sung the madrigal we had ensured our victory in the Inter-House Music Festival, Jenny was in love with me and Danny was ecstatic.

That was on a Friday—to be mundane for a moment. Afterwards I slipped a note into Jenny's schoolbag, asking her to meet me at the end of the Sunday service outside the Old Kirk. There was no answer from her but when Saturday had gone drearily by and the Sunday arrived, I hurried into church early to secure myself a pew in one of the transepts, from where I could be certain of a view of the divine Jenny.

Expectant and edgy though I was, I must confess that I was startled by her entrance. Sandwiched between her sedate parents, like a gorgeous book between two bibles, she filled the whitewashed silence of the ancient stones with a loud shout of sudden colour. She was wearing a poppy-red blouse with a large hat and shoes to match. Her skirt and jacket were white as milk. Set off by this outfit, her dark skin and midnight blue hair made her glow like a gypsy. O, she was ravishing, barbaric, the fairest flower of all the field, and she was mine! Soon to be. Except that she did not even once look at me. We rose and fell to the hymns, coughed and sighed through the hushed dusty prayers, examined the gilded motes that swirled in the stained sunbeams throughout an interminably long sermon on Galatians. Outside the firth glistened and crinkled again like tinfoil, the boats bobbed and creaked and cracked and oozed tar, the seaweeds steamed and birstled, flounders sunned themselves on the cool sandgreen harbour bed. The very old men slept in the sun, their pipes gone out, those who had been religious in their eighties but had gone right round the clock and were back to apostasy again. In a haze of distance the green cornfields were stacked like seats in an auditorium, the woods a dark froth on the inland skyline. A remembered gathering, silent upon a peak in Darien. The train flashing through the white world. My hand on fire with her pubic hair. A gull chattered briefly. Another screamed. The Galatians dragged on, hauling in their wake the smell of pandrops, mothballs and Sunday polish, a huge and birdless silence. *For the flesh lusteth against the spirit and the spirit against the flesh, the works of the flesh being adultery, fornication, uncleanness, lasciviousness, idolatry, witchcraft, hatred, variance, emulation, wrath, strife, seditions, heresies, envyings, murders, drunkenness, revellings* and putting my hand beneath that gorgeous red blouse and feeling Jenny's poppies for the first time. *And such like.*

It was over. The congregation was filing out, a black articulated crocodile, grinning its slow progress past the hand-shaking minister, then breaking up, stepping briskly, more cheerfully away to lunch in all directions, God having been fed, the women's coloured hats cast like flowers to the points of the compass.

But where was Jenny? The red hat and blouse were not to be seen. I panicked. She had taken to heart the message of the Galatians. She was saved from my carnal cravings. The spirit had prevailed against the lusts of the flesh. Her breasts were protected by the breastplate of righteousness (damn you, Paul! Oops, sorry, God!) and Fanny Fergusson had put the sword of celibacy into her hand, that would do more than circumcise. The truth was that it had all been in my mind, nothing more, and I faced the fact that she had not actually said a single word to me since the Friday madrigal practice. Not only had she not stayed behind, she had never even intended to come in the first place. Glumly I stood among the tombstones and watched the old sexton closing the doomsday doors with a double ecclesiastical clang, hobbling across the bridge to his burnside cottage, to his midday meal. Within minutes the fragrance of fried herring and oatmeal danced with the butterflies among the stones of the old salts, their bones packed deep in the cool and comfort of the kirkyard hill, away from the sweltering sun, the hot lusts and stirrings of the flesh.

'I had to go home first.'

The voice behind me made me jump. She was standing there still dressed as she had been in church.

'You haven't changed,' I said in a trembling voice, cursing myself for speaking words so obvious, so threadbare, so heavily banal. So ridiculously true.

'I wasn't allowed. Not if I'm going for a walk. Have to stay dolled up because it's Sunday.'

Her voice was naturally throaty. It didn't matter what *she* said. Coming out of her, every word seemed beautiful and correct. She looked at me and smiled.

'Come on, let's go.'

And she took me by the hand and we went.

Through the scythe-and-hourglass stones, across the flagstoned, flagrushed burn, past the herring-munching sexton's window with a wave, past the last houses, along the footpaths, the hawthorned hedgerows, over the fleece-hung fences, the smooth rubbed wood of cowpolished corner posts, skirting the dusty nettles, the frowning woods, the spiked purple of the thistles, electric with expectation and disapproval, and so on for miles upland and inland under the gloating sun, through campion and harebells, dogroses, daisies and old men's beards. Then we lay down in that field of buttercups and kissed.

O, all you young folks fresh and fair! Here I go again, I know, but what can I tell you, my seniors that are but juniors in love, as I once was? It was thirty years ago but I remember these kisses as the desert remembers water, as the exile remembers the country of his youth, my boys, my boys—she had kisses that would suck the very nails out of your boots! Kisses that would draw up salamanders from their fires! When her mouth attacked mine I was simply not prepared for the ferocity of her passion. My tongue felt as if it were being slowly extracted, anaesthetised by her barley breath, her sweet sucking saliva, tasting of Flora and the country green, dance and Provençal song and sunburnt mirth, the warm south, the true, the blushful Hippocrene, old wine, mandragora, all the drowsy syrups of the east, and beaded bubbles winking on her lips. They were the kisses of a girl who had never kissed before: a seventeen year old unopened hive of honey, bubbling and buzzing with the ferment of life, her natural juices brimming to bursting point, dammed back and damned down for countless Sundays by sermons on the Galatians and now, on this particular Sunday, clamouring like angels to be stickily tasted and drunk, yea, drunk abundantly. I tasted, I drank, and she opened up each hot clammy cell and poured herself out for me. All the time her

157

tongue darted like a little red snake inside my mouth, probing its recesses, thrusting in and out as though she were turned male, softly searching between my lips, showing me the way it would be when my maleness insisted on playing its appointed part inside her. How far would she let me go today? How far did she want me to go? How far dared I go with this soft firm bundle of sensations, joined to me unbrokenly by the insatiate mouth?

License my roving hands. I let my left hand drop lightly over her left breast. She kissed me all the harder and I squeezed the breast gently, feeling its fullness through the cup of her bra, one of that pair of stiff twin sentinels that guarded her bosom, protected its sanctity. Pulling her blouse out of her skirt and feeling my way up her grooved back, between her shoulder blades, I found the hooks of the brassiere and tried to undo them: a heaven for Houdini, a hell and a martyrdom for me. Jenny reached out with one hand and twitched the thing loose with a matter-of-fact grunt, lay back and closed her eyes, where all *did* become a burning mist . . . Nothing so true as a truism.

License my roving hands. Again left-handedly I approached the breast, this time prising up the loosened guard and pressing my fingers into the sudden thereness of the unseen mammary gland, the ivory orb of poesy. Its firm fluidity astonished me—the way it refused to obey the promptings of the surprised potter's hand but flowed instead like a mysterious clay through my new moulding, unpractised digits, always returning to its own shape. I reached out shiveringly with the tip of my third finger and touched the nipple, fascinated by its jealous possession too of a paradox: so rough yet so soft, so leathery in comparison with the surrounding flesh, yet so tender to the touch. No marvel that men killed for love, for this unclassifiable wonder of woman!

And yet this was but the surface of that sea that drew men to its bosom. Underneath the rustling hem of the tide lay the unseen secrets, the undiscovered country of the cunt. Sorry, Jenny, I mean you no dishonour, but the mind speaks unbidden. I dropped my hand now and touched the strange sandpaperiness of her nylon stockings, creeping fervently upwards past her parted knees, her sweat-pearled thighs, half stockinged, half naked, encountering on the way the curious clasp and stud of the suspender belt, that good old fixed rope with its taut strap that guided me up its elasticated length to where I had been before, six years previously, at the juncture of the thighs, the soft sweating curving crutch whose moist heat I could feel now passing into my fingers, through her knickers.

License my roving hands. How to proceed? The way I had done before-O. Of course. For old time's sake. My fingers found the navel again and crept fearfully downwards under the pants, terrified that perhaps the thing they sought was not there any more. Ah, but it was there, as it had been before-O. The same field of hair into which my fingertips burrowed now like grateful little mice, seeking the dark homely satisfaction of the nest, the fulfilment of an instinct uncategorised by all that has been written about it since the first hunters found the virgin forest and looked at one another, making no further progress in their thoughts for all their rough reachings than that first wild surmise.

License my roving hands. Shifting the knickers downward slightly with the back of my hand, creating a small space in which my mining fingers could crouch and work, I reached out in the underground and touched the iron gates of life, the keyhole in the door, the holy of holies, the thyng al rough and long yherd, the quaint honour so desired of man, so prized of the virgin, so monitored by the church, so dreamt of by the schoolboy, so euphemised, so stigmatised, so seldom sunned, so punned upon, so funned about, so fondled, so piddled through, so wiped, so washed, so opened and closed, so covered and uncovered and now so felt by me—the fanny, the female genitalia, the vulva, vagina and old Peronina, the crack, the quim, the pussy, the private, the purple fig, the front door, the secret cellar, the best seller, the pink gin, the mantrap, the cave of making, the rose of all the earth, mulieris pudenda, the glory, jest and piddle of the world.

The Cunt.

O, had I but time! As this fell janitor is strict in his closing of the school and the iron gates of Blair's are soon to shut upon me—O, I could tell you! I should eulogise the female part till a' the seas gang dry. I should write about it too, till my hand dropped off—whole volumes in folio, had I the patience for the pen, which I lack right now. Is there anything I would not do? Make me a willow cabin at those rosy gates of life and call upon my soul within the hole, write loyal cantons of

contemned love that would outdo the Chatterley ban, halloo
its name to the reverberate hills that all the babbling gossips
of the *Sun* would thus cry out 'Pudenda!' And the man's a
cunt. Even though Olivia, through her C's and U's and T's,
was wont to make her great P's, a missing N makes innuendo
just. Ach, well.

Back to the discovery.

Parting the pulpy, wetly furred lips, I slid my third finger
inside and searched about for experience, feeling at once how
the walls of the little room (infinite riches in!) expanded and
contracted, followed the finger wherever it went, closing in upon
it, sucking, oozing, like a tropical flower devouring the intruder,
hungry for prey. I inserted a second finger. Soft sucking sounds
came from within as I did so and Jenny moaned. It was with
quite a start that I realised she was still there! That, lying back
in the thick grass, crushing the buttercups with her now softly
shifting buttocks, was the girl who had grown up with me in
the same village, travelled to school with me, sat in the same
class, sung in the same madrigal group, read and rejected my
juvenilia, flashed me her scorn, surrendered so inexplicably
to the power of music and the chemistry of her sexuality,
sat through Galatians only two hours ago, come back for me
after church, and was now lying with her eyes closed, her
mouth open and my two fingers stuck well and truly up her
wet cunt.

I picture that scene often, behind my shut eyes. And at my back
I always hear, Fanny Fergusson drawing near . . .

It was all too much to believe. Had I gone too far? I removed
my hand, smoothed down her skirt and found her face again
with mine. She smiled, still with her eyes closed, and we clung
together and kissed. And kissed. And kissed.

Kisses that would tear up dandelions by the roots. Kisses that
would extract the marrow from your bones.

And so we lay and lay, the summery landscape all around us
dripping with passion and the sun, the hills twitching on the
horizon in the far heat, as we moved closer together, motionless
now, our minds racing, frightened secretive prisoners that we
were, clutching our frustrated longings, eager for one another
but slaves to the Galatians, genealogies of scripture and our
bible-punching forefathers, too tense and untutored to make
love. Instead we lay among buttercups, our right hands firmly

cemented with the fast balm of our sweat, my hand back between her thighs, sealed to her newly discovered cuntrie by the faster balm of that cuntrie's dew, our fingers intergrafted, our eyebeams twisted, eyes threaded hungrily together upon one double string, as we like sepulchral statues lay and we said nothing all the day, far miles from Arundel, lost climes from Darien, long years from Donne, but knowing our ecstasy springing out of innocence, babies reaching out and touching one another's worlds, silent, unspeaking among the buttercups, the excited butterflies, the bored, crapping cattle, the hovering light missiles of dragonflies, the bluebottles' buzzsawed anger, the moan of doves in immemorial elms and murmuring of innumerable bees . . .

'Oh, my God, my God!'

I sat up violently into the heat-crazed world. Jenny was staring at me, wild-eyed.

'What is it, Jenny? For God's sake, what's wrong?'

Had I made her pregnant just by *thinking* about it? Now that we were gods, was not thought sufficient to create worlds and to people them too? She was still staring at me, horrified.

I shook her—then followed her wide black stare to my own shirt front. For a second I too thought I was dying, dripping with blood from the nave to the chaps. Then we both saw what had really happened and doubled up laughing. The dye from her blouse had streamed out in the heat of the afternoon and stained my white Sunday shirt, branding me from collar to waist with the scarlet evidence of our long, close, passionate embrace.

'God, what'll I say?' I grimaced after we had stopped laughing.

Jenny thought for a minute.

'Say it was poppies,' she laughed.' Say you lay down among poppies. After all, what else could it have been?'

I looked at her streaked blouse.

'Yes, what else could it have been? But your blouse is ruined as well. What'll you say?'

She thought again.

'Passion!' she murmured, with deliberate huskiness. 'I'll say it was passion that made it run—and maybe it was!'

And she kissed me again hungrily.

I loved her. Suddenly she had grown up. The trees trembled like Elizabethan lutes and played this tune.

> *Whenas the rye reach to the chin,*
> *And chopcherry, chopcherry, ripe within,*
> *Strawberries swimming in the cream,*
> *And schoolboys playing in the stream,*
> *Then O, then O, then O, my true love said,*
> *Till that time come again*
> *She could not live a maid.*

The incident of the shirt and the blouse had broken the solemnity of our mutual initiation into the mysteries of love and as we stood together in the middle of this field of nowhere, even out of sight and sound of that gossiping old washerwoman, the sea, and with the nearest village roofs a series of tiny red smudges in the shimmering distance, we looked at one another and laughed hysterically.

'Come on,' Jenny giggled, 'take your things off—you're all red underneath too!'

And she started undoing my shirt buttons, her head falling onto my chest laughingly, helplessly. The smell of her hair maddened me. Following her fingers, I reached out and began unbuttoning her blouse, pulling it off along with my shirt. Her already unclasped brassiere flopped to her feet between us and her breasts bobbed out, as Miss Jones's had done. Her nipples were chocolate brown, the aureoles and teats staring at me like inverted mushrooms. I took a breast in each hand, lifting them delicately, feeling their heaviness and perfection, then I fell upon them breathlessly, taking a nipple conjecturally with lips and tongue, wondering what it would do. It grew erect and hard in a trice. Burying my face between the breasts, I pulled them about my head, smothering myself, seeing close up but from a great height, as it were, the pale blue Amazons of veins winding their way dreamily across the dusky hills and valley, their tributaries disappearing down out of sight, towards that other undiscovered cuntrie. Already my hands were fumbling with the fastenings of her skirt and she was helping me. Our legs and wrists shook as we undressed one another entirely, finally arriving naked together amid the strewn wreckage of our clothes, scattered flotsam and jetsam on a green sea crested with buttercups, the whole world round us beating backwards and forwards through hot watery veils.

Full nakedness.

It was impossible to think that Jenny unclothed was any longer the same being as strolled around Taft Academy in a blazer and socks. She was of another species, worlds removed from Gloria unclothed and all past years of Cranfordian crassness, her body creating, transcending these, far other worlds and other seas. I stood back a little from her, my eyes riveted to the Euclidean perfection of the pubic hair, such an absurdly available, unavoidable triangle, so startlingly incongruous, this black banner, flagging the unseen entrance to her underworld. The navel so secretive, the tits so curiously reached out like cunning nectarines, well above the dark roots of this incredible human tree—other black tufts fountaining out of the armpits as she branched out her arms and entwined herself around me, pulling me down among the burning buttercups. So delicately she extended her hand and caught hold of the abandoned, anguished cock, passing it through her fingerpoints several times with instinctive lightness of touch, having compassion upon its craving. The dark throbbing began. I knew that the moment had come. She knew it. She wanted it. We both did. Without a thought, it seemed, she had parted her thighs, raised her knees and placed the anxious tip of the prick like a petition between her soft, merciful, listening lips. I moved into her as gently as I could and she rose up to meet me, pushing softly with her pelvis. I struck deep, searching for I knew not what, rising and plunging on a wave of our own making, our onetogetherness. Then she was all open mouth and eyelashes armpits elbows black hair spilling out over the grass her heels digging into my calves legs coming up fast over me crossing over my waist she was nails and navel and knees and bare neck stretched like a dying swan and suddenly bucking buttocks and shuddering thighs and bruised black peaches where her breasts were and the dim discovered rivers blue miles below those blue remembered hills and I could feel the thrusting hardened coil deep in the roots of her being begin to hiss and sigh with voiceless triumph as she came nearer and nearer to knowing that she was naked that the forbidden fruit would make a girl a goddess for a suspended moment of ecstasy in Eden a moment which came as she shouted something to the huge listening sky came in a torrent of sap that seemed to shoot through her to fertilise the earth itself and rejuvenate the world for both of us a world emptied of all its people and one in which we ourselves were no longer alive so far off had we floated from this field of ours annihilated along with all that was ever made into a green unformulated furiously evaporating thought . . .

A green thought in a green shade.

When I came to, Jenny was sleeping and I was still inside her. My prick felt like an exploded battleship, hot and molten still, filling up a little harbour where it had crept for safety. Lifting my head out of the grass, I dug my fists into the ground and raised myself slowly, reluctantly, easing the war-torn vessel out of its haven, back onto the naked shingles of the world. Then I slid downwards, taking advantage of Jenny's unawareness, to gaze for the first time into that newly discovered cuntrie, that kingdom safeliest when with one man manned, the split halves of the parted thighs revealing the purple wound at the fruit's core, a long, red-lipped lesion, gaping poignantly among the tufts of normally protective hair, so rudely laid aside, but not rudely forced, Tereu, the ripe vulva suddenly open unto the fields and to the sky, the unruly sun brightening the buttercup pollen around the buttocks, making the drops of love-dew glisten on the gossamer hairs and catching the first trickle of seeds to come winding slowly out of the fissure from the land of milk and honey, a terrible trail of life-bearing lava . . .

Twit twit jug jug

The birds were singing.

O, sweet heavens! It was only then that I realised what I'd done. I had ruined us. A black wave swept through the countryside, blotting out the sun.

'Jenny! Jenny! Waken up!'

She half opened her eyes and smiled at me, a slow secretive smile.

'Jenny.'

'What's the matter?'

'Jenny, what if . . .'

She smiled again.

'Don't worry. My period's due in a day or so. We're safe.'

She yawned and stretched unashamedly.

We were safe. So she had said. *We*, she had said. There was now no he and she, no forked fates, nothing to come between us, we were our own, we were ours, one another's best, forever. And she had so casually mentioned her period to me, that sacred taboo, as carelessly as if it were a train due in. I was a callow youth no more. I was privy to the world's secretest business. One of life's merrie men. She saw me thinking this and laughed again.

'Stop worrying, will you? I'm not that daft. I'll tell you when I want a baby. Which I will, one day. O.K.?'

And she reached up and pulled my head deep down between her thighs, squeezing hard and long. I tasted our mingled milk and honey from the promised land, the newly charted cuntrie, and the fruit was sweet to my taste. Life with Jenny. Here in this field forever, with babies sprinkled round us like buttercups. All was yet young. And pleasant May was blooming. We walked naked together to the nearby burn—

> Quhare throu the grauel, bryght as ony gold,
> The cristall water ran so clere and cold.

It was absurd, I thought, as we washed ourselves down, our feet hurting on the hard cold pebbles—to think of *The Kingis Quhair* at a time like this. Even at the moment of orgasm my mind had managed to quote something to my defeated body, to make some kind of sense out of what was beyond all classifiable experience. Did that matter? When all was young? And pleasant May was blooming?

The world was all before us. We, hand in hand, with wandering steps and slow, through Eden took our solitary way.

It was 1963.

And when we arrived back within sight of the Old Kirk, the returning Sunday walkers were playing their transistors, fluting in the meadows, viols in the hall, Lennon and McCartney floating on the water.

> She loves you, yeah, yeah, yeah—
> With a love like that you know you should be glad.

It was true.
We were in love.
Yeah.

The next six weeks were ecstatic, as only those who have burst love's first grape against their palate fine will truly understand. We went through woods and fields, through the slowly ripening corn, between the acres of the rye, we pretty cuntrie folks, following the long curving ribbons of surf like the folds of a bright girdle furled, walking for miles past greens where the old wives bleached their

165

sheets, as maidens once they'd whitened summer smocks; we travelled the night roads white with moonlight and the summer dust, we kissed among stone skulls and angels of death in the kirkyard tombs, careless of mattock and pick, the dead skippers, the lichened emblems of mortality; we stood high on Kellie Law and knew that the kingdoms of this world were not for us, for our minds to us one kingdom were, that the world was all before us, where to choose our place of rest . . .

Bliss was it in that dawn to be alive, my friends—but to be young was very heaven! For true bliss lies not in revolution but in the inverted pyramid of a woman's pubic hair, the only isosceles triangle that ever meant anything to me; whose worth could not be measured by one of Mr Peter Periwinkle's protractors—that is if you happen to be in love with the lady who happens to be constructed around that cunning black corner of geometry, those three unalterable angles that add up to one hundred and eighty degrees, and yet whose downward angle plungeth to infinity. Into the cuntrie of the blind, my boys, where the one with one eye is king. Into the yawning yoni, whose worth's unknown although her length be measured. Although her depths be plumbed. Many waters cannot quench love, neither can the floods drown it. Nor any instrument that man has made begin to quantify its infinite mystery.

And so our days at Taft Academy wound to a bittersweet end: a mixture of Milton and madrigals and verse-laden kisses in the sea-flecked graveyards of the East Neuk.

As Jenny and I sat on one of the table tombstones after school one day in the last week of June, in the Skinfasthaven kirkyard, we happened to see Dr Orr down on the shore, far beneath our feet. The tide was out and he was walking against the wet sands with slow laborious plod, like some incredibly learned cormorant. Music crept past us on the far waters. Then he disappeared. We smiled, we that were young and uncelibate, held hands again, kissed, and swore to be true to one another. Minutes later the music we had heard upon the yellow sands came closer and Dr Orr appeared, walking slowly up the kirkyard steps, his broad hat first, then the rest of him, rising into view. To our amazement he was carrying a transistor radio. The disc jockey gave the title of the next number and it crackled fuzzily among the tombstones and fizzled away. Dr Orr saw us and approached us with stately tread.

Nonplussed, inadequate, the great scholar looked at the radio and handed it over to us beseechingly. We returned it to the station.

> *And when I touch you I feel happy inside*
> *It's such a feeling*
> *That my love I can't hide*
> *I can't hide, I can't hide*

'I was really awaiting the national news, of course,' he said, with a very deep smile.

And he turned away among the stones, carrying off the rest of the song along with the laborious arithmetic of his plod.

> *Yeah, you've got that something,*
> *I think you'll understand,*
> *When I feel that something,*
> *I wanna hold your hand*
> *I wanna hold your hand*
> *I wanna hold your hand*
> *I wanna hold your hand*

A cold feeling of something terrible came over me, and I looked at Jenny as she too looked at the doctor's slow ceremonious retreat.

I clutched her hand tighter and she smiled.

The session ended unforgettably with the whole school, pupils and teachers, six hundred and fifty strong, lined up on tiered benches out on the sports field—the custom always on the final day—to have a photograph taken. It was something of a joke, as the local photographer had run through the various stages of sand blindness and gravel blindness and was now reputed to be stone blind. He worked for the local newspaper and had scooped many's the dramatic shot at the Old Folks' Tea without a film in his camera.

But it was the moment Dave Logan of Pittenweem had been waiting for—he whose pater ran the Gents' Hairdressing Establishment which had provided us with our first glimpse of contraceptive technology. Logan had been planning this all session. For the past school year he had been filching a packet of three condoms per week from his father's shop and had distributed them this very morning, one to each boy in the senior school. As the teachers sat smiling in the front two rows, Dr Orr among them, they were unaware that each older boy had dipped into his pocket, quickly and quietly blown up a condom and knotted it, and on the aged photographer's 'Now!' we released our condoms every one to float over the heads of our fellows and the seated teachers and invade the pitch. The Shark was tight-lipped under his moustaches, Lachlan Campbell wore a huge grin and Mackay Mackay's glasses were steamed up and he had to take them off and wipe his eyes. Danny was red in the face with laughing and lit up a King Size. Only Fanny Fergusson went mad. Withdrawing an ever ready pin from her tweed lapel, she scuttled about the field like a crazed witch, her black gown flapping its pterodactyl wings, her finger jabbing and bursting wherever she could reach, shouting threats against our future employment and education and watching in hysterical despair as the barrage of condoms sailed out across the town roofs and headed for Norway.

Dr Orr sat on in the front row. He was wearing the most enigmatic of smiles.

Some of the condoms floated northward, symbolically, towards Aberdeen. Where Jenny and I followed them three months later.

10

AND THERE FOR us, in bonny Aberdeen, in 1963, began a new life.

Well, let us be both honest and accurate, shall we? What I should really have said is that up in the north, our common gateway to the glorious sixties, there began for us *two* new lives: one for Jenny and one for me. When a young man of eighteen enrols in the Faculty of Arts of a university and a young woman begins to train as a nurse in that same city, their orbits do not naturally intersect. We were two stones thrown into separate pools on the same shore and inevitably it happened that there radiated outward from each of us an ever-expanding series of concentric circles of friends and activities which had the effect of hemming us in from one another. We had to work very hard to keep ourselves as one. Jenny worked at it much harder than me, to her eternal credit, and I should applaud her to the very echo that should applaud again. It was mainly, let me tell you, because of her practical perserverance in love, that our relationship lasted three years, and, though frayed and fragile in places, wove through these three years like a golden thread. But look how I prattle, sweetings—I'm coming to that, all of that, all in good time. Let us first arrive in Aberdeen.

We went up together by train, holding hands by a moving magic casement that opened on cold sweeps of sea, like cut blue corn stacked in swathes, falling endlessly behind us. And bringing us eventually—would it have been a journey of over three hours in those days?—to the granite city, which spread before us like an El Dorado, gilded a sensible Scottish pewter, austerely eloquent in its northern way of fabulous nights and days to come, to give us solely sovereign sway and masterdom over our lives. We were away from home for the first time ever and would not now have to tramp for miles to be met and cloistered in caves of corn. No more lying down among cowpats and thistles to escape the harangues of the Galatians, the anti-fornication leagues of the Woman's Guild—and naturally grudging parents of post-Edwardian inertia. We would meet for lunch, discuss our courses, drink of an evening, and make love every night in our bedsitlands east of the harbour, where the cold poundings of the North Sea would echo through our open windows and remind us of home.

Ah, where did it go, the glory and the dream?

The horror and the awakening was that I found myself sitting at a heavily polished breakfast table in a substantially grey Victorian terraced house, run by a genteel white-haired landlady, a Miss MacDougall, who had hung her dwelling with formidable notices made out in large, aggressive letters. Please close vestibule door quietly; do not forget your key; main front door will be snibbed and chained and Chubb-locked in any case by eleven pm so be back by ten or sleep on the streets—not outside *my* house, if you please; any breakages must be paid for—in advance; silence must be observed in the drawing-room—it is agreed that it contains neither bodies nor books, but we'll let on it's a library or a morgue (same thing) if you'll be so kind; breakfast at 7.30 sharp or you'll go hungry, similarly tea at 4.30; don't stack your books against the wallpaper—it'll only mark it and maybe improve the existing pattern and we can't have that, you might feel at home and start taking bloody liberties, like breathing too loudly; do not smoke in your bedrooms, drop your filthy sodden fag-ends down the toilet, leave soapy bristles in the sink, forget to lift the seat when making water, or use more than two squares of tracing paper per visit—and get your aim straight, will you? furthermore don't dare to come back here boozed out of your minds to piss your student grants up against the wall and darken these respectable premises with your drunken goings-on; above all else, top of the list—and you'd better follow this one, *loons*—forget whatever plans you've made for four years' fucking at my expense, for you'll not be dipping your dirty wicks under this roof, turning me into a brothel while I'm still rattling my chains of asthma up and down the stairs each night, no, none of your sodomies and fancy women in this establishment so long as I'm on the prowl, let me tell you, especially having your ends away with your student nurses and radiographers and fresh young tarts who just can't wait to be pulling their knickers down to let you have your wicked ways with them, undoing all the good their mothers did them by getting themselves undone before freshers' week's even over, oh, yes, and to think of all the salt water that went over their fathers' heads, these fine fisherfolk, to send them here, scrimping and saving and hauling and dying, only for them to be shafted by the first spotty bastard in a brand new scarf to sneak them back here when my back is turned—no, it's not on, me buckos, for I'm a godfearing woman as the samplers will tell you, and I'm not mocked either, immaculate in my life as sacramental linen, untouched by man and private as the sphinx, never let any vile penis enter *my* front bedroom, for they are arrant knaves all, men, beasts and animals, just as sure as my mother told me, who ought to know, postmistress up in Elgin forty years with the world coming through her letterbox and me postmistress after her for another forty before I came to this, still a spinster and intend to be returned unopened to my sender and make *Him* pay the stamp (unperforated) my incorruption not once put on corruption by one iota, jot or prickle, untouched by any male part whatsoever, having remained so by the strength of my formidable knicker elastic and my good wholesome Scotch diet, served according to an unvaried seven-day cycle, as fixed and fossilised as the Gregorian calendar and boring as plainsong and which you will now start getting used to: poached egg on a Monday, kipper on a Tuesday, fried egg on a Wednesday, smokie on a Thursday, boiled egg on a Friday—no Catholic nonsense on Fridays up here, no fillet of Whore of Babylon, thank you—herring on a Saturday, sardines on a Sunday and don't expect any red meat, it'll only make you randy, it's a fish and vegetarian diet for you, my lads and porridge for every breakfast, oatcake and cheese for supper, that's all the protein it's safe to feed you and that's what you're going to be fed on, like it or lump it, and that'll keep your nasty tassles from their shameful erections, O, you brood of perverts, you litter of the sick sixties, but if it doesn't and I start hearing the bedsprings creak or find the sheets gone starchy in the mornings, if I once hear them crackle when I'm changing them, I'll be up with the garden shears before you can say John Thomas and off will come the cause of all the trouble in the world since time began—men, and their never-to-be-satisfied repulsive winklers, whoremasters every single one of you! Oh, and kindly put the light out when you go to sleep, please. And don't shag the cat—he'll shag you first, I'll be bound. Another rutting male on the rampage, a cock and balls on legs, that's all, only difference between you being—he's got four legs and more fur.

Having chewed my way through lump porridge and salt fish in the cold October company of students of agriculture, zoology, engineering, languages and law, all sitting round the same truculently scented table, antisepsis and oak on a threadbare carpet, all having come to Aberdeen to stick in— I made my way to the university on a crowded bus, clamorous with tongues from Oxford to Oban and well beyond in every direction. I found King's College in an academic dwaam, sunning itself among the ivied walls and cobbled streets of the quainter section of the city, Old Aberdeen, where let my due feet never fail to walk the studious cloisters' pale. No problem, Il Penseroso, old son, for there indeed they were, the cloisters of my Miltonically nurtured imagination, awaiting my anxious tread as I hurried along to a vast lecture hall to find myself on exhibition along with no fewer than six hundred students of Ordinary English (I hated the implication of that label and was itching already to get beyond it), all of us clutching blank writing pads in new ring binders, all flecked by hundreds of yellow price tabs from the university bookshop, not yet torn off, and all of us swathed in recently purchased scarves, the white and purple or yellow and blue showing up garishly over the Clerk of Oxenford gear—worn denims and baggy raggedy jumpers, as outrageously shabby as could be bought or battered into suitable shades and shapes of destitution. Several of the males were already hidden behind beads and beards. You could see the colour of the females' eyes by looking up the skirts they were almost wearing. No white thigh flesh flashing in the first generation of tights, no, no,—mini-skirts and suspenders cancelling one another out, you see. All progress leads to regress of some sort, all advances to a kind of recession. The demise of stockings led to the renaissance of legs—or was it the other way about? Someone would know. I don't. It hardly mattered, did it? Hundreds of female freshers sat with their feet up on the chairs in front, all of them advertising their limbs of propulsion from calf to crutch and laying the quiet respectable fields of Academe dangerously full of mines. See that you stick in, my lad. No distractions! But how many of these same tights, nylon or woollen, would be peeled off unlawfully some time in the next twenty-four hours? And how many virgins for defloration in bonny Aberdeen tonight, this night, Iago? Yes, that's right, remember you've come here to study English and the first lecture is on *Othello*. See that you stick in then. Yes, I'd love to stick mine in yours, sweetheart, yes, of course you can borrow my pen, you can borrow my pen any time, love. Wonder if she caught the heavy innuendo there? Lie? Lie with her, on her, in her—what you will. Oh, God, I'm sorry, Jenny, I shouldn't be thinking such thoughts, not on my very first morning. Still, I bet you're half in love already with some easeful greaseful medic who'll make things smoother for you by securing us the services of Madam Pill, the nonpareil of matchmakers and bawds.

Silence.

And now hangs expectation in the air.

There's so much to bloody well read! . . . Never mind about reading, there are so many to bloody well *ride*! . . . Which one do you fancy? Fancy riding *her*!

O what is that sound, said reader to rider? Is it the professor coming? Coming to teach us something about Othello.

An august personage swept in with an air of impregnable critical authority: a tiny little man with a scholar's humped shoulders and stoop, his black gown settling like wings as he arrived at the podium, golden eyes flashing now that we fell hushed under his imperious owlish scrutiny. This was THE UNIVERSITY personified, complete with cigar-stained teeth. This was what I had expected.

What's his name? Duthie. It's Professor Duthie. Great man. Over strong on Tillyard but studied with Dover Wilson. Old buddies, imagine. Expert on the Bad Quarto of *Hamlet*, Elizabethan shorthand, calligraphy, that sort of thing. Knows the lot. Looks fierce but reputed to be gentle with students. Also reputed to be dying. Doesn't look too gentle from here. Doesn't look too dead either. Looks bloody formidable. It's all right, don't worry, he'll put us at our ease. A few aptly chosen words. Yes indeed, I know you are all somewhat apprehensive, ladies and gentlemen (not schoolkids any more, you see, but ladies and gentlemen) and I understand that you are also considerably bewildered. Where do I find? How do I get? Whom do I tell? What must I do? But don't fret, you'll soon grow accustomed to it all. My name is Professor George Ian Duthie—some of you may know my work—and I'll soon get to know your names, all six hundred of them. After all, I'm cleverer than you, but with a little practice you'll soon be clever too. We may even make English scholars out of some of you. A few of you may go so far as to graduate! All right? Feel better now? Shall we begin? Good.

Several kindly chosen phrases such as these, edged with irony, naturally, from the lips of such a great man, but essentially benevolent. We sat back and waited for them.

What Professor Duthie actually *did* say, after a fleetingly belligerent scowl at the end wall of the lecture theatre, behind our heads, was this:

'In the tragedy of *Othello* Shakespeare is concerned with drama on three main levels: the personal, the political and the universal, or, to apply an alternative set of terminologies, the psychological, the social and the cosmic.'

Six hundred green scholars stared at one another, open-mouthed. With a wild surmise, did I omit to say? Certainly with a nasty surprise showing in each face. And it was with that verbal jolt that we realised that our university education had begun. Without preamble. Good one, Duthie. Let them have it. Wait a minute, what the hell was that he just said? God, he's off again! Six hundred pens started to scratch furiously on that first of four years' worth of days to come. Much ink to flow under many bridges. Into the valley of literary learning, into the jaws of critical dogma went the six hundred. And many shit themselves on that first day.

But for one who had studied under the histrionic Lachlan Campbell and the deep revolving witty Mackay Mackay, with their enlightened imagination, their impeccable scholarship and their freedom to teach the great tradition along with all the nuts and bolts of the job; for one who had been used to write the name of David Daiches thus—DVD DCHS—in vowel-less respect for his godlike academic authority (Guide us, O thou great Jehovah!); for one who had read the *Complete Works of William Shakespeare* from cover to cover five times in Senior Four and *Hamlet* fifty times, and the *Complete Works* of everyone else (excepting C.P. Snow) at least once; for one who had lived, eaten, drunk, dreamed, sweated and pissed out English literature with the lovely Jenny, who had felt everything on the page and off the page as on his own pulses, whose eyes, albeit unused to the melting mood, dropped tears as fast as the Arabian trees their medicinal gum; for one who had sat under the bookish sermonisings of Dr Andrew Orr M.A., B.Sc., B.D., D. Litt., D.D., and had carried into the summer holidays of '63 a complete understanding of the literal, symbolic, allegoric and anagogic meanings of Greek fire—for such a one Professor George Ian Duthie's first words were in no wise intimidating. Rather they were the draught of vintage that had been cooled a long age in the great Scottish professorial tradition and of which future students would never see the like again.

'Let us lay aside for the moment—but only for the moment—the second and third of these levels of dramatic concern, the political and the cosmic, and come first to the first level, the personal. For I would submit to you, ladies and gentlemen, that without question Shakespeare's principal preoccupation in the tragedy of *Othello* is a psychological one. Putting it another way, he is primarily interested in what goes on in people's minds . . .'

> *There are places I remember all my life,*
> *Though some have changed,*
> *Some forever, not for better,*
> *Some have gone and some remain.*

The generation who listened to Professor Duthie speak his Johnsonese had come from up and down the country between the Shetlands and the south of England, bringing with them a variety of accents and attitudes with which they bedecked the granite city. The city accepted them like a temporary dew, like the sparkle in its stones when the sun came out after rain and of no more consequence to these stones than that superficial glitter. The student population of any city is an unreal army, an occupying force of intellectual phantoms in a constant state of flux, one which never ages, never puts down roots, unlike the everyday citizens. It does not dig the city's drains, build its houses, operate its systems of transport, commerce, amenity, law, or any other of the manifold systems that constitute the life of the city. It inhabits but does not dwell; it feeds but does not provide, except in the slightest financial sense as a passing consumer. By and large the student is neither born nor buried in his university town. Even after he is dead his molecules do not feed its earth, its air. During his brief flirtation with it he may dwell in a number of its districts, as a bee populates this flower or that, possessing lightly, ephemerally. He will buy from its shops, board its buses, drink beer in its howffs and hostelries, thread his way through the loud noons of its thoroughfares—but remains essentially a foreign body travelling its arteries, pursuing goals that pass the place by.

Have you ever watched a lone student walking the streets, clasping his books and files? Observe his features, if you will. He wears an expression quite unlike that of the ordinary city-dweller, who goes from point to point in the certain knowledge that this is his world and the one in which he must remain and by which he is circumscribed. There is a something settled look in his face which is different from the scholar's. The latter has eyes but sees not the surrounding citizens, their habitations, their places of work; he has ears but hears not the music of that corporate humanity, a music that, whether it be still and sad or vibrant with optimism, is as unreal to him as he is to the unreal city. His thoughts, as he makes his way from A to B, are on other things, and, if he be a good student, on higher things. Thus neglecting worldly cares, he is dedicated to closeness and the bettering of his mind. Rather like the wandering scholar of the Middle Ages, you could say, his sack of meal on his back, his texts in his head, he is travelling light towards the ultimate light, the holy grails of learning and wisdom, so that even the ivory tower he heads for each day—King's College, in our case—possesses a spatial existence that is of secondary importance to the ideal abode that has been erected in his head. Its floors are in Florence, its walls in Paris, its halls in Bologna, its turrets and spires in Oxford, Cairo, Olympus. It is a place of ideals, a secular counterpart to St Augustine's *De Civitate Dei*, a city abiding in its Platonic reality, unserious in its absurd possession of architectural substance for the nonce—height, depth, volume, weight, and the irritatingly concrete necessities of seminar chambers, refectories, coffee rooms, recreational complexes, all made to accommodate the hampering demands of the silly flesh—and the Students' Union, with its beer bar, lounges, reading rooms, dining areas, bathrooms and showers and so on down to the lavatories and the pipes and sewers below us, that carried the most exquisitely learned excreta in the north into the North Sea. To me this all seemed—I have to confess it—as remote as it could be from the ultimate experience I felt I should be undergoing. Only in the monumentally hushed and awesome library did I feel close to the mystic intellectual heart of what I had conceived of as The University. The academic thought-force built up there by generations of concentrated minds, finely tuned each day and night to a million scholarly tomes, produced for me an atmosphere rarefied to the point of extra-terrestrial experience. This was the place where I should stick in. I would not move from here for the next four years except to sleep in my celibate cell under Miss MacDougall's spotless roof (on which no Aberdonian gull dared shit) and to attend all lectures. I should be a model student. I should be like Demosthenes, Milton, Mackay Mackay.

Very soon the demands of the world, the flesh and the devil prevailed and the university experience broke up over twelve terms and eleven vacations into an educational mosaic of pieces which at the time I could see neither steadily nor whole—mainly because I was frequently in my cups. We'll teach you to drink deep ere you depart was the watchword of the student community among whom I at once struck up sudden but fast friendships, pledged in oats for the drinking and oats for the sowing. We all needed one another for stimulation, sanity and relief and we met nightly in the Union beer bar where I began my drinking career with Black Velvets, moved on to heavy beer, and by the end of the first term had become a devotee of straight malt whisky, under the unshakeable hand of Torvil Nicolson, a scholarly crazed Shetlander with a powerful intellect, a genius for conversation, and an insatiable appetite for social intercourse, sexual intercourse, the Icelandic Sagas, English Romantic poetry and Glenfiddich—if possible all at the same time. But if two out of the list had to remain, they would be the Glenfiddich and the poetry and all else could go hang. Torvil would quote Byron to a brick wall while emptying against it his previously quaffed whisky in the time-honoured fashion.

'Well now, my friend, we'll just start off the evening with a wee treble, shall we?'

'What's that?'

'Good God Almighty man, don't show your ignorance, it's three Glenfiddichs in the one glass, what else would it be now? Cheers.'

Torvil could be counted on to disgrace himself at any professorial 'At Home'. On one of these exceedingly posh occasions the professor's wife stood at the door to her drawing room beside a table of drinks, supplying each guest on entry with his requested poison. If the guest accepted a glass of gin or vodka or whisky, she would ask imperiously: 'With?' Indicating with a wave of the hand the proferred range of soft drinks to reduce the alcohol to an appropriately genteel level of dilution. When it came to Torvil's turn he accepted a glass of whisky and was about to pass on when he was halted by the magisterial demand.

'With?'

Torvil's face assumed an expression of the wildest outrage and he knocked back the contents of the tumbler with exaggerated heartiness, downing the malt in one.

'With great appreciation!' he gasped, smacking his lips and holding out his glass for more.

He had a basement flat of his own quite close to the harbour. It was crammed with books on an astonishing variety of subjects. Torvil had changed course a number of times and no one was quite sure of what he was currently studying, or even in what Faculty, least of all his tutors, who seemed to have lost track of him. He was reputed to have been at the university for nine years and it was rumoured abroad that he had friends in some very low places.

If you're ever stuck for a bed for the night, my friend—there's the address. Always whisky in the jar and always the floor to sleep on, if you don't mind sharing it with a lot of other mad loons.

It was true. No matter when I visited Torvil, he was never around. But lots of other characters were—friends of his from all quarters who had found themselves locked out by their landladies or who were simply incapable or undesirous of finding their way across town in the small hours of the morning to brave a drainpipe or a lecture from a white tousled head. Ah, in those days we were Diana's foresters, gentlemen of the shade, minions of the moon. And Torvil's door was never locked—at one point there *was* no door at all—and the flat was never empty. Whenever a party had turned boring at three in the morning someone would be sure to say, 'Let's go to Torvil's place!' And there they'd all be. Students reading from the many books, sleeping it off in battered armchairs, footing it fiercely on the floor as they debated the relative merits and demerits of Platonic Realism and Aristotelian Nominalism, fighting over games of chess, and sometimes Norwegian sailors from the docks, sitting around among broken English and glasses, grinning or arguing. No one ever left without putting a little money in a tin on the mantlepiece, however minimal a recognition of Torvil's easy hospitality. Nor was anyone ever so crass as to sleep in Torvil's always available empty bed. In what strange beds abroad in the city did the absentee landlord find himself o' nights? The fact was that you couldn't go to a party—even if you attended three or four in one night—without finding Torvil in the corner, practising the gift of bi-location (or in his case poly-location), glass in hand, forefinger jabbing Socratically, pontificating or poeticising with a hearty laugh and a line from the Romantics, or, when he became dangerously drunk, jabbering in Old Norse. This was one of the subjects in his strange mixture of courses and he was the sole student of the course. After many wee trebles he would hold converse with his shadow in this weird tongue that sounded no wilder—possibly a trace more civilised—than his own Norse-influenced native Shetland, into which he also broke down at times when ecstatic or enraged.

Torvil Nicolson. First Class Honours in I can't remember what—and quite frankly I doubt if he remembered either at the time. Went back to Shetland after he'd graduated and took a berth on a fishing boat. Disappeared off the Faroes two years later, the sea in his mouth, (stopping it, like Shelley's, from speaking any more poems.) and in his hair, laving his oozy locks with nectar pure. Goodbye then, Torvil. Hence forth thou art the genius of the shore, and shalt be good to all that wander in that perilous flood.

11

All these places had their moments
With lovers and friends I still can recall.
Some are dead and some are living.
In my life I've loved them all.

—SO WHAT ARE you studying?

—English.

—Oh.

—Why, what are you studying?

—Economics.

—Oh.

—Yes, I'm going to make a fucking mint. That's what I'm here for. What else? I'm just sorry for the poor bastards I'm going to crush underfoot. What are you going to do—after you've got through all this garbage?

—Teach.

—A schoolteacher, you mean?

—Yes.

—Seriously?

—Seriously.

—Oh. See you, then.

—Yes, see you.

Perhaps not.

The voiceless velar plosive consonant is generally represented by c initially before liquid consonants and back vowels in Middle English as in Old English, as in comen (Old English cuman). Before secondary front vowels (i.e. those which became front in Old English as the result of i-mutation) and before the consonant n it is generally written k, as in kepen (Old English cepan), knight (Old English cniht). Medially and finally it is written c or k, as in clerc beside clerk (Old French clerc). Old English velar cc is generally written ck or kk medially, as in lockes beside lokkes pl. (Old English locc 'lock of hair').

'Ssh!' Jenny whispered, taking off her shoes and leading me by the hand up the creaking stairs. 'We mustn't waken my flatmates.'

The small room received us like a confessional. Jenny didn't switch on the light and the darkness was rich and heavy with her scent.

'Let's go to bed.'

We undressed and slipped between the sheets. Her nakedness shocked my flesh again.

'We can do what we like now, love,' she smiled, 'now that the Pill is working. And now I'm going to fuck *you*.'

And she began to lick the hairs on my chest.

> *But of all these friends and lovers*
> *There is no-one compares with you,*
> *And these memories lose their meaning*
> *When I think of love as something new.*

—So you wish to study Moral Philosophy? Well then, tell me what you think Moral Philosophy is.

—The study of ethics.

—What's ethics?

—A book by Aristotle.

—Ostensive definition. Don't try to be clever, it won't work in this department. You know what I want. Give me a definition. What's ethics?

—Moral codes.

—But 'moral' is one of the words I've asked you to define. Not much better. Try again.

—The principles of right and wrong.

—How do you know what is right and wrong?

—Well, some things are obvious. Stealing is wrong.

—Why? Give me an example.

—If it hurts society.

—Be more specific.

—Stealing an old widow's life-savings.

—Why is that wrong?

—It would hurt her.

—Supposing she didn't *know*?

181

—Well—

—Well, that's Moral Philosophy: doing precisely what we are doing now. Asking questions and proceeding by logic.

—But Professor Vernon—

—Yes?

—What do *you* believe?

—I beg your pardon?

—I mean the principle of stealing is still wrong, isn't it?

—I don't know. You haven't proved it yet, logically.

—But what do you believe?

—Believe? Believe! Good God, if you're going to start asking stupid questions like that, you'd better stop the course and go away and take up Bible Studies or something! I'm not interested in people who have beliefs, who have views about things, who stick out their chests and say 'I believe in X and I don't believe in Y', as if that were somehow supposed to be of some consequence to the universe. That is not philosophy. What I believe is of no consequence to the universe. I am concerned only with questions of logic and logic is all that matters. Believe? What nonsense! I don't have any beliefs, unless I stretch a point and say I believe in the law of logic. But no—that's not a belief, it's an intellectual position. No. I don't believe in *anything*.

Believe in the Lord Jesus Christ and thou shalt be saved. For as Paul said to the Galatians, knowing that a man is not justified by the works of the law, but by the faith of Jesus Christ, even we have believed in Jesus Christ, that we might be justified by the faith of Christ, and not by the works of the law: for by the works of the law shall no flesh be justified.

—Yes, but you have to put all that out of your mind now—now that we're students. Everything's cerebral, you see. Even moral philosophy isn't actually moral. You've got to stick to brainwork alone, old chap.

—You mean like Beethoven and Bach?

—What the hell are you talking about?

—Oh, nothing. I was just thinking about something somebody said to me once.

*   *   *

All these notes, lad—they didn't just come out of a human brain. They came into it first. Then they came out of it. The question is, where did they come *from?*

The greatest satire is written in anger, contempt or disgust, but uses laughter as a corrective, to promote self-knowledge on the part of individuals, institutions and societies, in the hope that laughter and knowledge, entertainment and instruction, will lead to right action. Discuss.

   —No, the brain isn't everything, it's just chemistry. And life's not chemistry.
   —Yes it is. You're just carbon and water.
   —I don't believe that.

Stan, stan, stanes, stane, stanas, stana, stanum.

Today, said Professor Duthie, today I am going to do something which I have never allowed myself to do in the course of my entire career. But I intend doing it today. I am going to permit myself to tell you what I believe to be the truth about something. I believe we are beginning to lose our way . . .

I looked at myself shaving in Miss MacDougall's bathroom mirror. The eyes were beginning to take on a haunted look. I'm not surprised—yes, it's you I'm talking to, you in the mirror! All that time gone by and exams coming up already. Ten weeks is nothing. Moral Philosophy, Psychology, English Literature, English Language—and a bloody Intelligence Test, of all things, to satisfy the psychologists! Essays translations, tutorials, getting bugger-all done, and you're starting to miss too many lectures already, oh, God and you haven't phoned Jenny for four nights in a row! This whole thing's going to pot, she'll ditch you if you're not careful, and maybe that would be the answer. The Clerk of Oxenford stuck to his pen. The perishing prick is going to be your downfall, mate . . . See that you stick in, son . . . I will, I will . . . You'll never have to take your jacket off, you'll be safe for life . . . We're safe, *we're* safe! . . . Let us go then, you and I . . .

Scip, scip, scipes, scipe, scipu, scipu, scipa, scipum.

* * *

The smell of yellow smoked fish filtered through the keyhole.

You fallen down the pan in there? Get a move on, for fuck's sake! The old bag's on the rampage and Vernon's on at nine.

Lufode, lufodest, lufodon, lufode, lufoden, gelufod.

Today we are going to examine the nature of power and authority in *The Republic*. Now I want every single one of you to hold one finger in the air and to do absolutely nothing else. Do you all think you can do that? Let's see. Fine. Ah, but ladies and gentlemen, you who are seated before me now (cunning) each with one finger held up in the air—you didn't just stick one finger up and nothing else (smirking), you stuck one finger up because I *told* you to! (triumphant) A world of difference there. Now let us move on to two fingers.

Oh, for fuck's sake!

Two fingers stuck up Jenny's slippery front as she finished licking me and, sweeping away the sheets, came on top, brushing my face lightly with her dangling breasts. There where my hand is set, my seal shall be.

Opening the cunt, she slid down onto the erection with a gasp and was impaled. To enter into these bonds is to be free. I grasped her haunches and she squirmed and slowly lowered her left nipple into my mouth, smothering my face with the increasing heaviness of the tit.

I can't breathe.

> *The luscious clusters of the vine*
> *Upon my mouth do crush their wine.*

—Marvell.
—You should be doing English, not nursing.
—If I wasn't doing nursing I might not have managed to get on the Pill so easily. Then you wouldn't be doing this to me.
—Who's doing what to whom?
—Try the other one.

> *The nectarine and curious peach*
> *Into my hands themselves do reach.*

—Seem to have heard that one too, somewhere before today. A tit in each hand and Jenny with her face buried in the

184

pillow, biting into my shoulder, her pelvis beginning to thrust against me.

—It makes me want to come too quickly when you're on top.

O come quickly, O come quickly, O come quickly, sweetest Lord,
And take my soul to rest!

—Remember the madrigals?
—Ssh.
—Do you think that's blasphemous?
—No, I just don't want you to waken Fiona and Jane with your bloody awful singing.
—Danny said I had a good voice.
—It's not your voice I want right now. Whoever heard of singing madrigals when making love!
—The two should always be taken together.
—Out of school hours!
—Only it was wine that was the second component, remember? Let's slosh back another glass before we go on.
—No, I want to come.

O come quickly, O come quickly, O come quickly, glorious Lord
And raise my sprite to thee!

—Why don't you think that's blasphemous?
—Because Donne is right. Sex is a sacrament. This is the most wonderful thing I've done. Ever. It's the ultimate experience and it brings me closer to God. O come quickly, glorious Lord—that makes me think of you—you are my glorious lord, made in God's image, and sex is the gift you bring me. It's a pity Paul hadn't realised that.
—Told you you should be taking the English degree. Maybe I should have said theology. It is better to marry than to burn, Paul said. Not much of an advert for marriage, eh?
—Silly twit, he just lacked experience.
—If he'd had you among the buttercups he'd have changed his mind.
—Maybe. To the pure all things are pure.
—And to the Puritan all things are impure.
—Paul was impure. I think Dr Orr was pure.
—Remember how he smiled at the condoms? Always assuming he knew what they were.

—He knew. He was pure. And so is this. Everything that we do together. Nothing of it can ever be impure, not when you're really in love, as we are. Even my erotic thoughts are spiritually beautiful. The genitals doing their work together, it's beyond words, the beauty of it.

—Little soft syllables of love, whispered by my prick to your cunt and so on back again, like ripples on the edge of the tide, our love-dew conversing eternally in a universal language—

—Not like Anglo-Saxon!

—God! One without inflexions, without barriers, lingam and yoni, penis and pudenda, what do the names matter, breaking the tower of Babel, reaching up to God—no, it's not beyond words, you see, it's just that it doesn't need words. Not when you're in love.

—As we are.

—As we are.

—As I am. I've never felt like this about anybody.

—So we're agreed then.

—About what?

—We're in love and we don't want to burn and it works between us—

—And so?

—And so, after we've graduated, we should marry. I'm sorry, love, that sounds clumsy.

—You want to marry me?

—You know I do. There'll never be anyone else but you.

—That's a song.

—Will you marry me?

—You know I will.

—Ic pe lufie. I don't know if that's right. I should.

—Say it in English then.

—It is English. I love you.

—I love you.

The Plough twisted slowly on its end round circumpolar Aberdeen.

The Northern Lights of Old Aberdeen
Mean home sweet home to me.

Jenny's flesh against mine, all night long. Man and woman one flesh.

*   *   *

186

—All flesh is grass, you see. Man is what he eats. You're just a collection of physical phenomena. Even your precious Shakespeare was just part of a chain from grass to grass.

—Yes, but there's one basic difference between Shakespeare and the grass.

—What's that?

—Shakespeare knew that he was part of a chain. Grass doesn't.

—Prove it.

—Thou art not thyself, For thou exists on many a thousand grains That issue out of dust.

—Don't see that makes any difference.

—You should read Pascal and you might change your mind. The universe is dying. I am dying. But the universe doesn't know that it's dying. I do. That makes me superior to the universe.

—Crap. Somebody will come and chuck some dirt over your head at the end of the day, one day. What difference will it make then? Death is a state when totally irreversible chemical changes have taken place in the body. The beauty of it is that your body then goes on to change the universe. The molecules that were Shakespeare exist now as parts of cows, coffee tables, ships, shit—

To what base uses we may return, Horatio.

—In theory your Jenny could contain something of Shakespeare.

'Twere to consider too curiously to consider so.

—Ever thought of that when you're fucking her?

—Don't talk about Jenny like that. She's not some tart.

—Why? She fucks, doesn't she?

—You've no conception, have you? You engineers. You remind me of a song called 'The Engineer's Wheel'. And of a chap called Cranford. God, I wonder who he's screwing now?

—Forget about Cranford. Your round, by the way. I've just proved your Shakespeare's a load of shit.

—You're forgetting about one thing.

—What's that?

—His plays.

—A load of bloody books.

*   *   *

Of making many books there is no end. And much study is a weariness of the flesh.

Cheers.

—Oh, but thank God for the vacations! Nice to be working out of doors for a few weeks, getting the good old sun.

—Nice do you call it? I've been doing this for forty fucking years! Too rough for fucking flymos, this. Here, try your hand at the scythe.

> *My mind was once the true survey*
> *Of all these meadows, fresh and gay,*
> *And in the greenness of the grass*
> *Did see its hopes as in a glass,*
> *Till Juliana came, and she*
> *What I do to the grass does to my thoughts and me.*

—I'll tell you what that fucking scythe will have done to your back and shoulders by the time you get home tonight. And I'll tell you what it'll do to my balls if you don't stop fucking swinging it about like that!

—Sorry. Have a fag?

—Ah, now you're talking. What is it you're studying again?

—English.

—Grunt.

—Hey, tell me something. If you do history you get called a historian, don't you?

—That's right.

—And if you do geography you're a geographer, right?

—Right.

—And the guys that do foreign languages are called linguists, yes?

—You sound quite Socratic.

—Aye, well what will you be when you've finished up?

—You've got me there.

—I mean, what do you learn from it exactly? Doing English? Even I can speak the fucking stuff without needing a fucking degree in it! What I'm asking is, what does it teach you?

—Life.

—Oh. You'll be a lifer then.

—Some truth in that. I'll be a Master of Arts anyway.

—Arts. What'll you do then?

—Be a teacher.

—A schoolteacher?

—Yes.

—Better be good with the fucking belt then. Bastards.

The Northern Lights of Aberdeen
Are all I long to see

The lady psychology professor looked at us in her American sort of way and directed us to what she had drawn on the board.

—This is a statistical graph of the intelligence test we adminis-tered last term. Your names are plotted on it according to your scores. Around the entire set of scores I have drawn a whale, its—er—snout, as it were, near the top left hand corner of the board, its tail at the bottom right.

—Flukes.

(A voice from the back of the lecture hall)

—Pardon? I cannot guarantee—

—No, no. Technically whales have flukes, not tails.

(Could be Torvil Nicolson's voice)

—Oh.

(Pause)

—Well, if your name is anywhere in the vicinity of the eye, you will have every hope of gaining a First Class Honours degree. If you are close to the gills—

—No gills.

—Pardon?

—Whales are mammals, prof.

—If you are down a bit, you should manage a Two One. Of course the great majority of you will gain a Two Two. The body of the fish.

—Mammal. Danish *hvalt*, meaning arched or vaulted.

—And if you are at the tail, then—well, you oughtn't to be, really, although I see that one or two of you are. I have to say that you are in some danger of a Third. Please remember I am talking statistically. I shall now quit this place and allow you to examine the results and your own personal placings at your leisure.

She left, to read Hermann Melville, and we crowded round the board like wasps round jam. Torvil and I found our names

189

eventually, sunk in one of the flukes. I also was to graduate with a First Class Honours.

Flukes?

Intelligence tests prove one thing very clearly: that you are good at doing intelligence tests. They also prove that lady professors of psychology from the States possess a curious lack of acquaintance with one of that country's greatest authors.

And with the human mind.

Odd.

Jenny turned over onto her back, panting, and reached out for my stiffness.

—Now you fuck me. Quickly.

—You're so wonderfully earthy. So Lawrentian.

—Leave Lawrence out of it. Lawrence never comes near what I feel. And that's because I think that, deep down, he despises women and despises himself for his bondage to their possessing cunts, degrades physical lovemaking in a big way, for all his superficial liberatedness. *Chatterley* was a brave gesture but in the end somebody is just fucking a cunt. *Chatterley's* not a great book, I know, by Lawrence's standards, but I get a horrid feeling from it that permeates the rest of his work, brings it all down in ruins. It's still a crude book and much of the rest is sham shagging. Lawrence was only interested in shagging himself in the end—no pun intended, though by your smiling you seem to say so—and even other men were second best to him. That, and putting us women in our places, was his message. And the only place he could ever think of putting us was either in a bed or in a book!

—Wow! Thanks for the lecture—shall I put all that in my next essay? And how come the noble art of nursing has made you so bloody articulate all of a sudden?

—I'm sorry, it's what I think. Revolutionary in its time, but saying *fuck* and *cunt* all the time is just a game with Lawrence. When I say it to you it's no game, it's something I feel deeper than I ever thought possible. I can say these words to you without feeling guilty or dirty as I used to when we were teenagers.

—You never swore once when we were teenagers.

—I thought them in my mind—and felt guilty, rightly so, I suppose, they were just symptoms of objectless eroticism. But now—our love beautifies any verbalisation of it, our eroticism

190

spiritualises my cunt, your cock. When you come into me you're coming into church.

—Now who's sounding like Lawrence again?

—No I'm not, I'm sounding like Donne—oh, now look what you've done with your literary talk! We'll have to start all over again. Isn't that a pity now? Fuck me.

I love you. You're grown up. But I love you.

> *Though I know I'll never lose affection*
> *For people and things that went before,*
> *I know I'll often stop and think about them,*
> *In my life I'll love you more.*

—Who the hell's sleeping in my bed?

—Oh, sorry, that's my friend from London.

—Well he can bloody well get out.

—He's a she.

—Oh. Can't tell with the hair these days.

—Pull back the covers and you'll tell all right.

—Don't think she'd go a bundle on that one.

—Yes she would—she drops them; She'd go on anything.

—God, why did I ever move into a flat?

You see, said Professor Duthie—he was speaking very quietly and this was a one-to-one tutorial—you see, he said slowly, Falstaff is said to have babbled o' green fields, but the phrase is a misreading of what Shakespeare actually wrote. The story begins with a curious misprint in the First Folio edition of *Henry V*, where what has gone through, in spite of the best intentions of Heminges and Condell, is the statement that, as Falstaff lay dying, 'his Nose was as Sharpe as a Pen and a Table of greene fields'. Patent nonsense as it stands. No acceptable meaning may be derived from the last five words, at least not in relation to Falstaff's nose, which is the subject of the line in question. Now when our friend Theobald, the eighteenth century editor of Shakespeare, came across the line, he at once made admirable sense out of it. Clearly—so he argued—what Shakespeare wrote, and what the printer mistook, was that 'a' babled', that is 'he babbled' of green fields. Admirable indeed, and an inspired reading, in my opinion. But (puffing at his dead cigar) an erroneous one, I can assure you. You wish to know what Shakespeare really did write, don't you? Of course. Who wouldn't? Well, I can tell you. I have never seen the actual manuscript, of course—would that it were extant!—but I can see it in my mind's eye, as Hamlet said to Horatio about his father's ghost. Very plainly. At this point I won't enter into the technicalities—the calligraphical technicalities, that is, of how I know this—it is, after all, a somewhat esoteric branch of Elizabethan scholarship, rather recherché even by the standards of some of my learned colleagues (cigar-stained grin), but without question, what William Shakespeare actually wrote down on his manuscript page was that Falstaff *talked* o' green fields, that's all. He talked of green fields. Yes, I see your face fall, young man, and I can well understand why. You are now about to tell me that you think Theobald superior to Shakespeare—in this one tiny instance, of course. And before you tell me that, I shall agree with you—again in this one small example. I have long thought it myself. *Babbled* is so much more evocative, euphonious, pertinent, poignant and true. In a word, more poetic. But it is not the only instance in the history of literature of an error's having resulted in an improvement. Much critical ink has been spilt in mistaken and unfounded praise of a printer's mistake.

And he gave the same deep, rather sad smile that I had seen on the face of Dr Andrew Orr as he wandered off among the tombs.

—Who's that cretinous looking individual over there?

—Oh, him. Doing a Ph.D. on Aspects of Symbiosis in the Fungus and the Orchid. Think it'll change the course of Biology?

—God, why do the bastards bother? Seems any bugger can do a science Ph. D. if he's prepared to waste three years of his life counting seeds or measuring waves, giving bloody rats electric shocks.

—It's a con, isn't it? Some of the cleverest men around here didn't even bother doing Ph.D.'s before they became lecturers—they had more intellect. You got any plans for a Ph.D.?

—Yup. Mine at least has some point to it. You wouldn't catch me spending the next three years looking at surface tension in a glass of water.

—No. What's yours going to be on?

—The Worm in English literature.

—The Worm?

—Yes.

—I like it.

—I mean, when a biologist looks at a worm, what does he see?

—A worm.

—A thing with segments. And that's all he sees. But I see beyond the worm, to dragons and serpents and pricks and fallen man. It's fantastic. There's just no end to the possibilities. *Beowulf*, the ballads, the bible, Milton, Shakespeare, Tennyson—all the way. It's an archetype. You take that poem by Blake, 'The Sick Rose'. Listen, you got time for this?

—Go on.

> *O Rose, thou art sick!*
> *The invisible worm*
> *That flies in the night,*
> *In the howling storm,*
>
> *Has found out thy bed*
> *Of crimson joy,*
> *And his dark secret love*
> *Does thy life destroy.*

—It's a powerful poem.

—Yes, but what does it mean? Blake has handed you a blank cheque, which is what symbolism is. You write your own meaning on it, whatever figuring out you arrive at.

—Within the confines of the poem, of course.

—Naturally. But within the confines of that particular poem there are a hiveful of possibilities. Is the rose in the poem the Tudor rose of England, being raped by capitalist bastards and reactionary governments? Is it the rose of religion, with Satan as the worm, sitting at its heart, eating the churches away with bogus Christianity? Is it a loving relationship that's been poisoned by guilt and deceit? Is the worm syphilis? Or is it the male phallus? Is the rose a virgin? Or is the rose the female vulva, being fucked by a prick that's not worthy of it? Oh, I tell you, I could write a Ph.D. on that one alone!

—Well, you're not going to be short of material.

—Listen, I think that I just might be able, through the archetypal worm, to provide the key to a better understanding of the major part of English literature.

—You sound rather like Dr Casaubon.

—Bugger off. He was a nobody—a harmless drudge, on a level with lexicographers, as The Great Cham himself once said. I intend going places, man.

He's a real nowhere man . . .

—After I graduate I'm going to get myself down to Oxford—or Cambridge, of course.

Sitting in his nowhere land . . .

—Take my Ph.D there and aim for the top—be a don, you know.

Making all his nowhere plans for nobody.

Or we walked, Jenny and I, along the miles of dunes, where the great North Sea went thundering whitely up the sands, rendering all sex, all scholarship, supremely irrelevant. Vietnam was someone else's bad dream.

—Jenny, I'm sorry I've been out of touch so long. Bogged down in this blasted work. Junior Honours. Listen—

—Ssh. Don't speak. We don't need words, remember? The sea makes them all beside the point anyway.

. . . the sea of green

—But what happens at the end of this year? When your course is finished? Where will you live?

And we lived beneath the waves

—Let's not think about it just now.

—But you've got to go somewhere. Where will you go?

In our yellow submarine

—Jenny.

—Ssh. I love you.

—I love you too.

*   *   *

> *Ah, love, let us be true*
> *To one another! for the world, which seems*
> *To lie before us like a land of dreams,*
> *So various, so beautiful, so new,*
> *Hath really neither joy, nor love, nor light,*
> *Nor certitude, nor peace, nor help for pain;*
> *And we are here as on a darkling plain,*
> *Swept with confused alarms of struggle and flight,*
> *Where ignorant armies clash by night.*

—Nixon's a bastard.
—And all Commies are cunts. What's worse than Vietnam?
—Anglo-fucking-Saxon.

Hey, you'll never guess! Professor Duthie was sitting in the staff coffee-room, pontificating away to one of his colleagues, don't know which one, you know, about Shakespeare and the usual stuff, and he was accompanying his sonorous statements with gestures to match, you know the way he does, when, quite by accident, his hand swept right up the skirt of Dr Imogen Huntly—yes, I know, she's rather nice, isn't she?—wouldn't say no to her—who happened to be sitting at the table. Well, she screamed, of course, when she felt her stockinged thigh being attacked and—this is the good bit—Professor Duthie turned from his colleague, and, without losing the thread of his sentence, swivelled round to face Dr Huntly and informed her, in parenthesis, that his gesture had been 'rhetorical and in no sense exploratory' and expressed his hope that the opposite was true of what he was saying to his colleague, whom he then turned to again and carried on with his sentence exactly where he had left off! How do you like that? What a man! They say he's not too well now.

> *It's been a hard day's night*
> *And I've been working like a dog,*
> *It's been a hard day's night,*
> *I should be sleeping like a log.*

And instead I found myself yet again in Torvil's place, pretty drunk. Jenny, I've let you down again. Wherever you are tonight. I know where I am. Standing swaying in a litter of broken glass and scattered books and bodies, I focussed on a Highlander standing in the open doorway. He was very dark and very straight-backed.

'Why don't you clear out of here?' he said, in quiet impeccable English, softened by centuries of Gaelic. 'You and your drunken bums.'

He was right. A crowd of drunken bums, sponging off the state when they ought to be working. Take a look at yourself, man. What art thou Faustus but a man condemned to die? All right then, the rot stops here. From now on it's work all the way.

Six months later, sitting in the catacombs of the library, reading about medieval monasteries, I reached out to turn a page—and just for one second, you needn't believe this, I could not see my own hand. I had disappeared into my own studies. Strange sensation.

Write the following essay:

'It was a nature of the spirit that the medieval poet sought to imitate. With Aristotle, he understood that poetry was philosophical and dealt in universals. He did not understand that in poetry universals are only felt as such when they are realised and individualised.'

Discuss.

No problem.

> *I've been a wanderer all my life*
> *And many's the sight I've seen*

Have you heard? My flatmate went to deliver his Moral Philosophy essay to the professor and didn't find him in his room so he sat down to wait. After a while he heard odd gruntings from behind a door and cottoned on to the fact that this was where the Prof had his private facilities. He coughed a bit to let old Vernon know he was around and—you'll never believe it—the door to the toilet opens just a fraction and this gnarled hand comes out and this even more gnarled voice (you know how old Vernon speaks) says: 'Give me your essay!' like something out of Boris Karloff. So my flatmate goes to the door and puts

his essay into this wizened claw, which immediately withdraws
the essay through the crack, with the message from the voice:
'Same time tomorrow!' and shuts the door. After that you can
guess, can't you? That's right, he heard the bog flushing on his
way out but he never saw his essay again! I said to my flatmate I
thought old Vernon had put on his essay exactly what he thought
it was worth. Goes off the Alpha to Gamma scale—a new concept
in critical evaluation. It's hilarious.

—An excellent essay, young man, even though I often do get the
feeling that you are drying the ink in the wind as you walk across
the quadrangle to read it to me. Up all night again, I expect? Well,
it does not smell of the lamp, I can assure you. Alpha minus.
    —Professor, why do I always get an alpha minus? Isn't it
possible to score a straight alpha?
    —Have you heard this little rhyme? Listen.

> *I dreamt last night that Shakespeare's ghost*
> *Sat for a Civil Service post.*
> *The English questions of the year*
> *Contained a question on 'King Lear',*
> *Which Shakespeare answered very badly—*
> *Because he hadn't studied Bradley!*

You see the point, of course.
    —Yes. No one can ever get a straight alpha.
    —Wrong. I can. I have studied both Shakespeare and Bradley.
    —But so have I, professor. What's the minus actually *for*?
    —Why, young man, the minus is merely to prove *my* superiority
to you!

> *God speed the day when I'm on my way*
> *To my home in Aberdeen*

In time the pieces of the mosaic began to assemble themselves and
there came a point where I saw what it was that I had been doing
for four years: refining my ignorance to the point where I was
supremely, almost arrogantly confident of it. Acquaintanceship
with a thousand years of English literature, its major texts and
authors, the language and changing styles, genres and traditions
in which they had written, the societies in which they had lived,

the world views they had accepted, had convinced me that there were no answers to the most important questions I might wish to ask; that if there were answers which were acceptable today, they need not necessarily be true tomorrow; and that one truth does not exclude its opposite. Professor Duthie and his team had done their work well. I had acquired the wisdom of humility, that endless attainment. That's why I'm so bloody proud of it. *Ars longa vita brevis.* No, Horace did not go far enough. Art is not long, it is infinite. I knew that from now on, as soon as I had reached the stage where I had begun to believe something, then a part of me would have gone dead. The more beliefs I acquired, the deader I should become, until eventually I should cease to exist. I realised that politicians, and indeed all propagandists, are largely dead inside, because they believe that they know the truth about something, that they are right about something and that someone else is therefore wrong. This position was no longer acceptable to me.

When I asked myself, therefore, what was it that I was now equipped to do, the answer seemed to be to teach people to think for themselves in a chosen discipline, yes; to expose themselves to the best that had been thought, written, said or done in the history of humankind, yes; to encourage them to read and write, not for the purposes of information and communication but for those of pleasure and enrichment, yes; to make them into autonomous beings, proud of their heritage; to make them more human, more tolerant, more aware of themselves and their fellow creatures, man, woman, bird, beast, fish and tree; to liberate them from bondage to the present moment, place, country, creed and circumstance, yes, yes, yes, all that and more; but above all these, surely, to lead them to see—(O thank you, Bronowski!)—that there are no decisions or morals or messages in literature, if it really is great literature, nothing to shut a door or close a mind. There are only the endless questions of art.

And I knew what was to be my vocation—to go forth and make the pupils that would be mine into citizens of a universe from which all mythologies of right and wrong had been eradicated.

I felt magnificently equipped so to do. My teachers at Taft had given me the vision: those in Aberdeen had provided me with the understanding and the wisdom. My tertiary education was complete.

12

WHEN I WENT on to prove, in ten Final Honours Papers, how well I knew nothing, they awarded me a First Class Honours, showered me with prizes and a medal, and offered me the opportunity of taking up a Research Fellowship at Cambridge.

Cambridge?

No, I think not, my masters. I'll not to Cambridge, I'll to schoolmastering instead, and to the trade my former teachers at Taft inspired me to take up.

And so: goodbye, Ph.D. on the influences of Charles Darwin and Charles Lyell on Victorian poetry, goodbye a lifetime in the ivory tower, goodbye bonny Aberdeen—and goodbye Jenny.

Jenny had completed her nurse's training one year before me, and had started work in a hospital in Cambridge the following year. The choice of Cambridge had been deliberate on Jenny's part. It had been no secret that I had been headed for a good degree, in spite of the whale's tail, but that I'd be top student was not a thing I counted on or even wished for. Jenny neither counted on it nor wished it: she knew it. She was sure of me. You'll win the Hewitt Fellowship all right, she said, and it's tenable only in Cambridge, and so that's where you'll be for three years after you graduate. And that's where I'll go before you, to prepare a place for you. Entreat me not to leave thee, or to return from following after thee, for where thou goest will I go and where thou lodgest will I lodge—I give you Ruth's pledge. Right, mate?

Right mate, flatmate, bedmate, soul's mate, first mate. And only mate.

And so she went before me to that honoured place.

To Ur of the Chaldees.

For Cambridge meant about as much to me as that. No. A good deal less, to be truthful.

And in short—I was afraid?

Well, no, I was not afraid, but I did not go after her.

Why?

I put love aside at that crucial moment in my life and I put career first. I put schoolteaching first. Let me strike a posture—just for a change, I hear you say!—and suggest to you that this was the supreme sacrifice for me. I lost a wife and what would have been, I am sure, a family, upon fortune's wheel. And for what? I have lost a career as well. Fortune's wheel is ever turning and we have not the gift to see ahead into the future. At the time I simply asked myself that if I were to pursue a career in Scottish schools, of what possible use would be three years spent in Cambridge? I was already supplied with all I needed for the task of pedagogy. What need any delay? Ah, but the prestige, the glamour, the reputation, the jobs! To say you'd been to Cambridge! One factor, quite apart from the reality that there was no professional need for me to accept the Fellowship, made me question its worth. Cranford was there! On the strength of his gift of the gab. And a string or two, nothing else. How many others were like him? Ingenuous, of course, but my mind ran along such lines. The real problem was Jenny. What to do, what to do? I decided to ask the opinion of the man who, above all others, had determined my future: Mackay Mackay. I crept fearfully back to Fife and put it to him.

He asked me only one question.

'What does your instinct tell you to do?'

My instinct spoke very loudly in the matter.

Life, as Milton said before me, in a great many words, is a matter of choices.

Jenny could not see it any other way but that I had betrayed her. Perhaps it was partly out of heartbreak and resentment, a touch of loneliness too, perhaps, that she began to go out with Cranford, a sentimental link with our mutual past. He was resitting in '67 when Jenny appeared in Cambridge, and re-sitting again in '68 when that hard mishap doomed the gentle swain, the gentle swain being with another filly at the time, as I must remind you.

Poor chap—I can say that now—he must not float upon his watery bier unwept and welter to the parching wind, without the meed of some melodious tear. Go on then, sister of the sacred well—marry the bastard. Take pity on him, Jenny, for pitee renneth sone in gentil herte, as I have made known to you. And Jenny was nothing if not noble-hearted. Generous to a fault, to the nth fucking degree. She did pity him. She stuck with it. She married the moron.

It is the stuff of fiction, isn't it? Would that it were! But after all we'd been through, Jenny and I, and after all I have told you about Cranford, you must be asking yourselves just how in the name of all that is holy and unholy, reasonable and unreasonable, could a girl like Jenny marry a man like Cranford. Believe me, I asked myself the same question. Many times. Naturally she had been hurt to the marrow by my decision and must have taken a grim satisfaction in thus committing marital and emotional suicide. It was rubbing her own face in the dirt and making me feel ashamed, I suppose. She knew what I thought of Cranford. But perhaps I'm being wildly uncharitable. I think you have to bear in mind the immediate circumstances. Jenny was a nurse, you see – and Cranford was whipped into the very hospital where she was working at the time. She looked after him herself, he came to depend on her, they talked of the old days, the old crappy violins, she was sorry for him, and it went on from there, I don't exactly know, do I, not being bloody well there? Anyway at the time I believe it was thought possible that they might manage a minor miracle with his mangled parts, cobble something together—you know, graft on a donkey's dick or something. But as time went by that hope faded. As a matter of fact I suspect Jenny knew he could never produce. Otherwise I can't imagine she would have gone ahead and married him. A child to Cranford was probably where she would have drawn the precise line of conjugal self-immolation. But she sacrificed herself in another way, poor girl, by entering on a life of childlessness, she whose instincts were so tender, and who had told me in a field of buttercups that she wanted a baby. My baby. That made me feel conscience-stricken, I can tell you. And when I heard the news of their marriage, a little golden light inside me flickered briefly and went out. O, we should be careful of each other, we should be kind, not fuck each other up. I had fucked up the best thing I ever had, and I knew it. The years to come seemed waste of breath.

That was in 1969. I had spent a year or two after my graduation pursuing my craft and sullen art, had published a slim volume of verses (no worse than many thereof) to which I had proudly given the authorial name of Campbell Mackay and was now training to be a schoolteacher at Moray House College of Education.

Which I shall pass over with the contemptuous disregard it deserves.

When George Bernard Shaw coined his famous witticism—that those who can, do, those who can't, teach, and those who can't teach, teach teachers—he got the first and third parts of his proposition correct. The error in the dismissive middle part consists in his failure to acknowledge the genius that goes into good teaching and the fact that teaching itself is an art form which many of 'those who can' simply lack the talent to practise. Shaw fails to distinguish between everyday educators—they that but teach bloody instructions—and the true teachers: a different breed entirely. But the dear old boy surely hit the nail most soundly on the head the third time. And, as no less a person than the Princess herself, in *Love's Labour's Lost*, thinks fit to say, *to teach a teacher ill beseemeth me*, the words should most certainly be arched in lead (but not in gold) over the dismal portals of Moray House.

By the time I enrolled there I had moved to Edinburgh and had taken a top flat in the Lawnmarket at the Castle end of the High Street, from where I dawdled down to the bottom of the Royal Mile each day to be taught how to teach by a tribe of wankers who had been too long out of the classroom and not long enough there in the first place—some of them never, I suspect. Fucking Florentines, as Iago might have said, that never set a squadron in the field and relied on their bookish theoric for effect. Mere prattle without practice was all their soldiership—the nadir of these nonentities being the sociology lecturers with their flow diagrams, their class plans and their reels of irrelevant statistics. Parts of the course did possess some inherent interest, mind you, such as the history of education, for example, always accepting that a knowledge of Spartan schooling, however fascinating in itself, would scarcely have proved likely to help you run your own schoolroom. But after the fire and water of school and university, I found the sodden clay of training college to be both intellectually degrading and a grim waste of time.

And I'm ashamed to say that in order to anaesthetise the awfulness of that sorry year, I threw in my lot with the pissheads. The drinking that took place then was of a different kind and quality from the university carousing which had been liberally laced with purposeful conviviality and spiked with the intellectual optimism of revellers who knew they were but breaking off the stately saraband of learning in order to dance a Bacchanalian dithyramb or two and please the learned Hermes with their cries. The Moray House drinking was of a more dogged type. It had a melancholy inexorableness about it that was almost sober. Gone was the ready belly laughter of our student days, replaced by what I can only describe as a kind of desperate glee, a determination to dowse the bleak flames of Hades with a steady flow of strong drink.

Putting it bluntly, we were in danger of becoming alcoholics. One or two of our circle certainly were so by the time the year ended and I think I must have just crept through by the skin of my teeth. Either God or the Devil—on second thoughts I believe an agreement was struck between them—must have so arranged matters that Moray House training college stood at the very bottom of a long line of pubs, from the 'Ensign Ewart' on the high ground to 'The Snuff Box' lower down. It was hard to make one's way to college without stopping off at one or another of these taverns, with the frequent result that the sojourn lasted all day—all day and all night too, i' faith. 'The World's End', 'The Allan Ramsay', 'The Blue Blanket' became our homes from home, our Lichfield, our Chatham, our Eastcheap, our Boar's Head. And of other anonymous howffs in that inebriate mile, one or more was not without its Mistress Quickly and, more to the prick o' the matter, its Doll Tearsheet too, to whom a man could say in his beer, I prithee, good Doll, do not speak like a death's head, bid me not remember mine end, bid me goodnight instead, and in thine own bed, sweet Doll—as indeed she would. And did. Unless of course she had a prior engagement. But for the price of a few drinks her time could be bought and a wakeful scholar could say goodnight to her all through the night as often as he wished. Goodnight, good Doll, goodnight, goodnight, for this life (a life intellectually and emotionally empty) is such unsweet sorrow that I shall say goodnight till it be morrow. Goodnight then, Doll, goodnight, Dame O Come Quickly, goodnight Ophelia, goodnight, dear Jenny, goonight Lil, goonight Lu. Goodnight, ladies, goodnight, sweet ladies, goodnight, goodnight.

Goodnight.

The drinking, as I have said, accompanied by a little mild whoring, was a rather desperate and morose affair, designed to keep us semi-comatose throughout the miserable desert of this year.

In which there were but two oases. One was teaching practice itself; the other was the College Dramatic Society's production of *King Lear*, for which I was auditioned and, being nothing if not an actor—thank you, kind darlings,—cast for the part of Edgar, who, as you know, plays a part within a part in the middle of the play. Right up my street.

It was while rehearsing *Lear* that I first met Gladstone MacLeod and Leroy Vintner.

The chap playing Oswald broke his leg outside 'Jingling Geordie's' and as we were pretty close to the first night, the college producer called upon a seasoned thespian who had suffered under the Moray House regime in years gone by, had taught for a score of years or more, and had frequently returned to help out in terms when acting talent in the college was thin on the ground.

A ton of man was Gladstone John MacLeod—no, don't even ask me about the first name God gave him—Falstaff with a cigarette holder, Sir John in his crimson leather boots, Jack in a polo neck sweater and gold medallion, and Falstaffian in all his habits save for wenching. Gentlemen's refreshment, as he called it, was his chief pleasure—beer's for expanding my tum, women a pain in the bum—and when called upon to sup up and move smartly along to rehearsals for fear of the producer's gathering wrath, would settle himself even more firmly in his chair and content himself with the rhetorical query, delivered in his marshmallow voice,—Shall I not take mine ease in mine inn?

He came strolling on stage one night, puffing at a Black Sobranie in its holder and reaching out his hand warmly.

'Gladstone MacLeod, old chap—but middle name's John, if you prefer. Teach English and History at Robert Blair's up there— ' (jerking his thumb through the proscenium in the vague direction of Arthur's Seat). 'Hear you're coming to land on us for a while.'

'Not as far as I know,' I said, surprised by the news. 'I haven't been told—

'Oh, that's neither here nor there, old fruit. Tell you nothing, these bastards. Lists arrived at the school—saw them this morning. You'll be with us the second half of next term. Looking forward to seeing you. Ah! Here's my ancient, trusty, drouthy crony, Monsieur Le Roi—who's going to prompt, but don't you believe it.'

And on swanned his friend and colleague in the English Department of Blair's, Leroy Vintner, another elaborately bowing thespian with the remover cream ever about his ears and—as he himself made confession—liable to pull on a pair of tights to go to work. In absent-minded error, of course, old boy—fear me not, fear me not! His physique, it seemed, had marked him out to play Sir Andrew Aguecheek to Gladstone's Sir Toby, Shallow to his portly colleague's Sir John. An act they frequently performed in their frequent cups.

I was introduced and I asked why I shouldn't believe the bit about his prompting.

'You have heard of fools who came to scoff and remained to pray, I take it?' Leroy inquired of me.

'Goldsmith—*The Deserted Village*,' I answered.

Leroy leapt back a full two paces with greatly exaggerated surprise and, whipping out his handkerchief and holding it by the corner, performed a fluttering Restoration bow.

'O wise young judge! How much more elder art thou than thy looks! O upright young man! Well, learned Theban, perchance I should say, I am that one who often came to prompt but remained to *play*!'

I ventured my opinion, based soundly on having possessed thirty seconds of his acquaintance, that therein lay his greater strength.

'O excellent young scholar! Come, good Athenian, you'll blow the froth off a pint o' mine afore we speak a single line o' blank verse!'

And he took me by the arm, Gladstone thirstily following, and propelled me vigorously in the direction of 'The Blue Blanket.'

Leroy did indeed end up on stage instead of in the wings. He played brother Edmund on alternate nights, pronouncing himself infinitely superior by nature if not by art to my Tuesday-Thursday bro., who, he said, was clearly much less of a bastard.

'Come on Wednesday and Friday, good people,' he roared up and down the Royal Mile, 'if you wish to see the greater bastard!'

The play was an astonishing success. Every tosspot in our year seemed to be up on stage at some point in that week, each playing his part in order to dull the pain of living. My worst moment came on the Saturday night of the final performance when, after killing Oswald/Gladstone with a hefty sword, I had to remove from his pouch Goneril's letter to Edmund, the evidence of her murderous adultery. As is the custom of the stage, this parchment-like square of material was kept blank, the lines of the message being written only on the walls of my remembering brain. It was with the greatest difficulty therefore that I kept myself from giggling at this dramatic moment in the play, as I prepared to read the letter to the audience. Gladstone had scrawled across it in large letters: Up yours, Edgar—and fuck the Pope!

An ungracious paper indeed, I complained to him afterwards as he stood at the celebratory party, puffing gold-tipped cheroots and sipping champagne.

'Not to worry, old bean—you got through. Now drink up that bubbly and make wanton the night with it. 'Tis our only drink, *n'est-ce-pas*, Monsieur Le Roi?'

'Oh, là, sir! But of course, sir! You overpower me with good breeding, sir! How well you know your wine, sir! Water is for beasts, milk for babies, tea for women, beer for Germans—but wine is the drink of the gods.'

'And,' added Gladstone, 'wine is the poetry of water—and champagne is the poetry of wine.'

We all ended up on the floor.

When I saw Gladstone and Leroy again they had assumed the perpendicular and were looking very upright indeed as they sailed along the corridors of Robert Blair's College, resplendent in their academic gowns.

When Gladstone had jerked his large thumb in the direction of Blair's College, he was indicating an establishment quite as imposing in its topographical situation as it had been in its comparatively brief educational history: brief, that is, in comparison with the rest of the famous Edinburgh schools, but celebrated nevertheless. Glorious things of thee are spoken, Robbie's, City of the Crags! There is little need for me to waste time in telling you about your own school, dear boys, its stupendous location, its soaring magnificence, its glittering façades. God knows you have heard it often enough, right down to the roots, through thirteen Founder's Days. Except that custom hath made it in you a property of easiness.

Colonel Robert James Blair, returning from the Crimea in 1854 to a tidy inheritance and with a soldier's newly inherited predilection for rolled cigarettes, decides to combine business with pleasure, and out of his spiralling tobacco enterprises comes the bequest that will, after his death in 1881, found and build your very own Robert Blair's. (Ironic, isn't it, boyos, that we pedagogues spend half our waking existences invading the school bogs to stop you smoking, when if truth were faced, all our hope on the weed itself was founded. Quite literally. Who will be the first educational philanthropist, I wonder, to build on the great French Letter industry? Not Condor but *Condom* College, *Playsafe* not Players, *Virgin* as opposed to Virginia.) A curious coincidence too that the building itself went up five years later, completed in the very same year as Taft Academy, 1886: twin towers of learning and castles of the foam, overlooking the Forth from different sides.

What you must understand, however, is the impression first made on me, (a little old country boy), by the sheer physical presence of this exalted establishment and its situation, every inch matching its academic reputation. Untravelled as I was in my youth, geographically immobilised and socially circumscribed, and with the morning train trundling north from Edinburgh seeming to me to be emerging in primordial steam from the other side of the world—I could hardly fail to be struck by Robert Blair's College as a distant and awesome image of that mighty world. After all, what does he see who stands on the Fife side of the firth and lets his eye travel along the horizon from east to south? He sees—across the gull's way and the highly irregular whale's way—the crenellated cliffs of the May Island, the growling hump of the Bass Rock, and the Euclidean apex of Berwick Law: a castle, a pyramid and a bear, all blue with distance on the skyline; then, coming south now, the rolling whalebacks of the Pentland Hills, coursing through time, and, crouched in their contours, static, statuary, fabulous, the blue beast of the southern skyline, Edinburgh's Acropolis, Arthur's Seat, all highly charged images to the impressionable and insular adolescent eye.

The crowning glory of the prospect was undoubtedly Blair's.

The engineering feat which had placed it on the Salisbury Crags, to tower over Edinburgh even loftier than Arthur's Seat itself, was perhaps no more remarkable than those performed by the medieval masons, who stuck castles on crags if kings waved their cheque books (or their truncheons, or anything else you care to name) and built on slopes steeper than Salisbury's by a long chalk. What gave Blair's its particular magic, for me, was not only the sovereignty of its setting, as I have described it to you from the Skinfasthaven side, but its architectural splendour, towers, turrets and delicate spires, all soaring skywards in a dreamy Gothicism that intoxicated the imagination and adumbrated the most hectic extravaganzas of Walt Disney, whilst remaining tasteful and somehow, amazingly, real. Tangible yet chimerical, like the Castle of the Green Knight as seen by Sir Gawain on that fateful Christmas Eve when a warm winecup, a winter wager and a woman's wiles (forgive the passing influence of the 14th century alliterative revival there) stepped in suddenly between him and a brutal beheading, early in the cold New Year. It seemed like a dream.

There was nothing dream-like about Robert Blair, whose Aberdonian ancestry inspired him, as you know, to have the school built entirely of granite, hewn from Rubislaw and shipped and railroaded here at enormous expense. Long before I saw the combined effects of sun and rain on my old university city, I watched it on Blair's from the other side of the water, through my grandfather's old spyglass—and was entranced. O, how that glittering taketh me, as dear old Herrick said! These sparkling spires under which I speak even now, they were like ringed fingers beckoning unto me from over the firth. And when the sun rose over the sea at the start of a clear day, it highlighted that other remarkable feature of Blair's: its myriad windows. They took fire with the dawn and set a morning star over Edinburgh to nurture a dream. Looking out across here from the tower of Taft Academy one morning during a period of practical mathematics, Mr Peter Periwinkle had pointed over the dancing white acres of waves and said to us, 'Robert Blair's College: a star for seamen. Tackle your trigonometry and you could arrive at it, teach there some day. Some hope.' The rest, as they say, is history, my personal history. That was the dream and you are the reality. Whacko. To be honest, though, it was not a dream that meant anything to me at the time. I never really *meant* to come here at all. Like most things in life, it just happened.

When I did arrive in Edinburgh and saw Blair's for the first time, from the south side with the eye of the city dweller, I was even more awe-struck. In fact I was intimidated by its pinnacled prominence and its multi-windowed grandeur, so close at hand: a castle of academic excellence, far out-soaring the grumpy solidity of Edinburgh's other famous castle. The one was of the earth, earthy, brooding over the city: the other reached into the elements of air and fire and unseen Promethean heat. I looked at it and instantly thought of Lachlan Campbell's favourite line from Tennyson: *On the hills like gods together, careless of mankind*. And I said, ye shall be as gods. Gods with intestines, though, as my trembling bowels affirmed. Picture if you will, dear hearers (forgiving the Charles Lamb tone and the Arthur Marshall inflexion)—picture if you will a young man of twenty-four, new to the notion of schoolmastering in the city and not well acquainted with it either, gazing up in expectant dread at this august edifice as it stood perched majestically on its crags, like some impregnable fortress of old time, a Krak des Chevaliers of learning and thinking, 'God help me—I'm actually going to have to walk in there on Monday morning and teach!'

As teach I did.

The men (mostly) who taught here twenty years ago and more were of a breed who knew there was but one way to train a student to be a teacher and that was to let the poor bastard teach. This was the determined view of the then Head of the English Department. When I walked into his classroom on my first morning, I saw a short stocky gentleman, red-faced and monocled, with a white handlebar moustache, who looked every inch a stage soldier. I was convinced I'd strayed straight into the school dramatic society and was impressed by the standard of the make-up. It looked real.

It was real.

I introduced myself.

'Colonel Stubbes,' he replied shortly. 'So you want to be a teacher, yes?'

I agreed that this seemed to be the general idea behind my being there at that particular moment.

'Very well then—teach.'

And he thrust an open book into my hand and glared at the class.

'You are now about to be taught by a young man who wishes to learn how to teach. I have only one word to say to you: cooperate. No, three words: cooperate, or else!'

I stared at the book. It was *Oliver Twist*. Colonel Stubbes had opened it at Chapter Ten, the scene in which Oliver sees the Dodger remove Mr Brownlow's pocket handkerchief and is then himself pursued, innocent victim as he is, by a vengeful crowd, screaming 'Stop thief!'

My first tack was to try vocabulary, a simple expedient when the teacher is not sure what to say or cannot be bothered to think. I asked the class the meaning of the word 'expatiate' in the second paragraph.

'They won't know!' snapped the colonel, who was sitting in the corner, grimacing. He rose from his seat and stormed at the intent faces.

'And why won't they know? Because they don't *read*, do they? Don't take dictionaries to bed with 'em, as I used to do, keeping myself pure for the army, my only mistress, throughout the long winter nights. And what do they take to bed with them instead?'

The answer came in deafening unison from thirty delighted fresh male faces of the first year.

'Girls!'

'Girls, *sir*!' roared the colonel.

'Girls—yes *sir*!' came the multi-voiced response.

It was clearly an oft rehearsed scene and I was amazed to see how quickly the class and the colonel had apparently changed their mood and personality. But Colonel Stubbes had not yet finished.

'No, they don't really take girls to bed with them, Mr Mackay—I simply feed their perverted little lusts. They'd like to, mind you, but they wouldn't dare, would you?'

'No, sir!'

No, sir. (The colonel was off.) So they take dirty magazines instead and read them under the blankets. Magazines which they daren't buy in Princes Street for fear of discovery and swift nemesis, but which the boarders buy abroad when they fly out to see their old colonial folks.—You weesh to buy feelthy book, sahib? Or you weesh to buy my leetle seester instead? And naturally it's got to be the filthy book, hasn't it? Even their gin-sodden maters and paters would draw the line at twelve-year-old concubines—too young for conkers yet, my lads—and they can't bring those sort of conkers back here to Blair's now, can they? They'd be spotted, don't you know? Subtle differences and all that. So they have to make do with picture books of the naughty sort and they gawp at them all night long when they should be studying Dickens and dictionaries and such like educational publications, with the result that when they come in here of a morning they're too damned shagged out and sleepy to answer questions, aren't you? Even supposing you knew the blasted answers in the first place, which you don't, do you?

The class was one huge grin. They obviously loved him, knew it was all an act, and went along with him for the fun of it.

'You'll find they'll be more receptive now,' whispered the colonel to me on his way back to his seat in the corner.

And so they were.

Colonel Stubbes interrupted me only once more. When I reached the chase sequence I asked how many had seen the film of the book and whether they felt that they'd rather see the chase on moving celluloid or read it in print, bearing in mind the relative merits and demerits of visual and verbal effects.

'I should think they'd much prefer to see the film, Mr Mackay. At least during a film they'd not have to answer bloody awkward questions like that!'

He chortled and his eyes twinkled. I carried on.

At the end of the lesson, after the class had filed out, Colonel Stubbes advised me.

'Don't bore the backsides off them with the right approach—the Moray House approach. Not to begin with. Forget all that, it'll come after you've got them on your side. But to get them on your side in the first place you've got to perform—and go on performing.'

Then to my surprise he shook me warmly by the hand and told me that he thought I had actually done pretty well. Still holding my hand firmly and looking me straight in the eye, he said this.

'You strike me as a fine young chap—intelligent, gifted, and with great potential. A natural for the classroom. Take my advice, will you? Don't come into teaching!'

I asked him why.

Because you'll be despised. Not by your pupils—they won't despise you. But those who make their way to the top of the profession, over your more talented head—they'll despise you all right, for being the mug who stays in the classroom and teaches for drawing-pin money, instead of going for the bigger money and status got by those who count your drawing-pins *for* you. Not that you actually need them counted, mind you—but administrators have a different view, naturally. Make no mistake about it, the only way forward in the teaching profession is outside the classroom. That's where respect is going to be found, in a very short time from now. Time was it was the man inside the classroom who earned the respect. That had a long run but it's just about over. You're a born teacher. As such you'd be a king in your own room, but you'd be a pawn for the jackals of the trade, and you mark my words, the jackals are on the move. In another generation there won't be any real teachers left. Coffee?

There ended the first lesson.

Colonel Stubbes took me along to the staffroom, where several old buffers sat around, dwarfed by their moss-green hairy tweeds and enveloped in skeins of blue tobacco smoke as they puffed their old pal pipes and cracked jokes out of Catullus. A monastic hum pervaded the place. The air was heavy with irony. I recognised the scene at once, of course. It was a fee-paying version of Taft Academy, an exclusive club of pedagogic eccentrics. The fact that money changed hands between the pupils' parents and the school's governing council was an educational irrelevance, a socio-economic matter about which people could argue forever on the élitist or the anti-élitist side as a matter of political principle—or the lack of it, dependent on your point of view: in much the same way as the debating insect divided the animal kingdom into cruel, bloodthirsty creatures such as ducks and hens, and noble, peaceful beings such as lions and tigers, again much according to its point of view. The fact remains that money cannot generate intelligence, act as a substitute for study, or indeed buy or create a superior teaching talent. It came to me in a flash how privileged I had been to have schooled at Taft Academy, where the Dannies and the Goofs and the Fat Boys proliferated, drawn there in the first instance perhaps by the relative smallness of the school itself and its enviable situation, cupped in the quiet palm of the East Neuk and serving a breed whose lives and outlooks were determined by the rhythms of land and sea. It was a privilege which had not cost my parents a single penny.

As I looked around the staffroom I formed the immediate notion that here was a place where I myself could happily teach. At the far end a wiry saturnine looking fellow was making his way round and under one of the large tables purely by means of his hands, his feet never touching the floor. The strength in his arms was clearly considerable. His movements were being closely monitored by several of his colleagues, their heads in solemn conclave, the stem of a pipe occasionally jabbing in the wiry fellow's direction as he negotiated a corner like an inverted squirrel. The wiry fellow's own pipe was still in his mouth and once he paused on one hand only, his entire frame at rest on a single arm, in order to remove the pipe and examine the condition of its bowl. This was carried out purely for effect and the desired result was easily obtained: loud and sustained cheers and applause from the greybeards who in a few minutes' time would be off gravely—or perhaps hilariously—teaching Latin and Greek to their pupils. I was reminded of Lachlan Campbell's victorious assaults upon the lampshades.

'Henry Archibald,' commented Colonel Stubbes, passing me a cup of coffee.' Teaches German.'

He seemed to think that no other comment was really required.

I asked what he was doing.

'Oh, that . . . demonstrating pressure holds, that's all. Goes round and underneath his classroom table just like that when the kids are getting restless. That quietens 'em down no end.'

'Why should that quieten them?' I asked.

The colonel gave me a bleakly sympathetic look.

'Would you relish the thought of six of the best from a man with arms like Archibald?'

I admitted I had been rather slow to appreciate the point.

'He doesn't even have to give the belt any more—clever sod!'

Henry Frederick Archibald. Mountaineer extraordinaire. Cycled into Glencoe when he was thirteen and climbed Buchaille Etive Mor by himself. One would have to know little about mountains not to appreciate the point of that, taken in conjunction with the fact that he then biked it to Torridon and climbed the Liathach ridge on the same day. Bagged every Munro before he was eighteen. Dawdled across the Alps one winter, went lightly armed up Annapurna the following summer, came back to Scotland, rubbed his hands and said, 'Fie upon this quiet life, I want work!' Decided upon schoolmastering as an appropriate challenge. Known to the pupils as Drak—not so much for his Transylvanian scowl as for his legendary ascents of the Salisbury Crags without rope or pitons, and one famous occasion when, using only fist-jams between the ancient stones, he climbed the front wall of the school to gain access to a colleague's room, from which that colleague had been locked out by an unruly class one hot summer. Appeared through the open window, pipe in teeth, of course, and said calmly, 'Now I'm going to beat you.' Which he did. Six each to the entire class. One hundred and eighty of the belt. Since when he decided to go in for pressure holds round the table, he said—much less strenuous.

Master of the *mot juste*, Henry Archibald possessed the power to emasculate a pupil or a colleague with laconic relish. Once during my period of training, a particularly effete young man with a mouthful of Oxford marbles had just given his colleagues the umpteenth demonstration of his pusillaniminity. Henry F. turned to me, took his pipe from his mouth, scowled, and said, 'Do you think he dresses himself?'

Before I could answer the rhetorical question, he asked me another.

'You're hoping to be an English teacher, aren't you?'

I confirmed his suspicion.

'What's anacoluthon?'

I gave the answer.

'And what is the word 'lift' when it's a noun and has nothing to do with portering or transportation?'

I told him that it was related to the German word for sky and that it appeared substantively in one of the Scottish ballads.

'You've been well taught and are well read,' growled the pipe, 'or perhaps you are just lucky.'

Then he asked me, 'What are the last words of *Love's Labour's Lost?*'

'You that way: we this way.'

'Hm, some people get the this and that the wrong way round. Actually I meant the words just before that final exeunt.'

'The words of Mercury are harsh after the songs of Apollo.'

The pipe puffed for a few seconds in silence.

Then—'You'll do,' it said, and the man behind the pipe held out his hand.

'Henry F. Archibald.'

'I know,' I said. 'I've heard all about you.'

'Well—it's all true,' he snarled, and got up to go.

Halfway to the door he turned back.

'You wouldn't happen to know the German for "conical flask", would you?'

I shook my head.

'Pity—I'll have to go and look up the dictionary. Don't like being defeated.'

At the door he turned again.

'On second thoughts, thank God for that! I was beginning to think you're cleverer than I am. You're not. But you'll do.'

And he disappeared in a puff of smoke.

Henry Frederick Archibald.

In my five weeks at Blair's, observing the teaching of Colonel Stubbes, Gladstone MacLeod and Leroy Vintner, I learned enough about teaching to last me the rest of my career. Everything since then has been polishing up from the inside, nothing more.

When teaching *Naming of Parts* the colonel appeared in full uniform and brandishing an army rifle, with which he demonstrated the weapon's parts and their functions according to the poem, and, when not receiving a satisfactory answer from a pupil, firing off a blank straight at him, as it were, to the delight of the rest of the class.

'The boy left alive at the end of the lesson gets to keep the rifle!' he bellowed.

By the end of the poem he had shot the entire class.

'Trouble with that is,' he said, 'the buggers know it's harmless.'

Next day he arrived carrying a javelin, armed for parts of speech.

'Now boy!' he thundered, 'parse or die!'

And he drew back his arm, the muscles of his face and eye assuming every sign of carrying out the threatened intention if the correct answer did not come forth. The primitive nakedness of the gesture with steel was considerably more alarming than the rifle shots

Colonel Stubbes had one basic tenet: never stick to the point. That was for instructors, that was for bores. Digression is the stuff of teaching. Literature itself is full of it. Just look at Dickens. Even the classical Milton was carried away by it. What are the best bits of *Paradise Lost*? The wonderful epic similes which interrupt and inlay the poem itself with a myriad little vignettes of life: the whale slumbering on the Norway foam, mistaken by the pilot of the small, night-foundered skiff for a restful island, anchor fixed in ignorance in the scaly rind as he moors by his side, under the lee, and night invests the sea and wished-for morn delays; the Tuscan artist studying the moon through optic glass from the top of Fesole, or in Valdarno to descry new lands, rivers and mountains in her spotty globe; and angel forms that lay entranced, thick as autumnal leaves that strow the brooks in Vallombrosa, a multitude like which the populous north poured never from her frozen loins to pass the Rhine or the Danube, when her barbarous sons came like a deluge on the south and spread beneath Gibraltar to the Libyan sands. Or bees in springtime when the sun with Taurus rides—or faery elves whose midnight revels by a forest-side or fountain some belated peasant sees, or dreams he sees, while moonlight laves his pale spellbound face and joy and fear co-mingled invade his heart. For a book about heaven and hell, what a marvellous variety of actual life it contains—and so it should be with teaching. One must always be digressing, dear Sancho, and, when not digressing, alluding and comparing. Metaphor is the key to teaching, as it is the soul of literature, and metaphor *is* digression: a sudden window on another world, allowing you intellectual egress, emotional exit for the moment, but making you think again about what is in the room. Even as I say *that*, I use metaphor, the honey that I generate, the sticky, true virtue of my trade. There I go again.

The colonel prized Gladstone and Leroy above all his department and allocated me to their classes for the bulk of my time at Blair's. Leroy psyched himself up for each lesson, holding the class at the door for a few seconds at the start of the period while he ascended his podium and declaimed the opening lines of *O, for a Muse of fire.'* to an empty classroom, sometimes delivering the entire speech to the rows of desks. He then gave a little Laurence Olivier cough and ushered in his audience, to whom he played with every ounce of his undoubted intellectual and emotional energy. It was a constant giving on his part.

'By the end of the day,' he said to me, 'if you're not shagged out, you haven't been teaching properly, you've only been talking. That's no good.'

From his pupils he expected a high return.

Come on, you useless bloody lot—you look like a pile of frozen turds on a frosty morning! Let's have some life about you! No? All right then, there's only one answer—touch a tree!

Yes, that's right, watch my lips and you'll see what I'm saying, go on everybody, touch a tree and come back, but don't come back here until you've touched one, every single one of you! Now go! Now!

The class shot out of the desks to a man and sprinted down the corridors. We stood at the window and watched them running down into Hunter's Bog, across Holyrood Park.

Nearest tree six hundred yards, laughed Leroy. Who hath measured the ground? (parenthetical imitation of the Constable of France) And it's a long haul back uphill. That gives us ten minutes for coffee and by the time they're back here the little buggers will at least have some oxygen round their mouldering brains. They'll also be ponging at the armpits but there's always a price to pay if you want something out of the punters.

I watched him string along a class of moderately intelligent fifth formers for an entire period by developing a theory that Hamlet's friend, Horatio, was really a medieval Irishman in disguise. This took its rise from the opening line of Hamlet's sixth soliloquy, when the hero is just preparing to stab the praying Claudius in the back, and whispers fervently to this Viking Dubliner who is hiding in the wings, 'Now might I do it, *pat*, now he is praying!'

Leroy's performances were deliberately heightened. Gladstone's were looser and lower key, more inclined in the direction of intellectual buffoonery. His pupils were not fooled, though: they were well aware of the penetrating mind and astonishing fund of knowledge that were so carelessly disguised by the big joviality of the man, his easy wit and bubbling laughter. I attended some of his history lessons too, which were brought alive with typical Gladstonian unorthodoxy when the first years made Iron Age villages out of dried grass and unused matchsticks, which the second years, as Viking marauders, were then allowed to burn down—a quick practical lesson then following on the methods of the early Fire Fighting Service and why they were unsatisfactory! The entire operation was filmed and played back the following week, the illusion marred only by several leering faces and V-signs thrust in front of the camera. Gladstone refused to have these edited out on the grounds that they actually added to the realistic presentation of the Vikings' unmannerly ferocity.

Oh, naturally I highlight the dotty features, the mad moments, the many eccentricities that characterised the atmosphere of the place—and I do so to let you understand how much at home I felt in this highly civilised asylum, whose teaching inmates had long since discarded sanity as society's long sleep and the badge of boredom. They knew by instinct, as the men and women of Taft had known, that in order to go forward dynamically one must leave the educational treadmill and foot it featly and more than a little foolishly at times. Otherwise the process of learning becomes a sterile circle of handing out information, a constant passing the parcel to dulled minds that will pass it on again and keep on passing it on with ever decreasing enthusiasm to the next generation until there is no longer any joy left in learning and a race of dullards inherits the earth.

But in those days there *were* giants on the earth, as the Scriptures tell us, and I have mentioned but a few of them. Were I to go through the entire staff of the establishment as it then was, I should have to compose another *Lament for the Makars* in order that I might catalogue that loss. And with some justification too. For the Middle Scots word for poet is a perfect translation of the Greek *poietes*—*poieein*, to create, to make. A true teacher must be a poet. A poet of his craft.

On the second last day of my teaching practice two things happened.

At morning coffee break the staffroom door burst open and a somewhat windswept character breezed in, quite literally stubbly with goodness. He had been around, that much one could see.

There was instant tumult.

Good God Almighty, it's old Stanislav! Shiver me phallic mainmast, me hearties, splice me bollocks, jolly jack tars, take care and batten your hatches, all ye fair Spanish ladies, the mad matelot's back! He'll board you—and down goes your topsails! Come in on deck, Stan—compass gone wonky, has it, that you've found your way back into this old port? Girl in every port and a bottle o' port in every girl . . .

These and many more nautical leg-pulls from a score of voices was my introduction to Stan Gorgerge (pronounced *Yoryerga*), a man of indeterminate nationality, but believed, genealogically speaking, to inhabit an ethnic area somewhere between Eastern Europe and Scandinavia. Not one to suffer fools gladly, Stan had finally lost the rag during an inspection of his department (Biology) the previous year and had left the room with the immortal words on his lips, 'Righto, Herr Inspektor, if you still know so much about teaching after twenty years out of the sodding classroom, you can do the sodding job for me—I'm sodding off!'

And sod off he did.

Out of the school gates and down the crags and down to Leith, and within five days had sold his flat and was sailing his beloved boat single-handed to South Africa. Amazingly, the Principal, a man of enlightenment and huge ability, had kept his job open for him, putting in an acting Head of Department on the understanding that the job would be temporary or otherwise depending on whether Stan embraced the sea or the sea Stan, for a season or for perperuity, betting heavily on the side of his safe and willing return.

'Let him get it out of his system—he was due for a blow-out in any case. He'll be fine when he comes back.'

Which he did on that very morning—to beg a bed in my Lawnmarket flat. Just until he got himself sorted out.

The second occurrence was that the oldest member of Colonel Stubbes's department announced his retirement at the end of the session. No sooner was this known than the colonel, together with Gladstone and Leroy, bore down upon me in a determined trio and would not let me go until I had promised to apply for the job.

As it happened I did not even have to apply for it.

'No point, is there?' boomed the Principal, who had asked to see me in his study. 'If there's one thing I can't be bothered with, it's these damn sham interviews when anyone with a brain in his head on the campus can see who the job's going to go to in any case. Sheer hypocrisy, putting short leeters through all that charade. No, when I know my man, that's it—and Colonel Stubbes always knows his. Which is good enough for me. Au revoir, my boy, see you after the summer—and welcome to Blair's!'

I left his study in a slight daze.

At the door he stopped me.

'Just one thing.'

He placed his hand very firmly on my shoulder and I felt the sheer strength of his grip.

'I don't think I have to say this to you, but I say it to all my staff, so I'll say it anyway. Education should be fun. The day you stop getting any fun out of teaching—get out.'

13

AND NOW I *am* getting out, dear boys, for the fun lasted only ten years, you see. After which decade the dram of eale was introduced which doth all the noble substance often dout to his own scandal, and Robert Blair's did, in the general censure, take corruption from that particular fault. The poisonous drop being that cretinous cipher, that ball-less nonentity, that one-legged clerk of works, Cranford. Came in 1980 and blighted my career, didn't he? Blighted the fucking school too.

But there I get ahead of myself again. Why do we wish our lives away as we do, forever posting on in spirit to the evil years, when a man shall say, I have no pleasure in them? Is not a decade of happiness worth a brief word or two?

Return again, Alpheus.

Stan Gorgerge stayed with me for the first of these years, the bed for the night having run to rather longer than either of us had anticipated. Neither of us regretted Stan's sojourn, though: we found we shared a mutual mistress in the sea, for the only lady in my life was now lost to me forever and the only woman in Stan's was his boat. He liked nothing better than to get inside her, oil her engine, get twenty knots out of her and let her take him to paradise and back and take six months about it, just the two of them—as he put it. We sat and drank late o' nights in the Lawnmarket and talked sea talk, Stan sleepily evoking the long white beaches of Africa like Hemingway's old philosopher of the sea.

Feel like taking off forever, old sport, sailing west of sunset, not come to land, world's a bloody disaster anyways, is that not so? going to get lot worse, lessyouanme, matey, lessyouanme take off in morning, cast off, nevvr comeback t'shore . . .

They wouldn't keep his post open a second time, I told him, and they wouldn't keep mine vacant at all. Only been in the job five minutes.

'In any case,' I said, 'you can't bloody well get up in the mornings. You'd never catch a tide these days.'

Getting Stan up in time for school was the morning version of a nightmare. I liked to be in at my desk at least an hour before the classes arrived, especially during the winter and well before sunrise, so that I might enjoy the sheer unspoiled serenity of the mornings—(the janitors going about the corridors like surgeons in their green wellie boots)—and take in the gorgeous views of the Forth from Blair's high windows. The trouble was that Stan drove a vintage banger, a dazzling display of chrome and wood and leather, which he insisted could easily have us in front of our first classes in five minutes flat—from the flat. Which meant not having to leave the house until 8.40. Which in turn meant not getting out of bed until 8.39, in Stan's case, and, more than once, climbing straight into trousers and jacket still wearing his striped pyjamas and putting on a tie with the pyjama top.

Not a problem is there, old son? Looks remarkably like a striped shirt to me—and I am close up to it. Nice blue and white, a little rumpled perchance, but sod it all, dear boy, what do they expect, I ask you, when we are batching it as we are? Not hitched up yet and no little lady to iron out the creases and all that.

'That's not what's worrying me,' I said. 'It's more the thought of all that foetid air trapped inside.'

Oh, bollocks to that, old man—have a swim second period. You ready then? Once more unto the teach, dear friend, once more!

No taming Stan. Even the sea could not tame him. He went his own way.

As soon as he was snoring his passage through the doldrums of his dreams (Can't stop dreaming about school, old boy—fancy having boring dreams!) I liked to lie back in my narrow little bed up in the gods—one of my chief pleasures in the world, this, as a matter of fact—lights out, window open, well on round the clock, listening to the sound of the night trains thundering in and out of Waverley Station a few hundred feet below. Did I forget to mention the glass of grog in my hand, put there by Stan? (Night, night, matey, see you in morning, but not at eight bells, if you please to be so kind!) Sipping some of Stan's Old Navy rum, semi-asleep, each little gulp of molasses and fire preventing my pillowed head from nodding off into the night, I imagined that I lay for hours and hours of hearing the trains, though I probably drifted in and out of only several minutes, minutes as large as haystacks, before finally blanking out for the night. But for these few minutes or hours or something in between, I used to derive enormous satisfaction, peopling the long lines of carriages with the travellers of my imagination.

Great thing about the imagination, as Coleridge knew more than anyone else—mining away underground with its secret lamp stuck to your head while the body slumbers on and never does a stroke. Anyway I used to imagine this little old lady travelling up north to catch the Inverness train in the morning, to chug her daintily all the way up to Thurso, from where she'd take the ferry to Orkney and be back among her islands and hens and webs of weather, having travelled down to Edinburgh to see her ninety year old sister cremated. Terrible goings-on these days, Orkney folk going to live in Edinburgh and folk burning folk there, just like in the days of the heathens, mercy me . . . And muttering her little frets to herself she'd get back to her croft to die and then completely forget what it was she got back for.

Sitting across from her was a tousle-haired university student, unshaven and swathed in his scarf. It was the next best thing to a poncho, which he couldn't afford, and in any case he wasn't Clint Eastwood, he was Rory Henderson or Hamish Stewart and he was going back to Dingwall for the weekend because his grant had run out and he was going to beg a little more subsistence from his folks, stretching their patient and much abused generosity by another few pounds. He had exams to come back to on Monday and the book in his hands was a torture to him. It was open at a passage on Grimm's Law. He was really concentrating hard on the question of whether he had made his girlfriend pregnant during their last intercourse in her flat. Through the dancing print telling him about the shifts from voiced to voiceless plosives and from voiceless plosives to voiceless fricatives he kept seeing and sensing the unexpected white flowering of his member and wondering if he had withdrawn it in time. For the seventy-seventh time he was counting days in his head. Yet he kept looking at the book. It would still be open at the same page as the fields and firths fled by and the train grumbled into Dingwall in a slow leaden dawn.

There were some oil-men, littering their carriage with cards and cans and oaths, fuck-you, fuck-me and big fucking money last year and fuck-all fucking money this year. No one else entered their carriage.

I don't know quite why the little Russian girl was on the train,

222

or where she had come from or was bound for, but she was always there, all right, smuggled in from Turgenev, perhaps, by my meandering mazy mind. Smothered in furs, Cossack-booted, muffed and dark-eyelashed, she was regarding icily the young Polish musician, who in turn fed hungrily with his romantic stare on the red red lips of the brocaded madamoiselle in the corner, her secret love-life winking behind her dreamy brow, lighting up the inside of her head in sudden flares and flashes as the train flitted in and out of tunnels.

You can see how it got out of hand, once sleep started to take over and controlling reason slumped down in his sentry box, letting the tribes of fancy run riot over me. But I didn't enjoy my actual dreams so much and still don't. It's like descending into the ungovernable sea, where frightening things gloom hugely, through your unconsciousness like Moray eels (or Moray *House* eels, even worse!) and do what they will with you, *to* you. No, I enjoyed those few hour-minutes or minute-hours just before sleep, when the very wheels of the trains ticked like tetrameters, each carriage a stanza, each coach a sonnet, pretty rooms built for pretty people, the whole train a poem, a sequence, a cycle, one moving north, one south, others to east and west and back again and round about, boxing the compass, the whole rail network of these islands a pulsating corpus of texts, British poetry from John o' Groat's to Land's End, the iron lines of the night alive with the literature of my head.

I was not a much travelled man, I need hardly remind you, but once or twice I had taken a night sleeper to London in my year or so between university and schoolteaching. It must have been to arrange something with a publisher. My narrow bed in the Lawnmarket flat reminded me rather of the bunk in the railway sleeper, and as I lay in the dark letting the sounds of the wheels carry me along, I could easily imagine I was aboard one of these sleepers again, being whisked through the night like a Pharaoh through the long tunnel of sleep, my beaker in my hand, my book of the dead by my side, into the next world . . .

I'd wake up with a dried sweet stain of sugar-cane sticking together the hairs of my chest where the last mouthful of rum had splashed from the glass, missing my sleeping mouth—and the glass itself on the floor, not rolling about, though, as I noticed with some surprise at first. The train must have stopped at the Lawnmarket. No, wait a minute, this *was* the Lawnmarket but it certainly wasn't a train and it certainly was time to get up. Stan! Occasionally I'd wake up with the glass of rum still clutched in my hand, not a drop spilt—or perhaps perched by itself on my breastbone, my chest still as a shelf, its owner having slept the sleep of the just.

I mention all this, using the past tense, because my capacity to wake and sleep in this fairly civilised fashion—a pretty basic thing, after all, sleep—is yet another casualty of the Age of Cranford. The false thane murdered sleep, didn't he? Show me the good teacher now who still knits up the ravelled sleave of care o' nights. He sleeps not in my bed, I can tell you!

Stan was a great sleeper. After he had left and found a flat of his own—precisely two floors beneath me, as it happened—I took to rising much earlier and running down the Royal Mile to work in tracksuit and trainers, in a conscious effort to re-attain that standard of fitness I had enjoyed under The Goof. It struck me that I'd spent seven years in an athletic wilderness and that the time had come to do something about it. Within a short time I had developed a much more exacting circuit than was really necessary: down the Mile, through Holyrood, up Arthur's Seat itself, sprinting up onto the haunch and so, over the spine and onto the leonine head, then, if time allowed, along the Radical Road, climbing slowly up the Salisbury Crags, just beneath the school, past Henry Archibald's Leap (!) smelling the toffee-scented whinflowers with the morning rain on them, newly washed gold, and so on round to the Hunter's Bog, climbing up again to bring me to the school gates further up the crags and a quick shower or swim before first period. Stan, who was physically as hard as nails, sometimes did come with me, but on the whole preferred the long lie and the slumberwear shirt for the day.

From these very windows here (I have had no cause to change rooms these past twenty years and more) I could command the stunning views that you are all so well used to by now: southwards across Edinburgh to where the Pentlands pause in a great frozen wave, white whales in winter, greenbacked in summer, stopping short of engulfing the city after all, and so on round the skyline to the borders and the southern hills—thence I looked towards England, and sweet Jenny, O, no more o' that, Master Shallow, no more o' that!—where I saw rain falling and RLS ghosting and the rainbow drawn on Lammermuir and hearkening, heard again, in that precipitous city, beaten bells winnow the keen sea-wind,

224

the wind itself turning with me eastwards and northwards then to look out over the white sea-horses flashing their manes in the Forth, and on a clear day to ascend the school tower and bring so close, *so* close through the observatory telescope that landmark which is but a faint full stop on the skyline to the naked eye—the answering tower of Taft Academy, catching the sun's fire and bouncing it back to me over the firth. Who could not teach well, given such a start to his day? Who could not have looked forward to a lifetime of teaching thus well? A giving back of what had been given, within this aerial view of the spire of the giver. A turning back into life of a great harvest, dreams happy as her day, and hearts at peace . . .

And in these circumstances I did indeed teach happily.

For ten good years.

And as I taught, I learned: from my pupils, from my colleagues, from myself—and each year ploughed back again what I'd learned into the next session's teaching. My objectives were very clear in my mind and I have made these clear unto you already. Suffice it to say, I felt myself to be continually handling and passing on with bright hands those live flames from the torches of my former teachers who themselves had carried out that action in relation to those who went before them, so that I experienced, burning within me, a fire that went back to Prometheus, and so to God.

I pinned up on my wall in my very first year the verse from *Ecclesiasticus* which all of you can still see there today. *And for some their daily work is their prayer.* From every lesson I taught there arose this narrow plume of spiritual smoke, a quiet feathering from the fire of my own academic offering to the Almighty. It did not mingle with the reek from the lums of old Edinburgh. It was invisible, intangible, but was, so I believed, scented by angels, who looked at it and said: Ah! that's a good period's work being done down there in Blair's. I can detect a little bit of heaven in that lesson, can't you, Gabriel? They'll never make that guy a Headmaster! Still, better to serve in heaven than reign in hell, what?

But though the spirit of the prayer never altered, the words were, by the same token, forever changing. For I can honestly say I never taught the same lesson twice. How could I? No man is the same person that he was one year ago. I have taught *Hamlet* twenty-five times, perhaps, in the course of my career, and have never failed to marvel at the different ethos of the play each time I inhabit it, disappear into it, to teach it to another generation, from the inside outwards. One thing that never alters in that play, though, and is the reason why I have continued to teach it, is its quality of enigma. It can never be brought under control, in just the same way as, thank God, we cannot civilise the sea. Hamlet's sea of troubles is the living mystery that is at the paradoxical heart of all humanity. The hero is the most mature person in the play—or the most immature; he is a teenager—or he is a grown man, or he is both, as Macbeth is both a milkman and a butcher. He is the life-force or he is the death-force, obsessed by eternity, death's pale ambassador stalking the castle walls, Elsinore's negative pole, destroying the positive, warm, comfortably corrupt and essentially human lives of the murderers, adulterers, intriguers, sycophants and shallow sensualists within. He cannot act because he is a manic depressive, a melancholic suffering a nervous breakdown. Or because he is in love with his mother. Or because he is suffering from some other psychoneurosis, sexual nausea or a panoply of related or semi-related complaints. Or because he is too sensitive and moral. Or because he is too callous and vengeful. Or because he is caught between conflicting codes of honour. Or because he has no proof. Or because he is crushed by a weight of difficulties, including the great mystery of life hereafter which he needs to understand in order to sift the evidence. Or because he is an irresolute intellectual who cannot make up his mind. Or because he is a character in a play whose creator has theatrical or psychological or psychic reasons for making the drama move along certain lines. Or because the play in which he appears is an unsatisfactory grafting onto the genre of older stock. Or because he is simply world-weary in the deepest possible sense: he has looked into the corrupt abyss of human life and has realised the futility of performing any act, has realised that the preacher's proposition is correct. *Vanitas vanitatum et omnia vanitas*. He has understood. And understanding has killed action. Paradoxically he has attained a form of freedom, like Pierre in *War And Peace*. A freedom of the mind and soul.

Teaching this play throughout my professional life, I have kept a passage from Tolstoy, as it happens, firmly in the forefront of my mind. It is about bees.

If a bee, Tolstoy says, stings a child, the youngster becomes afraid of bees and naturally concludes that the purpose of a bee is to sting children. The artist, however, with his poet's soul, loves to watch the bee sipping nectar from the chalices of flowers and satisfies himself that the purpose of a bee is to gather nectar for itself. The bee-keeper knows that this is only part of the truth because he has seen the bee carry away the pollen to its hive and his view is that a bee's purpose is to make honey, while one of his craft who has studied the life of the swarm more closely, argues that the bee collects pollen in order to feed the young bees and produce queens, thus continuing the species. Finally the botanist, observing the fact that a pollen-laden bee alighting upon the pistil of a flower happens to fertilise the plant, concludes that that is the ultimate purpose of the insect. Contemporary biologists would not, of course, think along Tolstoy's teleological lines. Nevertheless, as the great Russian argues, the ultimate purpose of bees is not exhausted by any such purposes for them as may be conceived by the human mind. The higher the human intellect soars in its conception of possible purposes, the more must it recognise and acknowledge that all such purposes lie beyond its comprehension.

Putting it another way, and leaving aside the fact that nowadays there are many who would argue that all purposes exist only in the human mind, the truth would seem to be as I have stated it already: we know nothing except that we know nothing—and that is the sum total of human wisdom.

That is the spirit in which I began my professional life, and in carrying out the steps in the child's game of trying to reach the wall by halving the distance between the wall and yourself each time. I have long since abandoned the faintest wish ever to reach it on this side of eternity. I see around me too many people who think they have already arrived and who actually have the temerity to believe that they know the truth about what is behind the wall. Let me repeat Cromwell's famous words to them for the last time in this lesson. I beseech you, in the bowels of Christ, think it possible that you may be mistaken. That is the only premiss from which I have ever proceeded. I have tried to produce, out of this bubble of learning, high up in the clouds above Edinburgh, this aery womb, a race of pupils who will go forth and multiply in the name of my proud humility. A humility which must at times appear to bear the stamp of the defeatist and the sceptic—all things are a cheat and a disappointment, life is unreal etcetera—but which may also move quietly forward in its own way to the acquisition of a certain kind of knowledge, and a wisdom that is beyond the classroom but which may be sown in the classroom, a wisdom which Francis Bacon writes of when he says that if a man will begin with certainties he will end in doubts, but if he will be content to begin in doubts, he shall end in certainties. If the man is a true thinker, that will never happen finally and absolutely, but that need not prevent him from getting as close to the wall as he can, the wall being the point where death and truth conjoin, as King Alfred the Great suggested long ago. I first read it in his plain old-fashioned Anglo-Saxon Wessex prose but it is as fresh as new paint in my mind today. Let a rough translation suffice: He seems to me to be a very foolish man and a very wretched one who will not increase his understanding while he is in the world, and ever wish and long to reach that endless life where all shall be made clear.

Such has been my aim and objective, Herr Inspektor, Herr Examiner, as old Stan would have said—if you wish me to be so philosophic so that you can fill in your form and collect your pay. Most practising teachers don't have the time *actually* to be so fucking philosophical. If you really want to know, my immediate objective is to reach the end of the period—and indeed the day. My short-term objective is to reach Friday—and especially the last Friday of term. My long-term objective is to reach the end of session—and finally arrive at the very last session and so safely retire. Looks like I'm almost there, too, much too soon, *nel mezzo del cammin di nostra vita*, in point of fact, and as Ovid and Faustus prayed, *O lente, lente, currite noctis equi*! But my ultimate objective is, if I be not cynical, to do as Alfred suggests and reach that endless life where all shall be made clear; to reach the wall, in fact, and to prevent any pupil of mine leaving this room for the last time thinking he has reached it already. If he thinks that, then I have failed.

And yes—I must have had many failures.

Too many odds stacking up, I suppose, in a shitheap of a world, discouraging the young. The global and spiritual threats: population explosion, food shortage, the dwindling of resources, pollution, nuclear energy ticking away like a time-bomb, rabid technology, the veneration of science, blind materialism, the death of God, famines, wars, genocide, terrorism, Saddam Hussein, Bosnia, Somalia, the Wet West the good man's failure, the disintegration of the family, juvenile immorality, mass unemployment, divorce, disasters cultural and physical, no time to name them all, no, nobody knows de trouble ah sees—oh, yes, and apathy. Apathy above all, governments thinking only five years ahead and everybody after the fast buck and nobody giving a fuck. O, my friends, my friends, I do not pretend it has been easy for you in such a world, so changed as it is from the easy world of masts and madrigals that so bedecked my seatown seat of learning in the golden age. No fleeting the time carelessly now, in good sooth, for youth's a stuff will not endure.

And today's youth hath cottoned on to that old saw with a venom, in good streetwise time, determined to smash and grab and rape and lie and cheat and beat the system while the going's good, i'faith, before the shadows fall, and the devil take the wimps and wallies that fall behind, especially them that no can do—the wankers we call 'teachers.'

Ah, but stay with me just a little longer yet, my boys, bear with me, not too much further now, and I will show you where the iron crosses grow . . .

They grow—the iron crosses—on the graves of all my former teachers: Lachlan Campbell, Mackay Mackay and Danny Dalyell, all of whom died in the last decade, Danny being the last to go. They had lived long enough through the educational revolution to see most of their lives' work undone.

And they grow—the iron crosses—on the graves of all my dearest hopes. My children that never were.

Let me tell you, then, how they died in the womb, my children.

One after the other.

It started, I need hardly say, with the coming of Cranford. You can imagine how I felt when, after our Principal announced at the end of the seventies that he was retiring the following year and his post was advertised in the press, the grapevine brought the news that among the applicants for the job was one John T. Cranford, Headmaster of a tuppence halfpenny public school somewhere in the south-east of England, off the official educational map. I'd heard he was already a headmaster—that wasn't the surprise and why should it be? He'd been active on the bureaucratic face of schoolteaching for some years, getting his name known at conferences. In Scotland the Oxbridge degree is the key to all mythologies and conference-crawling is the keyhole in the door. No, the surprise consisted in how even Cranford could have thought himself remotely capable of taking on a school like Blair's, so full of clever people.

'Simple,' the Colonel said. 'If he gets the job, all the clever men will sod off, leaving him king of the cretins.'

'No,' I said.' He's not clever enough to think that one through. Anyway, it's academic—he'll never even smell the job.'

He smelt it all right. They practically rammed it up his backside. His predecessor had been a law into himself and now they needed a cipher, a John Major, a grey man.

I'll spare you the tedious formalities of the first staff meeting at the opening of the new session. I sat well to the back of the staff room, my face buried in my file, wincing through his shocking delivery. Now and again I allowed myself a little peep at the guy over the top of Gladstone's mop of curls. He'd changed, of course, according to that grimly unavoidable pattern referred to previously in the lesson—fatter in the face, generally a lot flabbier, hair thinned out, and a considerable explosion of paunch. These deteriorations were partly due to the accident which had ended his spurious athleticism. The one-legged limp had been obvious from the moment he'd walked on. Otherwise he was still the same old Cranford, ugly as ever. But it was while I sat there listening to his uninspired verbiage that the first dram of poison entered my ear.

Envy.

And ire.

Anger and jealousy, resentment and hatred, two of the deadlies, call them by what names you will, well covered by the Ten Commandments, highlighted by Christ and forbidden by the Church, formed their leperous distilment and coursing through the natural gates and alleys of the body made me sick at heart.

It was a sudden and loathsome cocktail. I had drunk and seen the spider. Already something was rotten in the state of Blair's.

I coveted my neighbour's wife.

My God, boys, it was worse than that. The wife I coveted was not simply my neighbour's—she was my fucking headmaster's! Think of it! The very idea put toys of desperation into my brain. That deplorably untalented ruffian up there on the dais, who had come to lord it over a breed of men many times more gifted than himself, was actually married to my Jenny, the girl I had felt on a train, made love to among buttercups and sun-drenched cows, written sonnets to—nay, more than that, our two minds and souls had grown together as one—and that maladroit idiot up there (I was really beginning to rail silently now like a dumb frustrated Thersites) standing on one good leg and with a plentiful lack of prick to play with, O horrible! O horrible! most horrible!—he went to bed with Jenny every night, showered with her like a stork, undressed her, caressed her, sucked her nipples, kneaded her buttocks, bit her ears, fondled her crutch, licked her navel, kissed her armpits—

Or did he?

Maybe they slept in twin beds. Separate rooms. Did they even talk any more? I had to know. It was with a shock that I calculated I had not seen Jenny once in fourteen years, that all of us, she, Cranford and I, were now thirty-six years old. And they had no family. Thirty-six. It was just possible—my mind was racing—no, it was easily possible, that she could still have her baby. By me. For from his loins no hopeful branch could spring, to cross me from the golden time I looked for. We'd elope together and make a new life for ourselves. It was all so easy. I knew in my heart's core what she must have suffered all those years, how empty her days and nights must have been without me—sticking plasters on Etonian rejects and handing out prizes under abominable hats, among benchfuls of even more abominable human beings. She would drop all that and her knickers in a moment when she discovered that her old Antony was here, at this very school, and that the flame, although allowed to soften to the merest flicker, had never gone out, had shot up again in a moment, in the twinkling of an eye, and I was now ready to throw her manfully over the bonnet of my clapped out old Cortina and abscond with her up the M90, or over the borders and far away. Why weep ye by the tide, ladie? Have done, have done, for your Jock o' Hazeldean, not a headmaster but a simple teacher, your Lochinvar is here, not so young as he used to be, but willing to tread but one measure and quaff but one goblet and fuck but one lady if he can before he die and wave *adios amigo* to that laggard in love and that dastard in war who could stay at Blair's till pension time counting pins and paper clips and wanking off what was left of his stumpy knob in impotent rage. O wonderful: most wonderful! Would he were wasted, marrow, bones and all!

But first I had to play things cleverly—not upset the bastard too much, worm my way in, that kind of thing. The meeting was breaking up. I made my way out by the side exit and shot back to my classroom to see to necessary chores. Twenty minutes later I was standing outside his study. God, I thought to myself—study! Cranford in a study! Gengis Khan in a vestry. The stud that once through Taftian halls was now masquerading as a headmaster in a study. Lord, what fools these mortals be. None o' that right now if you wish to play it cool, my boy. Away and mock the time with fairest show—false face must hide what the false heart doth know.

I knocked on the door.

'Enter!'

I laughed at that. Enter indeed. Not 'come in' but 'enter' and kiss my papal toe, or my unprotesting knob—what remains of it. What, ho, is Horatio there? A piece of him. What happened to the other pieces?

'Enter!'

More loudly this time. I wiped the grin off my face and walked in.

Of course as soon as I did so I burst out laughing—partly at the sight of him standing there behind that enormous table and him not knowing his arse from his elbow intellectually. It was also impossible not to laugh quite spontaneously at the sheer absurdity, the incongruity of the meeting. For a moment I actually felt rather warm and sentimental.

I held out my hand with a cheeky wink.

'Hello, you fucking old wanker!'

I honestly thought I was going to have to run over and catch the bastard. He turned pure white and tottered. The shock would have been bad enough for him had he had two legs to his name, but with one dodgy pin he was at an understandable disadvantage. If there hadn't been one of these revolving chairs right behind him he'd have been arse over tit on the floor, like a medieval knight awaiting the can opener or the misericorde. Luckily he dropped straight onto the chair with a ferocious clattering of plastic and stainless steel and sat there swivelling helplessly for a few seconds, the dummy clown's leg stuck straight out in front of him. I decided it would be best to keep grinning.

'Sorry to give you such a shock, old buddy,' I said with as much breeze as I could muster. 'I thought it would be advisable to let you know as soon as I could— '

He stopped me with an uplifted hand, like a stunned, sedentary traffic copper. The other hand was fumbling frantically at a manilla folder. His scalp was scabby in patches, I could see, through his fast fleeing hair. Believe me, those endearing young charms, if charms they ever were, had gone the way of all flesh. He brought out the staff list.

'But you're not here . . . I examined every name— '

This time I stopped him. Not strong on contemporary verse, old Cranford. He needed a quick lesson.

'Campbell Mackay. Writer's name, see? Nom de plume. Author's alias. (It was sinking in.) I am not what I am.'

The penny dropped.

'God!'

My assumed grin became difficult to hold and in any case I could see it was hopelessly out of place, Cranford was so obviously upset and dismayed.

'Is there a problem?' I asked, acting the daft lad.

He stared back at me blankly, wearily, over the deskful of work, his new job stretching between us across acres of paper.

'Oh, come on,' I chirped, deciding to have one more go at the easy affability act,' just because we were once fellow wankers doesn't mean— '

'Stop!'

I stopped.

Cranford took a set of keys from his jacket pocket and started to rub them between his fingers. I was at once reminded of old Bogey doing Captain Queeg in *The Caine Mutiny*.

'Playing with your marbles?' I asked, without thinking.

Playing with your marbles?

It was the unkindest cut of all, though there was no *double entendre* intended and it had been the keys, pure and simply, that had sparked off the question in my mind. But Cranford read it quite naturally as a declaration of war and it was at that point that I could see how the poor guy had become paranoid about his missing parts. I must be careful not to mention legs, I thought. Make a mental note there.

The Principal (*Principal*! I still couldn't get over it) fiddled furiously with his keys for several seconds longer and seemed to regain a little of his accustomed floridity. He looked at me with real venom in his eye.

'I don't want you to refer to me in that way again, ever. It's an ungentlemanly— '

I started to protest that I had intended no insult.

'Don't interrupt me, please! I was about to say that we shall behave like gentlemen and colleagues from now on, as we are certainly the latter, forgetting the past and putting it behind us. All of it.'

I could see the things he was thinking. I was thinking them too. I couldn't help asking.

'Jenny?'

The muscles in his slack jaw twitched violently.

'Mrs Cranford—to you—is not with me as yet. She—she has remained south— '

It was curious listening to him attempting to speak formal English.

'There are a number of affairs to be settled, schoolhouse, transactions, no concern of anyone's but ours. She—she will join me—later—in time.'

I knew he was lying and my heart sank. He saw it, read my thoughts and nearly smiled a bitter smile. She would never join him. Jenny was not coming back into his life or mine. Ever again. God, what a cunt is time, to turn our lives to shit!

'And now you'll have a great deal of work to be getting on with and so have I.'

I took the hint and made for the door.

'I will say one thing, though, *Mister* Mackay.'

I waited.

'Should you wish to leave this teaching establishment in the near or immediate future, I should of course provide you with excellent references.'

We were sworn enemies from that moment on. But I have to insist that, irrespective of our entwined biographies, we should have clashed anyway. Cranford clashed with just about everyone on the staff. The grudge he bore each member of the human race that went upon two legs and packed a couple of six-shooting balls to boot—well, that turned out to be unfortunate for us at Blair's, where every single one of us was blessed with two balls and legs in good working order. I can't speak for the couple of spinsters on the

234

staff, never having peered that far into their private dimensions, even though one of them was at that time young and attractive, myself not being given to promiscuity but dedicated to teaching and the Muse and, as in my student days, to closeness and the bettering of my mind. But for the rest of us on the male staff, we were rock solid in those anatomical departments that filled Cranford with such resentment and—when he thought he was being got-at for his deficiencies—with paranoiac fury. Indeed his savage tendency to react violently against suspected slights grew quite out of order and Leroy and Gladstone produced in secret for the staff a handbook of forbidden phrases, anatomical anathemas and possible puns, expressions not to be used on any account when engaged in conversation with Cranford whether privately or in public forum.

As examples, the following were banned.

But if you say that, Headmaster, you won't have a leg to stand on. (Oops!)

Oh, but Headmaster, if you do that, don't you see, you'll shoot yourself in the foot? (Hell!)

He's only doing one leg of the two-year course, isn't he? (Ah.)

Can't you stump up just this once? (What I mean to say is . . .)

For two pins I'd have belted him. (Er, not that I . . .)

Well, you'll just have to put your best foot forward. (Oh, I didn't actually . . .)

A similar catalogue of inadmissible phrases pertained to balls, pricks, cocks, members, yards and so forth. *Pinprick*, for example, was considered a double insult. Absolutely taboo. If such words were used, they had to be employed with extreme care as to their contextual aura and penumbra of possibilities—in a word, their connotations. As soon as Cranford believed himself to be the victim of cruel and deliberate innuendo, he'd turn on the most uncontrolled tantrums, turn white with anger and thump the table like an irate but anaemic chimpanzee.

So, because you cannot win against me by the force of intellectual argument, you descend to the level of vindictive personal jibes. Is that it?

Thump thump.

Unhappily Gladstone and Leroy's light-hearted little booklet, which had been produced on school equipment, was left by a careless colleague in one of the staff bogs—you couldn't even have an entertaining crap without repercussions—and discovered by Cranford when he was stumping around on the snoop. All hell broke loose and from then on there was just no having any conversation with him. Sentence structure broke down, the resources of the English vocabulary in all its linguistic and literary richness were played out to the point where they could not cope. The unfortunate result of this was that the staff retreated more and more from intelligent conversation and showed a tendency to jabber monosyllabically. Cranford's features began to assume an expression of growing triumph. He believed he was getting the better of his staff and that they were at last bowing down to him. Rather than let this happen, I'm afraid that some of us went the other way and quite shamelessly taunted him with misquotations, spoonerisms, deliberately planted imputations and outrageous overtones, allusions to certain sea-cooks, mad whale-hunting captains and the like.

—Shall I be your first foot this Hogmanay, Headmaster?

Thump.

—Or your second?

Thump thump.

No need to be so testy about it! Forgot you were a bit of an odd ball about some things.

Thump thump thump.

Very well then.

Cranford was paranoid.

Do you think we gave him cause? Injustice, you see, hardened our hearts.

You'd think it unlikely that a man with his personal problems would have been appointed in the first place to a position of such authority, when he was clearly so unfitted for office. But was it so clear at the time? Clearly not. Otherwise the good men and true who elected him would not have voted him in. And let you as pupils ask yourselves, how much have you seen that is amiss in the school during your six years here? Robes and furred gowns hide all. And nine-tenths of the psychological iceberg lies inaccessible to that instant everyday analysis that is the stuff of interviews, I'm afraid. The school's governors probably saw in Cranford an unexciting but solid chap whom they could easily control. A dull dog. A bear—to alter the metaphor—of suitably little brain, to whose Pooh they might play Piglets and Tiggers and Eeyores. But they never dreamed that one day Christopher

Robin might have to take the pathetic little bastard to the shrink.

Cranford didn't go to the shrink: he went to the bottle. And he withdrew to his study, surrounding himself with jackasses and jackals, the former ready to bray for tuppence, the latter yapping for his job. He became, in fact, a paranoid schizophrenic and a dipsomaniac in one, a little Hitler and a nasty concoction of trouble and strife. And yet he managed all that while sitting on the fence. In fact he sat on fences so long he developed four buttocks instead of two: a perfect Celtic Cross at his rear end. More hole than holiness, but that's all one. Well, all nothing, actually. An unlovely, unglorious zero. That was Cranford. The sane retreated to their classrooms; communication began to break down. I speak, by the way, in terms of a decade, not in terms of terms, if you see what I mean. This was the pattern that set in and that followed its course with depressing inexorability. Oh, he had his good days. Once he even had a good term. (That was the term he was mostly away from school, sitting on committees.) But the school slowly, implacably, assumed its stern Wemmick face, rigid as a pillar box, tense, unsmiling, unrelaxed, afraid.

Were there not antidotes to the dram of eale, the leperous distilment, the cursed hebona?

Yes, of course there were. The greatest antidote to it all is teaching—and there was teaching. And there was friendship and fun, with Gladstone and Leroy doing their Falstaff, Shallow and Silence bit in the staffroom or in the lunchtime pub to which we were sometimes driven.

—Remember the night, old boy, when we lay in the fields at Penicuik? banging away we were?

—No more o' that, I prithee, gentle Leroy, no more o' that.

—Ha, it was a merry night! O, but Jesu, sweet Jesu, the days that we have seen, dear Gladstone, the mad days that we have seen, sweet knight!

—We have heard the chimes at midnight, Monsieur le Roi.

—That we have, that we have, that we have, Sir Gladstone, in Jesu's name we have. And shall we not have it away again, dear knight, with dear Jane Nightwork and that divine Doll Tearsheet?

—Old, old, sweet Leroy. We must remember our maker.

—Ah, thou sayest true, fat knight, death is certain, 'tis certain, as the psalmist says. We must all die. Jesu, Jesu, the mad days that I have spent—and to see how many of mine old acquaintance are dead and we must after them. We shall all follow. But to think of the mad days that we have seen. Jesu, Jesu.

This straight, unbottled stuff of the bard could go on throughout an entire lunchbreak unless Henry Archibald broke in with his ice axe and threatened murder. Or Stan sang *Henry Morgan* and served rum to every man.

Back in our classrooms we breathed in the free air of teaching according to the styles we knew best and that suited us best and which had produced generations of well taught pupils. Leroy in particular indulged his thespian foibles with a panache that was worthy of Lachlan Campbell. They were out of the same mould. Definitions were far from being a dreary affair in Leroy's room. It was one of the turret rooms, at the top of a winding staircase, with Gladstone's room being right at the bottom. Definition of a cataract, boy? What? you don't know what a cataract is? Bucket of water boy—bring! And the supplied bucket of water was sloshed down the spiral stones. Gladstone, teaching down below, merely glanced at the tide flooding underneath his door. Wonder what definition that was, boys. Any ideas? Leroy, up above, was already on to another. Beast of burden, boy? And the master of the dramatic was suddenly underneath his own far from undersized oaken desk, lifting it up on his bent back and humphing around the room with it in illustration of the phrase. If the word *sapping* came up, as it once did, the school grounds were not safe. To demonstrate the Roman chariot was no problem to Leroy: a Clydesdale horse was brought from the Cooperative Store and with cart attached, hurtled round the Radical Road with the class watching from above. And to create the atmosphere of boozy conviviality in *Tam O' Shanter*, a senior class was taken to the nearest pub—the landlord knew us well!—and an entire round supplied by the indefatigable Leroy.

Oh, yes, there were antidotes, and glorious remedies they were, too.

But alas, they could not last.

The trouble wasn't simply Cranford, you see—let's be fair. Just as Cranford had successfully hidden the bulk of his unspeakable personality when he came for interview, so Cranford himself was

238

but the visible tip of a colossal iceberg that was bearing down on HMS Blair's in the early eighties.

It was called educational change.

But it was change championed by Cranford (and his ilk) who had greased his way to the top by reproducing the packaged sentences, saying the expected things, parroting the pat phrases at and from the neverending conferences and conclaves of committees and the dreary debates throughout boring years of crawling and crapping until somebody finally grew weary of hearing him and, to shut him up, made him a headmaster.

A headmaster committed to change.

14

THE CHANGE TOOK various forms but the root of the cancer was the industrialisation and bureaucratisation of education: of syllabuses and schools, courses and careers, of the very philosophy, objectives, methods and even vocabulary of teaching.

Now at this point allow me to confess my greatest fear: that if even John Milton, who was said (remember?) to be most poetically successful where he was least didactic, failed to achieve complete poetic success when his theology took over, then what faint hope have I, Campbell Mackay, of succeeding, at such a juncture in this lesson? I pause for a reply. I know—none, Brutus, none. And all shall I offend. Well, it's none indeed, if you accept in the first place the truth of that old proposition about the great Puritan. I don't. But even if I did, I'd still swallow the roughage, the awkward lumps of didacticism floating in the porridge, still sit through every one of his lessons, just so as not to miss blowing the froth off a single pint of his poetry. In other words, dear chaps, this is the homily coming up, the pill beneath the sugar. Aha! Yet again you stand like greyhounds in the slips, straining upon the start of what is now for you the ultimate vacation, the last goodbye, the long farewell, the big sleep. O, weep me not dead with your faces! I was ever one to sugar the pill for you, I know. And now (you protest) does he offer us naked instruction? Does he threaten us with unashamed pedantry?

I do.

And you are going to hear it, you bastards, even if I have to perform the last trick left to me in order to command your flagging attention. I shall now take off all my clothes! Yes, by heaven! A garment per quotation from this point on until—oh là, sirs!—you will hear this pedantry from a quite naked pedant. The last refuge of a noble mind—to bring even boredom alive. Aha! Now that was a vague allusion rather than a straight quotation, I believe, I needn't begin to doff—but I'm generous. Half a sock? I shall undo my shoelace. Here goes. And bugger off, all ye who cannot take the punishment and are here only for the beer—I know you all, and will not uphold, this time, the unyoked humour of your idleness, no, by Janus, this be a place of learning, don't you know, on a high hill, cragged and steep, where truth stands among thorns, though I try to sow primroses where I can, and shall do even now. Farewell, shoe.

It all started in earnest the day the documents began rolling in from the Ironmills Kremlin: documents so impenetrable in their parlance that we could only laugh at the jargonising antics of the verbally inept somnambulists who had scattered them in the first place, embattled theorists that they were, to beset themselves by verbal thickets for yet another long snore in their castle of indolence, and keep the sleeping princess of education dying for but one kiss of life. Leroy ran out onto the crags, clutching one of these deeds of death, and shouted a couple of paragraphs aloud across Edinburgh—just to see, he said, if dogs would run howling down the streets and birds drop down dead from the sky, killed by cliché, bumped off by boredom.

How about this phrase, folks? *Summative assessment in relation to Grade Related Criteria.* I wonder how that one went off? Yes, by Jove, I think I've winged a seagull there! Oh gosh, try this one—double barrelled shotgun stuff, this. *Application of the Grade Related Criteria will call for a continual process of adjustment to arrive at a holistic assessment of pupil performance.* Brace of duck there, I believe, a seagull shit itself, and canine confusion down in Dumbiedykes. Lord, what fun!

It wasn't, of course: the fun was really over. The language of educational theory is a white-out of anaemic abstraction and truly civilised people cannot function in blizzards of concept and cottonwool. Once we had donned our snowglasses we began to understand the awful implications of the deeds of death, in which our souls had been written away. We were now being instructed to work much harder for less reward; we were sum-moned to conferences, workshops, lectures, some of these at the dreaded Moray House, where we were taught all over again how we should really have been teaching all along but for our lack of enlightenment. It has all been proved by educational science, comrades. After all, you wouldn't want Jones to return, would you? (skip skip) and the days of that horrid élitism? Dear me, no. Four legs good, two legs bad—or as Comrade

Cranford would say, one leg better. So you're just going to have to obey, aren't you? All taken care of, all decided for you. From now on you must split your classes into groups; you will use a tape-recorder and even a video camera; you will cease to be a talking head; you will refer to a checklist of guidelines criteria to see that you are teaching correctly; you will chew on our rubber tablets with your now rubber teeth and will not wipe your arses with our bumff, for we are now the shiten shepherdes and you the sillie sheep; you will not employ literary-critical jargon; you will burn your books and use units in their stead, photocopied at your own expense, and bloody expensive too—fuck the rainforests!—and if these include literary passages they will be from texts which are relevant to the lives of your pupils and that doesn't mean John bloody Milton, right Jimmy? you will teach oral pupil competence by promoting discussion on how to stop their spots, their smoking and their abortions—and N.B., debates about plays by William Shakespeare and novels by Charles Dickens are not considered a valid test of your pupils' oracy, we can't tell you why we believe this to be so, we're just fucking telling you, anyway who gives a toss about Dickens now, that's just oral diarrhoea, and oral English diarrhoea to boot and if you want to know the truth we don't consider a literary sensibility to be a socially useful skill any more, so you can forget all that and flush it down the bogs; moreover you will not rely on printed stimuli because modern man cannot rely on printed stimuli alone, we live in the age of the image and the button, the picture and the key, the sound and the graphics, the chopper and the slab, the power and the glory, the voice and the telescreen, we are the masters and you are the dead, for the Age of the Book is dead, is dead, and ours is the kingdom and thine is the hell, not forever and ever amen but just until the next round of changes when we can all justify our jobs by playing musical chairs with education again and might even get back to something approaching sanity but it will be too bloody late for you lot and a couple of million pupils by then, so pour out your old wine, your Chateau Mouton Rothschild, and bottle your cheeky wee worthless Beaujolais. Accept the inevitable and don't rock the boat, don't make waves. Quhy spurnis thow aganis the wall to sla thyself and mend nathing at all? Now who the bloody hell said that? None of your Henryson here! If you're going to do any of that Scots stuff, let it be Billy Connolly or Rabbie Burns.

Oh, and while we're on the subject of orders, get this into your heads: you are no longer teachers, you are Agents of the Board, officers of Ironmills, sub-postmen of the great Dalkeith sorting office, so please don't try to think for yourselves, just open the mail we send you, read it and pass it on—no inwardly digesting and all that Cranmer crap, that sounds suspiciously like thought-crime to us, and snobby high Anglican thought-crime too. Inspiration, aspiration, vision? Down wantons, down! Another quotation, I know—trousers off. And just cut out that sort of talk—there are no longer the good and the bad, there are only the ugly. Don't try to be Clint Eastwood or the Untouchables, you won't last three minutes. Dirty Harry is also dead. Not that we're in the Mob business in this little neck of the woods, oh dear me, no! the knock on the door at four in the morning, the wooden overcoat, the concrete wellies, the close shave, the hole in the head, the blade in the jugular, the cyanide in the scotch, the boot in the ribs, the truncheon in the penis, the stiletto heel in the testicles (oh, yes, we have willing dames enough, you know, matter of fact Scotland hath foisons to fill up their will and damage your willies, and enough jobs in Scotland to make our women fight for them like dogs—harder than the bleeding men, in fact), did I forget any items on the list? the poisoned book, the rotten apple, the treated comb, the unbated foil, the dram of eale (had that one), the cuddly toy (bang!), the half-sawn floorboards i' the privy, high over the moat (O, *merdres*! a fall into the eternal shit), the smother-proof pillow (sorry, defective), the electric food mixer (yourk!), the fast freezer (open the do—), the cuddly toy (had the cuddly toy), the thumbscrews, the boot, the strappado, the unction bought of a mountebank (stop fucking quoting!), sorry—goodbye, vest, the rope, the stake, the steak (said that), no, *steak*—different spelling (shut your face about spelling—middle-class convention, not worth a fart, sir!), pepperonied steak with nicely ground nuts from the poison tree, garnished with hemlock leaves and a dod of deadly night-shade jelly at the side, anything else now? yes, the red-hot pincers, the lime-pit, the in-service, the tweezers, the dentist's drill, the conference workshop, the seventeenth committee on talk moderation, the chain-saw, the garotte and many many more. But never a drop of arsenic on the arse! Come unto us all ye who are prepared to lick our arses and put your brains into neutral—and not one drop of arsenic will you get! You might

243

get other things but who would not take corruption from that particular fault for the sake of twenty-four years in power? But look, amazement on the pupils sits—seriously we're not in that kind of business, good God, no, this is Scotland, not so bonny as heretofore, but part of what was lately Mrs Thatcher's Britain, no, this isn't Germany, where they call you Herr Doktor, or France, where you're a professeur, or Italy, O professori! this is the brave new Scotland, where we don't supply any of these old élitist labels, this is Scotland the Brave, where they don't even call you a teacher any more, you're an Agent of the Board in our iron eyes, as said, you're an employee as far as the line managers in the New Schools are concerned, but to the public you're just a fucking wanker, never mind, we want you, Big Brother loves you and nothing nasty will happen to you here, so long as you toe the Party line, not like on the continent, where all those murderous Machiavells went to school, no, we'll simply remove you from office if you happen to be in a high place, and if you're not in a high place we'll just make sure you never get there, never even smell the prospect of promotion, that's hardly the gas chamber, is it? you don't hear the sound of screaming, do you? or the strains of nice German music?

O Freunde, nicht diese Tone!

Conformity will be rewarded. Be a worm, be a child again and you will never taste death's woe. Surely you will inherit the kingdom of Ironmills.

Wollust ward dem Wurm gegeben
Und der Cherub steht vor Gott!

Plodders will be welcomed, pedestrian crossings sanctioned. The lively, the intelligent, the charismatic, the creative, the thinkers—must go, must creep tearfully away from our charmed circle.

Freude trinken alle Wesen
An den Brusten der Natur

The wimpish wets, the stay-at-homes, will chomp on the fatted calf: the Prodigal Sons, who had a go, will never never be forgiven. This is bloodless revolution but it is war, war, total war

Laufet, Bruder, eure Bahn,
Freudig, wie ein Held zum Siegen.

And even a worm can be happy before Big Brother.

Got all that?

Are you sure?

And so we went to war.

Oh, yes, we went to war, we had our say. Our little Department in Blair's shook its fist at the big stick. We wrote to the Board, approached the very gates of Ironmills. How can you do this, we asked? Who will stand by our youngsters in the educational chaos that will prevail when all sane and intelligent individualists have fled the field? Who will ensure the survival of the dialect of the tribe in an age when our pupils are daily confronted by the abuse of English, not least by the members of Joint Working Parties with their canting twaddle, and the Examiners, Inspectors and ministers of education and officers of Ironmills? Who will protect our language and literature?—Our breakfast TV journalists? Our video editors? Our travel agents? Our computer buffs? Bruce Forsyth? Terry Wogan? *Eastenders*?

We saw quite clearly, and so we told our masters, that these impoverished and circumscribed courses, with their conversion and reduction of English into a nebulous assessment of life-skills and general ability, were taking us towards an educational black hole in which a generation would founder. As graduates and teachers and readers, even as civilised beings, we found ourselves at a loss when confronted by documents which instructed us to talk and think in terms of profiles, progress by accretion, norm-referencing, negotiated curricula. An essay was now an Instrument of Assessment. A pupil's vision was a Learning Outcome. But I believe it was when we read some documents headed *Module Descriptors* that we knew we were fighting a lost cause. This was gobbledygook aligned to Stardate Back to the Future, and only barbarians, imbeciles and climbers would boldly go along with it on board an Enterprise into which no reasonable man had ever gone before or ever would. In expressing themselves in this barbarous and inane phraseology the educationists had totally failed even to meet their own criteria. Such a language was in itself a negation of our ideals as English teachers and an annulment of much of our teaching. Whatever had happened to that quaint old idea which used to sustain us, that work in English was the unique and privileged educator of the imagination of the individual?

Quite a strong stand, yes? And was it not well done?

We might as well have held our peace. Cranford received a letter from Ironmills Road complaining about shit-stirring in the English Department at Blair's and if we had any shit to stir in the future could we kindly stir it through our professional Associations—our Unions? Direct contact with the gods is not permissible. Try to do so again and you may be consumed by fire. Intercession through a Union priest is the closest you can come to debate with us, they said, so fuck off, suckers.

After that we knew there was no hope, especially as the new kind of teaching was not slow to attract a new kind of teacher: subservient, unthinking, unprincipled, hungry for the cabbage, the dungheap, the cock o' the midden. At home in the shit, he stood there proudly and crowed. Crowed like Chanticleer that fools like us should be so deep contemplative. At one time this New Man might have opted for the Civil Service, advertising or industry. But with his businessman's brain and his manager's mentality and his snow-broth blood, he saw that children could be used as stepping stones and classrooms as springboards. The oftener he left the youngsters untaught and buggered off to collect more duplicated phrases from the in-service gurus, the more his superiors applauded him and recommended him for preferment. He was all for Grade Related Criteria, even though these fashionable shibboleths were already called into question in countries where criterion-referenced teaching had been well tried. He was for group teaching, naturally, and thus for reducing the influence and value of human contact between pupil and teacher, the methodology of a system which was so engineered to banish all sense of failure that it could not in itself deal with failure at its roots, a problem which remained—and remains—the prerogative and challenge of the old style teacher. The New Man valued instead the Procrustean Bed, life skills, middle-of-the-road books, calling literature 'writing' and comprehension 'reading' (not that the latter even required any actual knowledge of reading) so as to blur the lines of élitist division between Shakespeare and the latest pseudo-sociological trash dressed up as creativity. He could scarcely have stayed with the old language and literature nomenclature, could he? for though it would have been more logical and more honest, it would also have clearly indicated that the subject still anachronistically known as English was in some way concerned with the teaching of an academic discipline. Any such shocking admission our New Man disguised under these more pragmatic labels of reading and writing, which qualified as currently allowable social skills for living—as they still do. His reliance on snippets and illustrations rather than the traditional book as the stimulator of the imagination revealed his readiness to produce and accept competence and skill rather than insight and understanding, his willingness to make literature more of an option than it had been in the past (a time-consuming option, more likely than not to be shoved aside) and great literature less of a pastime than of a past time.

And, of course, talk.

Oh, yes, he was all for talk. He throve on it, endlessly crowing at one end and crapping it out at the other end, to fertilise the existing pile of garbage for more gasbags to come. And while he gassed his classes were taught by someone else. And when he came back to the classroom, filled with missionary zeal, he did not come back to teach—he came to talk. But not to talk literature. God, no! Not strong on the Graveyard Poets, our New Man. Not keen on grammar or Gutenberg or Gawain or Gunn. More on Glasgow and Gremlins, you could say. Ah, but he was a grand talker! He talked his way to the top job in no time at all and was soon busy encouraging another generation of youngsters to get talking instead of reading and writing. He knew his talk, all right. He was, after all, a communicator. Oh, did I forget to tell you? They stopped calling English *English* by the beginning of the nineties. Well, the term was still used in casual conversation, but I couldn't help noticing that publishers' circulars to Colonel Stubbes were posted to the school addressed to *The Head of Communications*, or some such phrase. To start with the Colonel used to send them back, labelled 'Not known at this address'. In time he simply chucked them in the bin.

Originally—as I intimated to you earlier—I believed all this to be a specifically Caledonian carcinoma. There also came a point at which I began genuinely to wonder, was it I? Myself and a few other dinosaurs left over from the Age of Mackay Mackay. Not that I ever teetered for one second in my convictions, but the moment was there when I asked myself about the rarity of my complaint: dinosauromania.

Picture my ecstasy when I heard that, in presenting the Thomas Cranmer Schools Prize in the Christmas of 1989, His Royal Highness, the Prince of Wales, had brought tidings to English teachers that were not tidings of great joy but consisted of a declaration that the English language had dwindled down into a dismal wasteland of banality, cliché and casual obscenity. He exhorted all teachers to give their pupils instead 'a vision of greatness'. I nearly grat with relief. I'm sorry about the strong language in this lesson, your Royal Highness, but I think that if you were seated in front of me now, you would agree that it is not synonymous with obscenity, that it is not four-letter words that constitute obscenity but the spirit in which they are said. And as to the vision, I try, I try.

As evidence of the New Rot, the Prince cited the pedestrian crassness of the New English Bible (the Devil take it!) and the Church of England's Alternative Service. O ye who worship fine language, say a prayer, please, of your charity, both for the Prince and for P.D. James who, as it so happened, said the same thing to the pundits of Bookerland! Charles then went on to proffer a personal illustration of what happens to Shakespeare when he is Made Easy for Schools. He was helped in this by a fellow prince (of Denmark) who once put the matter something like this, apparently.

> Well, frankly, the problem, as I see it
> At this moment in time, is whether I
> Should just lie down under all this hassle
> And let them walk all over me,
> Or whether I should just say: O.K.,
> I get the message, and do myself in.
> I mean, let's face it, I'm in a no-win
> Situation, and quite honestly
> I'm so stuffed up to here with the whole
> Stupid mess that, I can tell you, I've just
> Got a good mind to take the quick way out.
> That's the bottom line. The only problem is:
> What happens if I find that, when I've bumped
> Myself off, there's some kind of a, you know,
> All that mystical stuff about when you die,
> You might find you're still—know what I mean?

Yes, I know precisely what you mean—and well said, sweet

prince! If we encourage the use of mean, trite, ordinary language, we encourage a mean, trite, ordinary world—just exactly as you say, your Royal Highness. But flights of angels can sing your words to the century's rest for our educationists and for our educational publishers and for Brains of Britain like Julie Walters, who said, and bravely was it said: 'I'm all for this! It's exactly what kids need! I wish I'd had one when I did my O Levels! (She makes it sound like some new form of sexual aid.) And I'm sure one or two adults would be grateful for a quick translation on occasion!'

One or two, perhaps. Except why bother—if reading the guy is really that bad? Why not read something else? Jeffrey Archer, Wilbur Smith, Catherine Cookson, the script of *Neighbours*. Or why not just watch the box? Why read at all? To get away from the prince's ordinary world you would have to make an extraordinary effort, and extraordinariness is not what our educationists, whether Scots or English, are after—though the Scottish ones, I think we must confess, are much further on in the great race towards the ultimate banality for it suits their left-wing book, and while teachers in England even now kick back at the bureaucrats who are bleeding them dead, Scottish teachers accept this shit in the sacred name of social revolution. Ordinariness is precisely their goal and *know what I mean*? will suffice as the holy grail of literary wisdom in the brave new egalitarian wasteland they have mapped out for us, and whose broken images litter the route through the desert of the last decade, the legacy of Thatcherism: is art useful? does academic wisdom possess a palpable function? can you eat it, taste it, smell it, sell it? will it bring down inflation? keep out Labour. If not, then get rid of it, men and women of tomorrow! Send in the Ironmills squad to spray it out of existence, like poppies. England will follow thee—or die!

And in they went.

Not that I'd question their breathtaking idealism. But like all revolutionary idealists they do come rather short on the question of the practical flaws in all of this. The principal fracture running right down the middle of their entire scheme is that not all teachers are good at changing from the kind of teachers they were born to be, have been, always will be and are bloody good at being, to the kind of teachers the Board now requires them to be, insists that they be: in a word, instructors, educators in the

249

purely passive, formal, transactional sense. For myself I have to say that I could never be one of them even if I tried. I am an élitist, an old-fashioned fascist bastard. But call me what you will, I teach from an inner flame of conviction, enthusiasm, passion. I do not teach from a checklist. It is not a flame which an Ironmills document can kindle—or put out. You burn with it—or you don't. You cannot turn it down to a peep. You cannot dowse it. Because, in truth, it is the flame of love. Love of a subject. Of a vocation. And many waters cannot quench that love, neither can the floods drown it. Or, as the Alternative Version might put it, even the Water Board can't turn you off. I can die by it, if not live by it, this love of mine.

On the other hand, the new system, the scourge of the professional and the crutch of the weak pupil, is a boon to the bad teacher, for whom it is undoubtedly designed. Following the deadly drills of this ho-hum regime, the new instructors may sit for hours on their desk-bound backsides, scratching away at the cheerless files and forms that are such an inseparable part of this whole glum package and they may listen to their charges chattering for hours about everything under the *Sun* (tabloid version, of course) and imagine that they are actually teaching them.

And so the Promised land, as seen from Pisgah, down Dalkeith way, has turned out for me to be the mirage I knew it would be. All along the line.

There is also no missing the socio-vocational emphasis in the new courses and exams. But there are certain life-skills that the Iron Men of the Mills do not say much about. Vision, Judgement, Wisdom, the pursuit of Truth, Beauty and Goodness—those vital intangibles of human life that cannot be tested by Grade Related Criteria. Life is not merely about earning bread, as Christ taught us, and drilling is not teaching. In truth, the philistine and practical philosophy, spun in iron from the Mills, is disastrously *impractical*, while the stimulation of the imagination through art is as vital to life as breathing, as building, as hygiene. It is a vital enthusiasm that has to keep sparking between pupil and teacher as between Adam and God—yes, God!—and from the depths of the teacher's entire personality, part of which is, by definition, unconscious. And in order for this to happen the inspired teacher has to be left alone to do his work—*without* reference to Grade Related Criteria.

I for one cannot work with a sentence like the following assaulting my numbed brain:

When pupils are starting to write they will find real versions useful as models for structure and real information useful in providing them with something to say, and moving out from reading, real investigations and interactions with the world beyond the school will provide real audiences and purposes for the real exercise of all the modes!

Dull would he be of soul who could pass by a sentence so touching in its majesty! Only a man with the Ironmills in his soul could have written this. Or perhaps Antony Burgess, on a dawdle of a day for him, doing a clever imitation of the language of Attila the Hun. And yet this is the language employed by educationists who really believe they are qualified to teach teachers to teach English! A whole flock of gannets gone down into the Forth, Leroy? And in Dumbiedykes, cry 'Havoc!' and let slip the dogs of war, that this foul cant may smell above the earth, with gas-blown windbags groaning for burial.

It will not have escaped your notice that for some time now I have stood among you as a naked educator. And is there one among you that dare pretend that I am, in reality, fully clothed? That none of this is really happening. For it is so much easier to shut your eyes to the truth. Ah, Fat Boy, Fat Boy, perhaps you were, in such strange way, striving for our attention . . .

Listen again.

I am exhorted, in one of the many circulars, to consider *the value of Real Language Products, for Reading is a holistic activity and the techniques emerging from research, the now widely used group cloze and group sequencing activities are designed to encourage readers to be alert to the whole context of the text.*

How many dogs dead or fled now, pray, from Dumbiedykes?

This is the execrable jargon that is supposed to put you in the mood for teaching English. It does succeed in attracting our New Man into the civil service outposts of education, and even, sadly, into the classroom, but it is an insult to the language I write in, and teach in, and teach. And yet it is with such semantic sound and fury, signifying nothing, that the Dalkeith Daleks and their attendant zombies have sought to fill our heads and so equip us for the fight against the barbarism of ignorance.

Alas, such a language is a reversion to that barbarism. Don't they know that the more primitive the language the more complex its form? No, I don't suppose they know that. Not strong on historical linguistics, the men ... Ach, I grow tired of this and 'gin to be aweary of the sun. But at least I'll die with Dalkeith at my back. And with chalk in my hand and biro in my pocket. And books inside my head ...

If they could just have trusted me with these simple tools and left me to get on with the job!

But another crucial failing in the New Philosophie (which calls nothing in doubt and allows no room for doubt) is that the teacher who teaches from the inside is simply not permitted his privacy, his beliefs, not accorded that old-fashioned courtesy of getting on with the job. Of teaching. For accountability is now the name of the game and there is much too much else to do. Too much time to be soaked up by the anaemic blotting paper of the forms and the assessments and the checks and the profiles, the wearisome hours of stale air. This is a broken-backed education system for poor teachers who benefit from the proferred crutch, while the teacher of vision has to accept it in place of a perfectly good leg (Sorry, Cranford!). The highly structured system is a grid that comes down over all of us, trapping all alike. Can you imagine a world of literary criticism in which only one approach is allowed to be applied—and *must* be applied, like logarithms? Not only will there be few failed pupils in the new system, there will also be few failed teachers.

And no more Mackay Mackays.

Can you wonder that, in the face of all this, we felt trapped?

Intellectually trapped in a job which had become part of the Education Industry. Financially trapped by a system which had refused to acknowledge the paramount importance of the ordinary classroom teacher and had almost perversely lured him out of his room with the prospect of a fistful of filthy dollars on the other side. Philosophically trapped by uniformity, the pressures and demands of a system that aspired to safeness and sameness and tameness. Trapped by time: time spent listening to our child-centred new products, time spent clerking instead of teaching. They had poured the precious golden hours down the plughole of barren experimentation and political public convenience. The Chronicles of Wasted Time. And in a very real sense spatially trapped too—all around us the unweeded garden of paper. Not books, but units—the acres of pages filed away in their plain brown tidy boxes, the graveyards of literature, death by a thousand worksheets. In our worst nightmares we watched the rainforests of the world toppling to a planet peopled by life-skilled robots who had 'done the unit' on *Romeo and Juliet* but never actually studied Shakespeare's play. Seeing the video will do; it is not actually necessary to read the text! A helpful suggestion from an Exemplar Unit that was placed in front of our shocked white faces during a Moray House in-service, when the Shakespeare Made Easy approach to fair Verona brought it down as brutally as it could to the level of Leith—*Ra Nurse has a dirty mind . . . Up yours, Willy*—all of this to the grievous detriment of Leith, worth so much more than its patronising reductionists dare allow. No. Books, it was clear, would no longer be respected by our pupils because they were no longer respected by authority.

And so it continues.

Schools are becoming Palaces of Green Porcelain in which books stand as musty monuments to a dying tradition, to be blown to powder by the unit-literate, social-skilled travellers of tomorrow. Touch them and they crumble into dust. So the job I took over from my old masters is now a moribund and semi-remembered trade, akin to thatching, coopering, a craft practised by a shrinking band of brothers and sisters who rage against the dying of their light. Well, rave on, as Buddy Holly sayeth, for this brother here will *not* go gentle into the great goodnight, not so long as one hundred of us remain alive, no, they'll not destroy old Jock, old Campbell Mackay.

And not so long as occasional flashes of fire are heard issuing from high places. Such as from thee, Cardinal Basil Hume, who hath declared that as it is the teachers who really know how to teach, then it is they who should decide the curriculum. The educationists don't know how to teach and the curricula they have concocted are an impoverishment of the imagination. It is not the left-hand side of the brain but the right-hand side that really matters: God's Channel. Cardinal Hume (once a teacher), you can blow the froth off one o' mine any time you choose.

And so can you, your Royal Highness. Together we could build Jerusalem among the dark Satanic Mills of practical atheism which is at the cold heart of their philistine philosophies—and the vision of greatness will shine forth again upon your green and pleasant land. Give me a hearing, sir, or (should I say) *hearken unto my words*, for as somebody once said, using the language of

Not-Alternative Scripture, *Your old men shall dream dreams and your young men shall see visions*. And as somebody else once said—and it wasn't in Dalkeith—*Where there is no vision the people perish*.

Vision.

I had a vision . . . softly creeping . . . What a vision! . . . I had a dream . . . left its mark . . . I was not the only one . . . while I was sleeping . . . I heard a voice cry . . . The thane of Fife had a wife . . . Nor shall my sword . . . This nearly was mine . . . Sleep in my hand . . . Where is she now? . . . You may say I'm a dreamer . . . I will not cease from mental fight . . . In our yellow submarine . . . I hope some day you'll join me . . . At the round earth's imagined corners . . . In England's green and pleasant land . . . Blow your trumpets, angels . . . Shake off these scattered songs, death's counterfeit . . . And awake . . . Arise, you numberless infinities . . . In England's green and pleasant land . . . Swell! Swell! . . . In England's . . . Louder, louder! . . . I hear you, Danny Boy, peace, be still . . . Green and pleasant land.

What green and pleasant land? England? Did you say England? Alas, 'tis gone, 'tis gone. Where is the life that late it led? 'Tis gone, 'tis gone, the fields and farms, the shadows, meadows, lanes, the guildhalls and carved choirs, the bits of her broad bosom that I liked to see on holiday, like you, King Philip of Hull and Coventry and Oxenford and all those packed squares of wheat. Still, there'll be books, you reflected ruefully. In a pig's arse, mate, yet once more. Farewell, England!

And Scotland? Scotland hath need of thee, sweet prince, but in Scotland a great prince in prison lies, for poetry is a prince and Scotland's a prison, and the princely wrists, as they write, are laden with the shackles of the modern critical disease: *gritty realism*. Or rather, not gritty realism itself, but the absurd apotheosis of this crappy criterion by those who ought to know better, but who find that a free ride on a bandwagon is easier than thought. You see, when a cancer attacks an education system, it enters, tragically, the very lymph of the nation. It does not take long for the secondaries to develop, and one of the early casualties is that nation's art, its aesthetic consciousness and the public values and judgements that reach the young through—to take a simple example—literary excerpts presented for analysis in classroom or examination room, gift-wrapped in our case in no less a place than Ironmills Road. Here is your Scotland:

remove the bloody wrappings, witness the envious rents, look on our work, ye fustians, and despair! For gritty realism rules in Scotland (with glottal stop) and this, by definition, is the best we can do. A cancer brings out the ugly and the obscene in any body, its wretchedness and feet of clay, its crown of thorns without the nimbus of ecstasy, the golden flush of faith. The depressing force of limitation is felt in the blood. The anguished onlooker sees the corpse long before death occurs. Thus life goes on at its lowest level and Scotland gives birth in the gutter and her children are gritty realists, assessing her literary art by the numbers of fucks the books can manage. A fuck a line and you're a down-to-earth, no-nonsense, hard-headed, hard-nosed, unromantic, truthful, naturalistic, man-of-the-people, genuine, unsentimental—but not sober—absolutely authentic bastard. A gritty realist.

O Freude!

Oh, fuck off, Freude! Give us Freud instead, any Saturday night of the week. Never mind the sounds loosening themselves in agony from the knots in the Beethoven brow, forget the ecstasy, forget the Ninth, forget the last quartets, forget the early symphonies even, this is Paddy's Market, forget all that—where are the battleship turds, sludging through the sea of green, yellow submarine? Give us the composer's chamber pot, the shit and the piss, the immortal line, 'I want to go to the toilet', ah! now that is art, let's get get *beneath* the piano, below the boring technicalities, to the—to the—well, to coin a phrase, to the gritty realism of it all, the gritty realism of life, of art, for art is life, otherwise it is not art. Right, Jimmy?

I tell you if I come across this phrase once more, if I read but one more review in praise of gritty dialogue, gritty characters, gritty working class values, then I, who am as working class and bloody proud of it as the next man, must grit my gritty teeth, for O, Fool, I shall go mad, I shall go mad, O, Fool, I shall go mad. Poverty, pubs, boredom, violence, angst, ennui, urban deprivation, authorial malaise through the four-letter word and the rhetoric of the gutter—that is not real life any more than my teaching *Hamlet* was ever real life, with or without the fucks. It is a *part* of life—and that is all. O, but it offends me to the soul to hear some robust, grittily realistic critic tear a book to tatters because it has omitted the statutory strewn bowels, the rubbish tips, fractured heads, smashed glasses, big boots, bird brains, copulation, leather, and all the hard men whose occasional drolleries glint like broken bottles among the acres of monosyllabic obscenity. I hate the pretentious boredom of all this and the chronic Emperor's Clothes syndrome that makes the gritty realists afraid to see the naked lie. Not much grittly realism in *Lycidas*, eh? Just realism of another sort.

But what saddens and angers me above all else is that it is this simplified proletarian myth of Scotland which is fast gaining the greatest currency among the image-hunting pseuds who like to believe that they are hymning the people. We have seen rather less tartanism of late trailed across our silver screens and Brigadoon and Andy Stewart have had their day—nearly. But we are now being over exposed to the brutal edge of Scotland and the cult of the hard nut, the Jock, denizen of that nasty no-nonsense Scotland, no longer the land of the heather and the kilt, the mountain and the river, but the nation of big man realism, where they will have none of that imaginative shite. Let Hemingway kill Hamlet with an elephant gun and read the hero's destiny in his mangled intestines, pluck out the heart of his mystery thus—simple, for he is full of shit and we defy augury. Here's revolution an·we had the trick to see it. Some of us don't.

Of course we have always exhibited in our literature a deeper involvement with the working classes than English authors, but writers and critics who glorify this sham nobility to gross proportion are doing the working people no favours and the gritty critics perform a great disservice to a nation's art when they worship the writer who worships the country where they kill the imagination. All in the name of a droolingly downmarket cloth-cap brand of art. Unhappily such a critique does reflect an insidious suicidalism inherent in the Scottish psychology, a defeatist and inverted snobbery that has taken over from Scotland the Brave and Scotland the Sentimental and Scotland the Picturesque; a defeatist image of carefully defined ugliness that has worked the trick—the wider literary world has swallowed the current Scottish self-caricature. And we educate you, the young, into the accepted and acceptable image. And the image is perpetrated and scattered through the world. And thus we achieve our immortality.

From fairest creatures we desire increase?

That thereby beauty's rose may never die—yes, but it's not happening, is it? We are being invited instead to stick our heads down a toiletful of turds and call it art, brazen it out in letters of shit. *Exegi monumentum excremente perennius*. I am sorry, these are wild and whirling words, but I'm not myself, my wit's diseased, you see, I am not what I am and I'm sorry if they do offend you heartily, yes, faith, heartily. Be honest with yourself then, go to, for to be honest as this world goes is to be one man picked out of ten thousand. Very well, then, go to, I shall be honest—and this honesty will have me whipped in Scotland, yea, out of Scotland, perchance. O Scotland, Scotland! So to your pleasures—I am for other than for Glasgow measures!

But it's not just Scotland, is it? Stan was right: the whole world's a disaster. In the world of art shock tactics take the place of talent and Melvyn Bragg sucks forth the soul with his adenoidal kiss of death. From South Bank to South Bank—O, what a fall was there, my countrymen! Exit Shakespeare, enter Kathy Acker—and if you have yawns, prepare to show them. I'm truly sorry, all ye Acker devotees, but by the time I've pictured old Kath's protagoniste with her hand on her clit and her boyfriend sucking her cunt-juice through a straw, served chilled, if you please, with a little Del Boy umbrella stuck therein (and that's after the blow-jobs and the lick-outs, the incest and the buggery) I do begin to yawn just a little and say, Fie upon this quiet novel, I want filth! A *little* porn's a dangerous thing. Corrupting. Converted rainforests of the stuff, however, you do begin to take not too seriously. And seriously, what I do begin to miss is a little genuine *fun* from these O, so serious post-pornographers. You see, Hamlet doesn't really ask Ophelia if he can drink her cunt juice—he says, 'Lady, shall I lie in your lap? . . . Do you think I meant country matters?' And when she says,' I think nothing', he tells her that that is exactly what should be betwixt maids' legs: nothing. That is, a circle, a round hole. But if that is what virginity is—nothing, then to prize it too deeply is really to make too much ado about . . . nothing. Virginity's an empty hole. Nought plus nought equals nought, whereas nought plus a phallic one equals one. Ah, but it doesn't, you see, because nought plus one, sexually speaking, equals two, and spiritually, two true lovers, one plus one, equals one, while biologically nought plus one equals three. And that's the miracle of love, which transcends mathematics. And, while we're at it, transcends all things. O, see you, then, what can be done with this wonder of woman? And see you what a miracle she is? But Acker's not much interested

257

in miracles, is she? More in masturbation: the Cranfordian level, which most of us left behind with our tired adolescence.

Goodbye then, adolescence. Goodbye Kathy Acker. I'm doubly sorry, love, I'll say it once more, but I have supped full with horrors. Direness, familiar to my assaulted thought, cannot once startle me. The Men of Iron-mills have produced greater obscenities than anything you have ever written, or ever could. Their education system itself is an obscenity and their documents hit deeper pits than Dead-Eyed Dick screwing the arse off Lady Macbeth because he knows the sticking place and will not fail to come—and all that kind of crap. Yet another version of Up Yours, old Willy, transatlanticised, but I've had it already from arse to elbow, from Holyrood Road to Ironmills Road and I'm sick to fucking death of it. It's actually worse than Shakespeare Made Easy—it's the Old Bill brought with relevance and commitment and gritty realism to the streets of Manhattan, where the revolutionary hot-dog Kath sells her L.O.'s and her B.J.'s from her stand. No thanks, lady—it's not for me. Give me a Keatsian draught of vintage to a stein of cunt-dew any time, for your stories have gone so far that they simply cease to disturb. You've tried too hard, old girl. Too hard. You've gone the other way from Ironmills but you've ended up in the same place—you've ceased to disturb.

Now it is when literature stops disturbing us that a nation is in trouble—and literature does lose its power to disturb when it gets caught in the sterile white light of information. Ironmills Road information in particular. Somebody once said that happiness writes white. So does bureaucracy. So does intellect without emotion, reason without passion, communication without vision, clarity without insight, language without nuance, lucidity without depth, understanding without enigma, conviction without ambivalence. It is this quality of ambivalence in art which has been particularly threatened by the Ironmills Road-speak which refers to a book as a print stimulus, the clinical language that paints the world white and utterly destroys the sweet mystery of life. O, sons of the nineties, you are better fed, better doctored, better informed than ever before! But not better educated, that's for sure. The mystery has been taken away from you and you can see all, you can see all . . .

The Goof once told us another story out of Herodotus. It was about a king of Egypt who was conquered and captured by the Persians and put on public show. He was made to stand in front of the Persian king and watch all his beloved children and family pass before him in the chains of slavery. First came his son, then his daughter, and so on it went, a brutal parade of all his dear ones in bondage. And yet, like Job's, his composure did not break. Then, near the end of the line, among other prisoners, he saw one of his old servants, similarly chained. Faced with this sight he broke down suddenly and wept bitterly and could not be comforted.

Why?

There are no Grade Related Criteria that we can apply to that story, as a story. It is given by Herodotus without a further shred of information. Why did the Egyptian king crack only when he saw his old servant in irons instead of showing his grief at the sight of his own children chained and enslaved? The king simply said that some things lie too deep for tears, but that is not information. Because Herodotus has not supplied an explanation, the story remains in the mind forever, haunting the imagination, asking the endless questions of art. It is through such stories that we learn to be more human, that we learn more about what we really are.

We do not learn what we are from the Grade Related Criteria.

Or from the National Curriculum. Or from the New English Bible. Or from Shakespeare Made Easy. Or from all the other nine-day wonders of the world that extract the sweet mystery and hand us back the husk.

Such as the Word-Processor, the deity of Cranford's study, before which he abased himself each day. In the beginning was the Word and in the Age of Cranford was the Word Processor, ersatz substitute so often for ideas and for art. Appoint a New Man to a promoted post and within the hour he starts to use a word-processor, the status tool of the line manager. Well, I thank the old gods of the former dispensation that I never learned to bow down before the green screens of these graven images. Give me a pencil and a rubber and I will write a book, I say. But consider, if you will—one of the worst literary casualties of this powerful new god has been the death of the writer's notebook, revealing, as it used to do, the fascinating stages of his composition and local evolution of his art. Posterity will very shortly be in possession of aseptic acres of pristine white scripts with never a syllable out of place and all those hours of absorbing authorial effort gone the way of all paper. An entire branch of scholarship will have vanished over the technological night. No-one will be poring over the notebooks of the Dylan Thomases of the next millenium: they won't be there. And there will be no Bad Quartos of Hamlet to tease Professor Duthie out of thought. No bad thing, you could say? I wonder. For the want of an Elizabethan word-processor, Falstaff has forever babbled o' green fields. Just think—he might simply have talked about them instead, had Shakespeare used an Apple Mac.

Somewhere, over the Amiga Way, where Ataris fear to tread, there must be a Happy Land where all the vanished chapters and stories go to, like the Lost Boys in *Peter Pan*, if we could but penetrate behind the veil, behind the iron veil, the iron curtain of computer technology. There would be literary riches beyond the dreams of avarice. So: if there be an immortal soul but no heaven for it to go to, I pray that mine may go to that Happy Land where I may meet all those snuffed out sections and stories shunted into the Lethean sidings, there achieve reincarnation as a literary polymath and afterwards enjoy the fame and the girl and the money all at one sitting. But I know, of course, that there really is a heaven. There must be.

Because there certainly is a hell . . .

From this vantage point here in Blair's, I can stand like John Milton or Dante and view the entire cosmos. That dot upon the skyline over there, over the firth, there, where I point my finger, is the tower of Taft Academy, and if I ascend the tower of Robert Blair's and apply my eye to the optic glass, I can bring the spire of heaven close, as close as it will ever come now, for that is heaven over there, believe me, heaven as it was and always will be in my mind: the Paradiso. Now east of north, if you will, just where we stand, and what seest thou else? Arthur's Seat, the high hill, cragged and steep, the Edinburgh Acropolis, where Truth once stood. Squatting by the school now, frowning on the crags like the great Toad Work, Robert Blair's very own Hill of Difficulty: the Purgatorio. And if you turn your head beyond the hill and follow the old road south, you will see down there, far down among the distant brown folds of the earth, the place itself, Pandemonium, the seat of the Adversary, way down in Dalkeith Land, where the Chief Examiner sits like old Pharaoh and will not let us go: Ironmills Road and the Offices of the Infernal Board: the Inferno.

Hell.

And spread out beneath our feet—Edinburgh. And northwards the rest of Scotland, and southwards England, and eastwards Norway, and all about us continents and seas, the rest of the world, unfenced existence.

Where to choose our place of rest.

Rest?

Yes, perhaps I should rest there. Rest my case, as they say. The Naked Advocate takes up his briefs again, having laid himself bare before you as part of the art of education, unique instruction and the ultimate visual aid. To teach thee I was naked first. Never be afraid to take your clothes off. Let not our babbling dreams affright our souls. Richard's himself again. Human kind, after all, cannot bear too much reality, as I have said before-O, and you are but young human creatures, fresh and green. Yet so were we when Fat Boy walked among us, naked in Paradise . . .

But I ha' done. Dress me in borrowed robes again, on with the motley, and yet once more, O ye laurels! You've had enough of my schoolmastering I can see, and so have I, dear boys, so have I.

15

IT WAS INEVITABLE that Colonel Stubbes's prophecy would be fulfilled: that the clever men would look about them from this rough pinnacle and say, Sod it—I'm off! Men of integrity that they were, they would not spend an hour with such decay. On the other hand they might have stuck it longer had Cranford stood out against the shoddy new values and systems that were being imposed upon us from Mrs Thatcher downwards. In fact he ushered them in with undisguised zeal. Even if he'd had a brain in his head and understood the educational tragedy that was being enacted, he'd not have behaved any differently. A yesman, eager for Ironmills, perchance, and the post of Satan, bound to be vacated one day: Chief of the Fallen Angels in Dalkeith. I've already told you he had the face for it. Not the wings, though—-not strong on pinions, poor Cranford, unless it be paper pinions, passing out the interminable brown envelopes, the unbeauteous files, the jiffy bags of junk, with genuine satisfaction. Made him believe he was achieving something. It was just his cuppa. Offer him wine and he'd ask for water; bread and he'd prefer a stone; meat and he'd fancy a nice bit of scorpion. Not strong on taste, old Cranford. Not a man of palate. Instead he swallowed the view that teaching should no longer be considered a vocation but a business and surrounded himself with the flunkeys and functionaries to prove it, jacks-and-jills-in-office who would do his bidding and cause no trouble. Ensure a plentiful lack of ambivalence. And a moritorium on Herodotus.

It was all changed from the Taft days—shall I call them the daft days? the daft and happy days?—and indeed the early days of Blair's, golden days, McCann, believe me, golden days, when that single Headmaster and his Deputy did the lot and left the teachers to get on with it. As get on with it we did. Then no man had to defer to or instruct another because all teachers were equal. Nor did we have to consult job descriptions because we knew precisely what we were called upon to do.

All changed.

Cranford was no sooner in office than he bred a whole pigeon-loft of line managers who muted on us from above when they weren't actually in their pigeon-holes and who spent their days producing shit. Of course they also produced the paper to go with it, reams and reams of it, justifying their new jobs by the amount of paper they could generate. Do you want a statistic? Here it is anyway. Do you know how long the first Elizabethan government lasted? It was a long time. It may interest you to know that it ran an entire country for nearly half a century and in all that time produced less paper than Blair's produces in a single day. Think about it. So Blair's became a paper factory. And the line managers did less and less teaching. And the paper bred and bred. And none of it was really read. But it kept the books on the shelves, all right, kept the real teachers from their teaching, their preparation, their necessary reading. The school library began to take on a tinge of green.

'Good Lord, do I detect a touch of Porcelain about the old place today?' asked Colonel Stubbes of the librarian, as he poked his head through the door to inquire about a book on Gardening in Early Retirement. 'And have any of the Morlocks been in today to gobble up a wandering scholar or two? No? Then there's hope I may last another six months yet!'

The truly laughable part was that we could always tell when a New Man had been promoted, or was aiming at it. They changed their walks, you see. Now it's astonishing, but any psychologist will tell you that you cannot even cross a room without revealing fifteen things about your personality. Teachers on the move don't so much cross rooms as proceed along corridors and there was one basic division concerning the way these new nonentities walked, two categories of perambulation pertaining to the gutless grovellers. Either they speeded up their walks or they slowed them down drastically, so that what we saw was either steady quinquiremes and stately galleons—or dirty British coasters, depending on whether their psyches made them wish to appear calm and dignified or ruffled and pressed for time, so busy as they were with affairs of state.

I refer to Masefield there because Leroy penned a parody of *Cargoes* which took off the various walks and wallies:

Aspirant to Ironmills in distant Dalkeith,
Drifting down the corridors as if he'd seen the Queen,
With a cargo of apes,
Paper and parrots,
Gasteropods, hods and sods and lots of vaseline.

Dirty little bumboy with a bagful of brushes,
Chugging through the crowds in busy Robert Blair's,
With a cargo of floppy discs,
Fluff-remover, floor-polish—
And on his knees, from Cranford's room, a pile of carpet
*   hairs!*

There was more foolery yet, if I could but remember it—and
Colonel Stubbes spoke Greek—but there at least are two stanzas
for you.

'By their walks shall ye know them,' quipped Gladstone, and
taking off his shoes and diving out of the staffroom, went prancing
on his points, following one of the newly appointed New Men
down the corridor all the way to the front of school, all the time
carrying out a fierce burlesque of this particular toady's walk in
the silent hilarity of his socks. When he then interspersed his
antics with snippets from the John Cleese Ministry of Silly Walks
sketch, we could stand it no longer and were forced to retreat
into the staffroom, holding our mouths and our sides fit to burst.
When we dared look out again, Gladstone was crawling back up
the corridor towards us on his hands and knees, his tongue licking
the ground (in simulation) so recently trod on by the now august
personage who had just passed that way.

'Get back in here quickly, you bloody idiot!' spluttered Colonel
Stubbes, the tears streaming down his red face and wetting his
handlebars. 'The period bell's about to ring!'

La Damn Bell Sans Merci.

But Gladstone rolled in like Yogi Bear and stayed on his back,
waving his stumpy legs in the air and quoting the punch-line from
the old Highland joke about the ultimate Highland hospitality.

'Och, Fi-o-n-a, Fi-o-n-a, why aren't you aarching your baack
and keeping the poor shentleman's balls (voiceless plosive *p*alls)
off the stone cold floor!'

Poor gentleman indeed. When the bootlickers bent down they
needed machetes to find their way out of his carpet pile. He was
being paid a king's mint for fucking up the school and guzzling

the funds at the regular weekend conferences he'd concocted for himself and his minions, held in hotels down in Oxford and Cambridge, one every month. He even chartered private planes to take his team along with him and we walked the chartered corridors and stayed in our chartered rooms while he paid a grand a flight for a grand old time, all on the school, no problem. I kept thinking of all that rich food and wine going down their biological tubes and through the hotel's waste pipes and out along the sewage conduits, the classless society of turds, to the English Channel or the Irish Sea or wherever Oxford's egest goes to, treated or untreated––an expensive way of producing precious dung and curious excrements, as Donne reflected. Not too erudite an excrement, however. Not strong on Donne, the dung-producers, at their conferences, where they did their brainstorming and their tanking up, Donne not appearing on the agenda, and where they sped with such dexterity to incestuous sheets of waffle and to suck one another off down the one-way street of line management, to reinforce the pecking order all over again, to the glory of the one above and the greatest glory of Cranford himself. That's at least one thing Cranford was strong on: the hierarchy. Small wonder that he soon succeeded in splitting up the staff into two distinct camps: the teachers and the wankers—the latter led by the Great Wanker himself. O, how well we could have spared them, the wankers and the climbers. But the teachers dwindled and the climbers grew in number, enow of such as, for their bellies' sake, creep and intrude and climb into the fold! As still they do. Of other care they little reckoning make than how to scramble at the shearer's feast and shove away the worthy bidden guest. Blind mouths! that scarce themselves know how to hold a sheep hook or have learnt aught else the least that to the faithful herdman's art belongs! What recks it them? What need they? They are sped. And when they list, their lean and flashy songs grate on their scrannel pipes of wretched straw!

Flashy. Yes, by God, thank you, Milton! you use the right word there, as always. Spivs, a wise man called them more recently, and I couldn't have chosen two better words to fit together: flashy spivs promoting dull dog plodders to change the face of education in these days of market forces and benighted politics.

So now you know what *Lycidas* is really all about. What's the point in living? in working? in trying to make your job into a fine and noble art? when the good die young or get shoved aside and the glitzy turds rise to the top and start pretending they've developed brains at their top ends. Is there even any point in teaching *Lycidas*, I wonder, I really do? Well, I hope so, boys of Blair's, I hope so, though we must teach our elegies and wear our rue with a difference, perhaps. Still, we see what Milton saw before us, and life doesn't change that much across the centuries, does it? and maybe there's a lesson there and even a little hope. And there is yet another hope too—that when all else has failed you can at least write about it—as Milton did, and through your writing, hope to teach, as Milton did, what though the pen is yet one more infirmity of noble minds and writing itself a form of illness. What does that matter? Civilisation itself is but one gigantic neurosis—that's not to condemn it. Take up the pen, I beg you, for I can do no more. This is my long farewell to all my teaching.

And writing—writing makes me sick at heart. I'm no longer so sure, you see, about the therapy, the catharsis, the ultimate possession of truth, the universal embrace and all that stuff. Oh, and didactic writing is rather frowned upon these days, whereas teaching—well, teaching has always been a didactic occupation, has it not? Doesn't mean there's only one lesson to be learned though, does it? How many lessons have you learned this afternoon, for example? Or in the past six years? No, don't answer that; you lack the means of comparison, but I see a measuring stick that is twenty five years long and my ruined band of brothers and I, well, we saw the way things were going quite some time ago. The hungry sheep look up and are not fed and the grim wolf sits in Hell and smacks his chops. And the two-handed engine at the door, though it be strong to smite, is also slow to save and exceeding long in coming. Yet it will come. It must come, perforce. The readiness is all.

> *Our little systems have their day,*
> *They have their day and cease to be.*

But so, alas, do people.
One morning Leroy announced that he'd had enough. Went in and told Cranford to chew upon this: that he'd rather be a villager than to repute himself a son of Rome under these hard conditions as the time was like to lay upon us. When Cranford requested a translation (not strong on Caesar, the Principal) Leroy laid his

letter of resignation on the table and walked out. Gladstone announced that he would not stay a jot longer than his old friend and at the end of that week he too went along with his resignatioı., giving his notice up to the end of session. Surprisingly though, he came bouncing back into the staffroom, his eye alight with mischief.

'He's been given a Chair!' he shouted. 'Cranford's been given a Chair!'

Everybody stared.

What do you mean, a Chair? A Chair in what? Where? When?

'Follow me!'

We all hurried down the corridor at his heels, congregating uncertainly outside Cranford's room.

'It's all right, he's in Cambridge, at a conference,' said Gladstone, throwing open the door and waving us in like Manuel. 'Is all right—Mr Fawlty he no at home, you go in!'

Yes, Cranford had been given a Chair, all right. There it was, behind his desk. Impressive and expensive looking, but extremely odd in its design, with the most curious attachments. We stared at it, uncomprehending. Then Stan saw the joke.

'It's for his leg,' he laughed. 'It's an orthopaedic chair!'

The grey room was coloured briefly by our laughter. Even the shrouded word processor seemed to warm up a little as we stood and laughed.

'Yes, it's an orthopaedic chair,' Gladstone chuckled, 'and if you'd care to notice . . .'

He crept over the carpet and waved an outspread palm at it in mock triumph.

'. . . Empty!'

We laughed all the more.

Is the chair empty? Is the king dead? Is the sword unswayed? the empire unpossessed? No, the Chief Executive has simply swanned off on one leg to yet another *Spitting Image* gassing session, leaving his new chair free for us each one of us to dive into and do a turn, each outdoing the one before in an imitation of the utmost imbecility. He was always somewhere else, was Cranford, and the ordinary animals on the farm seldom saw him or his Chief Pigs. They lived in another world.

The ultimate insult, however, had yet to come.

It fell one day some time after Cranford had arranged for a hush-hush building project to be carried out for the start of what turned out to be Leroy and Gladstone's last summer term at Blair's. We arrived at school after the Easter vacation and saw the new extension off the front of school management suite. We were curious as to what it meant, naturally, and made our way in through the main conference room. Opening the new door that had been made in the wall, we walked through into what we assumed would be yet another office for yet another line manager. We were simply not prepared for what greeted us. I have to confess that we were knocked out, rendered speechless. We who throve on words were dumb to speak a single syllable to what was left of the crooked rose of virtue. For a full minute all we could do was to stare in silence and with, this time, the wildest of wild surmises, at the new discoverie which transcended by far all other worlds and all other seas.

Are you ready for this, then?

And don't dare talk to me about farce. The entire show was a fucking farce.

It was a jacuzzi!

A cauldron of unholy bubbles, foaming like the entrance to an antiseptic Acheron, or epic mere, at the bottom of which the mother of all intellectual frivolity might sit like Grendel's dam, generating an element fit for fools to sit in a circle and froth—filling the air around them with their insubstantial talk, a sterile coterie of disembodied heads, gassing amid the suds. Blue and green tiling, mosaic interior, muted underwater spotlights, in which soft lambency a carved dolphin swam, given fitful animation by the whirling flares of chemically treated water. Our eyes strayed to changing cubicles, glass-fronted drinks cabinets, exercise bicycles, dressing gowns, mini-conference table, and walls decorated with larger-than-life mosaics of insolent Greece and haughty Rome: victorious athletes being crowned by admiring girls, sandalled and braided and flowing with tresses and wine. A veritable theme-park of Cranford's youth, when he had not been short on legs and balls. Just on brains.

You know all about the jacuzzi, of course. It came last year. But I tell you this to try to give you some idea of how hard we were hit between the eyes by this latest insult to the poor sodding practising teacher. No longer content to fly down south to provide the Cam with their curious excrements formed from patois de foie gras, there to reinforce their incestuously conceived importance and actual educational impotence, the Principal and his team were going to do it to one another right here in Blair's, under our very noses, up to their necks in hot spume and their own hot air and God knows what else, sipping iced champers and brainstorming away four times as furiously as before, double double toil and trouble, wanking like Trojans and thinking like mad from their chins downwards, while we bloody infantry lazed around in the front line, looking after the sheep in No Man's Land (you poor buggers) and generally fleeting the time carelessly in our bucolic bliss, free from the cares of managerial responsibility.

It was a gathering of the Old Guard that stood in a wrathful circle that morning. Colonel Stubbes surveyed our faces grimly.

'Right, lads,' he snapped, 'pricks out! You know what to do!'

And to a man we emptied our bladders into Cranford's disgusting little cauldron.

'That's the most satisfying piss I've had in sixty years,' said Stubbes, zipping up his fly. 'And by the way—(looking at me)—you're on your own next session, boy. You'll be Acting Head of Department until such time as they've appointed some poor bastard to take my place!'

And the colonel walked off to pen his own letter of resignation.

And was quickly followed by Stan, who didn't even put pen to paper—not old Stan—but simply downed tools in the middle of a lesson and fucked off.

One of Cranford's eternal pieces of paper was the actual trigger. It was no different from any other piece of paper: just another form issued for the filling out thereof, another report to complete, another set of figures for the jackals and jackasses to re-jig in their jacuzzi, between gobfuls of Bollinger. The subject-matter matters not. And 'tis no matter. It simply represented the point at which Stan could take no more. O.K., he said, I'm out of here. And he chucked up everything, as the poet said, and just cleared off, ready once more for the audacious, purifying, elemental move, the stubble in the fo'c'sle, the swagger down the nut-strewn roads to Leith. O, Stanny! Why did you go? Why didn't you stay with your old Meg? Can't say why. It's one of the unanswerables of art, that question. One thing I can say, though. Stan's departure, poetic though it was, Larkinesque and all that, was not one of the fifth-hand wonders of hearsay. He came to me directly on his way to the front door, to say goodbye, stopped outside my room while I was teaching *Hamlet*, as it so happened. The ripple of laughter that went through the class made me turn to look at the door. Through its centre window pane I could see Stan's skeleton snapping its jaws in a cheery grin. He'd wired it up so as he could work it like a ventriloquist's dummy.

'Goodnight, sweet prince!' it squeaked shrilly through the glass, (Stan was good at voices) 'and tell his nibs I won't be coming back!'

I opened the door and Stan's face shot out from behind the skull. He was outwardly composed, but buzzing with rage, trembling almost audibly, like wires in the rain.

'There you are, matey,' he chirped with enforced gaiety, 'he's all yours (indicating Yorick), look after the dear old boy. I'll see you in Zanzibar—maybe—and may we always meet at Jenners!'

And he went.

First hand. Saying his own epitaph. Poor Stan. Drowned off Capè Lopez, all the way from Leith, and Lethe-wards hath sunk, in his dear little lady, *The Good Hope*. Have one with Torvil, mate—and may Fat Boy be the barman! See you at Jenners, Stan. Some day.

Some hope.

He wasn't the last Blair's casualty, courtesy of Cranford's bureaucratic crassness and time-wasting triviality and rigid little Hitlerism. Apart from Stan and Gladstone and Leroy and the Colonel, there were many others, the flowers o' the forest making way for the weeds, the springing thistles, the New Men. In point of fact the school's results had deteriorated markedly over the past year or so and the pupil roll had fallen, and so when the exodus began in earnest of the good old sturdy teaching stock, the merchant-minded governors were quick to see that this was no way to run a school, that perhaps they had, after all, made a mistake with Cranford, whose lack of vision had depressed so many able teachers into resigning and retiring well before their time. He was carpeted on his own piled carpet and told to get the ship back on course. Or maybe they all climbed into the jacuzzi together, he and the governors, and they held him under until he'd promised to do better. He responded with typical Cranfordian genius by planning more At Homes and Open Days. Breathtaking intellect, no? He also applied himself with even greater zeal to the solitary bottle. Sat in the sudsy seclusion of his little spa bath and knocked back the school, whisky, sherry, Beaujolais, watching the empties whizz about with the eddying bubbles like dodgems till they clashed and sank and he felt like going under himself. Such at least were the rumours that leaked out concerning him, and—do you know?—I actually started feeling sorry for the bastard. He was encompassed by talents greater than his own, even with the giants gone (mine, for example!) and was a contemptible nonentity in his own school, a purveyor of paper, a clerk of works, a breeder of boredom, a setter-up of sub-committees, a breaker-down of zeal, an enemy of fun, a killer of instinct, a stammerer, a wanker, a wet fart, an absentee landlord, an over-subsidised, subnormal little shit, a gin-drenched figurehead on a torn ship of fools, a grey mist on the sea's face and a grey sun setting . . . Oh, I give up, for fuck's sake, what's the use? What the fuck more can I say? The flyting of old Mackay is nearly done. Suffice it to say he was a John Balliol, a toom tabard. He was a nobody.

Years passed. As years do. With that increasing feeling of sameness that years take on. That lives endure. And in accordance with the deadening effect that years have and that lives eventually cease to feel, I lost all my anger and contempt and found that my bitterness towards Cranford—I had fucked up my own life, after all—had finally shaded off into a kind of grim pity.

Until Jenny came back.

Aha! that made you sit up, didn't it? I kept that one cleverly up my sleeve now, did I not? Worry not, boys, old Campbell Mackay has a sharp card or two to play yet, yes, by heaven, for I've seen the day that with my good falchion I have made them skip!

And so suddenly Jenny is back in the story. Much older, but with much greater power to transform the tale. And so the tale of Campbell and Jenny is not quite dead.

If this were played upon a stage now, would you condemn it as an unlikely fiction? Well, I should bloody well hope not—not after all I've taught you. You would simply observe (I trust) along with Professor Alan Stoll (*Art And Artifice in Shakespeare*) that improbability is not a problem in art: it is precisely what we expect from it and indeed demand from it. Who the fuck wants real life? And who wants *Lycidas* instead? (Hands up.) Such fine and fruitful situations as art provides us with—real life does not and cannot afford. So if I were writing a novel about the bastarding situation Jenny is exactly the character I should bring back into the plot at just this time, to catch the reader off guard, to gouge out his brains: the only way to kill off the crappy true-to-life criteria that bung up his thinking.

On the other hand I have to say to you that there was also something inevitable about Jenny's return, something right and true. I don't know if I can explain this to you, O ye of your ingenuous teens, but after all I am in the selling business, the old imaginative-leap trade, and still consider myself bloody good at it, so I'll have a try. Lay on, Macduff.

I ask you, first, to look at yourselves. Hard. What makes you tick? What juice do you run on? Let me answer that question for you in one word. Optimism. Belief in a future. The world is all before you and you cannot see it as anything other than your oyster, *your* oyster: university, a lovely wife, a cushy job, or at least a well-paid one, actually getting paid for doing precisely what you enjoy doing, fantastic house thrown in, well-balanced family in fine midsummer weather, holidays in Provence (or Florida, if you're on the Peter Mayle money and myth trail), a fat car and a fat pension, (inflation-proof, even Labour-Party-proof), a place in heaven, and never a thought in your youthful noodles that God or the Devil, disillusionment, disability, death or boredom is going to get in your way.

Dream on, dream on, you poor fuckers, it doesn't go like that. Not quite. Try it this way. You'll have three or four years of undergraduate fun and folly (though you'll be permanently short of dosh, courtesy of Mrs Thatcher and her Philistine government's slaughterous contempt for education in this country, not to be rectified by John Major or any other of the Tory wimps). This will be followed by: a frigid bitch in your bed (soon to shift into a single), long hours on crappy wages, if you're a gentleman and a scholar, surrounded by turds, unmitigated boredom, bills by the bushel, a leaky roof, dry rot, a clutch of kids deafening you with heavy metal and demands for your hard-won cash, loss of spiritual direction, loss of sexual drive, loss of teeth, hair, certainty, a rusty Ford, Sky TV screaming at you from the corner—and her mother coming to stay.

`Is that closer to the mark? I am here today to tell you that it is. Much. Not that this particular bespectacled schoolteaching sod was through *all* of that. But there comes a time in every man's life, if he's honest, when he starts to miss the girls he didn't screw. And starts to wank after those he did but didn't marry. In bed and bog they pursue him, the succubi of his handsome past. He shrugs them off. Or he lets them stay, to offer him their sweet torment. He looks in the mirror—and looks away, starts to fantasise, to dream about starting again, having the second fling, the crack of the whip (literally, possibly) in the cheeky wee bachelor pad. He lifts the telephone, starts in motion a train of events, following his train of thought . . .

He has marvelled, you see, that the menopause is so near, the executioner's assistant; that so much time has flown straight into nothingness, torn off unused, and cannot be repaid by faces and forks. More luncheons than lust, these days old son? Yes, yes, I well knew that Peter Porter feeling. It came upon me hard, hard upon the Philip Larkin feeling, made me realise just how far and how long teaching had pushed me to the side of my own life, especially these last years, just how efficiently it had pulled the plug on me. My spirits had gone glugging down the drains and Lethe-wards had sunk. Might as well have been the water of Leith, anyway.

So when I heard that Jenny was in the Athens of the North, that she was actually here, back over the border, what do you think I felt? My God, what did I not feel? I felt yet once more, let me tell you, like the Wild Rover, the Whistling Gypsy, and Jock o' Hazeldean and Young Lochinvar all rolled into one. Only this time it was no dream. The old menopause, having just got its foot in my flat door, was pretty niftily shown the tenement stair and I bowled the bastard down the Royal Mile as low as to the fiends.

I was sitting slumped in the flat at the time, facing a sideboard full of much-opened bottles and with my back to a bookcase full of much-unopened books, when the telephone shrilled. It was Leroy. You'll never believe it, old boy! What would I never believe? Cranford was dead, perchance? Far from it, far from it. Just seen the sodding bastard, stumping out of Waverley Station and into a taxi—with guess what?

A bit of fluff on his arm, you know—a bird, a shemale a child of our grandmother Eve, or, for thy more sweet understanding, a woman. And a bit of all right she was too—the sort he'd do well to get his leg over, and not his tin one, either, if he just had the engineer's wheel to go with it, that is. Couldn't be his estranged little missis, do you think? She who's never been seen?

She about whom I had never breathed a word to anybody——barely even to myself. All these years.

The phone must have picked up the statutory thump my heart gave as it skipped its statutory beat, but Leroy never mentioned it. He simply described Cranford's lady companion, as I bade him. Not that it took more than three words. Yes, it was Jenny, all right. She had come back, tender-hearted at the drop of a telephone, when he started going to pieces, back she came to cool his jacuzzi-cooled brow even further and to hold his trembling alcoholic's hand and to press her napkin to his salt and sorry rheum and to do everything she could in her estranged but strangely gentle nurse's way to comfort him: the vallium by day, the sleeping-pill by night, the needle, the narcotics, the stomach pump, the dull opiate, the perilous stuff, the sweet oblivious antidote, the bed chart, the physio, the hand that strokes the captain, hand on the helm (only there was no helm), the gentle touch then, the gentle touch. Gentle Jenny, sweetest girl, I love you.

Yes, it was too much for me and I'm sorry to say—no, I'm bloody glad to say—I couldn't take it, the thought of her moving into the schoolhouse with him above Dumbiedykes, living less than a mile away from me and massaging that bibulous bastard back into being. So, I decided to do what was perhaps the undecent: to woo her back to me and leave her shambles of a spouse to sink back into the ruination and oblivion he so deserved. I knew in my heart of hearts that she still loved me, as Lara loved Zhivago. (O, those sixties again!) that she would be unable to resist my emotional assault upon her. And lest you think me somewhat caddish, let me justify my action by stating the simple truth that I still loved her, though it was many a long year since I had seen her, longer than Shenandoah, oh yes, still I loved her, madly and beyond words, wildly enough to kill Cranford in his jacuzzi for her if I had to.

But I knew it need not come to that.

What must it come to, then? It did not take me long to come up with the answer. All I had to do was to write her a poem—it was not quite beyond words, you see—to let her understand that there had never ever been anyone else but her and never would be. I had written very sporadically over these past twelve years and had made no attempt to publish anything of what I'd written. I had lost my own style, which had become clouded and confused by a thousand love-affairs with other men's works. I just couldn't leave them alone, you see. It was a kind of alcoholism, worse, an adulterous obsession, like the kind of driving need some men have to possess all women and enter into them and master them and reflect their beauty. Only with me it wasn't women but books, authors. I had become a multi-ventriloquist, thinking and speaking in quotations. You've seen it for yourselves. As a teacher, of course, I could get away with it, this multiple fracturing of the mind and imagination. But as a writer I could see what was happening to me and dared not publish any more. I had become that literary Lost Boy, never grown up. Mackay Mackay had prophesied that something like this might happen if I didn't get the balance right. Very well then, I was ill, in a way, I suppose, but that did not matter to me very much at the point where I sat down, pen in hand, poised to write Jenny a love poem.

I had become, although I never read widely in foreign literature, an ardent admirer of the poetry of Pablo Neruda, and using all the Nerudian passion I could summon, I forged a white-hot lyric in the vein of the Chilean master.

If only you would fall again into my heart,
if only you would sweep like the sea into my heart
and drag me down in your sad ports,
ghost-girl of the golden storms.

Years have fallen like cities of trees since we severed,
years have wept like leaves on the wind
and left me lonely and wintered in waste places,
ghost-girl of the wind-torn woods.

I am tired of my loud successes and succession of days,
I am tired of my friends and the fixedness of feet,
and I'm tired, yes tired, of so many places without you,
ghost-girl of my ridiculous youth!

Bright the hooting of boats in the blistering bay,
bright the screams of gulls on forgotten beaches,
and I'm sick for the stars of the hunter over these places,
ghost-girl, in the fogs and squalls of my tears.

I don't want, one day, to be a soul on a lonely shore,
I don't want, one day, to be the spirit of the sea,
all I want, one day, is to sail madly back again,
ghost-girl, to the quiet harbour of your arms.

You held me close under the star-stabbed sky,
you rained wish-kisses like meteors on my mouth,
and your eyes, dear heart, were wide as absence—
ghost-girl, and your voice, my dear, as low as hope.

Your breasts were there for the drinking like goblets of snow,
your tongue a red bell beating against mine,
and the hugeness of seas and the sadness of waves breaking,
ghost-girl, quickened my sudden desire.

My kisses passed like gondolas along your lips,
like red embers wrested by fingers of the tide,
and my hands could hold no longer the torches of your words,
ghost-girl, I dropped them burning into the sea.

Oh, love me again, old friend, companion of past years—
don't leave me to founder on the flood of desire!
where I throw out my frantic net of words,
ghost-girl, to catch you like the drowned moon.

Everything is full of you tonight, the drenched gardens,
the city streets that soak up the headlamps and rain,
and the shining roofs and trains and deserted docks at dawn.
ghost-girl, are heavy with your pale gaze.

Your name is written on the wings of the south wind,
my words dying on your ears like tired geese,
yes, your name tinkles in the copper castles of the trees,
ghost-girl, throbbing in the year's dead-end gale.

The stars shiver like fish in the sky's firth,
hurricanes haul me out of the tents of sleep,
and pibrochs of passion throng the long winter sheets,
ghost-girl, where I freeze to the memory of your touch.

Closeness keeps you distant, but space is shrunk now
to rooms like counties, corn-stacked between us,
and the sentinel gull sits on my chimney top,
ghost-girl, like a sad captain, bearing you away.

Ah, the days flutter to earth, harden and die like anchors,
the planets pass like people over the hills,
and my aching arms reach out like old stone piers,
ghost-girl, cradling the empty waves.

And I'm wild with fear that you'll never be mine again,
ghost-girl, returning forever to another,
and the pen tingles like a duelling sword,
ghost-girl, fired by the true madness of love.

And if these be the last lines I write for you,
ghost-girl, I can see no ending but despair.

I've taught you enough about poetry for you to see why I couldn't publish verses like that. If I were to emigrate, however, and rewrite that piece in Spanish or Russian, publication would be no problem. Or if I were to stay at home and switch to Gaelic, all would be acceptable. The trouble is, you can't inhabit one literary world and write for another. As I completed it and sealed it up in an envelope, that, as it happened, was the last thing in my thoughts. This poem had been constructed as a grenade and was going to be lobbed at Jenny. That did not make it any the less sincere. If you were thinking that for one moment then you have not learned much about poetry or people.

The poem was written in the rainy lateness of the year, when the weeping Pleiads westered and I stayed up all night to get it right.

Not that I had been able to sleep much anyway, since the news of Jenny's return. I took the poem along with me to school in the morning and waited until I knew Cranford was busily brainstorming in the jacuzzi or however he spent his mornings, then I slipped out of Blair's in my tracksuit, the hood well up, went straight for the gradient beneath St Leonard's Bank, opposite the school, took it at a determined run, in spite of the wet grass, sped up the front path of the house, banged it through the letter-box like a bomb, making as much of a racket as I could manage—and shot off like a hound from hell. I didn't want to see her just yet. It felt a bit like the old days, really, only I'd come on a bit from the inchoate rubbish. Our lives don't change all that much, though, do they? It had been thirty years since I'd first sent Jenny my youthful poems and here I was again—sprinting back to school and all on edge already waiting for a response, like a youngster again. I couldn't concentrate on teaching and the classes knew I wasn't with them and made a paper aeroplane or two. That night I sat at home drinking, not hard but steadily, my stomach churning, waiting in vain for the telephone to ring or for Jenny to arrive at the door. Which was all rather silly really as she wouldn't even know my wherabouts. There are a great many Mackays in the Edinburgh Directory and I was pretty sure that Cranford would have come short on the subject of the identity and address of a certain mutual friend. It was even conceivable—it went through my mind—that he had not told her I taught at Blair's. I drank on into the dead watches.

Next day events took a certain course.

I received without warning a copy of a letter which the governors had sent to Cranford, asking me to apply for the post of Head of the English Department at Blair's and looking forward to meeting me at the forthcoming Principal's At Home, the following week, when we all might have an informal chat about the matter. This was a clear directive to Cranford, who was by this time a mere puppet of the governors. They probably wrote his At Home cards for him in a less shaky hand. Only now, I reflected, he had Jenny to do it for him and in any event he'd have to tell her about me now whether he felt like it or not. He could scarcely have me arriving on the doorstep like something out of Thomas Hardy after all these years. Little did he know that I had already surprised her. I hadn't signed the poem but she'd know who'd written it. Things were building up. When the invitation appeared in my pigeon-hole the following morning it burned my fingers. It was in her hand. How well I knew it—the neat, sloping hand with a tendency to the italic, confident and graceful in its black flow, like her hair. The days ground down to a stuttering crawl and I passed a weekend of nerves and snappishness, waving V-signs at myself in the mirror and chucking whisky at my reflection as there was nobody else around to get at.

At last the day came round.

It was very late in the year now, towards Christmas. I made my way after seven p.m. down a Royal Mile that was cold and wet but brightened by broken puddles of shop lights on the rain-soaked streets. When I reached the Cranford front door my heart sank at the sounds of the Hooray Henry socialites inside, yelling at one another in their loud voices, producing that kind of indeterminate animal braying that you hear from the Commons. They couldn't say either yes or no, it seemed: either monosyllable had to be prefixed with an 'oh' which in itself went through a couple of diphthongs in its flight before going on to the affirmative or the negative—a sort of *eyouh neyouh* or *eyouh yeaahs* sound, the guff of Eton strong in the breath. Snobs, every fucking one of them, I decided. Nothing like a generalisation on a doorstep to give you confidence. Fucking snobs, Cranford's circle, whether inverted or uninverted.

The latter had gone to Oxbridge and had come to despise their working class origins, for lowliness is young ambition's ladder, as I never tire of telling you, and they'd shed their rough accents and their families, like Pip, and begun to believe that the only clever men in the world were to be found under these sodding spires. The inverted snobs, on the other hand, were genuine products of the Oxbridge world. They had known nothing else—posh parents, private schools, pass the port, old poof, and keep the plum to the front of the mouth just to let other folks know you are superior—but they felt a weight of political guilt, you see, about being one of the privileged élite, so they hailed the virtues of the other side, went on marches, voted Labour (or said they did) and had a demned good mind to send their offspring to comprehensive schools, like Tony Benn, but didn't in the end because Blair's was so convenient, just round the corner, don't you know, or they just happened to know a good Labourite there, teaching History and Economics, or it was really his grandfather, don't you know, an old boy himself, who wanted the lad to go there and paid the fees, otherwise he'd be at the local, no question about it, but as long as the old buffer was still breathing, not quite gaga, and coughing up cash instead of blood—*you neyouh?*—and so on and so forth ad nauseam.

The inverted snobs and the uninverted snobs hated one another, though they let on that they were the best of pals, the uninverted snobs having to work a little harder at the hypocrisy because they hadn't been born into the world they'd attained and which they wished had been theirs by right. Always they feared some Duke of Buckingham standing in the corner under a lamp would fix them icily over his lowered glass and say, in his best Ralphie Richardson's draughtsmanlike tones, 'But I was *born* so high!'

All the same, being a hypocrite wasn't really all that bad for any of them. It was their trade. They'd chosen Cranford, realised what a boob he really was, and now they were all in there clapping him on the back and telling everybody else's wives what a fine chap he was. And Jenny, Jenny was actually in there along with them!

How could she bear it? How could I just walk in and start talking to her? The whole thing was mad. Why had she got herself stuck in this craphole in the first place? why are women such masochistic morons? I took my hand down from the bell. No. I should really walk away and let her . . . let her down? Again? You bloody fool, it was your own sweet fucking fault that things went this way and you've spent the last twenty-five years regretting it, now get in there and do what you have to do!

As my hand went up to the bell a second time the door suddenly opened and one of the Oxford accents raced out.

Eyouh heyleyouh, it said, *just fetching something from the caah*, (already halfway down the drive), *leave the dawh ajaah, would you, old men? Cehyouts upstehs.*

I did a quick unseen translation—coats upstairs—walked in and went straight up. A pile of leathers and furs and cashmeres and Burberry raincoats were lumped on one of the beds, about ten thousand quid's worth, I reckoned, that a handful of bastards had just taken off their backs, money from some other poor sod's backache and heartache, and their fat cars were squatting in the street out there, rejecting the just rain with a polish that came from an unreachable bracket. I looked quickly around. There was nothing feminine about this room. I went out and stood hesitating at the top of the stairs. Gusts of laughter from below swept upwards then died away a little as the blue accent on legs came running back through the open door and into the front room, where all the freaks were assembled, thankfully shutting the door on himself and them. I don't know what told me that Jenny was up here somewherabouts, but I opened a door—only to find myself in a bathroom. Well, she wasn't in the loo—nothing but a spare leg hanging from the shower rail, can you believe it? Would Cranford *never* learn any finesse? There were two more doors on the landing. I opened the nearest and went quietly inside, closing the door behind me.

Thick curtains and the sound of hurriedly taken breath.

'Who is it?'

'Jenny, it's me—where are you?'

'For God's sake!'

There was a sudden flurry of movement and the curtains were parted just enough to let in a little of the cold orange lamplight from the street. I could see her black eyes staring at me. She was in a nightdress. Her long white arm was still on the curtain. She was shaking her head in disbelief, her mouth fluttering like a rose. Still lovely, she was, still my Jenny, unchanged in the eyes of the transported lover. In another second I had her in my arms. She shivered.

'What's going on?' I whispered. 'Did he tell you? Why aren't you downstairs entertaining the VIPs, The Cambridge Cretins. The Oxford Arseholes. What the fuck are you—the first Mrs Rochester? And where's Grace Poole?'

'Oh shut up! you really are an incredible bastard, you know!'

She dragged her hands swiftly through her hair.

'Just don't insult me with that kind of talk, it's out of place and shows you up for what you've become, and don't ask me to spell it out for you! I'm not supposed to be here tonight. He begged me not to be seen, didn't want you to see me, but I was going to get a message to you anyway. He just felt it would all be much cleaner—with the governors—if I wasn't seen to be around.'

'Looking too much like his nurse, you mean—which is what you always were.'

'And always will be. He wants me to surface again once he's beaten the bottle, then it'll all be respectable once more— '

'But you can't— '

'Go back to him? What I can't do is just leave him to flounder.'

'For better or worse.'

'What would you know about that?'

Words, words, words.

There comes a point where they serve no purpose. That point had been reached, I decided and her last words had stung, though I'd asked for them and deserved them. I picked her up, dropped her onto the rumpled bed and threw myself alongside her, still wearing my wet overcoat. We looked at each other for just one moment before I kissed her. Kissed her after quarter of a century. And it was not long ere she gave them back to me—kisses that would suck the very nails out of your boots, kisses sweet as first love and wild with all regret. Nothing had changed between us. Nothing. I pulled her nightdress up to her neck and looked down at her. She looked up at me, unsmiling, exposed, sweetly, pitifully vulnerable. O, Jenny, I come to pluck your berries harsh and crude, your poor childless undrunk breasts, whose barren hurts I shall kiss away and with forced fingers rude scatter your sorrows before the end of the year.

—I love you.

—I love you.

The time was out of joint.

Yet once more, then, O ye lovely orbs, and once more ye nipples brown! Beyond a mortal man impassioned far, I buried my face in them, the luscious clusters of the vine, pillowed upon the nectarine, ripening, and curious peach, while she undid my trousers, with fingers rude, into her hand myself did reach, soft fall and swell, where my hand is set, cast no linen hence, no need but one, but blue remembered rivers, no, no penance, lost innocence, fuck me, at these voluptuous accents I arose, to enter into these bonds, I am sailing, to be with you, to be, to be, what needst thou have more covering, to be free, to die, ethereal, flushed and like a throbbing star and into her dream he melted as the rose, you mean he fucked her, oh, to be home again, to be deep, blendeth its odour, deep, with the violet, deep, solution sweet, deep as first love, love, and wild, wild as the wind and angry with time that took survey of all our world and had a stop, no stop, don't stop, don't stop, the clock upon a dial's point did ride, but at my back I always hear don't stop, amorous birds of prey, O Fanny Fergusson drawing near, the sounds of laughter from below, *eyouh neyouh*, oh yes, oh yes, oh yes oh yes oh yes, the time of life is short, so let us roll, willing soul, winged chariot hurrying near, to spend that shortness basely, all our strength and sweetness, were too long, if life did ride upon, sweet Jenny, one ball, one ball Cranford, sorry Cranford, no I'm not, *eyouh neyouh*, I'm not, *eyouh neyouh*, oh yes oh yes oh yes oh yes oh yes, these instant fires, sits on thy skin like morning dew, cunt dew, cunt so wide, prick of steel, sport us while we may, our time devour, and tear, tear, she was split from cunt to tit, tear our pleasures with rough strife, be rough, no, don't be gentle, no gentleman, no balls to you, Cranford, deserts of vast eternity for you, you worm, O worm, and time's winged alarm clock melting in the sands, impotent as Cranford Dali, fuck you, fuck you, through the iron gates of life, fuck me fuck me fuck me, O come quickly, for we cannot make our sun stand still, we cannot make our son, our son that never, we cannot make him run, run, O thou vile Cranford, thou usurping king, give me my son, O never never never never never, for at my back I always hear *eyouh neyouh*, O well kissed sir, an excellent courtesy, O well crawled sir, O you say true sir, O well licked sir, O yes, O come, O come quickly, O come quickly, O come quickly, no not yet, oh yes, no not yet, oh yes, sweetest lord, oh yes and raise my sprite to thee, but first we live and love to tread on kings, to kill a king, to kill a king? ay, lady, 'twas my word, to kill a king, yes, kill kill kill kill kill, for Gladstone, Scotland, England and for Stan, now therefore, now now now now now, so there's for them and there's for Leroy and there's for the Colonel and there's for Danny and there's for Goof and there's for Lachlan Campbell, there's for Henry Archibald and there's for the great Mackay Mackay, the death-blow that one, and there's for poor Campbell Mackay himself and his aborted life and unborn son and there's for Jenny and there's for thee, thou cuckoo-brained cuckold bastard, until at last the maiden cried, Enough, enough, I'm satisfied, but now we come to the tragic bit, for she makes hungry where most she satisfies, there was no way of stopping it, ha ha, so there, there there there there, you rat, you're dead for a ducat, dead dead dead dead dead, brave death we die when princes die with us, die, yes, we can die by it if not live by love, then die, die, die . . .

Not quite dead? Then I'll smother thee.

You're smothering me.

Thou'lt come no more.

Dead.

Dead together.

O pair of star-crossed lovers.

Dead.

O pair of undrunk breasts.

Dead.

Dead.

Jenny lay back with tears in her eyes.

The rain pattered against the window-pane, the quick sharp sleet, like love's alarum. Let's go, Jenny, 'tis dark, quick pattereth the flaw-blown sleet, this is no dream, my bride, 'tis dark, the iced gusts still rave and beat, I have a home for thee, do not stay here to fade and pine.

Still Jenny lay back, with tears like wet candles in her eyes. St Agnes moon hath set.

I love you. What is it? What's wrong, Jenny? For God's sake, what's wrong?

'You weren't fucking *me*,' she sobbed, 'you were fucking *him*.'

16

YES, IT WAS true, what she said. What had begun in love had ended in a kind of pornography. I had betrayed us yet again. Let not therefore your hearts be troubled, I said, neither be afraid. I'm all right now. A one-off, that's all. Something out of the system, something like that. Still she wouldn't come with me, though I pleaded, threatened.

—I'll stay here until they find us.

—I can't leave him, not yet.

—There's no better time.

The time is out of joint.

—Please go, please go.

Hurry up, please, it's time.

I said I shall go softly all my years in the bitterness of my soul.

But I closed the dew-splashed iron gates of life with a kiss.

And I went.

Into a kind of dark night of the soul, I suppose, during the start of which, absurdly, I did my Christmas shopping that Saturday. That was nothing. Around me on the bridges I saw thousands more benighted souls just like me, all as God made them and many of them much worse, all doing their pointless shopping. A crowd flowed over the North Bridge, so many, I had not thought death . . . Another over the South. And the two crowds met. Hell, in the midst of Christ's Nativity. Ironmills, I began to understand, had nothing on this. I came out of Thin's bookshop (I just want a nice book I can throw away after I've finished with it, mum . . . Why don't you try a Jilly Cooper then, dear, or a Jeffrey Archer?) and walked all the way up to Salisbury Corner in the rain, buying nothing. Then I boarded a bus to take me all the way down again to Princes Street, grimmest of miles on the Saturday before Christmas. All the way down the bus passed dozens of shops that at one time had been famous stores where the Duke and Duchess of Windsor might have popped in for a quick cuppa and bought a jewel from an Ethiop's ear. The Ethiops were Pakis now, Poundstretchers, the grand stores gone with the exorbitant rates down the political tubes. O, well done, Labour Party of Edinburgh, ye blind guides, ye blind mouths, improving services, creating jobs, selling cheap tin trays all the way down to the east end where only the Pakis can survive because they find the hours even God doesn't know about.

Scores of shops like these and swarms of insect shoppers buying up their trash, a vicious game of supply and demand with no genuine need behind it except the herd impulse to cooperate in the commercialisation of Christ. Rain on the grey metallic roofs of the bus-shelters, lying there in bitter pools like neutral blood, whipped up by the ruffling winds, blurring the skeletal images of trees. Tullymore, where are ye? The Northern Lights of Aberdeen mean home sweet home to me. The bus turned west along Princes Street, bringing the Castle into view, a great grey-black bulky nun with glowering brows and slippery stone skirts spilling voluminously in wet heavy folds down to the railway lines, where the trains crawled past her whinstone hem. O, look, there's my house up there, just as I left it, with its high windows! Yes. Home is so sad. There on the sad height. The nun frowned among the long lines of slavering serpentine clouds, keeping pace with the slow trains. Her skirts were impregnable. Who dare meddle wi' me? Begone, you mother-fucking trains! Only the worm, only the worm creeps under those great stone folds, the worm that feeds so sweetly when the nun dies, and your cunt honour turn to dust, the rusted iron gates of life, and into ashes all my lust. Lust? What lust? I have no lust, no desire. I am dead, Horatio, the potent poison quite o'ercrows my spirit. Dead, sweet prince, you are the dead. I am the dead . . .

For some reason I ended up in John Menzies. Standing there in a long queue, clutching something for somebody or nothing for nobody, I watched the escalator bringing down the interminable files of infinitely ugly people. Feet that go down to death, steps that take hold on hell, conveyer belt to the Inferno, no chance of catching Virgil or Dante on the way—an Eliot, perhaps, lurking among the cookery books. Can you recommend a nice novel I can throw away after I've read it? Certainly, madam, I can recommend about six thousand a year, minus six if you're lucky. These six I'm afraid you'd have to read! They're on the Booker list, you see. Oh, how awful! Yes, awful. And how astonishing too, the varieties of ugliness that evolution has managed to produce in the human frame. Not so much the sagging breasts and bellies, the bulging buttocks, bleary eyes, protruding lips, foul complexions, greasy hair, scraggy moustaches—not so much these as the expressions of bad temper and boredom in every eye. I never saw so many stupid sets of clothes in a row, everybody looking utterly pathetic in their cheap and crumby gear. And one born in a manger commands the beauteous files. O God, where was Jesus in this heart of hell? the infant, the star, the shepherds, the kings? What a terrifying perversion of the greatest story in the world! And what a dirty trick of Darwinism, the survival of the ugliest! and fittest for hell at the end of the sick mill in the Age of Ironmills! Why was it, I wondered, that I had never in my life seen an ugly cat? And yet, pouring down this escalator, endlessly, were the paragons of animals and every one of them ugly beyond measure . . .

I dropped my stupid package, whatever it was, and fled from the shop, taking the quick way home up the Mound and the Vennel, through the now steadily driving downpour, my soul sick unto death and my heart on fire in the rain for Jenny once again.

> *With love of one young maiden*
> *My heart hath ta'en its wound,*
> *And manifold the grief that I*
> *In love have found.*
>
> *If she would once take pity*
> *And take me to her side,*
> *And stepping down lean o'er me*
> *And so abide.*

When I reached the Lawnmarket I walked straight into my tracksuit, soaked as I was, and ran out into the slicing rain, headed for Arthur's Seat. The sun came out briefly just as

I reached the summit and all the windows of Blair's came ablaze, the sunlight bouncing off the rain-drenched roofs and spires of Edinburgh, turning them to black and silver, the raindrops splashing outwards and earthwards in wet flakes of fire. There was a streaming wind and the white clouds went like Agricola's armies, flagged and aflame, ribboning all the way down to Cramond and the Forth.

The physical effort of taking the summit at a run had eased my mind, as usual, leading me to that brief epiphany. I sat down on the hard wet rocks and allowed the rain to soak into me, my body drinking it up gratefully like a flower. After a while I lay flat, thirsting for every drop of it. I had laid me down like a gentleman in the shadow of the church, and the rainwater, blessed by contact with the holy edifice, was sanctifying my poor humbled bones. Or would it be better to be interred beneath the cold flagstones of the church floor and accept the penance of the priest's trampling feet? Mice or worms—which were the better companions in eternity? It did not matter. The body would be oblivious, as mine was now. I sat up. I was at peace as the afternoon thickened and twilight came on.

Ah, but how easily those tower blocks beyond Craigmillar would topple into that yellow postage-stamp of far-off field and all its useless lives be submerged; still leaving room for thousands upon thousands more! The houses under my feet—they seemed such an easy prey to the sucking edge of seagreen grass that would sweep them away when the time came, as come it would. O, come, O come, Emmanuel! A million ineffectual lives were spread out beneath me. A million lonelinesses. The enormity of that sudden perspective began to scare the shit out of me. To be down there and a living part of it, that was bearable because of the closeness, the oblivion, but from up here the million pointless salvations and damnations, the million lives or deaths or lives-in-deaths—were frightening. And beyond the city: blue water, blue hills and the four points of the compass, and the white endless meaningless air. An ampleness of acreage that numbed the brain, the blue ploughlands of the sea, the green waves of fields, the white light of eternity: a terrifyingly commodious triple bedcover for the earth's anonymous. I could barely see over to Fife now in the failed light.

The farms of home lie lost in even,
I see far off the steeple stand;
West and away from here to heaven
Still is the land.

The land is still by farm and steeple,
And still for me the land may stay:
There I was friends with perished people,
And there lie they.

And there if I went now, no dog would bark, no girl would greet me.

No girl would greet me.

And no girl did greet me as I came back heavily up the stairs to my cold flat and tumbled wetly into bed, too tired to dry myself or to see to food or fire.

But I lay listening to the trains again, for minute-months, mingled as they were with the cries of seagulls through the fog. And dreamt I was a seagull, flying over Edinburgh in the snow, soaring along above the long scar from the Castle to Holyrood and up again, to go skimming lightly over the railway tracks, following the black tangle of lines in the whiteness, sweeping under the Mound and underneath the National Gallery. I caught up with a train there in the darkness, and flying alongside the bright windows I could see inside, snug and warm, the travellers of my snowbound, sleepbound imagination: the little Orkney lady, the worried student, the Russian doll, the Polish musician, the brocaded belle, all of them bound for somewhere while I was condemned to keep on gliding along outside, following this cruel illusion of freedom while it was I, I who had nowhere to go but to flutter vainly opposite the oblivious figures, travelling as fast as I could but somehow remaining where I was, moving but motionless, frustrated, mad.

But I came out of it and left them to their journey, climbing skywards again and banking away sharply to the Botanic Gardens, white with winter, the scattered trees from above like frozen atomic mushrooms, dark and cancerous, sprinkling the white meadows. Northwards I glided then, over the Forth, turning east and dipping low to the wavetops, flitting in and out of the troughs, up and down, wetting my outspread wings in the white flying hair of the crests that stung my feathered eyes. Straight, straight I flew, coming off the firth and hitting the land where another train shot by me, an old puffer, flying along with a streamer of steam dancing to pieces behind it. I followed it up the coast and kept pace with difficulty, (for I was tiring), with one of its carriages, where, through the window, I could see a young boy and girl huddled in a corner, unspeaking, silent, the boy's hand hidden in the folds of the girl's navy skirt, invisible, eloquent with the poetic fire of her pubic hair as the train and I shot through the white surgical wards of the world and the low sun rose like a tangerine switched on in the early morning for getting me up and going to school. To school, to school, unwillingly to school. I reached out for the tangerine that hurt my eyes. To school, to school, I must arise and go now, I must get up and go to . . . Ssh, ssh, ssh, school's on holiday still, for Christmas, though it's past Christmas now, and you're ill. But what time . . .?

It was January.

The first month of the year.

And Jenny was looking after me.

I understood I was ill. I understood I had pneumonia. Pretty badly. And would have been hospitalised but for Jenny's being a State Registered Nurse. When I understood all that I sank back to sleep again. Content to ask no questions, to let her take care of me, to bend over me, to be my nurse and paramour, my mother dove, so full of tenderness and truth and pity.

> Ut mei misereatur,
> Ut me recipiat,
> Et declinetur ad me,
> Et ita desinat.

And she certainly took pity on me.

That was Jenny's trouble—too ready to pity others. But she was a wonderful nurse. It was some time until I understood just how ill I'd been and how well she'd looked after me. She bathed me, showered me, powdered me and I surrendered weakly. God. Left to myself under the shower that I'd rigged up in the bath, sitting there day after day, as I was growing a little stronger, I took a really close look at myself from the navel outwards and wondered how she could take the trouble. My feet, two pregnant s's, the soles intersnug, high arches, wrinkled sides, as is the ribbed sea-sand—and thou art long and lank and brown—yes, that's right, the feet of an ancient mariner who had to tell his tale. Two hairy legs (note that, Cranford! a weak smile here) the hairs darkened by the water. Two knees sporting all the cuts and grazes of childhood, the days when I needed my mother. Cried a bit. Thighs on the thin side, perhaps, but all muscle, no flab there. Belly tending to concertina just a bit when bending over for the soap that slid down to the plughole where the water dripped and gathered, like love. Not a paunch to be unproud of for one too well into his forties—be honest, you self-deluding bastard, you're nearer fifty. So what? Go to, go to, bend the head and let the water dance upon your neck, a galliard, gaze into the neat little tumbler of the navel (not one of these ugly black arseholes of belly buttons that you see on some, beset by wads of hairy fat). Modest shoulders, arms wiry rather than thin, and lanky wrists knotted by veins, like my grandfather's were, asleep in the chair at the end of the day. Chest hairs whitened, sadly, showing my ageing, hands dangling loosely over the knees, one hand only (my right) distinguished by the tell-tale shiny callous on the side of the little finger—the trade-mark of the teacher who still uses a pen, writes a lot, and has been bruised by his pen.

Did I forget anything. Oh yes, of course, and Percy himself, drooped onto the porcelain of the bath floor, played upon by droplets from my dripping hair and surrounded by sparking puddles of water, dear old Percy, down and out just for the moment, I'm afraid, and in need of renovation. Goodnight, Percy, goodnight, old son. Thy master's head hath need of sleep. And resting.

Sleep.

And resting.

When the spring term opened I was feeling a little better but a long way from home. Not strong on teaching, certainly, and Jenny insisted I should stay off at least a month and then take it from there, until I was returned to complete health and capability. I must admit I was still feeling rather shaky at the expiry of that month and so the month became two months and indeed the entire term. Quite apart from my state of health, of course, the thought of Blair's had added thorns to make me more than content to stay away. She had left Cranford, naturally, and was staying with me at the flat. It might surprise you, though, to hear me confess that we had not once made love since that awful night of the At Home——and that had not been love, well, not all love, but had contained altogether too much additive of poisonous and perverted revenge. More than a dram of eale returned to the inventor, I have to admit. Best forgotten.

So we lay together under the spring stars, in the Lawnmarket, throughout February and March, at one and at peace in our nakedness, and in our honesty and love for one another, my hand on her hair, my head on her breast, listening to the trains, while the iron crosses rusted on the graves of those I loved and the Plough rusted over our heads, with nothing else to do. The body was finding its strength again.

But not its sweetness.

The Lenten river ran blackly in the blood. Every Wednesday was Ash Wednesday. *Memento homo quod cinem est.* Ash was the anonymous address we were all headed for, written into human flesh. I took to reading Ecclesiastes again, and Marcus Aurelius, picturing him sitting in his sad tent among the soggy marshes of the Danube, charting human progress from yesterday's stinking drop to tomorrow's handful of dust, with copulation in between to keep us going: friction of the members and an ejaculatory discharge, producing the human cell, a twenty millionth of an ounce, programmed like an acorn for the grown man, fifty billion times that weight, a product of what he has eaten and drunk of his cannibalistic, self-consuming world. And yet this thing of grass that I was had come out of the stars, had known such infinite hopes, knew now such emptiness, such despair, the sensation of an empty circle, what shadows we are and what shadows we pursue, the image of a man in a cave, behind a windbreak, emerging to build cathedrals, starships, only to end up in the cave again, disease-ridden, wretched, short-lived, as Wells foresaw.

Somewhere in my Lenten reading I discovered a statistic that shook me to the bone, sucked out my marrow. That if we were to divide the last fifty thousand years of human existence by the average life span, we would find that we are now in the eight hundredth lifetime. Out of all these lifetimes six hundred and fifty were spent in caves and only in the last seventy of these lifetimes has it been possible to communicate from one generation to the next in the form of writing. Only in the last four lifetimes has it been possible to measure time accurately and only the last two have used an electric motor. Most of the material goods used in daily life today were developed in this last and eight hundredth lifetime. As to the knowledge of literature that had been my very heart's blood, it had been around for the merest fraction of human existence and although available to a very few meant nothing to the vast majority of mankind. Had I nurtured myself on a dream? a shadow's shadow? O, Jenny, you do me wrong to take me out o' the grave. Give me my wheel of fire and I'll not scream. For I have silence left.

'Why don't we go over to the East Neuk for Easter?' Jenny said to me one day.

I must have been hell to be with at that time.

I brightened at the thought and we drove over the Road Bridge and had a drink in Skinfasthaven. It was a brilliant April day. We came out of the pub and walked along to the kirkyard at Burial Brae.

'Oh, look, we can't go in yet,' Jenny said as we came round the corner,' there's a funeral going on.'

The narrow street was blocked by two heavy black cars and we could hear the words of the service booming among the tombs.

I am the Resurrection and the Life, saith the Lord.

That's not Dr Orr taking the service,' I said. 'It's not his voice.'

'Dr Orr will be dead centuries ago. Let's wait.'

After some minutes the few mourners came out slowly and the cars purred off. It hadn't been a large funeral.

The gravedigger and his assistant were busy spading in the clods when we went up the steps. Only one mourner was left and he turned to come away just as we passed by the grave. We all stared at one another.

It was the Goof.

He had wet eyes.

We shook hands and grinned at one another over what seemed like an immensely compressed distance. Then we asked who had just been buried.

'Ah,' the Goof shook his head, 'pity you hadn't known about it. You would have wanted to come across, you being in Edinburgh, just across the water. That was Dr Orr we laid to rest there. You just missed it.'

'Oh, but he must have been— '

'Ninety-seven,' interrupted the Goof.

Ninety-seven. Now isn't the mere passage of time remarkable,

I heard a sepulchral voice chuckling, and saw the ghost of a silver grin.

'But so small a funeral,' Jenny protested.

'The people who would have come—they're all in here already.'

And he took us over to see the graves of Danny and Lachlan Campbell. Mackay Mackay had been cremated and so there was no grave as such, except the whole earth, of course, and an iron cross of the mind, and right now a feeling again of being trapped inside an empty circle in which a white wind swirled, unable to escape to the liberating sea.

'Do you want to see the manse before you go?' asked the Goof. 'I'm responsible for clearing up all his things. There's a lot of books. Maybe you could help—I don't mean right this minute, of course.'

He took us along to the doctor's old residence. The church had let him stay on there even after he'd retired. He had been a most extraordinary minister. The study was very neat, though the books were dusty and had clearly been unread for a very long time. One shelf was tight with exercise jotters and hardbacked notebooks, learned sermons mostly. The doctor had left wide margins and here and there these had been filled with later doodlings of an abstrusely mathematical nature. The medieval monks in their scriptoria had offset their tedious chores with marginal art that gave them light relief: Dr Orr had offset learning with greater learning. That made me smile. I pointed out these esoteric scrawlings to the Goof.

'Relativity,' he said. 'Apparently. One of his abiding interests in later life. He and Pete Periwinkle used to have long talks on the subject. Pete always said he could only go so far along that road with him.'

'I think I remember something like that. Shouldn't Peter see these, if he's still alive?'

'Oh, he's still on the go. I've told him about it. But he doesn't want to look at them. He says he daren't find out now how ignorant he might have been when he was having talks with the doctor!'

I promised to come back and help with classifying the books, some to go to Taft Academy, the bulk to St Andrews University, the remainder to an Edinburgh bookseller.

'Before you go,' the Goof said, 'come and see my birthday present. I was seventy-five yesterday.'

We stopped at his trim garden on the way out of Skinfasthaven and he led us round to the back of the house, facing the sea. I expected to see an electric lawnmower or something, I suppose. At first I couldn't make out what it was I was meant to be admiring. There didn't seem to be anything obvious within view.

'That's it over there—up on the patio.'

The Goof pointed proudly.

It was a cement mixer.

For some absurd reason I burst into tears of joy.

The Goof had done it again. I had, if you like, come through.

At the start of the summer term—this summer term—I decided to give everything another whirl. I would not yield to kiss the ground before the Cranford feet. I would return to Blair's and champion the old values, be a thorn in the Cranford flesh. The governors knew my worth and as a matter of fact had written to me again asking me to apply for Colonel Stubbes's post despite my recent illness. This did actually touch me a little—perhaps there was hope yet for the failing world—and so I put in my application.

Naturally Cranford now hated me with a hatred that was vitriolic, diabolical, intense beyond belief. He wrote to me formally saying that in accordance with the new appraisal system now statutory in Blair's, he'd have to come into one of my classes and hear me teach; that is if I really wished to apply for the post of Head of English. I wrote back to him pointing out just how crass that suggestion was and that I'd refuse to go along with it. He'd be better employed listening to someone whose track record didn't speak for itself, as mine did. That suited him very well, was the reply. It meant that I could not be considered as a candidate for the post and in any case there were by this time several very strong applications from outside the school, in one of which the governors had developed an interest. It was at that point that I realised the battle was lost, but all the same, pricked into anger now, I decided to try the last. Resisting the temptation to study the passage about Ahab's leg, I prepared a safe Shakespearean sonnet and sent Cranford a note telling him I'd reconsidered and would, in the end, accept his grubbily irrelevant little appraisal. I should be ready to teach at his convenience.

He clanked in with a notepad, the stupid little beggar, all ready to scribble comments about me, even though I'd been in the place all my working life and he knew my worth just as surely as he knew his own ineptitude and knew no more about Elizabethan sonnets than he knew about how to grow another set of balls.

But, oh! the devil—he knew something, though. Yes, he did have at least one brain cell left in working order. Because a notepad wasn't all he brought with him: he brought one of the governors too—and this doubtless the corrupt little creep who had an 'interest' in what turned out to be the Cambridge candidate. His old buddy, perchance? his brother, brother-in-law, brother in business? What, could such things be and overcome us like a summer's cloud?

You bet they bloody can. For in the corrupted currents of this world, offence's gilded hand may shove by justice and management manipulation was at it again. I saw red, as they say. It was all so boringly predictable, like every fucking one of Blair's incestuous promotions. I was dead, all right.

But not quite yet.

I could at least sharpen the axe myself and hand it to them with a flourish. Go in style. Die a glorious death, as per old Macpherson's Rant.

> *Sae wantonly, sae dauntingly*
> *And sae flauntingly gaed he—*
> *He played a tune and he danced a roond*
> *Upon the gallows tree.*

I mentally bucketed the lesson on the sonnet and picking up my chalk prepared to play my fiddle.

Today's lesson, boys of the Fifth Form, is a grammatical one, illustrating the various forms and purposes of a single word and its grammatical relations. The word we are about to examine is that familiar four-letter Anglo-Saxon word, shunned by the majority of self-styled civilised men in public conversation, but used directly or allusively by a host of famous men, including Dunbar, Donne, D.H. Lawrence Philip Larkin and many contemporary celebrities including former President Richard Nixon and doubtless presidents before and after him.

It is the word fuck.

As soon as I said that everything in the room stopped. It was as quiet as a parson's arse.

Fuck. Substantively, a common noun (she's a good fuck, she's an expensive fuck) and may be used in the plural (I had three fucks last night).

Gender: neuter, ironically, for a noun so closely associated with male and female intimacy.

Case: may be used nominatively, accusatively or datively as fuck, and genitive usage (no connection with genitals for Principal's benefit: not strong on genitals, your Principal, or the genitive case either, for that matter) as in the common phrase, for fuck's sake, where the noun, as you can see, is personified.

Derivatively, we may say, what a fuck-up, or, he's a right fucker, where fucker does the job of a pronoun, more obviously seen in, for example, a sentence such as, take that fucker away with you.

Verbal usages are as follows:

Transitive Use: he fucked her.

Intransitive Use: she fucks.

Active Voice: He fucked her all night.

Passive Voice: She was fucked all right.

As a finite verb, fuck takes any appropriate subject. The three moods of this form of the verb are:

1. Indicative: He fucked.

2. Imperative: Fuck off.

3. Subjunctive: If you don't fuck off, you'll be in trouble.

The Interrogative form puts a popular question: Do you fuck? Here, if the answer is in the negative, the proposer's response ought then to be: do you mind lying down then, while I have one?

Although a strong word, fuck is grammatically in the category of weak rather than strong verbs, which means that it is of the conjugation of verbs that form their past tense by adding—d,—ed or—t, in the case of fuck,—ed: fucked. A strong conjugation might have taken the form of fuck, fock, fucken (speculatively), the last appearing phonetically in Scotland not as a past participle but as an adjective: shift your fùcken feet!

The forms of the Verb Infinite are: 1) the Infinitive Mood 2) the Gerund 3) the Past Participle.

1. The Infinitive Mood of the verb is used:
a) as a noun: to fuck is human, where to fuck is equivalent to a noun and is the subject of the sentence.
b) as an adverb of reason or purpose, as in: I came to fuck you, where to fuck is equivalent to an adverb modifying came.
c) as a complement: I must fuck you, where fuck completes the sense. Whether the complement is taken as a compliment depends entirely on the identity of the putative fucker and his relationship with the object of his desire.

N.B. Avoid the Split Infinitive, as in: she asked me to quickly fuck her, which should correctly be expressed: she asked me quickly to fuck her, or: she asked me to fuck her quickly. These denote two alternative actions from which the lady is free to choose, depending on whether she wishes a fast fuck when the gentleman is ready, or a slow fuck pronto. The Split Infinitive remains ambiguous.

2. The Gerund is the noun formed from the verb and ends in —ing.

If the verb is intransitive the gerund has the function of a noun. If the verb is transitive the gerund may have a following object and so retains the function of a verb:

Fucking is fun.

He had no difficulty in fucking her.

3. Participles resemble adjectives in their functions and present participles should be distinguished from adjectives and verbs, e.g.:

She is fucking (present participle).

She is a fucking tart (adjective qualifying tart).

She is fucking lovely (adverb modifying lovely). Thus fuck may perform the functions of nouns, adjectives, verbs and adverbs. Grammatically speaking it may also be used as an exclamation, interjection or expletive—always deleted in the case of Richard Nixon.

In context and with varied intonation it may be employed to purposes more versatile than the exclusively sexual.

It may be a valediction, as in: I'm fucking off.

It may be a salutation, as in: How the fuck are you? Or:

Hello, you fucking old wanker! (frequently used in the navy but must not be employed in Blair's).

It may convey surprise: fucking hell! Or: fuck me! (where the sense would not normally be taken as a directive but may be so interpreted if that is the bent of the person speaking or the person spoken to).

From the vast range of emotions covered by this word, we may pick out the following:

exasperation, dismay or distress: Oh, fuck it!
incompetence or error: You really fucked that up!
aggression: Fuck you! (often accompanied or symbolically replaced by the old Anglo-Saxon field sign from Agincourt which conveyed to the French that the archers still had their arrow fingers intact).
disappointment or frustration: What a fucking job!
disapproval or displeasure: What the fuck are you doing?
flippancy or promiscuity: Stop fucking around, will you?
disinterest: I don't give a fuck!

It may also denote extremes of size: fucking enormous! Or: sweet fuck all.

The list is really endless, and although history neglects to record many of its more famous uses, three have survived, all examples of famous last words:

Custer: Look at all them fucking Indians!
Captain Nolan (at Balaclava): Charge *which* fucking guns did you say?!
The Captain of the Titanic: Who's left the fucking taps running?

The origin of the word is uncertain, but we may discount the theory based on the contextual use of the word to denote bewilderment: Where the fuck are we? (sometimes thought to be the origin of the tribal name of certain pygmies whose natural habitat is elephant grass. They were discovered leaping around announcing—so the explorers thought—'We're the fukahwi'!)

This I quote to you at length because it is the kind of juvenile humour that Cranford himself would have hooted over in the old days, though I amused myself—and the class, as you will know from hearsay—by doing the whole thing in alternative Frank Muir and Arthur Marshall voices. That apart, I served him up a dish suitable to his intellect and his taste, with a couple of personal insults thrown in. To give him his due, he sat through all of it, with his sofa-freak friend, while the fifth form fell about in varying attitudes of mirth. Boys will be boys and I was one of them for the nonce.

After the class had rushed out to spread the gospel, Cranford surveyed me grimly from the back of the room.

'You've just committed Hari Krishna,' he said.

I couldn't help laughing.

'I think you mean something else, Headmaster, 'I said. Not strong on importations, our Cranford.

'But,' I went on, determined to brazen it out and keep on digging into his side, 'I don't imagine you'll find anything in my contract which prevents me from using a common Anglo-Saxon word as the subject of a lesson on grammar. The grammar itself is entirely accurate and the method is known in the profession as comic relief: a familiar aid to learning. As a wiser man than you once said to me, education should be fun.'

'We'll see about that,' was all he said, and stomped out, taking his puppeteer with him.

When I arrived back at the flat, Jenny had gone.

I sat around on edge all night, wondering where she had got to. She didn't appear next day or the following night. Into the weekend when she still hadn't come home I started to feel frantic and to drink quite heavily. Going in again on Monday to the teach was utter hell. When your heart's not in it, when the fun's gone out of it, as that wise man said, and wisely was it said, you should think of getting out. But what else was there to do? I plodded on. Ate little, drank much, ceased to read, to listen to the trains, to think, to care.

It was nearly three weeks until I heard from Jenny: a letter with no address but a London postmark. The few pained paragraphs said it all. Cranford had got to her, all right. The choice was hers: to leave me and go back to him, otherwise he now had all the ammunition he needed to shoot me down for good and end my career with an ignominious sacking. It would be the end of the line for me anywhere in teaching. I had gone over the top and everybody knew it. I knew it myself. Jenny knew it too. She was simply not going to allow him to do this to me, nor me to ruin everything for myself—not while she could make the sacrifice

299

herself. Which is what she was doing. Not that she was actually going back to him—that was unthinkable, but he'd accepted the compromise that she leave Edinburgh and me and that on that assurance alone would his friend the governor take no action concerning my removal. My teaching had been my whole life. She would not stand by and allow the teaching world to be deprived of a talent such as mine. I love you, she said, but I love you so much that I cannot see you destroyed, destroy yourself. This is not the end for us, of course it isn't, but I must embrace this as the immediate solution and so must you. And more words to that effect.

That is when I flipped.

I walked right out of the flat without even dressing properly and marched like a madman down the Royal Mile, up to the school and straight into his study to await his arrival. He was always in early himself, at least half an hour before anyone else, not out of a sense of duty but because it took him ten times longer than the average person to absorb a letter and think up a reply before lunch time. That was one thing about him: he had to work long hours.

In he came.

Most carefully upon his hour, as usual.

'You cunt!'

He shut the door and gave his evil grin, the one I'd seen on his face half a lifetime ago. God, he was ugly! Jenny must have been down as low as to the fiends to have become involved with him in the first place.

He stopped grinning.

'The choice was hers—and yours,' he said. 'You can have one another—I don't much care now—but you can't have your job along with that package. Any longer. You never really could manage your woman and your Muse at the same time, for very long. Could you now?'

'You bastard!'

'Rather short on words all of a sudden, aren't we—for an English teacher?'

'You wanker!'

'Wanking's what *you'll* have to go back to, my friend! Better save your breath for it!'

I looked at him smirking dully there and could read the deep misery in his face. That didn't stop me doing what I did, though.

I was out of control by now. But he was right, after all—breath was wasted in this room. I walked quickly over to where he was standing and kicked savagely at his dummy leg. He went down like a tree, giving a scream as if his roots were coming out. I looked down at him. He'd cut his mouth in falling on one of the metal projections from the famous orthopaedic chair and a scarlet ooze was already gathering on the carpet in a foaming gob.

The sight of the blood made me even madder. I wanted to kill him. A bust of Shakespeare stood on its pedestal in the corner: a huge Victorian thing. I had often begged him to let me have it for my room but he would never let it go. As he couldn't actually read Shakespeare himself it did his ego good to pretend. What a wonderful piece of poetic justice—to brain him now with the bard! I didn't, of course. What did you think you were getting? Tales of the Unexpected? This is a school and an English lesson, nothing more. But I was tempted, I can tell you, just as surely as I've often dreamed o' nights of drowning him in the malmsey-butt jacuzzi of his own useless piss and pissing in after him, making a sop of him, making the green go red because I'd punctured him first in three and thirty places, O wonderful! O, most horribly wonderful! My thoughts were ripe for murder.

I ran over to the bust, picked it up and stood over him like Achilles holding a rock in one of his rages. He stared up at me in real terror, his arm upraised, mouthing something indistinct through bloody teeth.

'You stupid little wanker!' I screamed at him. 'Do you really think I'd do you that favour? I may be short on words this morning but I'm not Billy bloody Budd! Fuck you!'

And I smashed the bust down on his duff leg. It gave a great thud and there was a tremendous splintering sound.

I stood there trembling.

Then I really let him have it, verbally, for everything he'd done to education and to the school, he and his kind, over the years, how he'd been a wanker quite literally from the very first day I'd set eyes on him and he'd wanked his way into office and surrounded himself with dummies who wouldn't or couldn't use their tools but played with them instead, people like himself who were ready to sterilise the imagination and take the balls out of learning for the sake of a few years in office, castrated little prickless wonders that would go down next century as the blindest leading the blindest in the whole history of education, and they'd fucked up people's personal lives too, people like me, men of choice and rarest parts like Gladstone and Leroy, Colonel Stubbes and Stan and all the men who'd taught me, who'd taught from the heart and felt things on their pulses, while Cranford's one-legged mob had tried to make me stand on one leg too and cut my balls off, to lop away my effectiveness as a maker of visions for the young, and for why? because they were afraid of people like me who would not accept mediocrity as a principle because we were ruled by our passions and saw things whole, felt our thoughts like roses and saw roses as our thoughts, yoked everything together, the sound of the typewriter, the smell of cooking, the philosophy of Spinoza, falling in love, our intellects were married to our emotions and now my emotional life was in ruins again and hot tears were on me now, staining my man's cheeks with noble anger, but I'd be revenged on the whole pack of them, yes, by heaven, pour on, I will endure, I said, the hell, the darkness, the sulphurous pit, the burning, scalding, stench, corruption, the dogs obeyed in office, Blanche and Sweetheart, drest in a little brief authority, strutting the stage of fools, why dost thou lash that Muse? hold thou thy bloody hand! give me an ounce of sanity, good apothecary, to sweeten my imagination, no, not a French Letter, it smells of mortality, silent upon a peak in Darien, like my old masters, on Kellie Law, they're dead and rotten and thou art a disease that's in my flesh, but ere I shall be brought to knee your throne and pension beg to keep base life afoot, be slave and sumpter to your detested grooms, up yours, Gladstone, and fuck the Pope, I shall go mad and my heart break into an hundred thousand flaws ere I do weep, for I shall have such revenges on you all, what they are yet I know not but they shall be the teachers of the earth, yes, I shall teach you such a lesson as will never be forgotten, so long as men can breathe or eyes can see, so long lives this and this gives life to thee, and thee, and thee, old men, my masters, 'tis a mad world, my masters, old men of dreams and young men all before me now, young men of visions as I was once, for sure, before the Palace of Green Porcelain stood on Salisbury Crag in the shadow of Purgatorio, bidding farewell tò Michelangelo and Romeo and Prospero, Vincentio, Antonio, Orlando, Petruchio, Othello, Mercutio, Don Adriano De Armado, O, farewell! and welcome now Malvolio, O, O, O, O, that

Shakespearian rag, and farewell cakes and ale, bid them farewell, young masters, bid them farewell as I do now, and say farewell to me, farewell, a long farewell to all my greatness, and after the lesson's over, do as I do now—nay, come, let's do't together, come, let's take old Stanislav's skeleton, come down, old boy, down from your corner, how are you, old chap? and place it in my chair, like this, behind my desk, thus, draped in my teacher's gown, think you? very well, then, I take it off, the toga given to me by Colonel Stubbes to carry on the work of Caesar, off, off, you lendings, now, place one bony leg athwart the arm o' the chair, like so, so casual like, and one lank hand and fingers resting on the works of Shakespeare, forbidden books, yes? like this, just so, and a fag between the teeth, think you? do I have one herabouts? no? why, when did I stop smoking now? they will not give me matches, that's the trick, very well then, a rose, a rose from the plastic vase, I cannot cut myself on thorns, they reckon, though I fall upon the thorns of life, I bleed, yet that's not much, for I am declined into the vale of years, when I have plucked the rose I cannot give it vital growth again, it needs must wither, there now, O crooked rose, rest you in Stanny's teeth, how does that suit you? not one now to mock your own grinning, old Stanny Boy, O, Danny Boy, I love you so, but enough o' that, no more o' that, Master Leroy, no more o' that, the Thane of Fife had a wife, peace, peace, where is she now? dead, for a ducat! Jesu, and is Jenny Miller yet with us, friend? dead, for a ducat! Jesu, Jesu, dead! ha, 'twas a merry night when we lay all night in the fields, babbled o'green fields, talked, talked, I say, no more o' that, but how we made love i' the fields, old, old, Master Shallow, ha, Jenny, art thou gone? no more, I prithee, but to think how many of mine old acquaintance are dead! we have heard the chimes at midnight, that we have, Stan, that we have, that we have, that we have, indeed we have, in Jesu's name, we have! so, Stan, there you are, settled in my chair, is the chair empty? not while old Stan yet grinneth here, not quite chopfallen, there you go, old Stan, you'll do the job so well now for the next decade o' years, the dead teaching the dead from the works o' the dead in the house o' the dead, thus runs the world away, and so to your pleasures, I am for other than for dancing measures—and when the parents arrive for their next meeting and the punters for the hundred and seventeenth Open Day i' the name o' Cranford, and the pupils to be taught, this is what they'll see, this fellow of infinite jest and most excellent fancy, whose gibes and gambols and songs and flashes of merriment were wont to set the classroom on a roar. O yes, I have seen the day when with my falchion wit I ha' made them skip, have I not fellows? but they'll never note the difference now, will they? they are the dead, we are the dead, I am dead, Horatio, so I'll walk out on the whole crowd right now, the time is out of joint, I'm ready to chuck up everything and just clear off, surely I can if Stan did, of course I can, I'm going, I'm going, look how I go, thought I never would, the lesson's over, you thought it never would, but soft you, a word or two before I go, ha! got you there! I have done the school some service and they know it, no more o' that, I pray you, but in your letters, when you shall these unlucky deeds relate, speak of me as I am, nothing extenuate, nor set down aught in malice, then must you speak of one that loved not wisely but too well, loved two ladies in his life, lady literature and his dear sweet Jenny, no more o' that, taught the one and was taught by the other, no more o' that, and had to make the choice, ah choice, and since my choice was made for me long before the beginning o' the world, I'll go now, you and I, like a patient etherised, over the blue firth like a bird to Fife, like a seagull on the train, where a lady sweet and kind awaits me, and I shall lay me down in that field o' golden buttercups with my serpent of old Nile, for it is June, jug jug, and things will be as they were, till that time come again, look at the strawberries in the cream, the schoolboys playing in the stream, and there we'll make pure love, me and my lass unparalleled, whose deep hurts could not be smoothed away by lipstick and powder that she puts on of late, and other unguents to hide her tears, but no more needs such flattery to beautify her face than the old moon needs a Sidney or a Shelley to court her in her age, and so we shall go out again like Adam and Eve from that green field, a sadder and a wiser pair, the world all before us where to choose our place of rest, and hand in hand with wandering steps and slow, we'll take our solitary way once more through our old Eden, and it will be Sunday, for it will always be Sunday, as it is now, is now, for listen, listen, do you hear this? is not the church bell ringing? is it not? and is this Jenny, come to take me? is she not? is she not come? O come, O come, O come, Emmanuel, la damn bell sans merci hath me in thrall, save me, O my true belle dame, but which is the church bell, pray, and which is Blair's? oh, they never let you finish, do they? leave me, friends, I'll burn my books, always a lesson too late in the learning, yet once more then, O ye laurels, I'll hang my harp on a weeping willow tree and build Jerusalem among these dark Satanic mills, where many pass through and are thus ground small and knowledge shall be increased and wisdom put to sleep, we shall not all sleep, no, I will not cease from mental fight, nor shall my sword sleep in my hand in Wanker's Wynd, where Cranford was harmless once, even with his vital parts intact, O Hamlet, thou has cleft my heart in twain, O dear Ophelia, I am ill at these numbers, for my words are not mine, I am ill, I am ill, an will he not come again? no, no, he is gone, my true love she's gone too, she's come to say goodbye, goodbye, goodbye, goodbye Bugsy, goodbye, Fat Boy, say goodbye to Bulldog too, untouched strangely by that bastard, O, these men knew something of life, the pathos of living, sunt lacrimae rerum, absurd idealists that they were, Minto Munro, Jock Cassidy, Pete Periwinkle, Donald Forsyth, Jimmy Macdonald, Herbert Sterne, Wilf Sutter, Colin Lees, Hector Green, Alastair Blair—what, will the line stretch out until the crack o' doom? thou'lt come no more, heaven lay about us in our infancy, where are the Lost Boys? then let the rains come down on Scotland, Scotland farewell, England hath not anything to show more fair, perchance, unless the sweet prince prevail? in a pig's arse, Charles, then it's goobye, enter Faustus and is torn apart by devils before he can ever open a book, exit Antigonus pursued by a bear, and exit Lachlan Campbell, Mackay Mackay, Danny Dalyell and the dear Goof and Dr Orr and George Duthie and Stan Gorgerge and Leroy Vintner and Gladstone Macleod and Colonel Stubbes and John Milton and English literature from Beowulf to Virginia Woolf—how did Cranford kill them all? how did power come to fester in filthy fingers? was it for this the clay grew tall? a plague on all your houses! a plague upon you, traitors all! I might ha' saved her! now she's gone for ever! O Swallow, Swallow, flying, flying south, fly to her and tell her what I tell to thee, the whole world's in a terrible state o' chassis, shall I at least set my lands in order? tell her brief is life but love is long, between our fates how long! ungelic is us, fate is forked, her voice was ever soft, gentle and low, an excellent thing in woman, O lente, lente, currite noctis equi, O Swallow, flying from the golden woods, Hieronymo's mad againe, fly to her and pipe and woo her and make her mine, you see, young man, *The Waste Land* does not end in complete gibberish, it only looks that way, as it had to, O, I'm glad to hear you say so, Professor Duthie, for I thought you were dead, unless thou art a soul in bliss, you say true, professor, O professor, tell her, tell her that I follow thee, no, that way madness lies, better be with the dead, why then I'le fit you, let me fit you with this, dear, they'd put them pincers on your head, they'd have you fixed, no, no, get off my head, you cannot control my mind, though you can fret upon me you cannot play me, no, don't struggle, say not the struggle naught availeth, not when she's here, she's here, patience upon a monument, smiling at grief, O ye do me wrong to take me out o' my grave, but look, look here, look here, do you see this? look on her, look! her lips, her lips! and bind me on a wheel of fire, bound to my head, kisses that would suck the very nails out of your boots, look there, look there, look up to Pentland's towering top, to Salisbury Crag, there is no Robert Blair's, was there ever? O pardon, gentles all, for I am punished with a sore distraction, was 't Hamlet that wronged Cranford? was it the baseless fabric of a vision, out of my weakness and my melancholy, dissolved, and like this insubstantial pageant faded, left not a wrack behind? or did I disappear that day, through the keyhole of my studies, through the iron gates of life, reborn? would it have mattered? or am I here or am I here? are you hearing me? were you ever listening? why do you never listen? were such things here as I do speak about or have I eaten on the insane root that takes the reason prisoner? hello, Jenny, I'm sorry I've been out o' touch so long, so long, between our fates how long, the room is empty but for you, and the janitors patrol the corridors like doctors, or doctors like janitors, green-booted and quiet, I see them speak like fish behind the glass, here on the sad height, be it Blair House or mad house, and you, my lovely girl, so like a nurse again, who art so lovely fair and smell'st so sweet that the sense aches at thee, would'st thou had never been—O take me by the hand, we'll go together and sing like birds in a cage and laugh at gilded butterflies and hear poor rogues talk of school news, who loses and who wins, who's in, who's out, and take upon's the mystery of things as if we were God's spies and we'll wear out the packs and sects of great ones that ebb and flow by the moon and stretch us out no more upon the rack of this tough world, this stage-play world, for the play is over, the lesson's taught, why so, being done, I am a man again, can such things be and overcome us as a summer's cloud? 'tis but our fantasy, world's a stage, must play his part, thank you, nurse, and mine a sad one, art thou my Jenny? you must not think me mad, I am but mad north-north-west and if the wind blows southerly, blow the wind southerly and brings back my bonny to me, to me, then all may yet be well and I'll be so much better, feeling better, feeling better? better already, yes, of course, it never was aught but an act, you know, teaching's an act, learning is fun, or let me die, better be with the dead, no, better it's over now, now that's done and I'm glad it's over, thank you, thank you, gentles all, for attending the play, I am not mad, I'm in control now, only a little mad, perhaps, when the play was on, the game afoot, Watson, for if we are not a little mad at least, then where's the fun? and naked instruction is not fun but instruction there must be, or where's the point? didactic? yes, of course, bloody didactic and bloodily didactic too, for what's literature or a lesson, pray, unless it hath a palpable design? no time for silly questions here, and madness? ecstasy? O, my friends, my pulse as yours doth temperately keep time and makes as healthful music, lay not that flattering unction to your souls that not your tresspass but my madness speaks, that be the easy way, to shift the guilt, tell that to Timon if you will, or Lear, or Hamlet, Keller, Kesey, Orwell, Swift, and all the blessed company of lunatics and lovers, and the poets too, of one imagination all compact, do the sane therefore have a corner in truth? I see a cherub that sees them and sees more, yea more besides, when I lay me down and roar, bewailing my poor wits, great wits are sure to madness near allied and thin partitions do their bounds divide, fear not Dryden, piss off, Plato, for most things that were well done were done in madness, what think you on't? was 't not well done? did not great Bugsy bleed for Cranford's sake and was 't not perfect conscience to quit him with this arm? well, may them that come after me do as well and may you see things well done here, but I'll not end there, I'll finish as I started and I've started so I'll finish, for I started as I meant to finish, with what i' the name o' Beelzebub? with a borrowed line, of course, ha! you see? I do know even when the blood burns how prodigal the mind lends the tongue lines, so Hieronymo's well again! old Campbell Hieronymo Macpherson's Rant Mackay is himself again, Richard's himself again and is not about to resist a quotation at the very end now, is he? that fatal

Cleopatra for which he lost the world, all for love, the world well lost for love, but that's not it, no that's not it, what shall it then be? there's only one, you know and it's been a long time in the coming, a long long way from home, but it's coming now from long way off, I can feel it, a positive and noble number to suit my so unmuddied mind, for I'm in the clear, yes, all's light at last and so I thank God that they may say of me that he left the classroom in grand style, that he did, Sir John, never the middle flight for him, no, he soared above the Aonian Mount—oh, but that's not the one, no, that's not what he did, no, I'll tell you what he did, I'll tell you at last, at last, at last, at last, at last . . .

> *At last he rose and twitched his mantle blue,*
> *Tomorrow to fresh woods and pastures new.*